# BROKEN DOLLS

## A JEFFERSON WINTER THRILLER

### JAMES CAROL

LARGE
PRINT

First published in Great Britain 2014
by
Faber and Faber Limited

First Isis Edition
published 2015
by arrangement with
Faber and Faber Limited

A catalogue record for this book is available
from the British Library.

ISBN 978–1–78541–062–8 (hb)
ISBN 978–1–78541–067–3 (pb)

Published by
F. A. Thorpe (Publishing)
Anstey, Leicestershire

Set by Words & Graphics Ltd.
Anstey, Leicestershire
Printed and bound in Great Britain by
T. J. International Ltd., Padstow, Cornwall

This book is printed on acid-free paper

# BROKEN DOLLS

Ex-FBI star profiler and eccentric genius Jefferson Winter is no ordinary investigator. Haunted by the legacy of his notorious serial killer father, he possesses a phenomenal insight into the psychology that drives the criminals he hunts. When Detective Inspector Mark Hatcher calls from Scotland Yard about a particularly disturbing case, Winter leaves his native California for the chilly streets of London to help track down a sadistic serial kidnapper. Four victims, all young women, all tortured and then lobotomised. None of them able to tell the police the name of their attacker. Just broken dolls, played with then discarded. When another young woman goes missing, Winter has to race against the clock to identify the attacker and find the latest victim before it's too late.

For Karen, Niamh and Finn.
Love you guys.

# Prologue

The last time I saw my father alive he was strapped to a padded prison gurney, arms outstretched like he was about to be crucified. All the appeals had been filed, and denied. There would be no last-minute stay of execution. He had a catheter in each arm, the IVs already attached. Only one line was needed to get the job done. The second was there purely as a back-up. A monitor counted off the final beats of his heart, the rate a steady, relaxed seventy-five a minute despite the circumstances.

There was a crowd of a couple of dozen witnesses in the viewing gallery. Parents of the victims, prison officials, a man in a crisp no-nonsense suit representing the Governor of California. Everyone was rustling and shifting, getting comfortable for the main feature, but I was only partially aware of this.

My father looked through the thick Plexiglas and the intensity of his gaze cut right into me. At that moment it was just the two of us. I stared back, curious to know what he was thinking. I had met and studied enough psychopaths to know he wasn't sorry for what he had done, that he was incapable of showing remorse for his crimes.

Over a twelve-year period my father murdered fifteen young women. He abducted them and took them to the wide rolling forests of Oregon, where he set them free and hunted them down with a high-powered rifle. He couldn't care less about those fifteen girls. To him they were playthings.

I kept my father's gaze. Held it. His eyes were bright green with a golden yellow halo around the iris. They were exactly like mine, just one of the many genetic traits we share. Looking at him was like looking down a long dark tunnel that led into my future. We're both five foot nine, slim and over-caffeinated, and we both have bright snow-white hair, the result of a rogue gene somewhere in our ancestry. My hair had turned when I was in my early twenties, my father had been even younger.

There were three main reasons he managed to keep killing for so many years. First off, he had the intelligence to stay one step ahead of the people hunting him. Secondly, he had one of those faces that was instantly forgettable, a face that merged into the crowd. The third reason was hair dye. It didn't matter how forgettable your face was if you had instantly recognisable hair.

The brief smile that flickered across my father's lips was there and gone in a fraction of a second. It was a cruel smile. A bully's smile. He mouthed three words and my lungs and heart froze in my chest. Those three words spoke directly to a secret part of me, a part I'd kept well hidden, even from myself. He must have seen something change in my expression because he fired another of those brief cutting smiles, and then he shut his eyes for the final time.

The prison governor asked if there were any last words, but my father just blanked him. He asked again, gave my father almost a whole minute to respond and then, when he didn't, signalled for the execution to begin.

Pentobarbital was pumped through the catheter first, the anaesthetic working quickly, rendering him unconscious within seconds. Next, he received a dose of pancuronium bromide, which paralysed his respiratory muscles. Finally, he was injected with potassium chloride to stop his heart. Six minutes and twenty-three seconds later my father was pronounced dead.

Behind me, the mother of one of the victims was sobbing openly and being comforted by her husband. The woman had the glassy-eyed stare of the self-medicated. She wasn't alone in her chemical lethargy. A glance around the gallery confirmed that. The legacy left behind by my father was long and hard and filled with a misery that would echo far into the future. The father of another victim whispered under his breath that he'd gotten off too easily, a sentiment shared by most of the people in the viewing gallery. I'd seen the crime-scene photographs and read the autopsy reports, so I wasn't about to disagree. Each one of those fifteen girls had suffered a slow, terrifying death, a death that was the polar opposite of my father's.

I filed out with everyone else and made my way to the parking lot. For a time I just sat in my rental car, the key dangling from the ignition, and tried to shake the fog filling my brain. Those three words my father mouthed were playing on an endless loop inside my head. I knew he was wrong, knew that he was just screwing with my head, but I couldn't shake the feeling that there was a shred of truth in there. And if that was the case, what did that make me? We build the foundations of our lives on faultlines and shifting sand, and in his last moments my father had managed to send a Richter-nine quake rattling through mine, destroying everything I'd held as right and true.

I turned the key, put the car into gear and headed for the airport. My flight to Washington, DC, left at six thirty the next morning, but I never made it. Instead, I drove past the turning to the airport and just kept going, all the way back to Virginia. There was no real hurry. I wasn't expected back at Quantico until the next week, but that didn't stop me wanting to get the hell out of California as fast as possible, to keep moving.

The static soul-sucking limbo of an airport departure lounge was something I could definitely live without. Minutes crawling into hours, hours crawling into days, days crawling into years. That's what I told myself as the speedometer needle crept higher, and it was the truth, albeit a small part of a much larger truth. The real truth was that I was trying to outrun those three words. The problem was that it didn't matter how far I drove, or how fast, I couldn't escape them.

Even now, almost eighteen months on, those three words still haunt me, jumping into my head when least expected. Time and memory have warped those mouthed shapes into my father's lazy Californian drawl, the same easy voice he used to charm his victims. I can hear him now as clearly as if he was sat right next to me.

*We're the same.*

# CHAPTER
# ONE

The woman in the hospital bed could have been dead. She should have been dead. The only reason I knew she was alive was because of the soft, insistent beep of the heart monitor and the gentle rise and fall of her blankets. Her face was slack. Emotionless. This wasn't the deep relaxation that came with sleep, it was more like the relaxation that came with death, like all the muscles in her face had been permanently switched off. I could have been looking at a corpse on a mortuary slab, or a body dumped in a lonely woodland, but I wasn't. A part of me wished I was.

Detective Inspector Mark Hatcher looked down at the sleeping woman and muttered a heartfelt "Jesus Christ" under his breath. He stared at her like he was hypnotised. An occasional shake of the head, a sigh, small gestures that spoke volumes. I'd first met Hatcher on a profiling course I'd run at Quantico for overseas police forces. He'd stood out from the crowd because he had been on the front row for every single lecture, and he wouldn't shut up with the questions. I liked Hatcher then, I liked him now. He was one of Scotland Yard's finest. Anyone who could stare into Nietzsche's abyss for thirty years and still feel something was all right in my book.

But those years hadn't been kind. They'd sucked all the colour from him, all the joy. His hair was grey, as was his skin, his outlook. He possessed a particular brand of cynicism you only found in cops who'd been on the job too long. His sad hound-dog eyes told the whole sorry story. They'd witnessed more than anyone should ever have to.

"Patricia Maynard is the fourth victim, right?" A rhetorical question, but one that needed asking to pull Hatcher back into the room.

"That's right." Hatcher let out a long, weary sigh and shook his head, then turned and looked me straight in the eye. "Sixteen months I've been chasing this bastard, and do you want to know the truth? The truth is that I don't think we're any closer to catching him than we were back at the start. It's like Snakes and Ladders, except someone's stolen all the bloody ladders and every other square has a snake's head on it." Another sigh, another shake of the head. "I thought I'd seen everything, Winter, but this is something else."

That was an understatement. There was no limit to the horrors serial criminals dreamt up, but even I had to admit this was new, and I have seen everything. There were some things worse than death, and Patricia Maynard was living proof of that.

I looked at her lying there in that claustrophobic private room, wired up to all those machines, an IV plugged into the catheter in the back of her hand, and it crossed my mind again that she would be better off dead. I knew exactly how I'd do it, too. Unplug the IV tube and use a syringe to pump air into the catheter.

The embolism would hit the right side of the heart first and from there it would travel to the lungs. The blood vessels in the lungs would constrict, raising the pressure in the right side of the heart until it was high enough to push the embolism to the left side. From there it had access to the rest of the body through the circulatory system. If it got lodged in the coronary artery it would cause a heart attack. If it reached the brain, it would cause a stroke.

A neat, simple solution. Unless someone looked really hard, the risk of doing prison time was minimal. And nobody would look too hard. Experience has taught me that people tend to see what they want to see. Over the last three and a half months Patricia Maynard had been held captive and put through hell. And if she died now? Well, we'd all want to believe her body had finally given up, and that would be that. Case closed.

"DNA?" I asked.

"Enough to tie her to the other three women, but nothing that gave a hit on our database."

"Anything new on the unsub?"

"The unknown subject," said Hatcher. "You know, I think the last time I heard that one used was on TV." He shook his head. "Nope, nothing new on the unsub."

"So basically we have four victims who aren't talking, and absolutely no idea who the bad guy is."

"That about sums it up." Hatcher sighed. "We need to find him before he gets his hands on someone else."

"Not going to happen. After the first victim was dumped two months passed before the second abduction took place. Only seventy-two hours passed between the dumping of victim number three and Patricia Maynard's abduction. Usually there's a cooling-off period, a time where the unsub's fantasies are strong enough to hold him in check. With this guy the fantasies no longer work. They're a poor substitute for the real thing, and he's got far too used to the real thing. This unsub is escalating. Patricia Maynard was found two nights ago, so my guess is that he'll kidnap the next one tonight."

"Just what I need. More bad news." Hatcher sighed again and rubbed at his tired face. "So what's the good news, Winter? Because you'd better have some. After all, that's what I brought you in for."

"The good news is that the more he devolves, the more likely it is that he'll make a mistake. The more mistakes he makes, the easier it'll be to catch him."

"That's fine in theory. The problem is there's a woman out there who's about to come face to face with her worst nightmare and there's absolutely nothing I can do to stop that. My job is to protect these people."

There was no response to that. I'd been in Hatcher's shoes plenty of times and knew exactly what he was feeling right now. The helplessness, the need to do something when you didn't have a clue what that something was. The anger was the hardest thing to deal with, though. Anger at yourself for not solving the puzzle, anger at a world where those puzzles even existed.

**10**

For a while we stood in a respectful silence and watched Patricia sleep. The heart monitor beeped, the bedcovers rose and fell, and the clock on the wall counted off the seconds.

Patricia was twenty-eight, brown-eyed, brunette. The second detail wasn't apparent because her eyes were swollen shut, and the last detail wasn't apparent because the unsub had shaved her head. The skin around her eyes was bruised, and her scalp was a shiny smooth pink dome under the bright hospital lights. There wasn't even a hint of stubble, which meant this had been done recently, probably in the hours before she was dumped. There was no way this was the first time the unsub had done this to her. This guy got off on humiliation, pain and torture.

I'd interviewed dozens of murderers in an attempt to get an insight into the impulses that drove them. I had made it my business to try to understand why one human being would hurt another for pleasure. But I was having a tough time getting my head around the fact that Patricia Maynard had been lobotomised.

Cardiopulmonary functions are controlled by the medulla oblongata, a part of the brain that hadn't been affected when Patricia was lobotomised. For as long as she lived, her medulla oblongata would keep her lungs pumping and her heart beating. Patricia wasn't even thirty yet. She could easily live for another forty or fifty years. Half a century trapped in a twilight prison, completely reliant on others for help in every aspect of her life, unable to feed herself or go to the bathroom, unable to string a thought or a sentence together. It didn't bear thinking about.

"And there's no scarring on the skull?" Another rhetorical question, this one necessary because I needed to find my way back into the room.

"That's because access to the brain was gained through the eye sockets." Hatcher was still staring at Patricia Maynard. "You seen enough, Winter?"

"More than enough." I was staring, too. I couldn't help it. "Okay, our next stop's St Albans. I need to talk to Graham Johnson."

"Is that necessary? My people have already interviewed him."

I tore my eyes away from Patricia Maynard and looked at Hatcher. "And I'm sure your people did a wonderful job. But it was Johnson who found Patricia, which means there are only two degrees of separation between him and the unsub. And since our victims aren't saying much, that's the closest I'm going to get to him right now. So yeah, I want to talk to him."

"Okay. Let me make a call. I'll find someone to drive you."

"And how much time will that waste? It would be better if you drove."

"No can do. I'm expected back at the office."

"You're the boss. You can do whatever the hell you want." I grinned. "Come on, Hatcher, it'll be fun."

"Fun! You know, Winter, you've got a pretty warped idea of what constitutes fun. Fun is a twenty-year-old blonde. Fun is partying all night on a billionaire's yacht. What we do is not fun."

12

"You know your problem, Hatcher? You've got too used to pushing a desk. When was the last time you did any real police work?" I grinned. "Come to think about it, when was the last time you did a twenty-year-old blonde?"

Hatcher let out another long, tired sigh. "I've got to get back."

"And I've just flown across the Atlantic to help save your ass. And did I mention it's thirty-six hours since I last saw a bed?"

"And that's emotional blackmail."

"Your point?"

Hatcher sighed again. "Okay. I'll drive."

# CHAPTER
# TWO

Hatcher drove fast and careful, the needle flickering around ninety and rarely dipping below eighty. We were headed north up the M1, an urban corridor on the outskirts of London. The motorway was flanked by dismal grey buildings that were made even more depressing by the dull December light.

Christmas was less than a week away but even the coloured fairy lights twinkling behind the windows we passed failed to brighten up the day. It was mid-afternoon, an hour before sundown, and the slate-grey sky was filled with dark storm clouds. According to the news reports, snow was on the way and people were already betting on whether or not it was going to be a white Christmas. I could understand the appeal of gambling but I didn't understand the appeal of snow. It was cold, wet and depressing. At heart I would always be a Californian. I crave sunshine the way an addict craves crack.

"I really appreciate you agreeing to take the case," said Hatcher. "I know how busy you are."

"Glad to be here," I said. *No you don't*, I thought. And that was the truth. Right now I could be in Singapore or Sydney or Miami. Hot, sunny places.

Instead I was in London on an icy December day, fighting off frostbite and hypothermia and wondering when the blizzard was going to hit.

I only had myself to blame. The main benefit of being your own boss was that you got to call the shots. I'd chosen to be in London for the simple reason that this case was unusual, and unusual made it interesting, and interesting was one of the few things that could trump sunshine.

Since quitting the FBI I'd travelled the world hunting serial criminals. Every day brought a new request for help, sometimes two or three requests. Choosing which cases to work was tough since declining a case could mean a death sentence for someone, often more than one someone since serial killers tend to keep going until they're stopped. This dilemma gave me plenty of sleepless nights during my FBI days. I slept better now, but that was the combination of sleeping pills, whisky and jet lag.

Unfortunately there was never going to be a shortage of monsters to hunt down. That was the way it had been since for ever, all the way back to when Cain murdered Abel. Serial criminals were like weeds. When you caught one another dozen sprang up to take their place. Some people believed there were as many as a hundred serial killers operating in the US alone. And that was just the killers. This figure didn't account for the arsonists or the rapists or any of those other monsters whose only goal in life was to bring pain and suffering into the lives of others.

I'd been your archetypal G-Man when I was with the FBI. A sharp suit, shoes spit-shined until they shone like mirrors, hair cut into a neat short back and sides. My hair was black back then, dyed so I wouldn't stand out. Put me in a line-up with a thousand other agents and I would have blended right in.

These day I'm more relaxed about my appearance. The starched white shirts and stiff suits have gone, replaced with jeans and dead-rock-star T-shirts and hooded tops. The shiny shoes have been swapped for comfortable, scuffed working boots. The dye ended up in the trash. I might not look as smart as I used to, but I felt a damn sight more comfortable. Those G-Men suits were like straitjackets.

"What are your first impressions?" Hatcher glanced over at me, one hand on the wheel, the needle pushing a hundred.

"There are only two ways this guy's going to stop. You catch him or he dies. Either from causes natural or unnatural. He likes what he does too much to stop on his own."

"Come on, Winter, this isn't some rookie you're talking to here. That description covers ninety-nine point nine per cent of serial criminals."

I laughed. Hatcher had got me there. "Okay, how about this? When you catch him, he's not going to come in easily. This one's a prime candidate for suicide by cop."

"What makes you say that?"

"Prison would kill him."

"Why?"

"This guy's all about control. He controls every aspect of his victims' lives. What they wear, what they eat, everything. He couldn't handle having that control taken away. Suicide by cop would appeal to him because he would be choosing the time and place of his death. In his mind, he'd still be in control."

"Let's hope you're wrong about that."

"I'm not."

While Hatcher drove, I went over the details of Patricia Maynard's kidnapping in my head. I would have liked more information, but that's nothing new. It doesn't matter how much information you've got, it's never enough.

According to the police reports, Martin Maynard had reported his wife missing on August twenty-third, and in doing so made himself the prime suspect. Most murders are committed by someone known to the victim. A spouse, a relative, a friend. At that point, this wasn't a murder investigation, but the cops were covering their bases.

Martin Maynard had had a string of affairs and the couple had been seeing a therapist in a last-ditch attempt to save a marriage that should have been signed off as terminal a long time ago. Add in a sizeable life insurance policy and there was plenty of motive. Murder was the logical conclusion.

After forty-eight hours of questions Martin Maynard was free to go. The cops kept an eye on him over the intervening months, but again, this was more about covering bases, and asses. When the cops assembled the puzzle pieces of Patricia Maynard's last movements, they established that she had gone missing some time during the evening of August twenty-second.

Martin's alibi was rock-solid and came in the form of his secretary, a woman he'd sworn to Patricia he was no longer seeing. On the night she disappeared he was supposed to be in Cardiff on business, but was actually still in London with his secretary. Hotel records and eyewitness accounts backed up his story.

For the next three and a half months, nothing. No ransom note, no telephone demands, no body. Patricia Maynard had disappeared off the face of the planet. Everyone assumed she was dead, then, two nights ago, she turned up in a park in St Albans, a small cathedral city situated thirty minutes north of London. She was disorientated and non-communicative, unable to answer even the most basic questions. Graham Johnson had been walking his dog, and found her wandering alone. He called in the local police, and they quickly identified their Jane Doe as Patricia Maynard. She was transferred to St Barts Hospital in London and Hatcher took over the case.

During her three and a half months in captivity, Patricia Maynard had been repeatedly tortured. Her body was covered in scars and bruising, some old, some new. This unsub liked to play with knives, and the tox screen showed that he used drugs to keep Patricia awake and hypersensitive while he had his fun. He had cut her fingers off one at a time, all except the ring finger on her left hand. The stumps were neatly cauterised. Curiously, he had avoided damaging her face, and even more curiously, there were traces of make-up that hadn't been properly wiped off. Another interesting point: aside from her injuries, Patricia was in pretty good shape. Her weight was appropriate for her height and build, and there were no signs of dehydration.

We reached the turn for St Albans and Hatcher hit the indicator and swerved left onto the off-ramp. Five minutes later we were driving through St Michael's, a part of the city made up of rickety terraces of little picture-postcard houses and larger properties that must have cost a small fortune. We drove past four bars. Too many for the number of houses, not to mention the demographic those houses represented. The area had tourist written all over it.

The cold hit me the second I got out the car. It was like charging head-first into a wall of solid ice. I was wearing my thickest jacket. Sheepskin on the inside to keep in the warmth, and waterproofed suede on the outside to keep out the worst of the wind and the wet. I could have been wearing shorts and a T-shirt for all the good it was doing. I lit a cigarette and Hatcher gave me a dirty look.

"We're outside," I said. "I'm not breaking any laws."

"Those things will kill you."

"So will a lot of things. I could get hit by a bus tomorrow."

"Or you could get diagnosed with lung cancer and die a slow, lingering, painful death."

I flashed Hatcher a tight grin. "Or maybe not. My great-grandpa smoked two packs a day and lived to be a hundred and three. Let's hope I take after him, eh?"

Graham Johnson's house was opposite the Six Bells. Like all the other houses along this stretch the front door opened directly onto the sidewalk. One of Hatcher's people had phoned ahead, so Johnson was expecting us. The living-room curtain fluttered down as we walked up to the house, and the door swung open before Hatcher had a chance to hit the bell. Johnson stood in the doorway, a Jack Russell yapping and bouncing hyperactively around his ankles. He was average height, average build, and his head brushed the top of the low doorframe.

According to the police reports, Johnson was seventy-five, and every single one of those years was etched into the lines that creased his worn, worried face. What little hair he had left was as white as mine and there were large bags under his rheumy blue eyes. He moved fluidly for his age, though, no stiffness despite the fact it was thirty degrees outside. Regular exercise rather than vitamins and joint supplements. Johnson didn't strike me as someone who would go down the vitamin route.

"Come on in."

Johnson stepped aside to let us into the living room. The dog was going nuts, yapping and twirling and chasing his tail. The old guy shouted a sharp "Barnaby, quiet!" and the dog shut up and bounced onto a chair, a guilty look on its face. I crushed my half-smoked cigarette out on the sidewalk and followed Hatcher inside. The dog's eyes followed us across the room. Johnson ushered us towards the sofa and we sat down.

20

The small fire burning in the grate warmed the room and cast a cosy orange glow.

"Can I get you anything?" he asked. "Tea? Coffee?"

"A coffee would be great," I said. "Black, two sugars, thanks."

Hatcher declined, and the old guy disappeared into the kitchen. I settled back on the sofa and checked out the room. My initial impression was that it was preserved like a museum exhibit. I'd noticed Johnson's wedding ring when he answered the door, and I'd also noticed that the living room had been decorated by a woman. What I hadn't noticed was a wife.

There were dusty ornaments on every spare surface, faded floral cushions on the chairs and sofas, faded floral curtains at the windows. An ancient framed wedding photograph had pride of place on the mantelpiece, and there were family photos everywhere, lots of smiling kids and grandkids. The hairstyles and clothes dated the photographs, with the most recent being about four years old. That's when Johnson's wife must have passed away.

Johnson came back with two steaming mugs of coffee, handed me one, then settled down in the chair next to the fireplace. My coffee was strong and packed with caffeine. Just how I liked it.

"Can you tell us how you found Patricia Maynard?" Hatcher asked.

"That was her name then," he said. "You know, I must have spoken to a dozen policemen since Monday night and no one bothered to tell me her name. Then again, I didn't ask, so I guess it's my fault as much as theirs. It doesn't seem right, though. Not finding out what she was called."

"Mr Johnson," said Hatcher.

The old guy snapped back into the here and now with a visible start. "Sorry," he said.

Hatcher waved the apology away. "Can you tell us what happened?"

"I was taking Barnaby out for his late-night walk. This would have been about ten. I take him out the same time every night. I actually take him out to the park two or three times a day. If I didn't he'd wreck the house."

"This was to Verulamium Park, right?"

"That's right. Verulamium Park. You probably passed the entrance on the way here. Anyway I got to the end of the lake and that's when I saw the woman. The reason I noticed her was because I thought she was about to go into the water." He stopped and drank some coffee. "Look, I don't mean to be rude but I've already told the police all this. I don't mind going over it all again, but I can't help feeling I'm wasting your time."

"You're not wasting our time." I glanced over at the Jack Russell. "I'd like to try something if you're up for it. Do you think Barnaby would like to go for a walk?"

The dog's ears pricked up when he heard the word "walk". He jumped off his chair and started barking and twirling, pirouetting like a circus dog. Johnson laughed. "I think you can take that as a yes," he said.

# CHAPTER
# THREE

It took us five minutes to walk to Verulamium Park, long enough to smoke a cigarette from tip to butt. Barnaby bounced all the way there, straining on his lead, half choking himself to death, and acting like this was the most exciting thing ever. Dark was descending fast and the streetlamps glowed a sickly sulphurous yellowy-orange in the heavy half-light. The snow wasn't far off and the air had a choking damp feel. I pulled my jacket in tighter to ward off the chill but it didn't help. The cold of a damp British winter day could penetrate an arctic suit.

"Do you do the same walk every time?" I asked Graham Johnson.

The old guy shook his head. "We've got a number of routes we take. It depends on the weather, how much time we've got, that sort of thing. It's a big park."

It was a big park. Off to the right, acres of grassland stretched as far as I could see, empty soccer fields marked out white on grey. The cathedral was off to the left, perched imposingly on a distant hill. Up ahead was a small lake that was separated from the main lake by a humpback bridge. Ducks and swans bobbed on the water, oblivious to the cold.

It was also dark and deserted, making it the perfect place for the unsub to dump Patricia Maynard.

"The night you found Patricia Maynard, which way did you go?"

Johnson pointed towards the cathedral side of the main lake. "We did a quick anticlockwise walk around the lake."

"And where did you see Patricia Maynard?"

The old guy pointed to the far end of the lake.

"Okay, let's go."

It took another five minutes to walk there. I got Johnson to sit down on an empty bench, then sat beside him. Barnaby was straining on the end of his lead, yapping and scratching at the concrete, desperate to get free so he could catch a duck. I glanced up at Hatcher, who quickly got the message. For this to work, the fewer distractions Johnson had the better. Hatcher took hold of Barnaby's lead and walked out of earshot.

A cognitive interview differs from a standard interview in that you're trying to get the subject to revisit the scene by reliving the feelings and impressions that were imprinted at the time. Rather than hitting the event head-on, you circle around it, looking at it through the different senses. The memories this evokes have been found to be much more reliable than those retrieved through the usual interview techniques. Strictly speaking, I didn't need to bring Johnson back here, but since we were just around the corner I didn't see the harm.

"I want you to close your eyes, Mr Johnson, and then I'm going to ask you some questions. Try not to censor your answers. I don't care how crazy they might seem, just say whatever comes into your head."

Johnson looked at me sceptically.

"It's okay. I've done this before."

Johnson gave another sceptical look then shut his eyes.

"I want you to think back to Monday night. You're taking Barnaby out for a walk like usual. What time is it?"

"Around ten. I always take him out around ten."

"Before or after?"

The old guy's face creased with concentration, then relaxed. "It was after ten. I'd just finished watching a TV programme. The news was about to start."

"What's the weather like?"

"It's raining."

"Describe the rain. Is it heavy? Light?"

"It's one of those misty, drizzly rains. You know the sort I mean. It doesn't seem heavy but you end up soaked."

"Is the park busy?"

"In that weather and at that time of night?" Johnson shook his head. "No, it's just me and Barnaby. And Patricia, of course."

I ignored the mention of Patricia Maynard because I wasn't ready to go there yet. "How are you feeling?"

"A bit annoyed to tell the truth. I'd taken the car to the garage earlier and been hit with a six-hundred-pound bill. Now I was out walking my dog in the rain. I'd had better days, let's put it that way."

"What can you smell?"

"Damp dirt. Wood smoke coming from my clothes."

"What can you see?"

"The cracks in the footpath. I've got my head down to stop the rain getting in my face."

"Are you walking quickly or slowly?"

"Quickly. I just want to get home out of the rain."

"What's Barnaby doing?"

A smile. "Pulling my arm off like usual. If he wasn't on a lead he'd be in that lake in two seconds flat."

"How do you become aware of Patricia?"

"Something catches my eye. A movement from the path at the far end of the lake that leads down from the Fighting Cocks."

The old guy gave an almost imperceptible nod of his head and I glanced in the direction he'd indicated. Even in the late afternoon half-light the dark, narrow path didn't look inviting.

"How's she moving?"

"Unsteadily. She's weaving like she's drunk. My first thought was that she'd had one too many at the Fighting Cocks. I don't want to stare, but you know how it is when you see an ambulance parked up at the side of the road. It's impossible not to look over, right? Anyway, I watch her weave out of the trees, and it strikes me as odd that she's on her own. There's no sign of a boyfriend. No girlfriends, either. It's dark and late. This is no place for a woman to be on her own. I watch more closely because she's got me worried and that's when I notice she's headed straight for the lake. I run over and just manage to grab her arm in time and spin

26

her away. If she'd gone into the lake at this time of year she would have ended up with hypothermia."

The rest of the story had been in the police reports. Johnson had tried to talk to her and when she didn't respond he'd taken her to the Fighting Cocks and got the bar owner to call the police. Graham Johnson was the first person I'd met in ages who didn't own a cellphone, a relic from a long-gone era.

"I want you to back up a couple of steps, Mr Johnson, think back to when you first become aware of Patricia. I don't want you to say anything, I just want you to picture the scene in your mind. Picture it as clearly as you can, every single detail, no matter how small or insignificant. What do you see? What do you hear? What do you smell? What do you feel?"

I gave Johnson a few moments then told him to open his eyes. The old guy had a strange look on his face.

"What is it?" I asked.

"You're going to think I'm paranoid."

"Paranoid or crazy, I don't care. I want to hear what you've got to say." I smiled reassuringly, waited for him to smile back. "So what happened? Were you abducted by aliens and transported up to the mother ship?"

Johnson's smile didn't last long. The old guy's face turned serious, and a little fearful. He pointed to a shadowy clump of trees and bushes off to his right. When he spoke, it was with absolute certainty. There was no doubt he believed every word he was saying.

"Someone was watching us from over there."

# CHAPTER
# FOUR

tesla: u there
ladyjade: yeah ☺
tesla: busy
ladyjade: u have no idea
tesla: still on for tonite
ladyjade: yeah
tesla: cant w8 2 meet u
ladyjade: me 2
tesla: gotta go works crazy here 2
ladyjade: ok cu l8r x
tesla: x

Rachel Morris shut down the IM box and her smile turned to a frown. What was she playing at? She was thirty, so why the hell was she acting like a lovesick teenager? It was crazy. She glanced through the window of her cubicle, convinced every set of eyes would be aimed in her direction, but everyone had their heads down. Rachel could hear the bang and clatter of the call centre on the other side of the glass, the chirping of the telephones, the mumble of dozens of one-sided conversations.

She stared at the report on her screen and willed the words to make sense. It didn't work. All she could think about was tonight. She'd told Jamie she was going out for a birthday drink with some of the girls after work. Not that he cared. She could have told him she was emigrating to Australia and she would have got the same uninterested, grunted non-response. It hadn't always been like this. Back at the start, they used to talk through the night, sharing their dreams and secrets. But those days were long gone, eroded away by the daily grind of six and a half years of marriage.

Underneath her desk was her bag, and inside the bag was her expensive perfume, her best underwear and her favourite little red dress. The dress highlighted all the good bits, hid all the bad bits, and was sexy without being slutty. That last part was important. She didn't think Tesla would appreciate slutty. There was something old-fashioned about him. He was a gentleman, in both senses of the word. It was his sensitivity that had attracted her in the first place, that probably more than anything else. It was nice to have someone who listened to her, someone who made her feel that what she said and thought actually mattered. Someone who appreciated her for who she was.

Rachel stared at the jumble of words on the screen and told herself there was still time to bail out. Then she thought about Jamie and all the hurt he'd caused her and she knew that wasn't going to happen. She'd been chatting with Tesla for the last couple of months and the more she got to know him, the more she liked him. She hadn't even met the guy, didn't even know his real name, but there was no getting away from the fact that he understood her in ways she had never been understood by anyone. He got her. *Really* got her. Jamie had never understood her so completely, not even back in the good days.

She glanced at the clock on her screen, saw it was only three thirty. Four and a half hours until they met up. Four and a half hours that were going to drag like the last day of school.

# CHAPTER
# FIVE

I stood with Hatcher at the end of the lake and watched Barnaby drag Graham Johnson home. The snow had finally started, fat flakes that hung suspended in the lamplight, trapped in slow motion. This was just a taste of things to come. The weathermen had promised blizzards and the newsreaders had promised chaos, and I saw no reason to argue with them. Johnson was already halfway along the lake. The old guy obviously wanted to get home before the snow really got going. I didn't blame him. Being stuck out here in a snowstorm was nobody's idea of fun. I tapped out a cigarette, lit it with my battered brass Zippo, and ignored the waves of disapproval coming from Hatcher.

"The unsub was here," I said.

"That's what Johnson said?" replied Hatcher.

"Not in so many words."

"So what did he say?"

"What he said wasn't important. What's important is what he felt. And what he felt was that someone was watching." I nodded to a nearby clump of trees. "From over there to be exact."

"What he *felt*," echoed Hatcher. "Not sure that one's going to stand up in court, Winter."

31

"And that's the problem with being a cop these days. You spend too much time thinking like a lawyer and not enough time thinking like a detective."

I headed over to the trees and peered into the gloom. Dark shadows moved with the swaying branches and the eerie whistle of the wind filled the air. Before Hatcher could lecture me on the dos and don'ts of contaminating crime scenes, I pushed through the undergrowth and the trees swallowed me up. Branches whipped against my face and flicked against my body. Mud splattered my boots and the bottoms of my jeans. Hatcher was a few steps behind, swearing and complaining and wanting to know what the hell I was doing.

I tuned him out and, for a while, just stood in that clump of trees, oblivious to the icy flakes of snow pricking my face. I knew with absolute certainty that the unsub had been here two nights ago. Hunting was in my blood.

When I was a kid my father used to take me on camping trips to the wide rolling forests of Oregon, the same forests he then took his victims to. He taught me how to shoot and how to track, taught me how to field-dress the animals we killed. Taught me that the strong endured while the weak perished, and that that was the way of the world. I lost count of the number of times I'd heard that one. It was a cynical piece of philosophy that made a hell of a lot more sense after the arrest.

I crouched down and moved around, searching for the best vantage point. From here the unsub would have had a great view of the lake, and the path that led up to the Fighting Cocks. The cathedral loomed off to my right, and I could see Johnson and Barnaby, two shadowy shapes in the distance. Hatcher's barked questions melded with the background noise as I slid into the zone and was transported back in time to that evening. I could picture the scene as clearly as if I'd been there.

There's Graham Johnson being dragged along the lakeside by Barnaby. He's walking into the rain with his head down, glancing up every now and again to check where he's going. He notices a movement on the path off to his left and freezes. He relaxes a little when he sees it's Patricia Maynard, and that she's alone. What threat could a woman on her own pose?

He doesn't relax all the way, though. The part of the brain that helped our cave-dwelling ancestors stay alive is whispering warnings and although we stopped listening to that voice generations ago, it still has the power to stop us in our tracks and pull the switches if need be, even if we don't realise. Graham looks over at Patricia, then glances over to where I'm hiding. He doesn't see me, but he senses my presence. I'm just one more shadow amongst all the other shadows. Patricia stumbles drunkenly towards the lake and Graham grabs her before she tumbles into the dark, icy water, a single spontaneous act that transforms him into the hero of the hour.

I clambered from the bushes, straightened out my jeans and took a drag on my cigarette. The snow was heavier than ever, the flakes fatter and thicker. That cold wind blowing down from the Arctic cut right through me. I pulled the hood of my top up and huddled deeper into my jacket but it didn't really help. Hatcher had given up bitching at me and was on his cellphone talking to someone from forensics.

"Okay, here's a question," I said. "You're the unsub. Why risk coming here? Why not just dump your victim and get the hell out?"

Hatcher killed the call and put his cell away. "Isn't that why we're paying you that large consultation fee? To answer those sorts of questions?"

"And why dump them in such a public place?" I added, ignoring him. "He did the same with the other victims. All three were dumped in public parks. Why take the risk? Why not dump them somewhere remote?"

I took another drag on my cigarette and thought about the unsub hiding in these bushes on a rainy evening. Watching and waiting. But waiting for what? And then I got it. I smiled and said, "He wants them to be found."

"Assuming you're right, then that answers the second question," said Hatcher. "But what about the first question? Why does he need to be here?"

"Because he wants to make sure they're found."

"Okay, I'll buy that. I guess the next question is, why is that so important to him?"

Hatcher was looking at me like he expected an answer, like he expected some momentous insight that was going to crack the case wide open. Unfortunately, I didn't have the answer he was looking for. Not yet.

It was almost four. Forty-eight hours earlier I'd been in Maine, dressed in Kevlar, watching a SWAT team descend on a snow-covered barn where a child-killer was hiding out. The killer ended up dead, shot by a marksman, which was a result. One less child-killer in the world is always going to qualify as a result.

I had already closed the book on that case. The bad guy was dead, time to move on. For me, the only thing that matters is the case I'm working on. Everything else is history, and I have no time for history. Rehashing past successes never saved anyone's life, and reliving the failures rarely achieved anything constructive. I'd got out of Maine before the back-slapping started, caught the first flight from Logan International to Heathrow, and hadn't looked back. Three thousand miles and five time zones later and nothing much had changed. Not really. It was still snowing, and I had another monster to hunt down.

"How about we head over to the Fighting Cocks for a drink?" I said.

# CHAPTER
# SIX

There was no argument from Hatcher on that score, not that I expected one. Another thing I remembered from his visit to Quantico was that he was always first to the bar. We made our way up the same narrow path that Patricia Maynard had stumbled down on Monday night. Halfway along, we crossed a small swollen river and the rush of water filled my ears.

The path opened out onto Abbey Mill Lane, a narrow road that had been built for horses and carts. From studying the maps, I knew Abbey Mill Lane was the only road in or out of this part of the city. Off to my left was Abbey Mill End, which finished in a dead end. I took a quick look around and tried to imagine things from the unsub's perspective. The fact it was so quiet was a plus, but the fact that parking was limited was a big negative.

On the other side of the lane was the Fighting Cocks. The place was old. *Really* old. It looked like something dreamed up by a Hollywood set designer, all strange angles and shapes, and black Tudor beams. We headed inside, past the framed news articles proclaiming it to be the oldest pub in Britain, and made our way through the maze of rooms to the main bar.

An old couple sitting at the table nearest the fire were the only customers. The miniature artificial Christmas tree on the bar had silver branches and a couple of pathetic red baubles and a crooked star on top. Christmas cards hung from a piece of string behind the bar. That was as far as the decorating went, and it was depressing rather than merry. Christmas as something to be forgotten rather than celebrated.

The guy behind the bar was skinny and bald with a large, easy smile. His hands were placed proprietorially on the surface of the bar and, from the way he stood there like he owned the place, it was a safe bet he did. His clothes were designer and there was a Rolex Submariner on his wrist. Hatcher ordered a pint of London Pride and I ordered a whisky. The drinks arrived and I drained mine to the halfway point, letting the alcohol burn away some of the snow that had seeped into my bones.

I put the glass on the bar. "You're Joe Slattery, right? The guy who owns this place."

"Depends who's asking. If you're after money, or you've been sent by my ex-wife, then I've never heard of Joe Slattery." The accent was Irish, the laugh infectious.

"You called the police on Monday night."

Slattery met my eye and his face turned serious. "Are you journalists? If you are then I'll ask you politely to drink up and leave. I've had enough of journalists."

Hatcher stepped in and flashed his ID. "I'm Detective Inspector Mark Hatcher and this is my colleague Jefferson Winter."

"Why didn't you say so?" Slattery's smile returned so suddenly it was like it had never been away. "You might even have got your drinks on the house."

I doubted that. Slattery's smile was big but it didn't reach his pockets. Here was someone who kept a sharp eye on the bottom line and a tight grip on the profits. That's why he could afford the Rolex. "According to your statement you didn't notice anything unusual."

"It was just a normal Monday night," Slattery agreed. "Until Graham came in with the girl, that is. Then it became anything but normal. Police, paramedics, journalists, it was a regular three-ring circus, I tell you. And what he did to that poor girl." Slattery shook his head and whispered a "Jesus, Mary and Joseph" under his breath. "They say he gave her a lobotomy. That's just sick."

"I'm interested in the parking around here," I said.

Slattery shook his head in disbelief. "This bastard cuts into people's brains and all you're interested in is the parking."

"Humour me."

Slattery looked at me, eyes narrowed. He was staring like he was trying to decide if I was being serious. I stared back, holding his gaze until he worked out that I was.

"The parking's a bloody nightmare," said Slattery. "Particularly in the summer. I'm always getting tourists filling up my car park. Then they use the lane. Like I said, it's a bloody nightmare."

"And that's why you had a security camera fitted in the car park."

"There are some other reasons, but that's the main one," Slattery agreed. "But, as you already know, that was broken on Sunday night. Originally I thought it was broken by some local kids, but obviously I know better now."

The police's theory was that the unsub had broken the camera. The way they saw it, he'd come down some time on Sunday night and broken it so he would be able to use the pub's parking lot when he dumped Patricia Maynard. I thanked Slattery for his time, finished my whisky in one, told Hatcher to drink up. We wound back through the tight low-ceilinged corridors and headed out into the cold.

"I agree with the police that the unsub broke the camera," I said. "But there's no way he parked here on Monday night. It's too easy. Too obvious. This guy does subtle. He doesn't do obvious."

"So what are you thinking?" Hatcher asked.

I stood and looked along Abbey Mill Lane. Full dark had descended and the lane glowed orange in the streetlamps. The snow was falling harder, the icy wind blowing it into swirls. It was already starting to lie, covering the road and the sidewalk.

"There's no way in hell he drove down here on Monday night," I said. "It's too risky. This is the only way in and out."

"So how did he get the girl here? Teleportation?"

I ignored the question, and the sarcasm, and did an about-turn and headed along Abbey Mill End. I stopped at the end of the narrow lane and tried to imagine the unsub walking along here, guiding Patricia

Maynard, one hand on her shoulder, gently coaxing her along. That felt right. More right than the idea of him driving down here and parking at the Fighting Cocks.

There was a small path straight ahead and I walked towards it. Hatcher was a few steps behind, complaining about the snow and the cold and the fact that we should be going the other way, back to the car, because he didn't want to end up stranded in St Albans. I tuned him out and carried on walking.

The path led to Pondwicks Close, another cul-de-sac. There was a school on my left, one for the younger kids judging by the brightly coloured play equipment. Pondwicks Close opened up onto Grove Road. Just one street away was the A5183, one of the main arteries that led in and out of the city. It was close enough to hear the rumble of traffic. I stood for a moment in the middle of Grove Road, snow settling on my head and shoulders. It pricked against my face and stuck to my eyelids, but I was oblivious. I nodded to myself then turned to Hatcher.

"This is where he parked," I said.

# CHAPTER
# SEVEN

Rachel felt as excited as she had done on her very first date. *Almost* as excited. She wasn't a teenager any more, so her excitement was tempered by a touch of trepidation. She knew all about disappointment, knew that reality rarely lived up to the dream and that hopes always outweighed expectations. She knew the agony of having your heart fed into a shredder. The red dress clung to her in all the right places and that made her feel good. She kept getting hit with little wafts of her favourite perfume and that made her feel good, too.

She stepped out of the Tube station into the cold night. The snow had slowed to a light flurry and the flakes drifted lazily, dancing and turning, blown on the breeze. Rachel had loved snow as a little girl, and had never really fallen out of love with it. Snow turned the world into a place of magic and romance. By tomorrow it would all be slush, but for now things were perfect. She pulled her coat tighter and picked up the pace, her bag banging against her side in time with her hurried footsteps.

The bar they'd arranged to meet in was large and anonymous. Tall wooden stools along the bar, wooden chairs and tables in the middle of the room, comfy leather sofas and coffee tables around the outside. Rachel scanned the customers. It didn't take long. There were only a couple of dozen people in a space that could easily fit a couple of hundred. They were spread throughout the room, mostly in groups of threes and fours. There were only a couple of solo drinkers. Rachel's eyes moved quickly from person to person. Tesla was in his mid-thirties and had short brown hair. He said he'd be wearing a long black woollen trench coat. The only person who came close was a man on one of the tall stools at the bar. He had the right sort of coat, but was too old by at least twenty years.

Rachel ordered a lemonade. Her plan was to stick to soft drinks until after they'd got through the preliminaries, then alternate her drinks, one lemonade for every glass of wine. She wanted to make a good impression, and to do that she needed a clear head. If tonight went well then Tesla might want to see her again. She really wanted to believe this was the start of something. A new beginning, a new chapter.

She took a sip of her drink and checked her watch. Ten minutes early. Rachel found a table with a good view of the door and sat down on the leather sofa to wait. The table was tucked away at the back, cosy and intimate.

Eight o'clock came and went. Twenty past eight. By half past her nerves were in tatters. She went to the bar and ordered a glass of red wine. Nine o'clock came and went. One wine became two. Rachel glanced over at the old guy in the black trench coat. Could it be him? Had Tesla lied about his age? The old guy paid no attention to her. He hadn't even noticed she existed. All he was worried about was the glass on the bar in front of him.

She checked her watch again, checked her mobile. Maybe Tesla was stuck at work, or maybe he'd been held up by the snow, or maybe he'd been involved in an accident and was in intensive care hooked up to a life-support machine.

By quarter past nine the excuses weren't working and Rachel was feeling foolish and angry. Her first date since for ever and she'd been stood up. She picked up her phone and checked again for messages. No texts, no missed calls. Not that she expected any. She'd thought Tesla was different, but he wasn't. He'd got cold feet and hadn't even bothered to contact her.

Rachel considered getting another wine, she considered getting a whole bottle, but that wouldn't solve anything. If anything, it would just make a bad situation worse. She'd wake up tomorrow with a hangover and nothing would have changed. Her life would still be a pathetic mess, and Jamie would still be the biggest mistake she'd ever made.

She drained her glass, pulled her coat on, grabbed her bag and headed outside. The pavements were still white, but the world had lost that magical, romantic glow. Now it just looked desolate and empty. The snow had stopped but the wind was still there. It whipped at her face and stung her skin.

The cold air hit Rachel straight away and two glasses of wine suddenly felt like four. Her head went woolly, her limbs felt lighter. She suddenly felt stupid. She *was* stupid. Stupid for believing that good things could happen to her. This whole evening was one she just wanted to forget in a hurry.

Rachel glanced right then left. There was no sign of Tesla, no sign of anyone. She turned right and hurried towards the Tube station. She just wanted to be home now, curled up in bed, cosy and warm. Someone shouted out behind her, the voice muffled by the snow but still loud in the silence. Rachel turned and saw a man about thirty metres away. He had his hands on his hips, like he'd been running and was trying to catch his breath.

She noticed the trench coat straight away. Black, knee-length. It was too dark to make out the colour of his hair, but Rachel thought it was brown. Hoped it was. The man started towards her and by the time he'd covered fifteen metres, Rachel saw he was smiling. Five metres later and she could see it was a very nice smile. Charming, relaxed, friendly, everything you'd want in a smile. And then he was standing right in front of her and she couldn't believe her luck. He was handsome enough to have been an actor. He would have looked great up on the big screen.

"I am so sorry I'm late," he said. "Work was manic and to top it all I've managed to lose my mobile. I had no way of contacting you to tell you I was running late. I'm just glad I caught you in time."

The accent was cultured and polished, the voice deep and sexy. Leather gloves, a black wool scarf, classy shoes. Brown eyes.

"It's okay," Rachel said.

"No it's not. It's anything but okay. You must have thought I'd stood you up."

Rachel smiled. "It crossed my mind."

"I need to make this up to you. Have you ever eaten at The Ivy?"

"Don't you need to book like six months in advance?"

"I know someone who works there, and I'm guessing with this weather they've probably had some cancellations. Look, I'm parked just around the corner. Let me buy you dinner. It's the least I can do."

"Okay. But I need to ask something first."

"Fire away."

"What's your name? Your real name?"

Another smile. This one as warm and charming as before. "Adam."

"Well, Adam, my name's Rachel, and it's great to meet you at last."

Rachel held her hand out and they shook. His grip was firm but gentle and his touch sent little bursts of fireworks shooting through her nervous system.

Adam's Porsche was parked down a nearby side street. He frowned when he saw the parking ticket stuck to the windscreen. Then he peeled it off and stuffed it into his coat pocket.

"One of those days," he said with a shake of his head.

He held the door open and Rachel slid into the passenger seat. She felt sophisticated and elegant, like Audrey Hepburn in one of those old black-and-white movies. Jamie never opened doors for her. Adam gently closed the door, locking her in with the smell of leather and a hint of aftershave. Rachel was grinning to herself. Good-looking and a great sense of humour. Two for two.

Adam climbed into the driver's seat and pulled his door closed. Rachel barely saw his arm move. It was just a blur in her peripheral vision. She felt a stinging sensation in her thigh and looked dumbly at her leg, looked at Adam. She saw the syringe, saw his expression change from charming to predatory. She grabbed for the door handle but it flapped uselessly in her hand. She reached for the button to unlock the door but noticed that it had been removed. Her limbs felt like they were made from lead and she couldn't move her arms. A ton weight pushed her deep into the seat. Her mind was screaming but nothing came out of her mouth.

"Hello Number Five," Adam whispered.

# CHAPTER
# EIGHT

The bar at the Cosmopolitan Hotel was sleek and completely devoid of character. Lots of polished wood and polished chrome and smooth, shiny leather. Artfully placed lights created strange shadows and made the leaves of the fake plants glow. Computerised versions of Christmas classics played quietly in the background. The sparse scattering of Christmas decorations wasn't worth the effort. There was a piano tucked away in the corner. According to the sign behind the bar, Tuesday night was jazz night.

Half a dozen customers were scattered among the tables, two pairs and two singles, mostly business people whose schedules had meant they were stranded here for a night or two. Plenty of laughter and chat, and plenty of drinking. The blonde girl behind the bar was pretty and bubbly and smiled a lot. Early twenties with an Eastern European accent. I ordered a whisky and sat down at the nearest empty table, rattled the ice cubes around the glass and took a sip. The alcohol made my throat burn.

One of the singles stood out because she kept stealing glances in my direction. She'd been here when I arrived, sitting quietly on her own at the table that gave the best view of the room. I drank my whisky and watched her from the corner of my eye, waiting for her to make her move. She gave it another five minutes before she stood up and made her way over.

She was an inch or so shorter than me, somewhere around the five-eight mark in flat shoes, and she moved with the self-contained, fluid grace of a dancer. She was absolutely stunning. Long blonde hair tied back in a ponytail and the bluest eyes I'd ever seen. Her body was to die for and whether this was the result of good genes or regular, vigorous workouts, I neither knew nor cared. All that mattered was the end result, and that end result was spectacular.

She put her glass on the table, pulled out the chair opposite me, then sat down and got comfortable. Head tilted slightly to the left, she checked me out. She made no attempt to disguise what she was doing. She started at my head and worked her way down to the tabletop, her eyes moving from left to right, like she was reading a book.

"What are you thinking?" she asked.

"I'm thinking you're not a businesswoman."

"And?"

"And I'm wondering why the hell you'd want to be a cop."

She smiled at that. "My dad was a policeman, and his dad, and his dad. I was supposed to be a boy."

"I take it he got over his disappointment," I said.

"He's very proud of me." She looked at me again. "You're not what I expected."

"In what way?"

"Your file says you're thirty-three."

"I've got a file?"

A nod. "You've got a file."

"I am thirty-three."

"You look older. It's probably the hair. You didn't have white hair in the file photo."

"That'll be all the stress and worry," I said.

"You could do with a haircut and a shave, too."

"And I guess I should be wearing a suit and shades. Once a G-Man always a G-Man. Is that it?"

"Something like that."

"Did Hatcher send you to babysit me?"

There was a slight hesitation. She broke eye contact and glanced left, a classic tell that indicated she was accessing the part of her brain where lies and half-truths were made. "Not exactly," she said.

"So why are you here?"

Her blue eyes locked onto mine again. "Curiosity. I've heard a lot about you." A wry grin. "Jefferson Winter, the big-shot American profiler."

"How did you know I'd be here?"

"Hatcher's told me a few war stories about the time he spent out at Quantico. Based on that I figured the bar of the hotel you were staying at was as good a place as any to start looking."

"Good call."

"Aren't you going to ask my name?"

"I already know it."

She raised an eyebrow.

"You're Detective Sergeant Sophie Templeton," I said.

Her face registered surprise, but she recovered quickly, cool and confident and back in control. The change was almost instantaneous, so quick you could have imagined it. Templeton was obviously someone who didn't get knocked off her game easily. Hatcher had mentioned her a couple of times, so it wasn't that difficult to put two and two together.

I nodded to her half-empty glass. "Can I get you another?"

Templeton shook her head. "Thanks, but no. I've got a busy day tomorrow."

"I can't twist your arm?"

"You could try, but I have to warn you I came out on top in all my self-defence classes."

Her comment sparked a whole load of interesting mental images. "I wasn't being literal," I said.

"And I was joking."

I smiled and she smiled back. It was a great smile, one that reached all the way from her mouth to her eyes and back again.

"You've only just got here," I said.

"It's a school night. I should have been home ages ago. I've got a busy day tomorrow." She rolled her eyes. "Not that that's anything new. Every day's a busy one. Particularly at the moment."

"We're going to catch him."

"And you're sure about that."

"Absolutely positive. No doubt about it whatsoever."

"Are you really as good as Hatcher says?"

I reached for my glass and took a sip. "And that's the real reason you're here, isn't it? So how did it go down? Did you all get together in the office and draw straws?"

Templeton drank some of her drink, a small sip followed by the tiniest licking of her lips. Jack Daniel's and Coke, judging by the smell and colour. "I'm not here to check you out, Winter."

I raised an eyebrow and said nothing.

"Okay, I am here to check you out. But, like I said earlier, I'm doing this for my own curiosity. I'm not reporting back to anyone." She paused and fixed me with those big blue eyes. "Nice deflection, by the way. Avoid the question by putting me on the defensive."

A shrug and a smile. Busted.

"So," she said. "Back to *my* question."

"I can't answer it."

"Can't or won't?"

"Can't. It's a trick question. The problem is that I don't know what Hatcher thinks of me."

"He says you're the best profiler in the business."

"In that case, he's right. I am the best."

Templeton laughed. "You don't do modesty then."

"Modesty has nothing to do with it. You've checked my track record. The stats speak for themselves."

"How do you know I've checked your track record?"

I raised an eyebrow again, said nothing. This time it was Templeton's turn to shrug and smile. She held her hand out over the table and we shook. Her skin was soft and warm, her grip confident yet feminine. That was good. She obviously didn't feel the need to overcompensate.

She smiled that great smile and said, "It's good to meet you, Winter. It's going to be interesting working with you."

# CHAPTER
# NINE

Templeton disappeared into the lobby and I was left wondering what the hell that was all about. I felt like I'd just done an exam or a job interview, but I had no idea what for, or why. For a while I just sat there nursing my drink and thought about Templeton. I'd ruled out the idea of anything happening between us the moment she walked over to my table and every male in the room had checked her out, both the married ones and the single ones.

It wasn't that I didn't want anything to happen, I was just being realistic. The bottom line: women like Templeton didn't happen to guys like me. If we'd been at college, Templeton would have been the head cheerleader and I would have been the straight-A student who ended up giving the valedictorian speech. Cheerleaders went for the jocks, they didn't go for guys who could count without using their fingers, or read without moving their lips. It was one of those laws that governed the universe, an unbreakable rule that made sure everything and everyone slotted into their rightful places.

When the music finally got too much, I drained my glass and headed upstairs. My suite at the Cosmopolitan was nothing special. On a scale of one to Vegas it scored a four. The decoration was as bland as the bar downstairs. The walls were white. So were the towels and the bedlinen. The sofa and chairs were cream. White rugs on the beige carpet, and black-and-white framed photographs on the walls. It was like all the colour had been leached from the room.

For the past eighteen months since the execution, home had been a series of hotel suites, each one as anonymous as this one. Whenever I take on a case I always insist on a suite instead of a room. This is non-negotiable. During my time with the FBI I'd slummed it in too many cheap motel rooms. This suite was my sanctuary, somewhere to escape to even if it was just for a few hours. The last thing I wanted was a bed where you could feel the springs, and a shower that didn't work, and walls so thin you could hear the neighbours breathing.

Everything I needed to get through the day was in my suitcase. It was still packed because there was no point unpacking. I'd be in London for a few days, a week max, then I'd move on to the next hotel. Off chasing the next monster. I still owned a house in Virginia. It had two bedrooms and a living room big enough for my Steinway baby grand not to look out of place. Once a week someone went in and checked the place hadn't been burgled, and once a month a groundskeeping firm tidied up the yard. I wasn't sure why I hadn't sold it. I guess everyone needs a place to call home, even if it is only a token effort.

My second condition when I take a case is that the suite comes with a complimentary bottle of single malt. The blended stuff is fine for everyday use, but when it comes to unwinding you can't beat a good single malt. Twelve-year-old is acceptable, fifteen-year-old is better than acceptable, and anything older is a bonus. Hatcher had come up with an eighteen-year-old Glenlivet that ticked all the appropriate boxes. I wired my portable speakers to my laptop, found Mozart's Jupiter Symphony, and hit play. Then I poured a drink and took a sip, savouring the smoky, peaty flavour.

Eyes closed, I let the beauty of the music wash over me. Mozart has the power to transport me into another world, a world that's light years from the one I usually inhabit. This is a place of beauty and life rather than a place of torture and screams, a place of hope rather than despair. My laptop contained the best performances I'd managed to find of Mozart's work. Everything the great man had ever written was on there. My goal was to own the defining performances of every single piece. It was a work in progress, a lifelong task.

The first movement drifted to an end and I opened my eyes. For a moment I just sat there and sipped my whisky. I'd lost track of how long it had been since I last slept, but even though I was so exhausted I could barely see straight, I wasn't ready to sleep. The second movement started up and I checked my emails. There was nothing much there. An update on the Maine case, a request from the San Francisco Police Department, a couple of junk emails.

I headed out to the balcony for a last smoke, the rich sound of the second movement following me, gentle and soothing. A blanket of snow lay over London, painting the city clean. Sounds were more muffled than usual, the streets emptier. High overhead, a lone passenger jet roared through the stratosphere. The London Eye stood still in the distance, lit up in blue and white. I finished my cigarette and flicked it out into the dark. The glowing orange tip tumbled end over end, getting smaller and smaller until it disappeared altogether. I went back inside and chased a sleeping tablet down with a shot of Glenlivet. My last thought before crashing in to sleep was of victim number five. We had no idea who she was yet, but the one thing I knew for sure was that right now she'd be more alone than she'd ever been.

All alone and living the nightmare.

# CHAPTER
# TEN

I'd promised Hatcher a profile by nine, but that wasn't going to happen. Sleep usually gave me a clearer perspective. Not this time. If anything, this case was hazier than ever. I had some ideas, but nothing worth sharing. My profile would influence the direction the investigation took, and if I got it wrong an innocent woman would suffer. A bad profile was one of the best ways to screw up a case.

This case was unlike any other I'd worked. For starters, there was usually a dead body or two to work with. That bugged me more than anything else. Performing a lobotomy would take time and skill. It would be easier to kill the victim. It didn't make sense, didn't tally with what I knew about this unsub. This guy was careful and tidy, and he didn't do anything without thinking it through first, so why go to all the trouble of performing a lobotomy? Also, this unsub got off on torturing his victims. He fed on their pain and screams. Once the lobotomy was carried out the fun would be over. No more pain, no more screams. So, at what point did he carry out the lobotomy? What was the trigger?

Another thing that bugged me was the contradictory way the victims were being treated. On one hand they were being brutally tortured. On the other hand they were being well cared for. It was possible the unsub was looking after his victims so he could prolong the torture. Possible, but the explanation didn't sit comfortably.

I showered quickly then towelled myself dry and got dressed. Yesterday's jeans still had some life left in them, but my T-shirt and hoodie were past their best. Today's T-shirt featured Nirvana, and today's hoodie was black. I ran a hand through my hair to tidy it up. I've never been sure whether one of my ancestors chose Winter as a surname because of that errant gene that caused our hair to turn white prematurely, or whether it was one of those cosmic flukes that occasionally happen. I wouldn't call it coincidence because I don't believe in coincidence or luck or fate. What I do believe is that in an almost infinite universe anything and everything is possible.

Like a kid in his early twenties with the surname Winter ending up with white hair. When you get down to it, as far as cosmic flukes go, it's really not that impressive. Impressive is when two high-school sweethearts separated by circumstance and oceans and half a century of living bump into each other on vacation in some bizarre out-of-the-way corner of the globe, and get to pick things up right where they left off all those years ago.

I ordered the full English breakfast from room service because God only knew when I'd get to eat again. The first coffee washed down my breakfast, the second came out onto the balcony with me. With the city waking up below me, I lit a cigarette and took a long drag. The sky was a bright, sharp blue that reminded me of the winter mornings back in Virginia. The lack of cloud cover meant it felt even colder than yesterday, the mercury struggling to stay in the twenties. My morning fix of caffeine and nicotine kickstarted my system, and by the time I got back inside I was good to go.

Hatcher had emailed through a folder that contained the before and after pictures of the victims. I started with Patricia Maynard's photos since she was the victim I knew best. The before picture was fairly typical in that it showed Patricia Maynard caught in a happy moment. These photos were supplied by the family and it was only natural that they would want their loved ones remembered with a rose-tinted glow. The truth was that Patricia Maynard was human. She had good days and bad days. Sometimes she was happy, sometimes she was sad, and sometimes she was angry. There were times she was a joy to be with, and times when she was a complete pain in the ass. The rollercoaster of emotions and moods of a normal life, in other words.

This photo froze her in a moment when she was at her best. It was taken in a restaurant and she was smiling as though she didn't have a care. There was no indication that she was going to end up colliding head-on with her worst nightmare, and that her life would effectively be over.

The photograph had been cropped to show Patricia Maynard's face, making it difficult to tell what the occasion was. Maybe it was her birthday, maybe it was

**58**

someone else's birthday. It had been a celebration of some sort. You didn't take photographs in a restaurant unless there was a reason you wanted to remember the occasion.

Her hair was brunette, her eyes brown, and she was attractive. Not stop-the-traffic gorgeous like Templeton, but she would definitely make a man look twice. She was in good shape, healthy and a good weight, and she was wearing a blouse with the top two buttons undone to show off a glimpse of her cleavage and the tiniest tease of lace. Patricia Maynard had been a happy, confident, attractive woman who'd had her whole life ahead of her.

The after photo had been taken by a police photographer and there was nothing rose-tinted about it whatsoever. This photograph was stark and brutal, and there wasn't a hint of the confident, attractive woman Patricia Maynard had once been. Her eyes were puffy and red and shut tight, like she'd gone fifteen rounds in a boxing ring. The slackness in her face made me think of stroke victims.

I went through the before and after photographs for the other three victims, the rose-tinted family shots and the cold, stark police shots. Sarah Flight, Margaret Smith, Caroline Brant. I pulled up the four after shots and arranged them in two neat rows. Sarah Flight and Margaret Smith were on the top row, Caroline Brant and Patricia Maynard were on the bottom. A prickle of excitement made the hairs on the back of my neck stand up. Laid out like that with their bald heads and their puffy boxer eyes, they could have been one person.

I opened a new screen and pulled up the before photos and laid them out in the same configuration as the after photos. I saw the resemblance immediately. I'd missed it earlier because two of the victims had dyed their hair. Hatcher answered his phone on the second ring.

"I've sent a car," he said. "It'll be there in a few minutes."

"That's great. I need the car, but I'm not coming in. Not this morning, anyway."

"What about the profile?"

"I need to do some more work on it."

"What the hell are you talking about, Winter? You said it would be ready by this morning."

"Shut up and listen a second. I don't have a profile for the unsub but I do have a profile for the next victim. Have you got a pen?"

There was a rustle of paper and plastic on the other end of the line, then Hatcher was back. "Okay, fire away."

# CHAPTER
# ELEVEN

"You're looking for a woman aged twenty-five to thirty-five." I kept it slow so Hatcher's pen could keep up. "She's going to be married, but there will be problems in the marriage. The husband will have had an affair. Possibly multiple affairs."

"I don't know if you can make that assumption, Winter. The Flights' marriage was sound. Granted there were problems in the other victims' marriages, but the Flights were fine."

"Were they?"

"We checked it out. They were as happy as Romeo and Juliet."

"Not the best example," I said.

"My people are good. If there had been anything going on they would have found it."

"And you're prepared to put your money where your mouth is?"

"Are you serious?"

"Let's say twenty pounds. No, let's make it interesting. How about fifty?"

"That isn't exactly ethical," said Hatcher.

"Firstly, you haven't said no. And secondly, that's loser talk."

"Fine, I'll be happy to take your money."

"Okay," I said. "The victim will be a brunette, brown eyes, and she'll be attractive, too. Bear in mind that her hair might be dyed, so don't rule out other colours. Caroline Brant and Margaret Smith both dyed their hair. What you're looking for is a natural brunette. She'll be a career woman, educated to university level. This is a high-risk target for our unsub."

"Why take that risk?" Hatcher asked. "If this guy's whole game is to make these women suffer, why not kidnap a prostitute or a junkie?"

"Because that's not his whole game. These women represent someone significant to him. His ex-wife, would be my initial guess. Whoever the real target is, she's the one he really wants to hurt, but he doesn't have the courage to do that yet. He's scared of her. Absolutely terrified. That makes him angry, and he takes that anger out on his victims."

"So, he's just practising with these other women, working up the courage to go after his ex."

"Pretty much," I agreed. "You need to get your people to look at every missing person report for the last three days. All of them. I'm particularly interested in anyone reported missing over the last twenty-four hours. If I'm right about the way this unsub is escalating then that's where we'll find our next victim."

"So you think he's already snatched someone?"

"Without a doubt."

"What sort of area are we looking at?"

"Everything north of the Thames."

Hatcher took a sharp intake of breath on the other end of the line, a reaction that was perfectly understandable since I'd just narrowed the search down to an area of hundreds of square miles and a population in the millions.

"It gets worse," I added. "It wouldn't surprise me if he starts targeting victims outside of London. That stunt with the car park security light in St Albans shows he's looking for ways to mislead us. From here on we need to assume he'll send us on a wild goose chase at every opportunity. That said, let's start with the area inside the M25 first. If we don't get any hits there we'll widen the search to take in the Home Counties."

"I'll get right on to it," said Hatcher.

"I'm going to need to see photographs ASAP. Send them to my cellphone."

"No problem. So when can I expect a full profile?"

"I'll have something for you by the end of the day."

I hung up, put my coat on, stuffed my cigarettes and Zippo into a pocket, then headed downstairs. An unmarked BMW was waiting outside and I had to smile when I saw the driver. I stepped from the Cosmopolitan's revolving door and walked over to the car.

"Morning, Templeton."

"Morning, Winter."

Templeton was leaning against the BMW dressed in a thick padded coat. Her jeans were so tight they clung to her legs like a second skin, and her blonde hair was scraped back in a ponytail. If anything, the daylight made her eyes appear even more spectacular. The way she was leaning on the car, she could have been in an advert.

"So you drew the short straw again," I said.

"Believe it or not, I volunteered for this. I'm interested in seeing you work first-hand."

"I'm flattered."

"You should be. Usually, I'd rather pull out my own wisdom teeth than play babysitter."

We got into the car and buckled up. A rock channel kicked in when the key was turned, classic Aerosmith pumping from the speakers. Templeton leant over the dash and turned the volume down. The engine had heated up during the drive from New Scotland Yard and the heater was working overtime to keep the chill out.

"You said babysitter rather than taxi driver," I said. "That means you've spoken to Hatcher."

Templeton nodded. "He called five minutes ago. He said you hadn't done the profile yet. He sounded pretty pissed off about it."

"What else did he say?"

"He told me to keep an eye on you and report back on everything you get up to."

"Will you?"

"That depends on what you get up to. So where do you want to go?"

"Enfield. I want to visit the first victim, Sarah Flight."

We turned right out of the Cosmopolitan's driveway and I flashed my cigarette pack at Templeton.

"Fine with me, so long as you're sharing," she said.

I lit two cigarettes and passed one to Templeton. The traffic was slow and sticky. Almost as bad as New York traffic, but nowhere near as bad as LA traffic. We drove in silence, Templeton concentrating on driving while I concentrated on the case. It was a comfortable silence, companionable, there was nothing forced about it.

I finished my cigarette and pitched the butt out of the window, hit a button on my door and the window buzzed shut. Thirty seconds later, Templeton followed suit. The buildings got smaller and greyer and bleaker the further north we drove. The winter sunshine made the architecture look better than it had yesterday, but not by much. The radio played a steady stream of classics. Hendrix, the Eagles, Led Zeppelin. Great tunes from a long-ago time.

"So what was he like?"

I'd heard that question plenty of times so I didn't need to ask who Templeton was referring to. Usually people waited until they knew me better, but I wasn't surprised she'd asked. She didn't strike me as someone who would tiptoe around a subject.

"He was completely plausible," I said. "A pillar of the community. He taught math at college and by all accounts he was popular with his colleagues. The kids liked him, too. He was outgoing and inspiring, your typical eccentric teacher. He had one of those brains that never switches off. While he was at San Quentin numerous attempts were made to measure his IQ but he just used them as an excuse to mess with the shrinks. All any of them could say for certain was that he'd easily qualify for Mensa."

"You didn't suspect anything?"

"If you mean, did I suspect that my father was a serial killer, then, no, I didn't."

"But there was something not quite right about him, wasn't there?"

I remembered a barbecue back when I was eight or nine, a couple of years before the FBI swooped in and arrested my father and my world turned upside down. The men were all gathered around the barbecue, and my father was in the middle of them. He was wearing a cook's apron, a beer in one hand, a set of tongs in the other. The beer had flowed freely all afternoon and everyone was laughing and joking and having a wonderful time. My father was laughing and joking right along with them. Except there was something a little too forced about his laughter. What I remembered most was that my father's laugh didn't quite reach his eyes.

"In hindsight, the signs were there," I said. "I like to think if I met him now I would see straight through him. But I was just a kid. I was eleven when the FBI arrested him. He murdered his first victim before I was born. At home he swung between being distant and being controlling, but he was no worse than my friends' fathers. In fact, he was better than most of them. Of course, all my buddies thought he was great, because that was the face he showed them."

"Why do I feel like I'm only being given the edited highlights?"

"Because you are."

"Look," said Templeton, "if you don't want to talk about this, that's fine. I understand."

"It's not that I don't want to talk about it, it's just that I don't really know what to say. If he was an unsub I could give you a complete profile, chapter and verse. But he was my father. I'm just too close to offer any sort of objectivity."

"You blame yourself, don't you? You think you could have done something to save those girls."

"And you sound like the shrink back at Quantico."

"You're dodging my question."

"Of course I am. We've only just met. Let's save the heavy stuff for when we know each other better."

I tapped another cigarette from my pack and offered one to Templeton. She declined with a shake of the head. A shaft of sunlight shone through the driver window and caught her just right. This was my first opportunity to study her profile up close. The view was every bit as impressive as the front view. She had great bone structure, a cute nose, high Scandinavian cheekbones.

She must have felt me staring because she glanced over and gave me a look. Front-on, her face had that perfect symmetry the camera loved. Break it down to a bunch of numbers and it would no doubt follow the Golden Ratio, 1:1.618, a ratio that had fascinated artists and mathematicians for the last two and a half thousand years. Evidence of the Golden Ratio could be found throughout nature, and it could be found in the driver's seat of the BMW.

I wondered why Templeton had opted for a breadline cop's salary when she could have earned a fortune trading off her looks. Following in Daddy's footsteps was a plausible explanation, but my gut feeling was that I was also getting the edited highlights. I cracked open my window and lit the cigarette. A Stones tune came on the radio and Templeton cranked up the volume. She was lost in the song, head bobbing in time with the beat, lips following the lyric word for word. I took another drag on my cigarette then went back to thinking about the case.

# CHAPTER
# TWELVE

Rachel's eyes sprang open but all she saw was a darkness that was so dense it consumed her. There was no light whatsoever, not so much as a single stray shaft sneaking through a window or around a door. Her heart was hammering as though it was about to burst through her chest and her breath came in short, sharp gasps, each one edging her closer to a full-blown panic attack. The dark took each breath and bounced it back, amplifying the sound.

Her mattress was so thin she could feel the cold, hard floor beneath her. The smell of bleach scratched at her nose and the back of her throat. Everything came flooding back at once. She saw herself sat in the front seat of the Porsche, grinning like she'd won the lottery. She saw the shiny steel glint of the needle.

Rachel tried to stand and a wave of nausea washed through her. She vomited, but managed to tip forward at the last second so most of it hit the floor rather than her clothes or the mattress. The smell of last night's red wine and stomach acid made her throw up again. She kept on gagging and vomiting until all that came up was bile. Rachel wiped her mouth with the back of her hand. Her head ached, her palms were clammy, and she felt shivery and shaky, like she was suffering from flu.

She slumped back onto the mattress and tried to control her breathing. Panic pulled at her and she forced herself back from the edge. Slowly. Gradually. She took a couple of deep breaths and the acidic stink of vomit stung her nose. She gagged, and would have been sick again if there had been anything left in her stomach. She coughed a couple of times and wiped her mouth, took another deep breath and told herself to get it together. Her breathing steadied.

Rachel waved a hand through the dark until she found a tiled wall. The tiles were smooth and cool beneath her hands, square like bathroom tiles, each side roughly fifteen centimetres long. Rachel used the wall to stand, little by little, moving slowly. Her head spun but her legs seemed to hold up okay.

The floor tiles were larger than the wall tiles, closer to a metre square, cold and glossy beneath her naked feet. She moved around tentatively, trying to get a sense of her surroundings. There was a door in the third wall she came to. It felt solid. Her hands slid over the painted surface until she found the handle. She tried it. Locked. Her heart started racing again and this time the panic got hold. A whooshing sound filled her ears and she had a sense of falling.

Then nothing.

When she opened her eyes everything was still pitch black. The floor was a cold crush against her back, and her limbs felt stiff and awkward. A bruise was growing on the side of her head from where she had hit the ground. She guessed she'd been out for a while, but couldn't say how long. Rachel got unsteadily to her feet and followed the wall back to the mattress. There were no more doors.

She slid down the wall and pressed herself into the corner, hugged her knees in tight and turned herself into a ball. She barely noticed the tears streaming down her face. This situation was as messed up as it got. She was going to die. She was certain of it. That wasn't what scared her the most, though. What terrified her more than anything was the fact that she was still alive.

She'd seen the way Adam's smile changed last night. One second it had been friendly and full of humour. *I'm going to be your best friend*, that smile had promised. *I'm going to take you away from your sorry excuse for a life and transport you into the sort of life you always dreamt of, the sort of life you always felt you deserved.* In a beat his smile had changed to that predator's smile. Rachel's stomach tightened and she thought she was going to be sick again. Her legs and arms turned to water and the tears flowed freely down her cheeks. She wondered if Jamie had called the police yet. That thought was followed swiftly by another, one that brought a fresh wave of tears.

Had he even noticed she was gone?

Had anyone noticed?

# CHAPTER
# THIRTEEN

The driveway was a minefield of potholes, but Templeton didn't seem to notice. She drove across them as though they didn't exist, the BMW's suspension complaining with every bump and jolt. She pulled into a walled courtyard and skidded to a halt, kicking up a spray of gravel that rattled against the underside of the car.

Dunscombe House was centuries old, older than America. Over the years new bits had been added here and there. Different styles, different periods, different architects. The building had an air of randomness, and a sense that it had been dislocated from time. It was big enough to be classed as a manor house, but nowhere near big enough to be a stately home.

We got out of the car and walked to the main entrance side by side. Templeton pressed the buzzer then took a step back and peered into the lens of the security camera. There was a look on her face like she was daring whoever was on the other end to deny us entry. Two seconds passed, three. The door clicked, the lock released, and Templeton strode in like she owned the place. Shoulders square, back straight, hips swinging. From behind, those tight jeans looked fantastic.

A Christmas tree opposite the reception desk was ten feet tall and totally over the top. It had dozens of glittering ornaments and baubles, hundreds of tiny white lights, yards upon yards of tinsel, and a large silver star on top. Templeton marched straight up to the reception desk and showed her ID.

"We're here to see Sarah Flight," she said.

The receptionist looked surprised.

"Is there a problem?" I asked.

The receptionist shook her head. "No, not at all. It's just that Sarah doesn't get many visitors."

"When you say not many, how many are we talking about?"

"Her mother visits every morning without fail. You've just missed her."

"Anyone else?"

A shake of the head.

"What about her husband?"

The receptionist hesitated. She glanced left then right, a classic tell for someone with a secret to share.

"He's never visited, has he?" I said.

"Not once."

"Where will we find Sarah?"

"She's in the day room." The receptionist pointed to a set of double doors opposite a wide old-fashioned staircase.

The day room was large and churchlike. Wood panelling, parquet flooring and a high vaulted ceiling. Someone had gone to town with the Christmas decorations, and there had to be a mile of tinsel and banners and strings of silver bells. The Christmas tree in front of the large fireplace wasn't as big as the one in reception, but it was still impressive. It was decorated in a similar style, probably by the same person.

The room stank of overcooked vegetables and gravy and cleaning products, and reminded me of every institution I'd ever been in. It was like something from *One Flew Over the Cuckoo's Nest*. The patients were being supervised by two orderlies, a black guy and a white woman who both looked bored to death. They were at a table near the door, killing time until their shift ended.

Sarah Flight's chair was positioned in front of one of the bay windows and she was staring blankly out at the grounds. Her hair had grown back. It was shiny and healthy and neatly styled, and it had been brushed recently, probably by her mother as part of their morning routine. There was no way the orderlies would have taken the time to do it. Sarah was dressed in loose, baggy clothes. Easy to get on, easy to get off. A hundred and twenty pounds of dead weight was hard to manage, and the orderlies would be looking to make their lives as easy as possible. A trickle of drool escaped from the corner of Sarah's mouth and dripped down the side of her chin.

"Have you got any tissues?" I asked Templeton.

Templeton fished a clean tissue from a pocket and I gently wiped the drool away. It was a small gesture, one that would go unnoticed, but Sarah deserved some dignity even if she wasn't aware of it.

My first thought when I saw Patricia Maynard yesterday was that she'd be better off dead, and I was thinking the same thing now. That's not a conclusion I'd come to lightly. Alive is always better than dead because any sort of life has to be better than a cold, lonely grave. If you're alive, it doesn't matter what horrors have been inflicted on you, there's a chance you can be fixed.

That said, not everyone can be fixed. I know that from bitter experience. My mother had never been physically abused by my father, but the psychological scars ran deep, and they ultimately killed her. There will always be a few survivors who turn to drink or drugs to numb the memories, and in the more extreme cases, things will become so intolerable they kill themselves. Most manage to pull together something that resembles a functioning life, though.

Alive is always better than dead.

I looked at Sarah Flight sat there staring into nothing through dead eyes, and wondered if this was the exception to that rule. Sarah would never be fixed. For her, this was as good as it got.

I positioned a chair alongside Sarah's, unzipped my sheepskin jacket, then pulled the hood of my top up and for a while just sat there sharing her view. Thoughts of the case tumbled randomly through my head and I did my best to ignore them. I wanted a few moments when my mind was as white and blank as the landscape on the other side of the glass. My biggest failing is getting too close, too involved. I want to solve the case so badly that the trees blur into one great big forest.

The winter sun made everything look sharper and more real, more defined. It reflected off the snow-covered lawn, dazzlingly bright, and the trees and bushes resembled white minimalist sculptures. The whole scene looked like a Christmas card. It depressed me that Sarah would never really see this.

For a split second my perspective shifted. The grounds blurred into the background and the window became a dull mirror that threw back a reflection of Sarah and myself. Because of the angle and the light and the lack of a reflective surface on the back of the glass, it was like the whole world had shrunk down until it was just the two of us.

And then my vision readjusted and I was back in the day room again. Templeton was standing behind me in a state of agitation. I could see her reflection in the window. She glanced at her watch, glanced at her cell, glanced over her shoulder at the patients. She sighed a couple of times, bit her lip. She was a woman with places to go and people to see.

I gave her another minute, a minute that was more like forty-five seconds. She crouched down and leant in close enough for me to get the full effect of her perfume. It was a good smell, one that monkeyed around with my overactive imagination and filled my head with all sorts of interesting and inappropriate notions.

"If you don't mind me asking, what the hell are we doing here, Winter?" She was talking in a low whisper, her breath tickling my ear. "The reason I ask is because it looks to me like you're sitting here watching the

76

flowers grow when we should be out chasing the bad guy."

"What I'm doing is getting some perspective."

I smiled and waited for Templeton to smile back.

"Okay," she said. "I'm listening."

"You do this job to catch the bad guys, right? That's your endgame. And you're good at it."

Templeton's head bobbed ambiguously from side to side, which was as close to an admission as she was ever going to give. There was no way she was going to admit something like that out loud.

"You're a classic overachiever," I added. "Driven and good at your job, and there's nothing wrong with that. Nothing wrong with that whatsoever."

"Your point?"

I nodded towards Sarah Flight. Another slither of drool had escaped from the corner of her mouth and I wiped it away with the tissue.

"She's the point. Her and every other person who's come up against a lunatic with a warped world perspective and a bunch of twisted fantasies. When you focus all your energies on the bad guy it's easy to forget the victims. Way too easy. I'm as guilty of that as anyone. That's why I came here. To remind myself that the real reason I do what I do is because of the victims. Catching the bad guys is just a bonus. Somewhere out there is a woman who has been snatched by our unsub, and if we don't do our job properly then she's going to end up like this."

I reached out and touched Sarah Flight's hand. Partly because I wanted to check she was real, but mostly because I *needed* to know. I half expected my hand to pass right through hers but it didn't. I expected her skin to be cold but it was as warm as my own. There was a space on her one remaining finger where her wedding band had once been. The stumps of her other fingers and thumbs had been cauterised and were covered in scar tissue. Who'd removed the ring? Her mother? One of Dunscombe's staff? A nurse or orderly Sarah would never know? One thing was for certain: Greg Flight hadn't removed it. I got up and headed for the door. Behind me, Templeton's footsteps sounded tentative and timid on the parquet floor, nowhere near as confident as when we'd walked in.

# CHAPTER
# FOURTEEN

Greg Flight's PA showed us into his large corner office on the top floor of a three-floor building leased by Fizz, a Soho-based advertising agency. The agency wasn't premier-league, but it wasn't a bottom-feeder, either. It sat comfortably in the middle, surviving on the crumbs dropped down from the tables of Saatchi and Saatchi and the other big boys.

Flight's office was large and uncluttered, so was his desk. The furniture had soft round edges and was made from dark wood, and the ego wall screamed out that Flight had low self-esteem and was desperate to be taken seriously. He was doing his best to hide his insecurities and, given his position as art director, for the most part he was succeeding.

The PA escorted us towards two seats near one of the windows. They were made from soft padded leather and had been positioned so that when the blinds were up, you'd end up squinting into the sun. Flight's chair was big and thronelike and positioned in front of the window so anyone talking to him would be forced to look in that direction. It was also a good three inches higher than the ones we were supposed to sit in. The power play was obvious and pathetic, and smacked of desperation.

Templeton stood beside me, tall and imposing and giving Flight her best cop stare. Greg Flight looked lost and nervous in his big chair. It was a major win for us. A total slam dunk. Flight had made his play, and couldn't have got it more wrong. He'd aimed to be the top dog and failed spectacularly. If he stood up now then he might as well wave a white flag. The golden rule with power plays was that you never made your move until you were absolutely certain what your opponent's move was going to be. Sun Tzu got it right two and a half millennia ago when he said you needed to know your enemy.

The PA flashed her boss a look, then shut the door gently behind her. She was in her early twenties, brunette and perky and no doubt useless at her job. What she lacked in competence she must have made up for with her athleticism. It was the only reason I could see for Flight hiring her.

I smiled down at Greg Flight, and he fired a smile right back at me. He was doing his best to save face, but he'd already lost, and didn't even know it. Flight also had a space on his ring finger. His way of dealing with what had happened was through denial, and he'd no doubt done a thorough job of erasing Sarah from his life. If this meeting had taken place at his home rather than his office, there wouldn't have been a single trace of their life together. No pictures, no mementos, no reminders whatsoever. There was a good chance he'd sold the house he shared with Sarah. It had taken some serious persuasion from Templeton to get five minutes of his time, not because he was busy, but because we were representatives from a past he was trying very hard to run away from.

"How long have you been screwing her?" I asked.

Flight looked confused, a man caught on the back foot, which was exactly where I wanted him. He knew what he'd heard, but couldn't be sure he'd heard right. "Excuse me?" he said.

I shrugged. "I was wondering how long you've been having sex with your PA. Does she know her days are numbered?" I nodded to myself. "Of course she does. Incompetent isn't the same as stupid. So were you screwing her before Sarah's kidnapping? She looks a lot like Sarah, you know."

Flight just stared, open-mouthed and dumbfounded.

I shook my head. "No. Sarah was kidnapped last year and I'm guessing there have been about six or seven women since then. A new one every couple of months would be about right. Did they all look like Sarah?"

Flight just carried on staring.

"You were screwing around with someone when your wife was kidnapped, though." I nodded to myself. "Of course you were. And before that there would have been someone else. It's what you do. You see a woman you like and you have to have her. It doesn't matter who you hurt."

A pause, then, "Did you ever really love Sarah? I mean *really* love her. I'm talking the sort of love where you would sacrifice your life." Another shake of the head. "Of course you didn't. You could never do that.

And the reason you couldn't do that is because you're a self-obsessed commitment-phobic asshole."

Greg Flight's face turned bright red. And then he launched himself at me. He moved quickly for someone who spent a large part of his life stuck behind a desk, covering the distance between us in seconds. He hit me hard in the chest and I stumbled backwards. One moment I was upright, the next I was flat on my back with Flight pinning me down. I tried to wriggle free but there was too much of him and not enough of me. He curled his hand into a fist. His face was twisted with rage, lips narrow, eyes bulging. I struggled some more and ran through the various scenarios, but it didn't matter which way I came at the situation, I was going to end up hurt. The question right now was how badly.

The punch never came.

The weight on my chest eased and when I opened my eyes Greg Flight was glaring at me side-on from about four inches away. He was close enough for me to smell the stale coffee on his breath. His right cheek was squashed into the carpet and Templeton was on top of him, pulling his right arm up behind his back.

"This is police harassment," Flight said, his voice muffled by the carpet.

I sat up, crossed my legs and looked down at him. As power plays went, this one was pretty good. I now had the height advantage by almost two feet. And he was being pinned down by a woman. The second part would have eaten into him more than the first. In Greg Flight's world women were still very much second-rate citizens.

"Technically it can't be police harassment since I'm not a cop," I said.

Templeton pulled Flight's arm higher and he grimaced. "Let me go."

I tilted my head to the side so we were looking at each other eye to eye. "Look, Greg, nobody's judging you here. To be honest, I really don't care who you're screwing. All I'm trying to do is get an idea of the state of your relationship with Sarah at the time she was kidnapped."

"Let me go," he repeated.

"We'll let you go when you start co-operating. And I'd think very carefully before answering my next question. Another couple of pounds of pressure and that shoulder's going to pop right out of the socket. It hurts like hell having it put back in, like someone's grinding glass into the joint."

I paused, gave him a second to process this. Flight was glaring across at me like he was dreaming up new and improved ways to hurt me.

"Okay, here's the million-dollar question, Greg: your marriage was a mess, wasn't it?"

"You don't know what you're talking about."

"And that's the wrong answer. I'm afraid you don't win the car."

"There was nothing wrong with my marriage."

"Yeah, that's what you told the police. And because they were so focused on finding your wife they didn't dig too hard, did they?" I paused, softened my voice, made it quieter, more intimate. "Every time you have sex with your PA all you can think about is Sarah. You think about her wasting away in that hospital and the guilt eats you up."

Flight's eyes darted downwards, seeking out his naked ring finger. Templeton pulled harder on his arm and he gave a yelp.

"I'm reckoning another pound of pressure before that shoulder pops out, Greg. You might want to think about that." I paused again. "You know, we've just been to see Sarah. That private hospital she's in isn't cheap, but you're doing well for yourself so I reckon you can probably afford it. Does it ease the guilt to see that payment going out of your bank account each month?"

Flight broke eye contact and turned his head downwards into the carpet. When he looked back up at me again I could tell he'd come to a decision, and that the decision was the right one.

"Things hadn't been good between us for a while," he whispered.

# CHAPTER
# FIFTEEN

The lights came on with a dull thud, harsh, bright halogens that burned Rachel's sight into blindness. The glare reflected off the white wall and floor tiles, dazzling her. It was too much, too soon.

Rachel put a hand up to her forehead to block out the light, but it was still too bright. She closed her eyes then opened them slowly, a millimetre at a time, letting the light filter in until they were fully open. She'd been right about there being no windows and only one door. The door was painted white, gloss rather than matt, and was almost as reflective as the tiles. There was a large dog flap fitted to the lower part of the door. The ceiling was painted white, the mattress was white, the blankets.

It was a cold, sterile space that made her think of a laboratory. *Easy to clean.* The thought made her shiver despite the heat. Adam had removed her favourite red dress and replaced it with a pair of shapeless grey jogging bottoms and a matching grey sweatshirt. He'd also removed her underwear, lace replaced with cotton.

Rachel saw all these things without really seeing them, registered them without really registering. She was only vaguely aware of the mattress, and the drying puddle of vomit, of the black plastic bucket in the corner. She'd wished herself out of the dark, and now she could see, she wished she was blind again because all she could see was the dentist's chair.

The chair was made from brushed steel and had cream upholstery. It was solid and heavy and identical to the sort of chair she sat in every six months when she went for her check-up. Identical except for one big difference: the straps. Padded straps to secure arms, padded straps to secure legs, a padded strap to hold the head in place. For a while she just sat on the mattress and stared at the chair. She didn't want to, but couldn't help herself. Just looking at that chair made her feel sick.

Rachel got up and walked over to the chair in a trance. The upholstery on the armrests was stained dark in places. She knew it was blood but didn't want to admit that to herself because then she'd be opening up the floodgates, and she wasn't ready to go there yet. She didn't know if she'd ever be ready.

"Number Five will walk over to the door."

Adam's voice came from all around her. It was distorted and robotic, so loud it was deafening. Rachel spun around in terror. Four speakers were hung high on the walls, one in each corner, all painted white. The cameras fitted next to each speaker were painted white, too, positioned so there were no blind spots.

"Number Five will walk over to the door," Adam repeated.

Rachel walked slowly to the door. She stared at the floor so she wouldn't have to look at the cameras, watched her feet move one in front of the other. Her legs felt like they belonged to someone else and her whole body was trembling. She was aware of the cameras following her every move. The dog flap swung open and a bucket was pushed through. The bucket was filled to the three-quarter mark with soapy water, a scrubbing brush floating on top. The dog flap swung shut with a clatter.

"Number Five will clean up her mess."

Rachel hesitated. She glanced at the speakers, glanced at the cameras, glanced at the pool of vomit next to the mattress. Then she looked at the dentist's chair. She picked up the bucket and carried it over to the mattress, got down on her hands and knees and scrubbed the floor clean. The smell of bleach got into her nose and made her eyes water. The chemicals burnt into her hands and made her skin itch. When she'd finished cleaning up, she carried the bucket back to the door. The dog flap opened when she was a few steps away.

"Number Five will put the bucket through the flap."

Rachel complied immediately. The flap clattered shut and the lights went out. Adam's footsteps faded into the distance, a door opened then closed. The only sound was the sound of her breathing. Rachel made her way back across the room, slowly, arms outstretched like a sleepwalker. She reached the far wall, followed it around until she found the mattress, then lowered herself down and wrapped a blanket around herself. She was searching for comfort, but all she found was a lonely sadness that gnawed away at what little hope she had left. She closed her eyes to fight off the tears and the backs of her lids burned white and pink in the darkness.

# CHAPTER
# SIXTEEN

The temperature outside the Fizz offices was at least fifty degrees colder than it had been inside. It was like walking into a freezer. Most of the snow had melted, leaving behind grey piles of slush and treacherous patches of pavement ice. I zipped my jacket up to my chin, pulled my hood over my head, and wished I was in California or Hawaii or Rio, anywhere that was sunny and warm. Anywhere but here.

"Do you want to press charges?" Templeton asked.

I gave her a look. "Why the hell would I do that?"

"Well, first off, Greg Flight assaulted you. And secondly, he's an arsehole. There's two good reasons to get you started."

"And thirdly, he told me what I wanted to know, and at the end of the day that's all that matters. If I press charges I'm just wasting time and energy that could be put to better use. Like tracking down the unsub."

"Fair enough, but if you change your mind I'll be more than happy to play witness."

I lit a cigarette, offered one to Templeton, then pulled out my cell and thumbed through the list of recent calls.

"Who are you phoning?" Templeton flicked the Zippo to life and touched the flame to the tip of the cigarette dangling from the corner of her mouth.

"Are you always this nosy?"

She laughed. "Of course I am. I'm a cop. It goes with the territory. So, who are you phoning?"

I ignored the question and hit the button to connect the call. Hatcher answered on the second ring.

"You owe me fifty pounds," I said.

"I'll need proof before I pay up," Hatcher replied.

"Templeton was there when Greg Flight confessed. She'll corroborate. Flight was having an affair at the time his wife was kidnapped. That means the pattern holds. All the victims' husbands were having affairs. Any hits on the victim profile yet?"

"Nothing so far, but it's still early days."

"As soon as you get anything I want photographs," I said.

"No problem. You were right about what happened in St Albans, by the way. Our man did park in Grove Road. A resident saw him."

"Did you get a description?"

"Get this," said Hatcher. "We're looking for a man of average height aged between thirty and fifty. He might have dark hair, then again he might not have. Probably white, but again he might not have been."

"What about the vehicle?"

Hatcher was shaking his head on the other end of the line. I could sense the gesture in the tone of the silence that followed my question. A sigh, then, "It was dark and he parked away from the streetlamps, so the description of the car is as useful as the description of the bad guy. According to our witness it was a standard four-door saloon. Could have been a Ford, or a Vauxhall, or a Skoda. Might've been five years old. Might've been ten. As for colour. Pick a shade of grey."

"Don't you just love witnesses?"

"Tell me about it."

"On the plus side, the fact he parked in Grove Road means my theory that he's trying to mislead the investigation holds up. We might not know what he looks like, or what sort of car he drives, but we have a better idea of how he operates. Remember, Hatcher, I want those photographs ASAP."

I killed the call and took a drag on my cigarette. Templeton was staring at me with those bright blue eyes.

"What?" I said.

"You made a bet with Hatcher on whether or not Greg Flight was having an affair. I'm sure there are rules and regulations prohibiting that sort of thing."

"Probably. But it's worth keeping in mind what's important here."

"And what would that be?"

"The fact I'm now fifty pounds richer means the drinks are on me tonight."

Templeton narrowed her eyes, giving me her cop stare. The difference between this one and the one she'd used on Greg Flight was that this time she was trying hard to keep a straight face. "I don't remember agreeing to meet you for a drink?"

"Granted," I said. "But let me put it another way. How many cops do you know who'll turn down the offer of a free drink?"

Templeton paused like she was giving this some serious thought. "What time?"

"How about eight?"

"Eight works for me. And just so we're totally clear here, it's going to take more than one drink to buy my silence."

"Have as many as you want," I said.

We reached the BMW and I crushed my cigarette out under my boot heel. I kicked the butt into a nearby drain, got into the passenger seat and went to work on my cellphone.

"Who are you calling now?" Templeton asked.

"I'm not calling anyone. I'm hoping my good friend Google can tell me who the best brain surgeon in London is."

# CHAPTER
# SEVENTEEN

Professor Alan Blake was the best brain surgeon in London. He was based at UCL's Institute of Neurology, an imposing red-brick building in Queen Square that was surrounded by other imposing buildings and lots of concrete. According to Blake's secretary, the professor wasn't just busy, he was hideously busy. Fortunately, he had a fifteen-minute window just before lunch. The emphasis she put on fifteen left me in no doubt that if we overran we would not live to see another sunrise.

Templeton used the blue lights to carve a course through the traffic and we got there with five minutes to spare. According to Wikipedia, four of the twelve most highly cited authors in neuroscience were based at the institute. Professor Blake was number two on that list. He'd been pipped to the post by a Professor Xi Yeung, who was based at Johns Hopkins in Maryland.

Professor Blake's office on the top floor was dusty and well lived in. It was the polar opposite to Greg Flight's office. There was no ego wall, partly because the professor's credentials spoke for themselves and he didn't need to shout about his achievements, but mostly because there was no space for one.

Floor-to-ceiling bookcases lined the walls and every single inch of space was taken up with books, hundreds of them, thousands. Paperwork was strewn across the desk and a tall stack of folders tottered precariously on the edge. Professor Blake greeted us at the door with handshakes and hellos. He had a pot belly, a wide, friendly face, grey hair and a neat beard. Delicate, precise hands. He cleared books and paperwork from a couple of chairs and waved us into them.

"So, you're working on that case where those girls were lobotomised." Blake's Scottish accent had been softened by years of living in England.

I nodded. "That's right."

Blake shook his head. "A terrible business. I've been following the story in the news."

"What can you tell me about lobotomies?"

"What do you want to know?"

I glanced at my watch. "Give me the thirteen-minute crash course."

"Don't worry about Glenda, her bark really is worse than her bite." Blake paused to compose himself. His face turned serious and his voice went into lecture mode. "Okay, a lobotomy involves cutting the connections that lead to and from the prefrontal cortex. That's the part of the brain that deals with personality and decision-making. The prefrontal cortex is crucial in that it enables us, amongst other things, to differentiate between conflicting thoughts, to determine what is good or bad, better or best, what is same and what is different. It's responsible for our ability to determine the consequences of our actions, and it enables us to envisage our expectations. It also deals with our social control, that is, our ability to suppress urges that, if not controlled, could lead to socially unacceptable behaviour. When you perform a lobotomy you are basically destroying someone's personality. Stealing their soul, if you like."

I thought about Sarah Flight staring blankly out the window at Dunscombe House, seeing but not seeing. That was exactly what had happened. She'd had her soul stolen.

"By present-day standards, the procedure is butchery rather than surgery," Blake went on. "It's on a par with using leeches. That said, the first thing you need to understand is that the technique was born out of desperation. Go back in time to the turn of the last century and you had asylums that were filled to bursting point with patients, and no real way of treating them. Along comes this miracle procedure which, on the surface, appears to help the patients. Of course, it's going to be welcomed with open arms. It's estimated that a total of forty thousand lobotomies were performed in America and seventeen thousand were performed here. Most were carried out between the early forties and the mid-fifties."

"That many," I said.

"That's the problem with so-called miracle cures. People get carried away, and by the time sanity prevails, the damage has been done. The Russians were the first to abandon the technique, in 1950. They concluded that it turned an insane person into an idiot, and they were right. The Americans were much slower to reach this conclusion. Lobotomies were still being performed in the US in the eighties."

"What does the procedure involve?"

"Your victims, did they have holes drilled into their skulls?"

I shook my head. "No."

"In that case, what you're dealing with is a transorbital lobotomy, or, as it is more commonly referred to, an ice-pick lobotomy. This procedure was developed by Walter Freeman in the mid-forties using an ice-pick and a grapefruit, hence the name. Freeman moved from grapefruits to cadavers before he started on real patients. With this sort of lobotomy, the upper eyelid is lifted up and a thin surgical instrument called an orbitoclast is pushed in until it touches the eye socket. A mallet is then used to drive the orbitoclast through the thin layer of bone and into the brain, where it is moved from side to side at various depths, destroying brain tissue. The orbitoclast is then inserted into the other eye and the procedure is repeated."

"I take it you'd need medical training."

"Not necessarily. Freeman is believed to have carried out almost three and a half thousand lobotomies despite having no surgical training whatsoever. He charged twenty-five dollars for each procedure." Blake shook his head. "Twenty-five dollars to destroy a life. It's impossible to imagine it happening, completely unreal, but it did happen. It was like something out of the Middle Ages. Freeman was completely evangelical about the procedure and travelled across the States in a van he nicknamed the Lobotomobile, visiting mental institutions to educate and train staff. More than anyone else, Freeman was responsible for the popularity of the procedure."

"Could I carry out a lobotomy?" I asked.

"Easily. Like I said earlier, what we're talking about here is butchery rather than anything that resembles surgery."

"That wasn't what I meant." I grinned. "What I'd like is for you to teach me how to perform a lobotomy."

# CHAPTER
# EIGHTEEN

A shrouded cadaver lay on the stainless-steel table in the middle of the dissection lab. It was the first thing you noticed when you stepped through the door. You couldn't help noticing it because it shouted out to be noticed. Even hidden beneath a green sheet, it still managed to command your complete attention. Templeton was staring, too. She was wearing blue medical scrubs and latex gloves. I was kitted out the same. The big difference was that she made the outfit look good. She looked like the main character in a TV medical drama, whereas I looked like an extra. My scrubs fitted badly and the latex gloves were tight and dry on my hands.

Fluorescent strip lights embedded in the suspended ceiling flooded the lab with light, while more focused lighting was provided by the movable surgery lamps on extendable arms that hung above the table. White was the dominant colour. Walls, floor tiles, roof tiles. It was the right colour for the environment. Sterile, fresh, practical. The long whiteboard that stretched the length of one wall was filled with notes written in black marker pen, and a powerful air-conditioning system worked hard to keep the air clean and cool.

"I appreciate you doing this," I said.

"Don't thank me," said Blake. "You've done me a favour. I'm supposed to be in a budget meeting right now."

The professor pulled the green sheet back from the cadaver's head and Templeton took a sharp intake of breath, all the colour draining from her face. I took a step closer to get a better look. I'd seen plenty of dead bodies in all sorts of states of decay and dismemberment, but I'd never seen anything quite like this. It was both gross and fascinating.

The cadaver had already been used by the students, probably more than once. The skin had been removed from the right-hand side of the neck and face to reveal the muscles and tendons. In places the skull was showing through. The hair and eyebrows had been shaved off and preservative chemicals had turned skin, tissue and bone a dirty, unhealthy orange colour. The left side of the face was still intact and the shape of the nose and chin suggested this had once been a male. I could have been looking at a wax model, except there was no way wax would smell this bad.

"Are you okay?" I asked Templeton.

"I'll be fine in a second. It's not what I was expecting, that's all. I assumed the body would be in one piece."

"Sorry," said Blake. "I should have warned you."

The professor pulled the surgery lights down, angled them so they lit up the face, then tilted the head back.

"Freeman used an ECT machine to render the patient unconscious," he said. "With older patients one shock was usually enough, however, younger, fitter patients sometimes required as many as six shocks. The patient would only be unconscious for a few minutes, but that's all the time he needed."

Blake picked up an eight-inch-long steel instrument that had a flat head at one end and tapered to a sharp point at the other. "I'm afraid I don't have an actual orbitoclast but this will do the job."

The professor lifted the cadaver's left eyelid and slid the sharp point into the socket above the eyeball. He hit the end of his makeshift orbitoclast with a small rubber mallet and there was a soft cracking sound as it punctured the thin bone at the back of the eye socket. The professor gave a running commentary while he worked. He was a good teacher, enthusiastic and informative. When he'd finished, he turned to me and held out the makeshift orbitoclast.

"Okay, your turn," he said.

I took the instrument from him. The steel was still warm from his hand. I looked at the cadaver for a moment, then shut my eyes and imagined myself in a place of torture and screams.

I work underground because of the noise, a basement or a cellar. There are brick walls on four sides, tons of dirt beyond the brickwork. Perfect noise insulation. The only place sound can get out is through the ceiling. Maybe I've used a false ceiling and rockwool to stop the screams escaping, or maybe I'm living somewhere remote enough for noise not to be a big deal. The woman strapped to my table has Sarah Flight's face.

The ritual is everything. What I'm doing here will get replayed over and over in my mind. I've already imagined this moment a thousand times.

First, I need to shave her head one last time.

I undo the wrist straps so she can sit up. She doesn't struggle or complain. She knows better than that. The lessons with the knife have been painful and memorable. I work slowly, enjoying every moment. I work until her head is smooth and perfect. She lies completely still while I secure her to the table, compliant and corpselike, her spirit shattered.

Now for the main feature.

I show her the orbitoclast and the mallet. During our time together she'll have seen these objects on numerous occasions. She'll know exactly what I intend to do with them. I won't have spared her a single detail. Her eyes widen when she sees the orbitoclast. She struggles, but there's no real intent there. These last few months have stripped the fight from her. That's why we've reached this point. When they stop fighting, they stop being fun.

I peel back her right eyelid and slide the orbitoclast in above the eyeball, keep on pushing until the tip touches bone. Her body bucks weakly but the leather strap holds her head completely still. She's making pathetic mewling noises. Compared to some of the screams I've had, these are nothing, yet it's still one of the most beautiful sounds I've ever heard. Her left eye is wide with fear.

I pick up the mallet and hit the orbitoclast with just enough force to pierce the bone. I've practised this and know exactly how much force to use. The bridge of the nose acts as a guide to help get the angle right. I keep going through the frontal lobes until the orbitoclast reaches a depth of two inches. It's just like piercing a grapefruit. I pull the orbitoclast forty-five degrees to the side and the tip cuts through the brain. Another tap with the mallet, another inch deeper into the frontal lobes. This time I pull the orbitoclast from side to side, twenty-eight degrees each way. I finish by forcing the butt of it upwards to sever the interhemispherical fissure.

At some point during the procedure my victim slipped into unconsciousness. I don't wait for her to come back around because there's no point. I'm not going to get any sort of worthwhile reaction from her. I feel a sense of anticlimax. The fun and games are over. This good thing has come to an end.

I peel back the left eyelid and go to work on the left side of her brain.

We shook hands at the lab door and the professor told me to call if I needed anything else. I walked into the corridor with Templeton and the door closed behind us. Within two steps the air smelled fresher. A faint trace of the cadaver still lingered, though. It was stuck to my clothing. A whisper of the smell remained in my nostrils.

"We need to talk to Hatcher," I said. "Someone needs to check museums and private collectors to see if anyone's missing an orbitoclast. I'm hoping our unsub's a traditionalist."

"And if he's not?" said Templeton.

"Then he's had an orbitoclast custom-made, which would be bad news for us since it makes it a lot more difficult to find out where he got it from."

"Maybe he made it himself."

"Unlikely. This unsub is not a blue-collar worker. He wouldn't have the skills to make something like that."

"We could do the same thing with ECT machines," Templeton suggested. "If he's a traditionalist then maybe someone's missing one."

"Nice idea, but it would be a waste of time. The reason Freeman used an ECT machine was to knock his patients out. Our guy wants his victims awake. He wants them aware of what's going on right up to the last moment."

"Jesus." Templeton went quiet for a moment. "Okay, where to now?"

"Somewhere that does a decent lunch. Do you know anywhere?"

"You can eat after that?"

"I can always eat."

# CHAPTER
# NINETEEN

Templeton pulled up outside a café in a narrow back street. The place had evidently been here for ever and had seen better days. The orange paintwork was peeling, and *Angelica's* was written in swirling faded black letters above the doorway. The shops on either side were boarded up with wood panels that were covered with graffiti and layer upon layer of posters advertising events that had long passed into history. I looked at the café, looked at Templeton.

"You've got to be kidding," I said.

Templeton shook her head. "I've never been more serious."

"We're in London, a city that has thousands of places to eat, a city that has some of the finest restaurants in the world, and this is the best you could come up with."

"Looks can be deceptive. Trust me, the food is amazing."

We went inside and the Italian guy behind the counter came around front and hugged Templeton like she was his long-lost daughter.

"And how's my favourite detective doing?" he said.

"Good, Federico."

"Still catching those bad guys so we can all sleep safe in our beds?"

"I'm doing my best."

Federico nodded toward me. "Who's your new boyfriend?"

"He's not my boyfriend." Templeton gave the café owner an indulgent look. "This is Jefferson Winter. He's helping us out on a case."

Federico held out his hand and we shook. He had to be pushing seventy, but he still had a decent grip on him.

"So what can I get for you guys?"

I ordered the lasagne, while Templeton opted for the all-day breakfast. The dissection lab was already a distant memory and she'd got her appetite back. It was a cop thing. There's a definite correlation between experience and the amount of time it takes to bounce back from something horrific. The more you've seen, the faster you bounce back. It had taken Templeton the best part of the drive to Angelica's to regain her equilibrium. I was good to go by the time we reached the door of the dissection lab.

The table by the window was empty. Window seats are great because you can watch the world go by. I unzipped my jacket, hung it on the back of my chair, then sat down and got comfortable. Outside, a steady stream of people walked past. Some were on cellphones, some walked purposefully, on a mission, all of them were wrapped up in their own private dramas. A cute girl wearing a dress much too short for the weather caught my eye because she had great legs. It was impossible not to look.

I stared out the window and went over what I'd learned this morning, adding new details to the profile, reassessing and changing others. Federico brought our drinks over and put them on the table. I stirred two sugars into my coffee. Templeton was staring across the table at me.

"What?" I said.

"You're miles away there. What are you thinking?"

"I'm wondering why you told me your dad was a cop."

"That wasn't what you were thinking."

"Maybe not, but that's what I'm thinking about now. So why did you feel the need to be disingenuous?"

"Are you calling me a liar?"

I laughed. "Tomato, tomato. Anyway, you're dodging the question. Your dad wasn't a cop, was he? Or his dad."

"No they weren't," Templeton admitted. "My father's an accountant."

"So, what's the story?"

"It's stupid." Her voice was small and lacking in confidence.

"I like stupid."

"Okay, I'll tell you. But promise you won't laugh, and promise you'll never breathe a word of this to another living soul. Not a word, Winter."

"Cross my heart."

"I've never told this to anyone."

"Tell me or don't tell me, but don't keep me hanging."

Templeton took a deep breath then went for it. The words came out quickly, like if she didn't get them out fast enough, she'd never get them out.

"When I was a kid I didn't want to be an actress or a ballet dancer or any of those things that little girls are supposed to want to grow up to be, I wanted to be a cop. Or, to be more accurate, I wanted to be a detective. Nancy Drew was my first hero. I read all the books. And I used to watch every cop show, even the really crap ones. Reruns from the seventies and early eighties, everything. *Cagney and Lacey* was my favourite."

Templeton cringed at this last admission, embarrassment written all over her face. I liked this version of Templeton as much as the tough, cocky cop version, perhaps more. It was somehow more real, a glimpse behind the mask. I understood why she presented herself the way she did. Law enforcement is still very much a male-dominated profession, and she had ambitions and big dreams. To get as far as she wanted to get, she needed to both understand and play the game. There was no way her career was going to stall at detective sergeant. She had the makings of a great detective inspector, a detective chief inspector. She could go all the way if she wanted, smash right through that glass ceiling.

"There's nothing wrong with *Cagney and Lacey*," I said.

"There was everything wrong with *Cagney and Lacey*. I bet you hated the programme."

"Okay, you've got me there. I was more of an *Equalizer* type of guy."

"A moody loner, out to save the world one person at a time. Yeah, I can see that. Although technically speaking it wasn't a cop show."

"Tomato, tomato."

Templeton laughed, and I laughed along with her.

"As for why I was so obsessed, I've no idea. It wasn't like I had brothers I needed to compete with, and my parents certainly weren't pushing me in that direction. I guess I believed it was a job where you could make a difference. As soon as I was old enough I joined the Met."

"Do you still believe you can make a difference?"

She considered this while she drank her tea. "Some days, yes, other days, no. On the whole, there are more yes days than no days. I guess if that changes then that's when I'll quit." She smiled that great smile. Her teeth were perfect, two neat white rows. "I reckon I've missed the boat for becoming a ballet dancer, but maybe it's not too late to become an actress."

Federico arrived with our lunch. My food came without any embellishment. No salad or bread, just a slab of lasagne on a plate. It didn't look much but Templeton was right, it tasted amazing. Templeton's plate was piled high with a cholesterol overdose. Bacon, sausage, egg, beans, the works. I looked at her plate and wondered how she kept so slim.

**108**

Templeton scraped some beans onto her fork. "So what about you? Why do you do what you do?"

"I became a cop because my father was a serial killer."

"That wasn't what I asked."

Templeton was right and we both knew it. She was staring again, but there was nothing warm and fuzzy about this stare. It was the sort of stare that would make an innocent man confess. This was the other side to Templeton, the cop side. The side Hatcher had warned me about. It was an uncomfortable insight into why she was so good at her job.

"That explains why you joined the FBI," she said. "But it doesn't explain why you left, and it doesn't explain why you do what you do now."

I fell quiet, debating the best way to answer. There were a number of reasons I could give. One big reason and a whole load of smaller ones. All of them were true, but none on their own gave the full picture. I'd given eleven years of my life to the FBI and for the last three I was their lead profiler. I'd been awarded the Medal of Valor for my part in a high-profile kidnapping that ended with the girl alive and the kidnapper dead.

On the face of it my FBI career was a success, however, the reality wasn't so clear-cut. I have always been an outsider, and I've always done things my own way. The problem is that the FBI isn't a place for outsiders, or people who do things their own way. The organisation is massive, thirty-four thousand employees and an eight-billion-dollar annual budget. The emphasis is on the team, and the higher up the ladder I climbed, the more obvious it was that I didn't fit in, that I would never really fit in anywhere. I made enemies in high places. Resentments festered. Politics came into play and I've never been much of a politician. Whenever my methods were called into question, I argued that I did what was needed to get the job done, but that argument wore thin pretty fast.

Those were the little reasons. The big reason was those three words mouthed in that execution chamber at San Quentin prison eighteen months ago.

*We're the same.*

Every major decision has a tipping point, a single event that shifts enough weight to one end of the scale or the other. That was the tipping point for me. I resigned from the FBI as soon as I got back to Virginia, just packed up my desk and left and never looked back. I knew my father was screwing with me, but it didn't make any difference. Those three words hit harder than any bullet. I'd never murdered anyone in cold blood, and I sure as hell hadn't gone out into a forest under a cold, dead moon and hunted down an innocent woman with a high-powered rifle and a night scope.

But knowing wasn't enough. I needed to prove to myself that we weren't the same, and I couldn't do that within the constraints of the FBI. That's why I'd chosen the path I had, and that's why I drove myself so hard.

We were not the same.

But.

My cellphone buzzed in my jeans pocket. Templeton was still staring across the table at me, expecting answers. She was going to have to wait. I thumbed the phone to life. Hatcher had sent two photographs. Both were grainy and indistinct on the cellphone's small screen, but I could see everything I needed to see. The woman in the first picture had dark hair and brown eyes, and had been reported missing forty-eight hours ago. She wasn't the one. I opened the second picture and a shiver shot up my spine. Everything about this woman was right. Her dark hair, her brown eyes, the confident way she held the gaze of the camera. I placed the cellphone on the table and spun it around so Templeton could see.

"Meet our next victim," I said.

# CHAPTER
# TWENTY

"Number Five will sit on the chair."

Adam's distorted voice boomed around the base-ment. It was loud and terrifying and filled Rachel's head with so much white noise it was impossible to think straight. The sound bounced off the smooth tiles and ricocheted throughout the room, creating strange, disturbing echoes. Rachel put her hands over her ears, crawled to the back of the mattress, and curled herself into a tight fetal ball. The lights were back on and she had her eyes shut tight to keep the glare out. To keep reality out. There was no way she was going to sit in that chair. It wasn't going to happen.

"Number Five will sit on the chair or face the consequences."

Rachel pushed herself right into the corner, her whole body trembling. Hot, salty tears leaked from under her eyelids.

"No," she whispered. "No, no, no, no, no."

The door slammed open and Rachel's head snapped towards it. Adam strode out of the brightness and stopped in front of the mattress. He was tapping an old-fashioned bamboo cane gently against his left palm. Rachel cowered deeper into the corner and tried to

**112**

make herself smaller. Without warning, he brought the cane down on her back, putting his full weight into the blow. The pain was so sudden, so unexpected. Rachel let out a screech that was more animal than human and tried to push herself even further into the corner.

"Number Five will sit on the chair."

Rachel didn't move.

The cane whistled through the air and bit into her back, and she let out another scream.

"Number Five will sit on the chair."

Adam tapped the cane against the tiled floor. *Tap tap tap*. The rhythm was monotonous and infuriating. All Rachel could hear was the sound of the cane. It obliterated all other noise. Adam stepped to the side and the dentist's chair loomed large in the middle of the room, filling her vision. Rachel looked at the cane then stood up and began walking. Adam followed her across the room, tapping the cane against the floor. *Tap tap tap*. The way he was watching her made her feel like a bug in a glass jar. The dentist's chair was only five metres away but those five metres felt like five miles. She hesitated in front of it, her eyes drawn to the dark stains on the cream-coloured armrests.

"Number Five will sit."

Rachel glanced over her shoulder and saw the cane, saw that Adam wouldn't hesitate to use it again. The skin on her back burned where he'd hit her. She sat down and the coldness of the vinyl through the sweatshirt made her skin crawl. How many other women had been strapped to this chair? What had happened to them? Rachel forced herself to stay in the chair, but it wasn't easy. All she wanted was to bolt across the room back to the illusionary safety of the mattress. All that stopped her was the thought of what Adam might do.

Adam leant across her to fasten the first arm strap and Rachel recoiled. His aftershave had smelled so good when she first met him, but now it turned her stomach. Adam spent a long time securing her to the chair, his fussy fingers fastening and refastening the buckles until he was satisfied. He attached the last leg restraint and straightened up, then flashed that charming smile she was learning to loathe.

"There," he said. "That wasn't so difficult now was it?"

# CHAPTER
# TWENTY-ONE

I sat with my feet propped on a desk, drank my coffee, and watched Jamie Morris on the screen. He was doing clockwise laps of the table bolted to the floor of the interview room, going around and around like a clockwork toy. I could sense the pent-up energy, the frustration, the anger. He was wound up tight, a trapped animal, scared and desperate to escape. Morris was a reluctant forty-year-old, someone who would do anything to create the illusion that he was younger than he was. Plastic surgery, a deal with the devil, anything.

Rachel Morris was thirty, ten years younger than he was, and that was one of the reasons he married her. The women he screwed around with would be younger still. Like Jagger and Picasso, and a whole long line of deluded men that stretched way back to the start of time, Jamie Morris believed that eternal youth could be attained through sex. Morris was five-eight with brown eyes. His hair was black and short, the grey made to disappear with dye. Manicured nails. He was casually dressed in expensive designer jeans and an expensive designer sweatshirt, an outfit that probably cost more than a halfway decent suit. Stress had left him ragged around the edges, and my initial impression was of someone who was used to being in control, but who'd had the rug well and truly pulled from under their feet.

Eventually Morris got tired of pacing and sat down. I took this as my cue and nodded to Hatcher. *Time to go*. On my way out, I grabbed a fresh coffee and stuffed a couple of tubs of milk and some sugar sachets into my pocket.

The smell hit me the second we stepped into the interview room. It was a smell I knew well from all the hours I'd spent in prisons interviewing psychopaths and serial criminals, a unique smell made up from stale sweat, soap and desperation. The smell permeated the room. It was embedded into the walls, the floor tiles, the wooden table, the plastic chairs. Morris sprang to his feet the second he saw us.

"Do I need a lawyer?" He talked fast, the words coming out in a rush. "I didn't do anything to Rachel. I swear to God I didn't. I loved her."

Loved instead of love. I noted the use of the past tense and filed that one away. "Relax," I said. "We know you don't have anything to do with Rachel's disappearance."

"So why have I been brought here?"

"We need to ask you a few questions," said Hatcher. "We're trying to build up a picture of what happened to your wife."

"She's dead, isn't she?"

"Why don't we all take a seat?"

Morris crumpled back into his chair. He looked small and defeated, weighed down by the weight of his

116

uncertainties. I took one of the seats opposite, the scarred wooden table separating us.

I'd spent a while studying Morris on the monitor, but it was different when you were up close and personal like this. The picture was clearer, more defined. Morris was nervous, but that was to be expected. Last night his wife hadn't come home, first thing this morning he'd reported her missing, and an hour ago a cop car had rolled up outside his apartment block and transported him here. The world he woke up to yesterday morning was very different from the world he now inhabited. I pushed the coffee, sugar and milk across the table.

"I thought you might like a coffee," I said.

"Thanks."

Morris stirred both tubs of milk into the mug, but left the sugar. His right hand shook a little, but, again, that was to be expected. There was a faint nicotine stain on his middle finger.

"I'm DI Mark Hatcher, and this is Jefferson Winter," Hatcher said. "We're going to record this interview, if that's okay with you."

Morris nodded that it was okay. Not that his acquiescence made any real difference. This interview was being recorded whether he liked it or not. I understood why Hatcher had asked. This was a softly-softly interview and he was giving Morris the illusion that he had some control over the situation. Illusion being the operative word.

"When did you last see your wife?" Hatcher asked.

"Yesterday morning. We had breakfast together."

"What time was that?"

"Around seven."

"Do you normally have breakfast together?"

"Most days. Rachel has further to commute so she tends to leave before me."

"And that's what happened yesterday?"

Morris nodded.

"Did you notice anything odd about your wife's behaviour?" asked Hatcher. "Anything different?"

Morris shook his head. "She seemed her normal self."

"And how would you describe her 'normal self'? And please be honest about this, Mr Morris."

"Okay, let's just say that Rachel isn't a morning person."

"Did you argue?" I asked.

"No."

"Did you say anything to one another?"

"Not really. She told me she was going out for drinks with some of her work friends so she wouldn't be back until late. I think it was someone's birthday."

"You think?" I said.

"I wasn't really listening. I'm not much of a morning person either."

"So, you went to work, then you came home, had a quiet evening, went to bed, and when you woke up your wife wasn't there."

Morris hesitated. The gesture was so small anyone else would have missed it.

"That's right," he said.

"What's her name?" I asked.

"Excuse me?"

"Yesterday morning, when Rachel told you she was going out for drinks, your ears pricked up, didn't they? It was too good an opportunity to miss. So did you go out for a meal, or did you go straight to your usual hotel?"

"I don't know what you're insinuating."

"Of course you know what I'm insinuating. You're emotionally dysfunctional, and your marriage is a sham, but you're not stupid."

"I love my wife."

"Of course you do."

"Look," said Hatcher. "We don't care what you've been up to. All we care about is getting Rachel back."

"Getting her back." Morris repeated the words in a whisper. His hand was shaking worse than ever. "You think someone's taken her?"

"We know someone's taken her," I said. "And before you say anything else I want you to listen very carefully. The man who took your wife is a sociopath. He enjoys watching his victims suffer. He spends hours watching them suffer. He had his last victim for three and a half months and during that time he repeatedly tortured her with knives, knitting needles, all sorts of things. He's very imaginative when it comes to his favourite pastime. And then, when he got bored with her, he lobotomised her. He took a sharp implement called an orbitoclast, wedged it into her eye, bashed it through the thin bone at the back of the eye socket, and destroyed her brain."

Morris's face drained of colour. "My God," he whispered.

"You said earlier that you loved your wife. Now I don't know if that was ever the case, but even if it wasn't you'll want to help get her back safely because it's the right thing to do. That means you need to co-operate with us. I'm talking full disclosure here."

Morris slumped back in his chair, a conflicted look on his face. He wanted to do the right thing, but at the same time he didn't want to.

"Helen Springfield," he said quietly.

"And how long have you been seeing Helen for?"

"A couple of months."

"And before that there were other Helens, weren't there? A whole string of them?"

Morris nodded.

"Did Rachel know about your affairs?"

"No, I don't think so."

I raised my eyebrows and gave him a look. People knew, particularly when their partner was a serial cheat. They might choose to deal with it through denial, but they knew.

"Maybe she suspected something," Morris admitted reluctantly.

"What time did you get home last night?"

"A little after eleven. Rachel said she'd be back by midnight, so I wanted to make sure I was back before her. I went to bed as soon as I got in and when I woke up in the morning she wasn't there. I sleep soundly, particularly when I've had a couple of drinks. As soon as I realised she wasn't there I tried calling her friends, but no one had heard from her. That's when I called the police."

"Was Rachel ever unfaithful?" I asked.

"Rachel? No way. Never."

"You're sure about that?"

"My wife would never cheat on me."

# CHAPTER
# TWENTY-TWO

"I'm ready to give the profile now," I told Hatcher. We were outside the interview room in a quiet, grey corridor, just the two of us. The corridor was long and lit with strip lights and smelled of disinfectant. It reminded me of a hospital corridor.

"In that case I'll go rally the troops."

"Not so fast. You owe me fifty pounds."

Hatcher pulled a wallet from his back pocket. He counted out two twenties and a ten and slapped them grudgingly into my hand.

"Double or quits," I said.

"I'm listening."

"Get one of your people to phone up Rachel Morris's workplace. I'm betting there was no birthday girl inviting anyone out for drinks."

Hatcher considered this, then shook his head. "Too rich for me, I can afford to take a fifty-quid hit, but a hundred would be pushing it. The wife would kill me if she found out."

"Fine, but get someone to make the call. I need confirmation on that one."

"How certain are you that Rachel Morris is the next victim?"

"Certain enough to leave my lunch half-eaten."

"Seriously, Winter."

"Rachel Morris is the next victim. If it makes you feel better you can have your people keep looking, but all you'll be doing is wasting time and resources that could be put to better use elsewhere. Like finding Rachel Morris."

"But how can you be so sure?"

"Because Rachel Morris did not go out for a birthday drink last night." I looked at my watch. "Give me ten minutes. I need a smoke before I give the profile."

"I'll get someone to make that call."

Hatcher strode off one way down the corridor, and I headed the other way. I took the elevator to the ground floor and went outside, found a quiet corner where nobody would bother me and lit up.

The thing that was most frustrating about this case was the lack of crime scenes. The police had no idea where the victims were being snatched, and there were no bodies, therefore no dump sites. I like to walk the same ground as the unsub. I like to see the same sights, to smell the same smells, to breathe the same air. It helps me feel closer to the people I'm hunting, which in turn helps me build a more detailed profile.

I huddled deeper into my sheepskin jacket in an attempt to ward off the cold and thought about Rachel Morris. She'd be alone right now, more alone than she'd ever been in her life. More terrified, too. There was nothing that could prepare her for what had happened, and nothing that could prepare her for what was about to happen. I dealt with this stuff day in, day out, and had built up a tolerance to the horror. I'd had to. It was all about self-preservation. Without that layer of insulation, I wouldn't be able to do my job. But Rachel Morris was just a normal person who'd led a normal life. No doubt there had been plenty of ups and downs, but no real danger, at least nothing to match this.

That mental snapshot of Sarah Flight dropped into my head again. One second I'd been thinking about Rachel and now I was thinking about Sarah. The image had been bugging me since this morning, dropping into my head without warning. My subconscious was trying to tell me something, but what? I pulled my hood up to block out the world, took a drag on my cigarette, then closed my eyes and drifted back in time a few hours. I could see our ghostly reflections in the glass but still couldn't see the significance.

And then I got it. I grinned to myself and shook my head and wondered how the hell I could be so dumb. So slow. That mental snapshot had nothing to do with Sarah Flight and everything to do with the unsub.

I smelled Templeton before I saw her. Her scent was subtle and sensuous. I turned around and there she was, smiling that great smile and looking gorgeous.

"Hatcher sent me to tell you we're ready," she said.

"I told him ten minutes. By my reckoning I've still got another five."

"He also wanted me to tell you that you were kind of right."

"Kind of?"

"Rachel Morris's colleagues did go out for a birthday drink last night."

"But Rachel wasn't with them," I finished for her. "That figures. All the best lies contain an element of truth."

"Rachel stayed behind, working late. She told her workmates she had a couple of jobs she needed to catch up on."

We headed back inside and rode the elevator to the fourth floor, where Hatcher's team had taken up residence in a large incident room. The room was cluttered with the detritus of a major investigation. A ton of paper, half-empty coffee mugs, overflowing wastepaper bins, fast-food containers and pizza boxes. Today there was a buzz in the air, a sense of collective purpose emanating from the cops working the case. There was nothing like a fresh development to get people motivated again.

Everyone turned to look when I entered, a dozen cops, all checking me out, suspicion and wariness in their eyes. Most of them wanted me here because they figured I could help, some tolerated me being here because they'd been ordered to, and a few resented me treading on their turf because they felt it reflected badly on them and made it look like they couldn't do their jobs properly.

It was the same every time I was called in to consult on a case. I couldn't care less what other people thought of me. That was one of the few positives that comes from having a serial killer for a father. If I'd let other people's opinions get to me, I would have been destroyed years ago, like my mother had been. She died three and a half years ago, a haunted woman who never got the peace and closure of knowing the man she'd called her husband for so many years was dead. She drank herself to death, a slow, slow suicide. I thought of her as my father's sixteenth victim.

Walking into that room was like walking into a new school for the first time, something I'd done plenty of times. My mother's way of dealing with what happened was to run. She started running when the FBI took her husband away, and kept running until she reached her grave. Between the ages of eleven and seventeen, I lived in fifteen cities in ten different states. Fifteen new homes, fifteen new schools. Every school was different but the same in that the new kid always started at the bottom. The trick was to get out from the bottom before any real damage was done, and you did that either by hitting first and hitting hardest, or by being smart. I chose smart.

On one wall was a large map of London with four red pushpins marking the places where the victims were found. Three were inside the M25, all north of the Thames. Patricia Maynard's was the only one outside. The five green pins scattered across London marked the last places the victims had been seen before they were kidnapped.

To the right of the map was a gallery of photographs of the victims. They were arranged in two neat rows, one on top of the other. The top row contained the five before shots and the bottom row contained the four after shots. Rachel Morris was the newest addition, and the only one who didn't have an after shot. She was striking a pose in front of the Eiffel Tower, smiling and clearly having a great time, obviously there for pleasure rather than business. Her dark hair was tied back and her brown eyes sparkled. Happy days with Jamie, the denial doing its job.

Hatcher shushed the room, did a quick introduction and waved me to the front. I walked into the space the detective had just vacated and turned to face the crowd. The detectives had arranged their chairs in two neat semicircles, five in the front row, six in the back. Aside from Templeton there was only one other woman there. The men included one guy who was overweight and grizzled and looked like he should have been put out to pasture a decade ago, and a kid who looked like he was too young to be playing with the big boys.

I cleared my throat, then said, "What we're dealing with here is a pairing. There are actually two unsubs."

# CHAPTER
# TWENTY-THREE

A wave of murmured speculation went through the crowd of detectives. The idea there were two unsubs working together had obviously not occurred to them. It hadn't occurred to me until a few minutes ago. I was prepared to wait their reaction out, though, let them get it out of their systems, but Hatcher wasn't as patient. The detective shouted for everyone to shut up and the incident room fell silent.

"Pairings are rare," I said, "but it's not unprecedented. You guys actually have the dubious honour of having two of the most famous pairings of all time. Ian Brady and Myra Hindley, and Fred and Rose West. The reason pairings are so rare is because, thankfully, we live in a society where psychopaths are the exception rather than the rule. That means the odds of these monsters coming into contact with one another is highly unlikely. This is good news for us generally, but bad news for you guys right now. There's strength in numbers. Two heads are better than one. Pick the cliché that fits. This strength can also be a weakness, though. One strategy we might consider is to try to drive a wedge between the unsubs. If we can undermine the relationship, if we can somehow get it to start unravelling, then they're going to make mistakes."

"How come you're so certain this is a *pairing?*"

This came from the grizzled old cop. He made the last word sound like a cuss word. Odds on he belonged to the subsection who felt their toes were being trodden on.

"What a great question. Maybe I took a guess, hoping to get lucky. Or how about this? Maybe I actually know what I'm talking about." I gave him the hard stare. "The reason I'm certain this is a pairing is because there are two very distinct signatures." Half the detectives nodded their heads, while the old guy and the rest looked blank. "You all know what a modus operandi is, right?"

Nods all round.

"Okay, so your MO is the way a crime is carried out, the methods used. The signature is very different. This is something unique to the unsub. With this case you have two distinct signatures. One of the unsubs gets off on performing DIY surgery. The other gets off on playing dolls."

"Playing dolls?" said Templeton.

"You had dolls when you were a kid, right?"

"Yeah, but I never played with them."

That figured.

"One of the unsubs likes to dress the victims up," I said. "She likes to do their make-up, that sort of thing. We know this because of the traces of make-up found on the victims. The main reason the victims have their heads shaved is to make it easier to play around with wigs."

"What are the other reasons?" Hatcher asked.

"Well, the other big reason is depersonalisation. The Nazis shaved heads in Auschwitz and Treblinka for much the same reason. When the victims were found they were all wearing identical unbranded grey sweatpants and sweatshirts, right? This is what they would have been dressed in most of the time. It's another part of the depersonalisation process. Also, the unsub who likes playing dolls would want to keep her dressing-up clothes in good condition."

I gave it a second for all that to sink in.

"With pairings you have one unsub who's dominant and one who's submissive. In this case our dominant unsub is the guy carrying out the DIY surgery. He's white, well educated, aged thirty to forty. These crimes are too complex to be carried out by a kid. He's highly organised. Everything he does is well thought out and planned to the nth degree. His fantasies run his life, and now he's started acting them out the only way he'll stop is if he is captured or killed. Also, he has money, probably from an inheritance."

I pointed to the map. "The fact that all the pins are north of the Thames indicates that he is based somewhere in this area. To do what he does he needs privacy. His victims are going to make a lot of noise, so that means a detached property that's far enough from the neighbours so he doesn't disturb them. Property in this area is expensive, particularly the sort of property large enough to allow him the space to have his fun."

"Fun," said the grizzled cop. "How the hell can you call what he does fun?"

"Believe me, this guy's having a ball," I replied. "You've seen the victims' tox screens, right? The first three all had traces of ecstasy, amphetamines and Valium in their systems. Patricia Maynard's will come back the same. He uses ecstasy and amphetamines because he wants the victims to experience as much pain as possible. Ecstasy makes them more sensitive to every slice of the knife. The amphetamines keep them conscious longer. The Valium is used to subdue them, to make them more compliant during the downtime when he's not having his fun. The choice of drugs is interesting in that they're all easy to get hold of. And the fact they'll all have been obtained illegally means there's no way to track the unsub down through that route."

"Maybe he's trying to mislead us," said Templeton. "Like the stunt with the broken camera he pulled in St Albans. Maybe he wants us to believe he's based north of the river, but he actually lives south of the river."

"Not a chance," I said. "Highly organised unsubs like this one are constantly looking for ways to improve their MO. The use of misdirection is something new. The fact he feels the need to do this tells us one of two things. Either something you guys are doing is working and he's feeling under pressure, or his paranoia is getting the better of him. Whichever one it is, it's a good sign. Add this to the fact that the kidnappings are coming closer together, and it's another indication that he's devolving. The more rapidly he devolves, the easier he'll be to capture."

"That's a pretty big haystack," said Templeton. She was staring at the map behind me.

"It is. And I'll do what I can to make it smaller."

"Could we be looking for an actual surgeon?" Hatcher asked.

I shook my head. "Nice idea, but no. This guy has no interest in helping people get well. The surgery he carries out enables him to keep his victims alive and prolong the torture. Very pragmatic when you think about it. That said, the unsub would have started a medical degree, but he would only have lasted a couple of semesters at most. There would have been some indiscretion that would have gotten him kicked out. You need to contact all the universities that offer medical degrees and check out anyone who got kicked out, particularly the incidents where there was some drama involved. Our unsub would not have gone peacefully. You might be talking nearly twenty years ago, so it's a bit of a long shot, however, I'm betting that whatever he did will be remembered."

I paused and scanned the faces to make sure I still had everyone's attention.

"Which brings us onto the second unsub. You're looking for a white female. She'll be a couple of years younger than her partner, shorter, too, and she would have dropped out of the education system before university. She's going to be smaller than him in every way. Smaller in size, personality and intellect. There's no way our guy could deal with anyone who could be

**132**

perceived as superior to him on any level. No way. She's going to be timid, too. Chances are they're lovers, maybe even husband and wife like the Wests, but don't rule out other types of relationship at this stage. They could be brother and sister, for example."

"You said she's female," said the grizzled detective. "You sure about that?"

"Yes, I'm sure. And the reason I'm sure is because she's the reason the victims are still alive. If we were dealing with two males then they would just keep going until the victim was dead. This unsub gets attached to her dolls. She looks after them, feeds them, keeps them healthy. She wouldn't be able to handle them being murdered, and the dominant partner understands this at some level. The lobotomy is a compromise. The victims are still alive but they might as well be dead. And of course, there's no way they can ID the unsubs. It's a neat solution. Another example of the dominant unsub's pragmatism."

"You sound like you admire this guy."

"And you wouldn't believe how far off the mark you are." I locked eyes with the grizzled cop. "Don't ever make the mistake that I admire these assholes, because I don't."

The old guy looked like he could have killed me where I stood. The fact there were almost a dozen witnesses in the room, all cops, would have made no difference. I held his gaze until he looked away first. It was like being back in the schoolyard all over again.

"Okay, moving on," I said. "The dominant partner is impotent, and this is a source of anger and frustration for him. This is one reason why the torture is so extreme. All the victims have stab injuries that were caused by a knitting needle or a skewer. In this case, stabbing is a substitute for sexual penetration. The same goes for the knife wounds."

"You said one reason. What's the other reason?" asked the female DC on the second row.

"Because he likes to hear them scream."

The DC's face drained of colour.

"One more thing," I said. "Despite what you guys think, this is actually a murder investigation."

"How do you figure that one?" asked Hatcher. "There have been four victims so far, and we've got them all back."

Hatcher almost said alive, but stopped himself at the last second. I could sense it there on the tip of his tongue.

"Because he needed to practise. The four victims we've got back were all successfully lobotomised. You don't get this proficient without practice, and I'm betting that his practising got messy. Look back at any unsolved murders or mysterious deaths that pre-date the first kidnapping. Cross-reference these with the victim profile I gave you and you should come up with a name. Okay, questions?"

This was met by a wall of silence that stretched out for a couple of seconds before it was shattered by a ringing telephone. One telephone was quickly followed by another, and another. Within ten seconds every phone in the incident room was ringing. For a second everyone just stared at them like they couldn't work out what they were. It was Hatcher who broke the spell. He grabbed the nearest telephone, listened and asked some questions, told the person on the other end that someone would get back in touch, then hung up.

"You're not going to believe this," he said. "Rachel Morris's father has just offered a million-pound reward for any information leading to the safe return of his daughter. It's all over the news channels. Photographs, a press conference, the works."

A collective groan went around the room.

"Great," I muttered.

# CHAPTER
# TWENTY-FOUR

Rachel heard the rattle of a trolley behind her and strained to turn around. The leather straps dug into her arms and legs, restricting her blood flow and making her fingers and toes tingle. She could see the walls either side of her, but she couldn't get far enough around to see the wall with the door in.

"Number Five will face the front," said Adam.

Rachel's head snapped forward and she stared at the mattress. She forced herself to breathe slowly, told herself to relax even though it was impossible. The growing bruises on her back throbbed in time with her racing heart, a painful reminder of the cane. The artificial pine stink of disinfectant made her head swim.

Adam took his time coming into the room. Slow footsteps behind her, the rubber squeak of the trolley wheels on the tiles. He stopped the trolley in front of her, positioning it so she got a good look. It was the sort of trolley found in any hospital. Stainless steel that glinted under the halogens, three shelves, black wheels. The trolley was crammed with an odd assortment of equipment. Most items she recognised, some she didn't. A mallet, a jigsaw, kidney bowls, safety goggles, knitting needles with heat-blackened ends. Clean clothes and a towel on the bottom shelf. Rachel tried to swallow but her mouth was bone-dry. Her back was on fire but, looking at the trolley, she realised there was much worse to come.

She stared at the collection of objects on the trolley, her mind spinning one dark nightmare after another. She was too young to die. This wasn't fair. There were still so many things she wanted to do. She wanted children and a happy ever after, she wanted to visit Mexico and New Orleans and the pyramids, she wanted to get to the end of her life and have no regrets. Right now all she had were regrets, a whole list of them, a ton of things she would have done differently.

"Number Five will sit still."

Adam picked up a pair of stainless-steel hairdressing scissors from the trolley and grabbed a handful of Rachel's hair. Instinct kicked in and she tried to pull away, but Adam dragged her head back into place with a sharp tug that almost ripped her hair out by the roots.

"Number Five will stay still or face the consequences."

The needle-sharp point of the scissors was only a couple of millimetres from her left eye. It was too close to focus on and all she saw was a grey, shiny blur. Rachel closed her eyes and waited for the thrust that would steal her sight. Seconds passed. Long seconds. There was a metallic *snick-snick* as the scissor blades separated then came together again. She opened her eyes and saw a clump of her hair tumble to the ground. Adam took hold of another handful of hair and hacked it off. This time Rachel didn't see it fall because her vision was smeared with tears.

Adam hacked at her hair until all that was left was a rough, uneven stubble. He dropped the scissors onto the trolley and the metallic clatter shattered the uneasy silence. Then he picked up a bottle of water and tipped the contents over her head. Rachel tried to move out of the way, but the restraints held her in place. She coughed and spluttered, convinced she was drowning. Adam shook out the last few drops of water then returned the bottle to the trolley. Rachel's sweatshirt was soaked through, a chilling damp that made her shiver. Adam picked up a can of shaving gel, squirted some into his hand, and massaged it into Rachel's scalp.

"Number Five will sit very still."

Adam went to work with the razor, and when he'd finished he stood back to admire his handiwork. He tilted his head from side to side, checking from all angles. Rachel just sat as still as she could, paralysed and dumb, not even daring to breathe. Adam unfastened the restraints then told her to stand up and take her clothes off. Rachel complied immediately. She didn't try to hide her nakedness. She just stood with her arms by her sides, trembling from head to toe, and stared at a spot on the floor so she wouldn't have to look at Adam. He handed her a towel and told her to dry herself, gave her a clean set of clothes and told her to put them on. He left with the trolley and the door banged shut. The halogens were abruptly switched off.

Darkness.

Rachel walked back to the mattress and sank down onto it. She squeezed herself tight into the corner, pulled the blankets around herself and hugged her knees, tears streaming down her face. Her naked head felt cold and strangely weightless.

Losing her hair was horrendous, but right now that was the least of her worries. Rachel had had her suspicions, but until Adam cut her hair, that's all they were: suspicions. She'd chosen denial because the truth was too frightening to contemplate, but the denial didn't work any more. She thought back to the conversation she'd had at work yesterday morning, and the tears came harder. She'd been talking with some of the girls about the woman who'd been found wandering in a park in St Albans. The woman had been kidnapped and held captive for almost four months. That was scary enough, but what scared Rachel even more was that her head had been shaved and she'd been given a lobotomy. According to police she'd been the fourth victim.

*Number Five.*

The memory of Adam's rich, cultured voice resonated through her mind, two words that contained a whole host of terrifying possibilities.

# CHAPTER
# TWENTY-FIVE

Donald Cole was an East End boy born and bred. He was also a poster boy for the rags-to-riches cliché. He'd dropped out of school at fourteen without a penny or a single qualification to his name, and built up a thriving property rental business, while somehow avoiding prison. He had done good and wanted everyone to know it. Rachel Morris was his only daughter.

The headquarters for Cole Properties was in Stratford, a part of London that had been given a new lease of life when the Olympic circus came to town. It was based in an old converted factory, a three-storey red-brick building with blacked-out windows on its south-facing side. Cole's surname was plastered across the sign on the front of the building in massive capital letters. The "properties" part of the logo was tiny in comparison, more a footnote than a statement. News trucks were parked out front, satellite dishes pointed to the heavens. Sky, BBC, ITV. Camera crews, sound technicians and reporters milled around waiting for something to happen.

Templeton abandoned the BMW on a set of double yellow lines as close to the entrance as she could get. We got out and slammed the car doors shut and dashed through the slush. The sky was bright blue, the temperature somewhere around thirty degrees. The reporters shouted questions at us as we breezed by, and the cameramen hustled to get their cameras pointed in our direction. We kept our heads down and our mouths shut and bowled through the double doors into the building, the heater above the door blasting hot air at us as we passed underneath it.

While I stamped the slush from my boots and unzipped my jacket, Templeton marched up to the receptionist and told her we were there to see Cole. The receptionist stuttered that there must be some mistake since Mr Cole had cancelled all his appointments for the rest of the day, and Templeton flashed her ID. One quick call later and we were riding the elevator to the third floor. Cole's PA met us off the elevator. She was in her forties, blonde and efficient. She must have been stunning when she was younger because she was still attractive now. She led us along a white-painted corridor that was decorated with bland black-and-white photographs that were trying too hard to be arty, and stopped outside a set of wide double doors. She knocked twice, then pushed one of the doors open and stepped aside to let us through.

Cole's office was as big as the incident room back at Scotland Yard. Unlike the incident room, though, it was clean and free from clutter, and smelled of orange groves and cigars rather than detectives.

There were two white leather sofas arranged in an L-shaped formation around a glass-topped coffee table for informal chats. The big oak desk with the huge high-backed leather chair was where the heavy business was carried out. Large expensive rugs covered most of the wooden floor and there were more of those bland black-and-white framed photos on the walls.

The silver-framed family pictures arranged carefully on the desk covered three generations of Coles. It was strange that there was no other family here. Given the circumstances, I'd at least expected Cole's wife to be here. The fact that she wasn't meant she probably wasn't handling things too well.

Donald Cole was standing in front of a large floor-to-ceiling tinted window, staring blankly out at the cityscape. Stood like that, looking without seeing, he reminded me of Sarah Flight. Cole had his back to us, a cigar burning between his fingers. He was a big man, tall and wide. His face was hard and worn with red drinkers' veins snaking across his nose and cheeks. He didn't have a broken nose, which meant he either hit first and asked questions later, or he paid someone else to do the hitting. Once he'd been muscled up, a real tough guy, but the years had softened that muscle to fat. He had a chunky gold bracelet, a sovereign ring, and a large expensive watch, unsubtle reminders of his wealth and success. His suit was bespoke and his shoes were handmade from expensive leather.

"Have you found the bastard who took my daughter?"

Cole's voice was a low, rough growl. He was still staring out the window.

"Bastards," I corrected. "There are two kidnappers."

142

The big man turned and stared, a move he had down to a fine art. It was a move designed to intimidate, and it had no doubt worked successfully for him in the past. He had both the look and presence to pull it off. I wasn't impressed. I'd been given the hard stare by men a lot more dangerous than Donald Cole, men who would cut you up before breakfast then eat your heart and liver for lunch, and laugh with glee while they were doing it.

"This isn't a joke. These bastards have got hold of my daughter and when I get hold of them I'm going to rip their heads off."

"No you're not," said Templeton. "What's going to happen is we're going to catch these people, and they're going to go to court, where they'll be tried and then they'll get sent to prison for a very long time."

"And how safe do you think they'll be in prison?"

"Is this a good point to mention that I'm wearing a wire?" I said.

Cole tried the hard stare again. This time I responded with a yawn and the big man's face turned a shade redder.

"Who is this Yank? And what the hell is he doing in my office?"

"Mr Cole," said Templeton, "we need you to retract your offer of a reward."

"Give me one good reason."

"I'll give you four good reasons." I walked over to the desk, reached into my pocket for the four after photographs I'd stolen from the incident room, and slapped them down like playing cards. Curiosity got the better of Cole. He walked over to his desk, glanced at the photos, then looked at me.

"What is this?"

"Take a look," I said. "This is what will happen to your daughter unless you retract the reward." Cole took a look and I watched him closely. His face wasn't giving away much, but small cracks of uncertainty were forming below the surface. "All these women had parents who loved them, parents like you who would have done anything to get their children back safe and sound. Unfortunately for these four that didn't happen."

"I just want my daughter back."

"I know that, but believe me, offering a million-pound reward isn't the way to do that." I paused and looked at the photos laid out on the desk and waited for Cole to do the same. "Right now, because of what you've done, Scotland Yard's telephone system is jammed solid. Anybody who has ever seen anyone who even slightly resembles your daughter is calling us up because it's lottery time and they all think they've got a shot at that million-pound prize."

Cole stared at the photographs without saying a word. His hands were gripping the edge of the desk, eyes narrow, lips tight. My guess was that it was Rachel's face staring back at him from all four photographs.

"Then you've got the lunatics," I continued. "The crazies who wear tinfoil hats and have a direct line to the mother ship and are convinced that Rachel's disappearance is the result of some government

**144**

conspiracy. And the thing is, Mr Cole, all of these calls need to be checked out. Do you have any idea how many man-hours will be wasted doing that? And those are man-hours that should be employed on something constructive, like, I don't know, finding your daughter. And here's the irony. Somewhere amongst all those calls there will probably be a genuine lead, and that lead would have come to light anyway even if you hadn't offered the reward. At worst it's going to get lost. At best it's going to get buried under a ton of useless crap and by the time we realise its significance it'll be too late to help Rachel."

I shrugged. "Of course, we might get lucky and spot it, but I'll tell you now, even though I'm a betting man, those aren't odds I'd bet on." I tapped the desk to make sure Cole's attention stayed on the photographs. "Unless you do what we ask then I'm going to be adding Rachel's picture to my collection."

Cole stared at the photos for a while longer, shadows of emotion flickering across his hard face. He picked up Patricia Maynard's photo and studied it closely.

"Okay, I'll retract the reward." Cole shot me a look that was both a challenge and a warning. "But you'd better get my little girl back."

Cole's PA escorted us to the elevator and waited with us until it arrived. We got inside and the doors closed and Templeton hit the button for the ground floor.

"You really get off on all that alpha-male stuff, don't you?" she said. "You like to lock horns? Do a little rutting?"

"For the record, we were not rutting."

"Antagonising Cole like that might not have been your best move. If you're not careful you're going to wake up with a horse's head in your bed."

Before I could respond, my cellphone rang. Hatcher's name was lit up on the screen. I answered and said hi.

"You're not going to believe this," said Hatcher. "Despite that stunt of Cole's, we might actually have got a halfway decent lead."

# CHAPTER
# TWENTY-SIX

Springers looked shabby, but most bars did in sunlight, even in an upscale area like Kensington. There was nothing like moonlight and streetlamps and tasteful lighting to paper over the cracks and make things appear more presentable than they were. The woodwork was purple, the lettering silver. Hippy colours, designer bohemian.

Most of the bar's frontage was taken up by four large windows that gave a good view of the interior. Three o'clock in the afternoon and there were ten drinkers inside. Most were dressed for work but I didn't see much business going on. The Christmas decorations were expensive and tasteful, nothing too garish.

"Fancy a small wager?" I said.

We were parked on the yellow lines outside the bar. The heater was on full and "Layla" was playing on the radio. This was the extended version rather than the radio edit. Slide guitars and piano and Clapton wailing away on his Fender Stratocaster.

"Okay, I'm listening," said Templeton.

"I'm betting Cole has a Bentley."

"What do you think I am, Winter? Stupid? You saw the car at his office."

"I didn't, but I can see how you might think that, so let's make it more interesting. Check the records and you'll see that he also drives a Maserati. The Bentley will be a Continental. The Maserati, a Gran Turismo."

"Okay, you're on. Ten quid. But you need to be right about both cars. Make and model."

"I am."

Templeton held out her hand and we shook to seal the deal. Her touch was electric and it lit up my synapses in a way that was better than any artificial stimulant. We got out the BMW and went inside.

Andrew Hitchin was waiting behind the bar for us. He introduced himself as Andy and got us some drinks on the house. Whisky for me, coffee for Templeton. Andy had a Budweiser straight from the bottle. He was Australian, a surfer-dude with scruffy black hair, a blue stone on a strand of leather around his neck, and enough of a tan to indicate he was still fairly new in town. His pupils were dilated and there was a sweet tinge to the tobacco smoke that clung to his clothes. He spoke carefully to hide the fact he was stoned. Templeton placed a photograph of Rachel Morris on the bar, the Eiffel Tower shot. It was blown up to the point where it was starting to lose definition.

"Yeah, that's her," said Andy. "I'm a hundred per cent sure. A hundred and ten per cent. She was sat over there." He pointed to a sofa and low table hidden away at the back of the room.

"Is she a regular?"

"I've never seen her before. Then again, I've only been here a couple of weeks. I showed the CCTV

148

footage to a couple of the other guys who've been working here longer, but they didn't recognise her, either."

"We're going to need that footage," said Templeton.

"Thought you might. I already checked with the manager and he said no worries."

"You obviously get a lot of people coming through here," I said. "How come you remembered Rachel?"

"We weren't all that busy last night because of the snow. Also, we don't get many women coming in on their own. Usually they're with their friends or partners. The ones who do come in alone don't tend to stay alone for long. They've just arrived early and are waiting for their friends. Men drink on their own, women don't."

"How long was she here for?"

"I'm not sure. Long enough to have a couple of glasses of wine."

"Red or white?" I asked.

"Red." Andy paused, thought for a second. "Wait a minute, I've just remembered something. It's probably not important, but she started off with a soft drink then switched to wine."

"That's good," I said. "Anything you remember, please tell me. You never know what might be important."

Andy smiled like he'd just been given a gold star and moved to the top of the class. He took a long pull on his beer.

"Okay," I added, "you said it wasn't busy, which means you had time on your hands. What do you do around here to kill time?"

"Load the dishwasher, empty it, tidy the bar. That sort of thing."

"Check out the women?"

I grinned and Andy grinned right back. "Busted."

"You thought Rachel was attractive, didn't you? At any rate, you thought she was attractive enough for you to keep tabs on what she was drinking."

Another grin. "Busted again."

"I want you to close your eyes."

Andy looked at me suspiciously.

"Probably best to humour him," said Templeton. "And don't worry, if he tries to make off with your wallet, I've got your back."

The barman shrugged. *What the hell.* He shut his eyes.

"Okay," I said. "I want you to imagine that it's last night. You're looking for things to do to keep busy. It's a cold one, and you're bored, so you're more aware than usual when the door opens. Every time it does you get a blast of cold air and you look over. The door opens and Rachel comes in. The reason you notice her is because she's on her own. What are you doing?"

"I'm just finishing serving someone."

"Is anything else going on at the bar?"

"Yeah. Lisa's just winding up her shift."

"What time does she clock off?"

"Eight. She needed to get home for her kid."

"Rachel comes over to the bar. Who serves her? You or Lisa?"

"Lisa."

"And because it's not too busy, and because she's on her own, you notice she has a soft drink."

Andy nodded.

"What happens next?"

"She goes over to her table." A nod towards the table he indicated earlier.

"What's she doing?"

"She's waiting."

"For what?"

A shrug. "Her date, I guess. Her phone's on the table next to her glass and she keeps checking it. Every time the door opens she looks over."

"Did you serve her when she came to the bar for a glass of wine?"

Andy nodded. "Yeah."

"Did she say much?"

"Not really. She was giving off a vibe that she didn't want to talk. Some people want to talk, some don't. Do this job long enough and it gets so you're pretty good at reading that one."

"She wasn't wearing a wedding ring, was she?"

Andy shook his head. "Nope, no wedding ring."

"Did her date turn up?"

Another shake of the head. "When did she leave?"

"Some time after nine but I'm not sure when exactly. Maybe quarter past, but it could have been later."

"You can open your eyes now."

Andy took a long pull on his Bud. "So does any of that help?"

I nodded. "It does. A lot. Thanks."

"No worries."

Templeton handed over a business card that had the Metropolitan Police's logo embossed at the top and her direct line printed at the bottom. She asked Andy to call if he remembered anything else. Handshakes all around, then we went over to the table Rachel Morris had sat at last night. I sat at one end of the sofa and Templeton sat at the other end, a patch of artificially distressed leather separating us. We had a good view of the door, and the bar, and the other customers. It was a good spot to watch what was going on without being noticed.

"Okay," said Templeton. "We know Rachel Morris got here just before eight, left some time after nine and likes red wine. Do you mind telling me how any of that helps?"

"It helps because I've now got a pretty good idea how the victims are kidnapped."

"And you got that from the fact that she prefers red wine to white."

"No, I got that from the fact she wasn't wearing a wedding ring."

Templeton started to ask something and I held up a hand to shush her. Without another word, I closed my eyes.

# CHAPTER
# TWENTY-SEVEN

I walk into the bar, stamp my feet on the mat, shake the snow from my coat, and for a second just stand there and check out the customers. My eyes flit from person to person, but don't linger. Just a quick glance, long enough to see if he's here, then on to the next. The unsub has given me a description, but nobody matches it. And the reason nobody matches it is because he's given me a false description.

And the reason he did that is because he's here right now, watching me.

I take another look at the customers. No, that doesn't work. The bar is too public. It's too risky. This unsub is careful. He wants to limit the amount of time he could be seen with his victim, limit the exposure. There's nothing to be gained from being here.

At the bar I order a drink. A cola or a lemonade, or maybe a soda water with a splash of lime. Money changes hands and I come over to this table. It's out of the way, which means nobody will bother me or try to chat me up. There's an unobstructed view of the main entrance, which is important because there's no way I'm going to miss my date when he arrives.

We've arranged to meet at eight because nobody ever arranges to meet at five minutes to or seven minutes after the hour but I'm early because this is all new and I'm wired, totally hyped. I walked too quickly from the Tube station. I'm doing everything too quickly.

I tell myself to relax but it's no use. Every time the door opens my head snaps towards it, heart pounding. At this stage it doesn't occur to me that he might not be coming. It's only just gone eight so he's not really late. Not yet. I check my phone for messages or missed calls. There won't be any, but I check anyway. There's got to be a logical explanation why he hasn't got here yet. Maybe he's been held up at work. Maybe he's been held up by the snow. I put the phone on the table and try not to stare at it.

Time passes. I drink my drink, watch the door, wait. Every time the door opens and it's another false alarm, I feel more foolish, and angry. The longer this goes on, the more likely it is that I've been stood up. I go to the bar and get a glass of wine.

Back at the table, I drink my wine and check my phone and wait some more. How long do I wait? According to Andy, about an hour and a half. That feels about right. If my date hasn't got here by then, and he hasn't phoned, you can bet he isn't about to turn up any time soon. I finish my wine, check my phone one last time, then put my coat on and head for the door.

I opened my eyes and drained my glass. The alcohol seared my throat and burnt my gut, heating me up from the inside out. Templeton was staring across the table.

"Wedding rings," she prompted.

I ignored her. "Take a look at the customers and tell me what you see."

"A bunch of business people. So what?"

"Now take another look and tell me what you don't see."

"Alcoholics, homeless people, down-and-outs. Factory workers."

"Statistically speaking there's at least one alcoholic in the room right now, probably a coke addict, too, but yeah, you've hit the nail on the head."

We stood up and headed for the door. The second we stepped outside a blast of arctic air hit us. The harsh wind cut away at my face and I pulled my coat in tighter and hitched the collar up as high as it would go. A discreet camera was hidden above the doorway, positioned to catch the faces of anyone entering. The bar owner had no interest in the people leaving because once they'd left his premises they were someone else's problem. I made a mental note to make sure we got the footage from all the cameras.

I stopped on the sidewalk, looked right, looked left. Late afternoon, daylight fading to dusk, the streetlights already on. This street wasn't a main thoroughfare, but it wasn't a dark alleyway, either. It sat somewhere between those two extremes, busy with cars and taxis and people who were hurrying more than they would in the summer because they wanted out of the cold.

"Look at the shops," I said. "Look at the restaurants, the cars, the people. What do you see?"

"Money."

"This is our unsub's hunting ground. He feels comfortable here, he feels at home. He blends in."

"Which backs up your theory that he comes from money."

"Predators stalk their prey. They pick a spot in the tall grass and they wait. So where's the tall grass around here?"

I glanced around and spotted a small café on the other side of the street. It wasn't directly opposite, but it was worth checking out. I crossed the road, dodging around the back of a Mercedes that swerved so it wouldn't hit me. There were two tables for the smokers outside. *Mulberry's* was painted in friendly red letters on the window. Hot air blasted from the heater above the door as we entered. Mulberry's was a medium-sized establishment, big enough to offer anonymity, which was all the unsub cared about.

There were two window tables, and both offered a great view of Springers. From here we could see right inside those four big windows. The interior of the bar was lit up like a jack-o'-lantern. I could make out individual faces and I could see lips moving in conversation and I could see the Christmas decorations and coloured lights. I saw Andy the barman zip up his coat and make for the door. The sofa where Rachel Morris had sat was tucked away in the shadows, but I could just about make it out.

"This is the tall grass. Now, there are two ways I see this playing out. Either you have the unsub here, watching and waiting for Rachel, or his partner." I thought about this for a second, then shook my head. "No, that doesn't work. It has to be the dominant partner. Remember what Andy the barman said. A woman on her own would have stood out."

"So what was the partner's role in all this?" asked Templeton.

"She was probably driving the getaway car."

"A car rather than a van? A van would be more practical for hiding someone."

"If the kidnappings were taking place during the day then I'd agree with that. There's nothing more anonymous than a plain white delivery van, right? But at night, in an area like this, a van's going to stand out."

"Isn't that risky, though?" said Templeton. "Hanging around here waiting for Rachel to get fed up and come out of the bar."

"It's less risky than hanging around on the street. If our unsub had done that then someone would definitely have noticed him."

"But why bother waiting at all? All waiting does is increase the exposure time, which increases the risk of being seen, which increases the risk of being caught. Cutting Jack knows Rachel's coming here so why not snatch her before she gets to the bar?"

"Cutting Jack! Jesus Christ you've given him a nickname. I hate nicknames. It legitimises the unsub, turns them from assholes into legends."

"Back to my question, Winter. Why wait?"

"Because the unsub wants to catch his prey off-guard. He wants them to let their defences down. Here's a question for you. What do people do in bars? Don't think too hard. Just say the first thing that pops into your head. The obvious thing."

"They drink."

Templeton looked at me like this was the dumbest question she'd ever been asked, and the dumbest answer she'd ever given.

"Exactly. They drink. Alcohol is one of the most effective drugs there is for reducing social inhibitions. You want someone to let their guard down, give them a couple of drinks. What's more, alcohol is totally legal and you can get it anywhere." I nodded to myself, a smile spreading across my face. "This guy's clever. Really clever. Do you want to know why you haven't caught him yet?"

"Enlighten me."

"It's because he gets his victims to do all the hard work."

# CHAPTER
# TWENTY-EIGHT

Rachel paced the basement in the dark, building a mental map of her prison. She thought of the mattress as north and the door as south. If each of her strides was more or less a metre, then it was ten metres from the mattress to the chair, and another ten metres from the chair to the door. East to west, the width of the room was twenty metres. Each wall was a uniform twenty metres in length.

The dentist's chair had been positioned in the exact centre of the room.

Rachel's measurements tallied with the last time she'd done this, and the time before that. She'd lost count of the number of times she'd done this. It gave her something to do, something to relieve the boredom and stop her thinking. Something to stop her imagination running away with her, at least for a short while.

Rachel went over to the door and pressed her hands against the dog flap. The plastic was cold and smooth beneath her palms. She felt her way around the edge until she found the rough area near the bottom where the manufacturer's name and logo had been cast into the plastic. She pushed against the flap. Gently.

Carefully. It was locked, just like all the other times she'd tried.

Even if it had been open she didn't know what she would have done. She could imagine herself crawling through the flap and making a run for it, but she was terrified of what Adam would do if he caught her. The fact it was locked wasn't really a barrier anyway. The dog flap was made from plastic and all that held it locked was a small red plastic clip. If she wanted to, she could easily kick her way to freedom.

And Adam knew that.

Rachel walked back through the dark to the mattress, found the blankets and wound them around herself like a cocoon. She was building a picture of where she was being held. The house was big and old, and definitely detached. She had a sense of large rooms and space above her. Her hearing compensated for her blindness, the dark amplifying any sounds. There was a big boiler nearby that made a heavy thump whenever it kicked in, and the whoosh and rattle of pipes both distant and near added to her sense of being somewhere large. Occasionally she would hear a floorboard creak. Again, some of those sounds were distant, some close.

Noise wasn't an issue. Adam had demonstrated that clearly with the speakers. Also, he hadn't seemed bothered by how loud she'd screamed when he hit her with the cane. Then there were those bloodstains on the armrests. Whoever left those stains would not have done so quietly. If anyone lived close, or anyone was passing on a nearby street, the police would have been called by now and Adam would be in prison. Then

**160**

there was the fact that the dog flap could easily be smashed open. Adam obviously believed that if she did get out, she wouldn't get far. He was confident he could contain her, that there was nobody nearby who could help her.

All this added up to a large, detached house situated well away from any curious neighbours or passers-by.

Rachel ran a hand over her smooth skull and tried to tell herself it was just hair and that it would grow back. It didn't work. It wasn't just hair, it was *her* hair, and Adam had stolen it.

She wished her father was here, not because it was his job to make the monsters go away, but so that he could break Adam's legs. Rachel had overheard the whispering conversations when she was little, the one-sided telephone calls. Her brothers had passed on the rumours and the speculation, and when she put it all together it was obvious what her father was. Rachel had come to terms with what he did long ago, and although she didn't agree with the way he carried out his business, there was no doubt he loved her and would do anything for her, and that included breaking bones.

The dark was disorientating. There was nothing she could use to track the passing of time, no boarded-up windows with telltale shafts of daylight sneaking through, no cracks in the floorboards above her head. The corridor beyond the dog flap was as dark as the basement.

Rachel had no idea how long she'd been here. She reckoned at least a day, but couldn't be sure because she had no reference point to work from. She remembered getting into Adam's Porsche, then nothing until she woke up here. She might have been out for a couple of hours, but it could have been longer. Or it could have been less time. She just didn't know.

How much time had to pass before she was officially classed as missing and the police started looking for her? Forty-eight hours was the figure in her head, but she wasn't sure if that was the case, or if this was something she'd picked up from television.

Had Jamie contacted the police yet? Rachel wanted to believe that he had. She couldn't see why he wouldn't have. If he'd got home early and gone straight to bed then he might not have noticed that she hadn't come home. He slept so heavily that bombs and earthquakes wouldn't wake him, but he would have noticed she wasn't there at breakfast. He would have contacted her friends to see if anyone knew where she was, and when he came up empty there he would have contacted the police.

It was the obvious thing to do, the only thing to do. A slither of doubt slid across Rachel's heart. This was Jamie she was talking about. Obvious and Jamie didn't necessarily go together.

She thought back to the conversation with the girls at work and wished she'd paid more attention. She remembered a few vague details, but nothing substantial. Torture, lobotomies, things being done with knitting needles. At the time these details had just struck her as gross. Tabloid titbits. Everybody's reaction had been the same. Revulsion and disgust and total disbelief. Nobody

162

could understand how anyone could do those things to another person.

A couple of the girls had even wondered out loud what it would be like, but only in a vague sort of way. They hadn't considered what it would really be like to be at the mercy of a psycho who wanted to hurt you for kicks, someone who, when he'd finished getting his kicks, intended to mess your brain up and turn you into a vegetable. And why would they? It wasn't as though anything like this was ever going to happen to any of them. The odds of winning the lottery were shorter than the odds of that ever happening.

Except it had happened to her.

The dog flap clattered and Rachel's head snapped towards the sound. A wave of adrenalin hit, doubling her heart rate in the space of a single beat. Her mouth went dry, her palms turned clammy, and all she could think about was running even though there was nowhere to run.

The lights slammed on and Rachel automatically shut her eyes. A second wave hit and she started hyperventilating. Rachel forced herself to take a couple of deep breaths, told herself to calm down. Losing it every time the lights came on was not going to help. She opened her eyes slowly so she could adjust to the brightness. The anger hit as hard and suddenly as the adrenalin. She was angry with herself for letting Adam's games get to her, absolutely furious that she'd been stupid enough to get in this situation in the first place.

Rachel noticed the smell of food before she saw the tray. Eating was the last thing on her mind, but that smell changed everything. Her stomach rumbled and her mouth flooded with saliva. Aside from a Mars bar, the last thing she had eaten was a BLT. That could have been twenty-four hours ago. It could have been longer. Rachel glanced anxiously at the speakers in the corners of the room, her head moving from one to the other. She was waiting for Adam's distorted voice to boom through the speakers and tell her what to do. For once she wanted to hear that voice.

Rachel chewed one of her nails without noticing, paring it back to the quick, something she hadn't done since she was a child. The speakers stayed silent. Was this another game? Some sort of test? If she moved towards the tray before she was told to, would it be taken away? Rachel decided to give it two minutes and started counting off the seconds in her head. If the speakers stayed silent after two minutes she would take the risk and go over. If the tray was taken away it meant Adam never intended letting her eat, that he was just playing mind games with her again.

Two minutes passed.

Rachel left it a little longer, just in case. She took one final look at the speakers, then got up unsteadily and went over to the door, giving the dentist's chair a wide berth. The tray was still there when she reached the door.

There was a tall glass filled with water on the tray, a plate of ravioli, cutlery and a napkin. She took a closer look. The plate was antique bone china, so thin she could see veins and shadows, and the glass was crystal. Rachel turned the fork over and saw the hallmark imprinted on the back. Solid silver. The white linen napkin was neatly folded and pressed, the edges military-straight. The ravioli had come straight from a tin, though.

Rachel looked over at the chair with its straps and bloodstains, then looked back at the tray. She felt a sense of dislocation. Two universes had collided and she was trapped in the middle of them. She was Alice, tumbling down the rabbit hole.

She tentatively tried the ravioli, wondering what the catch was, wondering when Adam would charge in and snatch the tray away. Rachel took another forkful, then another. She got herself as comfortable as she could, her back against the wall, the tray balanced on her lap, and made herself keep eating way past the point she was full because she had no idea when she would be fed again.

She put the plate back on the tray and wiped her mouth with the napkin. After everything that had happened she still couldn't get away from the idea that this was some sort of trick, that something terrible was about to happen. For a while she just sat there with her back against the wall, the tiled floor cold beneath her.

The seconds ticked by.

Nothing happened.

Rachel tidied the tray and placed it back in front of the dog flap. She got up and walked across the room to the mattress. A voice stopped her in her tracks. This voice wasn't booming from the speakers, and it wasn't Adam's. It was soft and timid, female rather than male. "Did you enjoy your dinner?"

# CHAPTER
# TWENTY-NINE

Mulberry's was busy and full of sound. Snippets of conversation, the rattle of spoons and cups and plates, the gurgle and rush of the espresso machine. The smell of coffee hung heavy in the air. Tinsel had been draped over the picture frames and a tree surrounded by presents glittered colourfully in the far corner. I glanced over the road at Springers. The bar glowed warmly on the other side of those four large panes of glass. The people inside made me think of ants trapped in an ant farm.

The girl behind the counter had finally noticed us, but didn't seem bothered that we hadn't ordered anything. There was a brief moment of eye contact and then she went back to her customers. This got me wondering. Once a customer placed their order they became part of the background noise, they were dealt with then forgotten about, move on to the next customer. I was certain the unsub had been here last night. It felt like the sort of thing he'd do. He might even have sat at this very same table. He would have ordered his espresso or his latte then he would have done his best to become invisible. Go back in time and it wouldn't be Templeton sat opposite, it would be the unsub. I caught the waitress's eye and waved her over. She swerved around the counter and came across.

"Hi."

The waitress was in her early twenties. She had a tasteful nose stud, dyed black hair, and her baggy jeans hung low around her hips, hiding her shape. Combat boots rather than shoes, worn in and comfortable. A student working her way through university was my guess, someone whose parents weren't loaded.

"Bit of a long shot," I said, "but I don't suppose you were working here last night?"

The girl shook her head.

"Any idea who was?"

Another shake of the head. "I'm only part-time. I do a couple of afternoons a week." She glanced at Templeton then looked back at me. "So, who are you guys? Are you police or something?"

Templeton flashed her ID. "I'm going to need a contact number for your boss."

"And I'm going to need a coffee to go," I said. "Black, two sugars, please."

Raised eyebrows and a smile for each of us. "No problem."

The waitress hustled back to the counter and got busy.

"Wedding rings, Winter."

Templeton gave me a look that left me in no doubt that the gloves were about to come off and things were going to get unpleasant.

"Okay, wedding rings," I said. "There are four distinct phases with these sorts of crimes. Stalking, acquisition, enactment, and disposal. Acquisition is the riskiest phase. Why?"

"Because with the other three it's easier to control the situation, the environment and the variables."

"Exactly. That's why so many serial criminals target low-risk victims. Prostitutes, drug addicts, homeless people. These targets have lifestyles that make it easy to isolate them, which reduces the risk of being caught. A prostitute will get into a car with a stranger. She might think twice about doing it, but she's going to do it anyway because if she doesn't then her pimp's going to beat her up. A well-educated businesswoman won't get into a car with a stranger. Fact. So what does that tell you?"

"That our victims know Cutting Jack."

"But the victims have never met the unsub," I said. "So how do they recognise him?"

"I know what you're getting at, Winter. We've already looked at the internet angle and come up empty-handed."

"Look harder. You also need to check to see if the victims have any secret cellphone accounts their husbands don't know about. This unsub builds up a relationship with his victims and this is done over time. We're talking months rather than days. By the time he's ready to reel them in, they're prepared to lie to their husbands and friends. They're prepared to take off their wedding rings and hide them in their purses. And they're prepared to get into a car with someone they've only just met."

"Why bother taking off their rings? Surely Cutting Jack already knows they're married."

"They do it partly to make the unsub feel better, and partly to ease their own guilt. They don't want the unsub to think of them as married. They don't want to think of *themselves* as being married. They want the unsub to see them as young, free and single. Ironically, that's what they want to believe, too, since it makes the guilt easier to handle. Did you notice Sarah Flight wasn't wearing a wedding ring?"

Templeton shook her head.

"At the time I wondered who'd taken it off. I wasn't sure if it was her mother or someone who worked at Dunscombe House. It wasn't either. Sarah Flight took it off and hid it in her purse or her bag or wherever. The unsub found it when he went through her stuff and kept it as a trophy."

The waitress came over with my coffee. She handed a business card to Templeton. It was decorated with the Mulberry's logo and had the manager's cellphone number scribbled on the back.

"Okay, what now?" Templeton asked.

"Are you into role-playing?"

The look she gave me was priceless.

# CHAPTER
# THIRTY

I stopped in front of Springers' tall glass windows and took a good look all around, getting a feel for the environment. Left, right. North, south, east, west. The unsub had been sitting across the road in Mulberry's last night. What had he seen? What had he heard? What had he done? Lazy trails of smoke wound upwards from my cigarette, twisting through the light that spilled from the bar. The throwaway cup was hot in my hand despite the cardboard collar. My breathing and heart rate increased as I slipped into the zone. Smells, sights and sounds were suddenly sharper.

"Okay, you're Rachel Morris," I said to Templeton. "You've been stood up and you're feeling angry. The weather's lousy. It's cold and it's snowing. You come out of the bar. What's the first thing you do?"

"I head for home. I've had a crap evening and I just want to be tucked up in bed."

I shook my head. "You're jumping the gun. Yes, you want to get home as quick as you can, but, despite the cold, you're still going to stand in that doorway and check the street one last time to see if your date's going to turn up. And the reason you're going to do that is because you feel foolish for getting yourself in this situation in the first place, and if your date does make a miracle appearance then you won't feel so foolish. It's basic human nature. Psychology 101."

Templeton moved into the doorway and made a big show of checking the street. "Looking left, looking right," she said. "No sign of the bad guy."

"That's because I'm over in Mulberry's, watching you. Okay, you came here on the Underground. The CCTV footage from the station showed that. Odds on you're going to go back the same way. Except you didn't. The CCTV footage showed that, too."

"Maybe I spoiled myself and got a cab."

I shook my head. "That doesn't work. You're a commuter. You use the Underground every day. It's what you're familiar with, and familiarity is what we use to give the illusion of safety. Also, a cab would be expensive and you're already bummed at wasting your money on an evening out that never happened. Then you've got the hassle of flagging a cab down. There's no way you're taking a cab."

We turned right and started walking towards the Underground station. It wasn't far, about eight hundred yards. I could see the sign up ahead.

"Now that you're headed home, you want to get there as quickly as possible, so you're walking fast, covering the ground. Meanwhile, I've now left Mulberry's and crossed the road to your side. You haven't seen me yet because you've got your head down and all you can think about is getting home. I call out to get your attention. You stop and turn around."

Templeton stopped and turned to look behind her.

"What do you see?" I asked.

"I see you walking towards me."

"It's dark and you've never seen me before, but you're not spooked. Why?"

"Because I recognise you. Either you've sent me a photograph or you've sent me a description."

I shook my head. "Not a photograph. Way too risky. If the police got hold of a photograph then that would be my fun and games finished when I've just got warmed up. A written description is more likely because it can be specific and ambiguous all at the same time. If I tell you what I'm wearing and the colour of my hair and my age, then you'll recognise me, but I'm really not giving anything away. I still want to see that description, though, so get your computer people to keep digging."

"They didn't find anything."

"They haven't found anything *yet*." I took a drag on my cigarette and drank my coffee and let the mix of nicotine and caffeine do its thing. "So what happens next?"

"You walk up to me. Your body language is relaxed. You're not a threat."

"And what's the first thing I say to you?"

"Sorry."

I smiled at that and Templeton smiled back, smug *na-na-na-na-na* smiles from both of us.

"Which makes me appear even less threatening," I said. "So I tell you I'm sorry, give you some story about why I'm late, tell you I'm sorry again, and by the time

I've finished you're going to think I'm as dangerous as Mother Teresa."

"And those couple of glasses of wine will be making me feel all warm and fuzzy, so I'm happy to get sucked into the fantasy," said Templeton.

"This is your chance to salvage something from the evening, so when I suggest we go grab a drink or a meal, you jump at the offer. I tell you I'm parked close by, let's go."

"So where are you parked?"

"Good question."

I stood for a second and smoked my cigarette and looked up and down the street. There was a right turn a hundred yards further along and we headed towards it. The street was narrow, with double yellow lines along both sides.

"This is where he parked," I said.

"I'll get someone to check if any parking tickets were issued last night. This part of Kensington, I'd be more surprised if he didn't get a ticket."

"Good idea."

Templeton narrowed her blue eyes. She was almost squinting, but still managed to look sexy. It was a neat trick.

"And what's that supposed to mean?" she said.

"It means it's a good idea."

"Yeah, that's what you said. But the way you said it makes it sound like it's a stupid idea."

"Get someone to check it out," I said. "So, Rachel Morris climbs into the car and they drive off into the night. What's wrong with this scenario?"

"Two things. Firstly, the place where Cutting Jack makes contact with Rachel is all wrong. If he was late and parked here, why would he be coming up on Rachel from behind? He should be coming from the front. I know she'd had a couple of drinks but I think she'd notice that one."

"That's easy. He waits until she's gone past this street and then he approaches her. That way they can turn around and head back to the car without Rachel getting spooked. What's the second thing?"

"He needs to incapacitate Rachel as soon as she gets into the car," said Templeton. "At some point she's going to realise something's wrong, and if he's driving when that happens that puts him in a vulnerable position. He can't tie her up and gag her and dump her in the boot because someone would see him. So he drugs her and straps her into the passenger seat. Even if he's stopped by the police he could claim she was sleeping, or she'd had a few too many drinks, and that would be plausible."

"That's pretty much how I see it. So, we've got an MO for how he abducts his victims. The next question is how does he stalk them?"

Templeton sighed. "On the internet."

"It's the only explanation. Okay, next stop Geek Central. I want to chat with the best computer wizard you've got."

# CHAPTER
# THIRTY-ONE

"What did you say?"

Rachel wanted to hear that voice again because she needed to convince herself the woman on the other side of the locked door wasn't a figment of her imagination, that she hadn't dreamt up an imaginary friend to keep her company as she slid into madness. The silence lasted long enough for Rachel to convince herself her imagination was playing tricks, then the woman spoke again.

"I asked if you enjoyed your dinner. I made it myself. It's my favourite."

The woman was talking quietly, almost whispering, and Rachel had to strain to hear. But that didn't matter because she was real. Rachel suddenly realised something. Whoever this woman was, she wanted to please her. She didn't just want to know if Rachel liked the food, she *wanted* her to like it. This wasn't just any old meal, this was her favourite. The food was average at best, there was only so much you could do with a tin of ravioli, but Rachel wasn't about to tell her that. If this woman wanted to hear this was the best meal she'd ever eaten, then that's what she was going to hear.

"It was very nice," said Rachel.

"Thank you."

Rachel heard the brightness in the woman's voice and knew she'd got that one right. "What's your name?" she asked, and immediately wished she hadn't. The silence that followed this question went on much longer, long enough for Rachel to start beating herself up for pushing too hard, too soon. She strained to hear what was happening on the other side of the heavy door, imagining that if she listened hard enough she would hear the woman breathing, hear the beat of her heart. All she heard was the dull, distant rumble of the heating system.

"Eve," the woman said eventually.

Rachel smiled. Eve. She would use it wherever she could, anything to build the trust between them. That's what had happened in every hostage movie she'd ever seen. The negotiator would use the bad guy's name wherever possible. He'd talk calmly and do his best to keep things relaxed and use that name like they were best friends sharing a couple of drinks.

"Hi Eve. My name's Rachel."

"I know."

Rachel didn't say anything for a moment. She sensed there was an opportunity here, but wasn't sure of the best way to play it. The answer came to her in two sudden flashes of insight that hit one after the other.

"Is Adam your brother, Eve?"

There was another of those long silences. Rachel figured that Eve had learned to be careful what she said around Adam.

"Yes," she said. "Adam's my brother."

Of course he was. Adam and Eve. It was so obvious when she thought about it. Rachel's first insight had been correct. She hoped her second one was, too.

"He hurt me," Rachel said.

"I'm sorry. I've asked him not to hurt the girls, but he doesn't listen. He gets angry."

"And when he gets angry, he hits you, doesn't he, Eve?"

This pause was followed by a rush of words, short staccato sentences filled with misplaced justifications. "Sometimes. But he doesn't mean to. And he only does it because I make him angry. And he's always sorry afterwards."

Rachel smiled. Two for two. She'd been right to play the empathy card. For the first time since she got here she could see a glimmer of hope. It was only the tiniest glimpse but right now she would take whatever she could get.

"I really should go. I shouldn't be here. Adam would be angry if he knew I was talking to you."

Rachel heard a shuffling on the other side of the door and panicked. Eve was getting up, and then she was going to leave, and if Eve left, she would be on her own again. Alone in the dark. Rachel wanted her to stay. She *needed* her to stay. The loneliness of the situation suddenly hit her and she bit back the tears. She didn't know anything about Eve, didn't know how she fitted into this madhouse, but what she did know was that she wasn't Adam. Adam had shaved her head and reduced her to a number. Talking to Eve reminded her she was still a person, that she was more than a number.

178

"Please don't go, Eve." Rachel heard the desperation in her voice, but didn't care.

"I guess I can stay for a little while. Adam's not due back yet."

"Thank you, Eve."

Rachel stared across at the dentist's chair and lapsed into silence. Bright light reflected off the steel and porcelain. The tiles were hard and cold beneath her, numbing her muscles. How the hell had she ended up here? It wasn't fair. She wasn't a bad person. Her thoughts caught up with her, and when she realised how naive they were she almost laughed out loud. Life wasn't fair, and bad things happened to good people all the time. Karma was bullshit.

A childhood memory surfaced from her subconscious, something she hadn't thought about in years, decades even, a long-forgotten memory. She was about five or six, young enough to still believe her father was a superhero. They were at the villa, walking along a beach together, and for once she had her dad all to herself. It was just the two of them. No mum, no annoying brothers. The sand was warm between her toes and the setting sun behind their heads stretched long shadows out in front of them. Her hand was tiny in his rough, callused one. They were talking and laughing, making up stories, and she had never felt so loved, so safe.

Rachel grabbed on to the memory. She wasn't in that bright cellar any more, she was in a place where the air smelled of salt and exotic food and heat, a safe time and place where the only monsters she had to worry about were the imaginary ones living under her bed.

"Are you all right?" asked Eve. "You've gone really quiet."

The sunlight faded and Rachel was back in the basement. "I'm fine," she said. "Just thinking, that's all."

"About what?"

"About the sunshine," said Rachel.

"And that makes you sad."

"No, it actually makes me happy."

"I don't get it."

Before Rachel could stop herself, she was sharing the memory with Eve.

"You're lucky," said Eve. "I don't remember my father."

"What happened to him, Eve?"

"He died."

From the flat, abrupt way Eve answered, Rachel sensed it was time to back off. She'd pushed hard enough for one day and didn't want to alienate her.

"I should go," said Eve.

"Will you come back and talk to me again? It gets so lonely."

"I'll try. But I need to be careful. I'll need to wait until Adam goes out again."

"Bye, Eve. Thanks for talking to me." Rachel paused. "And thanks for dinner. I appreciate it."

"I'll come back soon. Promise and cross my heart."

The lights went out and Rachel made her way over to the mattress, dodging to the left to avoid the chair. She was halfway across the room when the dog flap clattered. She turned and saw the shadowy silhouette of the tray disappear through the hole in the door. Rachel reached the mattress and wrapped the blankets tightly around herself.

Alone in the dark again.

Rachel had learned a number of interesting things from talking to Eve, and one important thing.

The most interesting thing was that Eve was lonely. She craved approval and wanted friendship, and that's why she'd initiated the conversation. Rachel was more than happy to be Eve's friend. She would be her Best Friend Forever if it helped her get out of here.

And the important thing: there were occasions when Adam went out and left Eve alone to guard her.

Rachel needed to get Eve on her side. If she could somehow persuade the girl to view her as a person rather than a prisoner, she had a much better chance of manipulating her into helping her escape. Rachel let that thought hang there, then told herself she was being ridiculous. What the hell did she think was going to happen here? That if she made nice, Eve would help her escape?

But it could work. It was a long shot, and she might be letting her fantasies run away her, but what was the alternative? Should she just give up? Resign herself to a fate that ended with a psycho slicing into her brain? There was no decision to be made here, not really. Donald Cole had not raised his daughter to be a quitter.

# CHAPTER
# THIRTY-TWO

Templeton stopped at a door halfway along a subterranean corridor, gave a sharp, staccato *rat-a-tat-tat* knock, then pushed it open. The room on the other side was small and crammed with computer gear. Servers hummed and clicked, cooling fans spun and whirred. An air-con unit kept the temperature at a comfortable level, not too hot, not too cold.

Two wizards worked the terminals, one male, one female. They turned from their screens in unison, like they were being operated off the same wires, and checked us out. Neither adhered to the computer geek stereotype. They weren't wearing ripped jeans or stained four-day-old T-shirts or thick bottle-bottom glasses, and they didn't have Jabba the Hutt physiques. Both were slim and in their early thirties and well turned out. They looked like lawyers or accountants.

The girl wizard was Indian, pretty with wide almond eyes and a way of looking at you like she knew something you didn't. She was wearing an engagement ring but no wedding band. The boy wizard had ginger hair and a permanent blush. No rings, but his Tag Heuer appeared genuine.

"Meet Alex Irvine and Sumati Chatterjee," said Templeton.

"Hi," they said in unison.

Given their names and appearance, I expected them to have accents. They didn't. They sounded like they'd been shipped in straight from Oxford or Cambridge, or the Massachusetts Institute of Technology.

"So, which one of you is the best?" I asked.

"I am." They weren't quite in sync this time. Sumati won by a nose. They turned to look at each other, then launched into a full-blown argument. I leant back against the door to watch and Templeton sidled up next to me. She was standing close enough for me to catch small scent clouds of her perfume.

"You did that on purpose," she whispered.

"Of course I did. They might not look like computer geeks, but looks can be deceptive. You don't have to peel away too many layers before their true nature comes to light. So, who has the biggest collection of *Star Wars* memorabilia?"

"That'll be Sumati. Except it's not *Star Wars* she's into, she's a Trekkie."

"Does she speak Klingon?"

Templeton shrugged. "How the hell should I know?"

"*BIjatlh 'e' yImev!*" I shouted.

Sumati stopped in mid-rant and stared at me like I was an alien. Templeton was staring too. "I've got a real good memory," I whispered to her. "It's great for quizzes, and exams, and for surprising complete strangers."

**183**

"Actually," said Sumati. "*BIjatlh 'e' yImev* is fine if you're telling one person to shut up."

"But if you're talking to more than one person it would be more correct to say *sujatlh 'e' yImev*. Yeah, yeah, I know. I just wanted to make sure I'd got your attention." I turned to Alex. "It looks like you lost this one. I'm going to go with Sumati."

"Because she speaks Klingon?"

"No, because she's a woman who can obviously more than hold her own in a male-dominated profession, which means she's got to be at least ten times smarter than you are."

"So what can I do for you, Mr Winter?" asked Sumati.

"I guess this is the point where I ask how you know my name so you can prove how smart you are."

She grinned. "The internet."

"That figures. You know which case I'm working?"

"Of course. The Cutting Jack case."

"Our principal unsub is stalking his victims on the internet. I need you to take a look at their computers, see what you can find."

"We've already done that. We didn't find anything."

"That's because you didn't look hard enough. Go back and have another look, and this time work from the assumption that he might be smarter than you guys rather than some dumb schmuck who can barely navigate his way around Internet Explorer. Start with Rachel Morris's computers since she's the latest victim. You won't have had a chance to look at them yet, so you'll be able to approach them with fresh eyes. Look

**184**

hard enough and you will find something. I guarantee it."

"And I guess you want this done by yesterday."

"Of course."

"Leave it with me."

Templeton opened the door.

"Your Klingon," said Sumati. "I'm impressed, but you need to work on your pronunciation."

"*Qapla'*." This time I really hammered those guttural syllables.

"Better," she said.

Templeton pulled the door shut and we headed back along the corridor to the elevator.

"I take it that meant 'screw you'," she said. "At any rate, that's what it sounded like. It certainly didn't sound like you were wishing her a long life filled with health, wealth and happiness."

"The literal translation is 'success', but it's used to say goodbye. There's no translation for 'screw you'. Say that to a Klingon and you'd be inviting a battle to the death."

Templeton laughed. "Nobody likes a smartass, you know. Particularly one who's a closet nerd."

"I am not a closet nerd."

"Yeah, right, so says the man who speaks fluent Klingon and can no doubt reel off the title of every episode of *Star Trek*."

"I can't name every title."

We stopped walking and Templeton stared me straight in the eye.

"Okay," I said. "I can name every title. But only for the original series. And, for the record, that doesn't make me a closet nerd. It just makes me someone who likes to know things."

Templeton flashed a smug grin. "Yeah, so says you."

# CHAPTER
# THIRTY-THREE

I sat at the Cosmopolitan's piano and rattled off some quick C-major scales. One from the bottom register, one from the middle, one from the top. The keys were heavy and sluggish and nowhere near as responsive as my Steinway, but at least the piano was in tune. The fact it had a decent enough tone was a bonus.

The barmaid had looked relieved when I suggested she turn off the music and let me play. She'd jumped at the suggestion. Hadn't even asked about my level of skill. Not that she cared either way. Anything had to be better than that insipid computerised Christmas music. Ten minutes of that crap and I was ready to jam pointed sticks in my ears. How she managed to last a whole shift was beyond me.

I went straight into the second movement of Mozart's Piano Concerto 21. By the third phrase, London and the bar had phased away. The heaviness in my heart and chest eased. All that mattered was the music. All that existed was the music.

Eyes closed, my fingers instinctively found the next note, the next phrase. They didn't let me down. This wasn't one of Mozart's flashy show-off pieces, but that didn't mean it was easy to play. The music has a forward momentum that makes you want to play faster, but if you do that you kill the mood. The trick is to keep it slow and easy. I reached the final phrase, the final note, paused a moment with my eyes still closed and waited for silence.

"That was beautiful."

Templeton was standing beside the piano stool. She had a strange expression on her face that was difficult to read. She was five minutes late, which was an acceptable level of lateness given the circumstances. Early wouldn't have been cool, and any later would have been rude. I was already halfway through my first whisky and contemplating a second.

"I mean it," she said. "You play really well. Where did you learn?"

"My mother was a music teacher. She taught me to play. I studied music at college, as well."

"I thought your degree was in criminal psychology."

"It was. I did the music degree in my spare time."

"Most people tend to party in their spare time."

I laughed, remembering a boy who'd thought every night was party night. "I was fortunate," I said. "I found the academic stuff easy, which left plenty of time for all the extra-curricular stuff."

Templeton's eyes narrowed and she fixed me with her cop stare. "Just how clever are you?"

"That's not what you're really asking, is it? You want to know what my IQ is."

"Okay, what's your IQ?"

"It's well above average, but a damn sight lower than da Vinci's."

"You're not going to tell me, are you?"

I shook my head. "It's just a meaningless number. It's what you do with your life that matters. Our actions define us. On paper my father was a genius, and he chose to use that gift to destroy."

"And you choose to use your genius to try to undo his wrongs. To balance things out again."

I shrugged, but didn't deny it.

Templeton gave me a sly look. "It annoys you that da Vinci had a higher IQ than you, doesn't it?"

"The question is irrelevant. The IQ test wasn't invented until 1904, so any figure attributed to da Vinci is just some so-called expert's best guess."

"See, it does annoy you."

The mat my drink was on was at an angle, so I straightened it up, moving it until the edges lined up just right. Ice rattled against glass. "It doesn't annoy me."

"You say it's just a meaningless number, but I'm betting you could tell me who invented it, where it was invented. I bet you could tell me the whole story. So here's my question: if it is so meaningless why won't you tell me what your IQ is?"

"Because I don't want you to define me by a number."

Templeton reached for my glass and took a sip. She grimaced and put the glass back down. The mat shifted and I straightened it again.

"Interesting choice of words, Winter. You could have said that you didn't want to be defined by a number.

Instead you said that you didn't want *me* to define you by a number."

"A slip of the tongue."

Templeton gave me a look. "So you say."

"Remind me again why you're pulling a cop's salary. You would make a great lawyer."

"There's not enough money in the world, Winter."

I laughed. "Yeah, you've got a point there."

"When you said earlier that your mother *was* a music teacher, you didn't mean that she was retired, did you?"

My laughter died away and I shook my head. "No she isn't. She passed away a few years back."

"I'm sorry."

"Don't be. It was probably for the best. She never really came to terms with what my father was."

"Have you?"

"I'm working on it." I linked my fingers together and stretched them out. "Okay, enough with the heavy stuff. I'm warmed up now. Any requests?"

Templeton thought for a second, then said, "Do you know 'A Whiter Shade of Pale'? That's always been one of my favourites."

"So, what are those lyrics all about?"

Templeton smiled one of those great smiles. "You're the genius, you tell me."

"Well, the fandango is a dance that originated in Spain. And a cartwheel is an acrobatic movement."

Templeton punched me playfully on the arm. "Some questions aren't meant to have answers."

"Every question needs an answer. At any rate, we need to at least attempt to answer them because that's how we progress. If we ignored the tough questions, we'd still be swinging from the trees blissfully unaware of the fact that our opposable thumbs made us the kings of the jungle."

"Just shut up and play."

I laid my fingers on the keys and closed my eyes. The melody lit up inside my head, each note a different colour. I worked out some simple chords to support the tune then started to play. The song owes a huge debt of gratitude to Bach and I really emphasised that in my interpretation. I threw in a couple of Mozart-inspired flourishes because they seemed to fit. When I'd finished Templeton was looking at me with that strange, unreadable expression again.

"This might be a stupid question," she said. "But have you ever played that song before?"

I shook my head.

"That was amazing, Winter. Seriously impressive. I mean, how the hell did you do that? It's like you're Rain Man or something."

"Hopefully my social skills are better. And I promise I've never had a complete meltdown because I missed my favourite TV programme."

"So you say."

I laughed at that. "Let's go find a table."

# CHAPTER
# THIRTY-FOUR

Templeton led the way to a table near the bar. Like earlier, she was wearing jeans, and like earlier, these ones were tight and clung in all the right places. She shook off her coat and took a seat. Her plain black wool jumper tried hard to hide her body, and failed miserably. Templeton could wear a burlap sack and make it look sexy. Her hair was still damp from the shower. The shampoo she'd used had apples in, and the smell brought a memory of summer into the room.

She reached into a pocket, pulled out a ten-pound note, slapped it down onto the table. Her expression was all mock annoyance and pretend indignation.

"How the hell did you know what cars Donald Cole owned?" she asked.

"When you eliminate the impossible, whatever remains, no matter how improbable, must be the truth."

Templeton gave me a stern look. "How did you know, Winter?"

"He had pictures of the cars on his office wall."

"He had lots of pictures on his wall."

"He did," I agreed. "There was a picture of his boat, a picture of his Mediterranean villa, pictures of his

**192**

racehorses. Donald Cole doesn't have a single qualification. No diplomas, no doctorates, no certificates. Given his background, it's unlikely that any Nobel Prize winners or American presidents will be lining up to have their picture taken with him any time soon. The pictures are just another version of an ego wall. Cole defines his success by his status symbols, and he wants to show them off. Did you notice the family photographs?"

"Yeah. They were on his desk."

"Did you notice they were facing towards him? That they were difficult to see?"

"So he has good feng shui. What's the big deal?"

"He's happy for the world to see his status symbols, but not his family. He's protective of his family. He wants to keep them close. He wants to keep them safe."

"What father wouldn't?"

"You'd be surprised. Take my own father. On the surface he looked like the perfect dad, but scratch away at the surface and there was a psychopath lurking underneath. He wouldn't have thought twice about killing my mother or me if it had served his needs."

"Sorry, I didn't think."

I waved the apology away. "The point is that Donald Cole feels responsible for his daughter's kidnapping. He'll be racked with guilt. He has a ton of cash, he doesn't trust the police, and he comes from a world where you hit first and ask questions later. Not a good combination. Keep tabs on him. If he decides to go vigilante that would cause you guys a major headache.

**193**

Not to mention putting Rachel into even more danger than she's already in."

"How could she be in any more danger than she already is?"

"These unsubs keep their victims for an average of three months. However, if Cole does something stupid, like reinstating the reward, for example, then that could lead them to decide that she's not worth the trouble. The dominant partner ups his timescale, fits three months of fun into a couple of days, lobotomises Rachel and dumps her. Game over. In cases where the victim is kept alive, things can always get worse. Remember that."

"Point taken." Templeton nodded to the ten-pound note on the table. "I'm dying of thirst here."

"Jack Daniel's and Coke?"

"How did you know?" She shook her head. "Actually I don't need to know. What I do need is a drink."

I stood up, grabbed the ten-pound note from the table and headed for the bar. The barmaid was the same one as yesterday. We'd got talking earlier and I'd found out she was Polish and her name was Irena, and she was single. I took the drinks back to the table, handed Templeton hers, tipped what was left of my old drink into my new glass. Then I sat down, swirled the ice cubes around my glass, took a sip, and wished you could still smoke inside. The ban was a pain in the ass. Alcohol and nicotine were meant to go together, like peaches and cream, only not as wholesome.

"Cutting Jack did get a parking ticket," said Templeton. "He drives a Porsche."

"But."

"Nobody likes a smartass."

I raised an eyebrow and Templeton sighed.

"According to the DVLA he drives a five-year-old silver Ford Mondeo. He switched the plates, so no ID there. But you already knew that. So, why did you leave the FBI, Winter?"

Templeton was staring at me, those sharp blue eyes fixed on mine. She wasn't about to let this one go any time soon. I took a slow sip of my drink.

"You ducked the question earlier because we didn't know each other well enough," she said.

"And we know each other so much better now."

"We've spent a lot of quality time together today. More than most married couples. Anyway, I told you why I became a cop. Quid pro quo, Winter. It's only fair."

The distant echo of my father whispering that three-word curse in his lazy Californian drawl drifted through my head. *We're the same.* The easy answer seemed the better option. I placed my glass carefully on the table.

"My superiors didn't agree with some of my methods. They felt I took unnecessary risks. I got a reputation for being a loose cannon, and in an organisation like the FBI where the team is everything, loose cannons aren't tolerated for long. I left before I got asked to leave."

"Were you taking unnecessary risks?"

"I did what I needed to do to get the job done. Same as I do now."

"That doesn't answer my question."

"I was solving cases," I said, "bringing the bad guys in. How I was doing that shouldn't have been an issue."

"Of course it should," said Templeton. "You get a police force that isn't regulated, and all you've got is a bunch of vigilantes. We're talking one step up from a lynch mob."

"And I suppose you always play by the rules. Do you expect me to believe there's never been an occasion when you bent a rule or two so you could get the job done?"

Templeton hesitated. She opened her mouth to speak, closed it again.

"Of course you've bent the rules," I said. "There isn't a cop around who hasn't. At least, there isn't a cop who's halfway decent who hasn't. I'm not saying that we shouldn't have rules, but those rules can't be so rigid that they stop us doing our job."

"And who decides where the line gets drawn?"

"That one comes down to common sense and your conscience. And for the record, I have no problems with any of the decisions I've made. No regrets. I sleep like a baby."

"Liar. There's not a single cop who doesn't wish they'd done something different, that they'd made at least one call differently."

When I didn't respond, Templeton flashed me a *told-you-so* smile. She reached for her drink. "Something's bugging you about the case. What?"

"Who says anything's bugging me?"

"Cutting Jack and his girlfriend are still out there. Until they're caught there will always be something about this case that bugs you. It's the way you're wired. So 'fess up. What's bugging you?"

"The fact they lobotomise their victims."

"In your briefing you said the lobotomies were a compromise between the two partners. The dominant wants the victims dead. The submissive wants them alive. It makes sense to me."

"It does make sense," I agreed. "But I've been thinking about that one all day, and the more I think about it, the more convinced I am that I've missed something."

"Could you be overanalysing the situation?"

"I'm not overanalysing. The lobotomy is the key to solving this case."

"So, what are you thinking?"

"That's the problem. At this stage I'm all out of ideas."

"What? Not even half an idea? A quarter of an idea? A hunch?"

"Not even that," I admitted.

"So, there's nothing cooking in that planet-sized brain of yours?"

I shook my head and sighed. "Nothing's cooking."

"Remind me again: what was da Vinci's IQ?"

"I never told you what it was in the first place, so how can I remind you?" Templeton arched her eyebrows and gave me that cop stare. "Two hundred and twenty," I said.

"And he was smarter than you," Templeton said.

"Way smarter," I replied. "But remember, it was just a guesstimate."

Templeton sipped her drink then smiled at me over the rim of her glass. "It really does annoy the hell out of you, doesn't it?"

# CHAPTER
# THIRTY-FIVE

"Number Five will use the bucket."

Adam's distorted robotic voice boomed around the room, bouncing off the walls and making her head pound. Rachel blinked away the brightness, shook off the blankets, and got up from the mattress. Her limbs felt both heavy and light. She was aware she was moving, but felt like she was going the wrong way on an airport travelator. She sleepwalked across the room in a daze, slid the grey jogging bottoms and panties over her hips, then squatted down. When she was done, she stood, pulled up her panties and jogging bottoms, then waited for her next instruction.

"Number Five will bring the bucket to the door."

Rachel carried the bucket across the room and placed it on the floor with the handle facing the door, just like she'd been told to do. The first time they'd gone through this routine, Adam had been very clear with his instructions. So clear she knew that he'd spent a long time thinking it through, and if she deviated he wouldn't think twice about punishing her. The bruises on her back were all the motivation she needed to make sure she followed his instructions to the letter.

"Number Five will go to the chair."

Rachel looked at the dentist's chair and felt nothing. No racing heart, no cold sweats, no shakes. Just the mention of the chair would usually send her into a panic, but not this time. A strange bubble of calmness had enveloped her, a feeling that whatever happened, she would deal with it.

*Drugged*.

The thought emerged slowly from the sludge inside her brain, and the fact it had taken so long for her to reach this conclusion meant she was right. Eve must have put something in the food. It was the only explanation.

"Number Five will go to the chair or face the consequences."

Rachel looked up at the nearest camera and for a moment she just stared into the lens, confused and disorientated and not too sure what was going on or where she was. And then she remembered. The chair. She was supposed to go to the chair. Rachel walked to the middle of the room and was about to sit down when Adam's voice boomed around the basement again.

"Stop!"

She froze with one hand on the bloodstained armrest.

"Number Five will take off her clothes."

Rachel paused long enough for the order to penetrate the fog in her head, then started to undress.

"Number Five will fold her clothes neatly."

She crouched down and did as she was told, slowly and with difficulty, her hands refusing to co-operate with the vague messages coming from her brain.

"Number Five will sit in the chair."

Rachel sat. The vinyl was cold against her naked skin, but she barely noticed. She heard the door open, heard footsteps come into the room, heard the plastic scrape of the bucket being lifted out, heard the hollow thump of a clean, empty bucket being put down. Rachel didn't bother to turn around to look. She was familiar with the routine. In her current state of mind, it was something she couldn't care less about. She didn't resist when Adam fastened the leg and arm straps. Didn't even flinch when he fastened the head restraint for the first time. The leather was soft against her bald head. Adam checked the straps were secure then left the basement.

Time passed.

When Adam returned he was pushing a medical monitor in front of him. He placed a plastic sleeve over her left index finger and switched the machine on. Her heart was beating at a steady seventy, the beep echoing brightly off the basement tiles. Adam left again and returned with the trolley. Rachel followed his progress all the way along the corridor, the sound of his footsteps getting progressively louder. He stopped in front of her then picked up a length of rubber tubing from the trolley.

Rachel felt dissociated from what was happening. It was like she was here but not here, like she was watching a film where everything was happening to the Rachel on the screen. From a distance, she watched Adam tie the rubber tubing around her right arm and pull it tight. Her lower arm throbbed in sync with her heartbeat, the monitor beeping in time. Her fingertips tingled. Adam picked up a syringe, tapped away any air bubbles, then tapped up a vein. Rachel saw her vein thicken and turn a darker shade of blue. She saw the tip of the needle pierce her skin and sink into it. She had always hated injections, but right now Adam could stick her with a hundred needles and she wouldn't care.

Adam pushed the plunger all the way down then removed the needle and untied the rubber tubing. A couple of seconds later the drug hit and the heart monitor suddenly jumped to 140, the beeping going from steady to frantic in a beat. Rachel felt indestructible. It was like someone had lit a load of fireworks inside her head. She'd never experienced anything like this. It was amazing. All her senses were heightened and she felt like she could dance for ever. She needed to dance, needed to move. It was the only way to burn off all the restless energy stored up inside her body. And she wanted to talk and talk and talk, wanted to share all these good thoughts and feelings with everyone and anyone.

She opened her mouth and Adam slapped her hard enough to leave a throbbing red handprint on her left arm. Pain jagged through her body, more pain than anyone could endure. This was worse than the time he'd hit her with the cane. Much worse. Rachel screamed and the heart monitor jumped up another twenty beats a minute. It pushed past the 160 mark before slowly settling back to 140.

"Number Five will not speak. Not. A. Word."

202

Rachel struggled against the restraints, desperate to escape, but they held firm, the leather digging into her arms. She wanted to crawl back into that narcotic bubble she'd been in earlier. She'd felt warm and safe in the bubble. Nothing had mattered. There had been no pain, no screams. Adam reached for a hunting knife and she shrank back into the dentist's chair. The blade was razor-sharp and glinted beneath the bright lights, six inches of wicked steel.

She looked at the knife, then looked at Adam.

The heart monitor beeped faster.

"This is really going to hurt," he said.

# CHAPTER
# THIRTY-SIX

By the time I'd showered and dressed, room service had arrived. Another full breakfast, a cholesterol-heavy injection of protein and calories to recharge my batteries. Plenty of coffee to wash it all down. I've got a hyperactive constitution, the sort of metabolism supermodels would kill for. I never put on weight. The downside is that my blood sugar level can crash without warning, and when that happens things can get real messy real fast.

I ate quickly then took my coffee out onto the balcony. The grey skies were back and the darkness was heavy and oppressive. There was more snow on the way. Six storeys below people hurried through the cold, wrapped up warm and moving fast. It was still an hour until sunup. Tomorrow was the shortest day. In forty-eight hours the days would start to get longer again, and in five days it would be Christmas. I'd still be around in two days, I'd probably be around in five. Hopefully these unsubs would be in custody by the New Year, though, so I could get the hell out of Siberia.

I lit a cigarette and called Hatcher. Seven o'clock and the detective was already at his desk. He told me about the parking ticket and I made all the appropriate noises you made when you heard something for the first time. Aside from that, nothing much was happening. They'd found plenty of disgraced medical students, but none who fitted the profile. No sign of the unsub's practice victim, either.

Hatcher was talking but I wasn't really listening. Something Professor Blake said yesterday had jumped into my head and I could have kicked myself for not spotting its significance earlier. It's the smallest of details that make or break an investigation. They can be the difference between alive and dead. It wasn't just God who was in the details, the devil was in there, too, and he was just waiting to trip you up. Professor Blake had told me that Freeman had progressed from experimenting on grapefruits to experimenting on cadavers.

Grapefruits and cadavers. Plural rather than singular.

I'd told Hatcher to look for one murder victim, but it was possible the unsub had needed more than one person to experiment on.

"We need to expand the search parameters for the practice victim," I told Hatcher. "First off, we could be looking for more than one victim. The exact number will depend on how quickly the dominant unsub taught himself to perform a lobotomy. Also, we're looking for a female or a male. Any age from thirteen or fourteen upwards. The victim will be low-risk. A prostitute or a junkie, or a homeless person. They're going to be under sixty, since the older they are the easier it would be to kill them accidentally. However, I wouldn't be too concerned about placing an upper age limit since this will be self-regulating. Junkies don't tend to live to be old. And forget about anyone who fits the original victim profile. He was experimenting, so he knew these ones were going to die. Part of his signature is that he doesn't kill, so you're looking for someone who doesn't fit the criteria he uses to choose his usual victims. That means no brown-eyed, brunette career women."

"Great," said Hatcher. "Can you narrow it down any less?"

"The victim will stand out," I assured him. "This unsub was practising his surgical skills so there will be evidence of the brain being mutilated. Get your people to call every coroner in the city. Even if it was a couple of years ago, someone's going to remember something like this. He may well have attempted to disguise what he'd done."

"How?"

"Maybe he used a hammer to smash in the front of the skull, destroying any evidence of mutilation to the prefrontal cortex. Or perhaps he removed the head and disposed of it separately. Get imaginative".

"Get imaginative," echoed Hatcher.

There was frustration in his voice, a stress that comes from chasing shadows and ghosts and feeling like you're getting nowhere. I could imagine him hunched over his desk, shaking his head wearily and rubbing those basset hound eyes and wishing he'd been an engineer or an accountant or a grocery store bagger, anything but a cop.

"We're going to catch them," I said.

"Well it had better happen sooner rather than later."

Hatcher let go of a sigh that was loaded with a ton of hidden implications.

"What's going on?" I asked.

Another sigh, this one longer and even more loaded.

"This stays between you and me," he said. "Okay?"

"You could be talking to your priest," I replied.

"There's a rumour going around that I'm going to be taken off the investigation."

"Ignore it. There are always rumours, and there always will be. And do you know the thing about rumours? Nine times out of ten there's no substance behind them. They're just smoke. Usually what you're dealing with is some asshole with a grudge, or someone playing politics. Bottom line: you're the best person for the job, Hatcher."

"Thanks for the vote of confidence, but this is the one time in ten where the rumour has substance. The media is putting pressure on the people upstairs, and that pressure is being passed down the line to me. It's scapegoat time, and I'm right up there at the top of the hit list. Everyone wants to know why we haven't caught this bastard yet. And by *we* they mean *me*. And rightly so. I've had over a year to catch him and he's still out there. Rachel Morris's kidnapping has sent the press into a feeding frenzy. You want to see this morning's papers, it's not good. The media has cranked up the fear level. People are scared."

"Then let's throw the media a bone."

"What have you got in mind, Winter?"

"Give me a couple of hours to sort some things out."

"You're not going to tell me. Fine." Another sigh. "But be quick. I need you here."

"I'll be there as soon as I can."

I killed the call, took a last drag on my cigarette, pitched the butt over the railing and headed inside, back into the warm. Downstairs at reception, the concierge ordered a cab. The car arrived five minutes later. I climbed inside, gave an address to the driver, then settled back in my seat.

I realised we were being tailed the second we turned out of the Cosmopolitan's driveway.

# CHAPTER
# THIRTY-SEVEN

The X-Type Jag was right behind us, close enough for me to make out the two guys up front. The guy behind the wheel was in his late forties, skinny and tense-looking. His buddy was younger, and much bigger, tall and wide and bulky. A linebacker rather than a quarterback. The driver did nothing to hide the fact he was following. He matched us move for move, turn for turn. Whenever my driver indicated, he indicated. I rapped my knuckle on the partition and the cabby slid it open.

"Yeah," he said.

The cabby was a white guy in his late fifties. He had a beer belly and a jolly demeanour and had probably driven cabs his whole life. I nodded to the rear-view mirror.

"See that Jag behind us? I'll give you an extra twenty if you can lose it."

"No problem."

The cabby put his foot down and I held on tight. He turned down side streets without indicating, bullied his way through jams, cut across traffic to a discordant chorus of blaring horns. I lost count of the number of near misses we had. My adrenalin was pumping and my knuckles were shining white from gripping the seatbelt. I kept catching glimpses of the cabby's reflection in the rear-view mirror. He was grinning a wide dopey grin and clearly having a ball. He looked like a little boy who'd fallen through the big screen and ended up in a Hollywood action movie.

My guy was good. *Really* good. Unfortunately the skinny guy driving the Jag was better. He rode the rollercoaster the whole way, never falling more than two vehicles behind. We turned into Dunscombe House and made our way up the potholed drive, swerving from side to side to avoid the worst of the craters. The cab rolled to a stop at the front door, and the Jag rolled to a stop in a parking lot about fifty yards away.

"Sorry, I gave it my best shot," the cabby said.

"No problem," I told him, and gave him the extra twenty anyway.

The cab did an about-turn and disappeared down the drive. The Jag stayed put. I gave the driver a small salute then made my way to the front door and rang the bell.

The same receptionist as yesterday was behind the counter. She called me Detective Winter and I didn't bother to correct her since it saved on long explanations and made my life a whole lot easier. She got me to sign in and I headed past the tall Christmas tree into the day room.

Sarah Flight was in the exact same spot she'd occupied yesterday, her chair pushed into the bay window, the unseen grounds stretching out on the other side of the glass. I carried a chair over and sat down beside her.

Today's crowd was the same as yesterday's, a dozen or so patients floating twenty miles high. Like yesterday, some were playing cards and some were talking to themselves, while others were staring off into space. The same two orderlies were on duty. They had a table to themselves and looked as bored as they had the previous day. The TV high up in the corner had the volume down too low to hear anything anyone was saying.

If I came here tomorrow, or a year from now, or ten years, the scene would be pretty much the same. The faces would change, but that TV would still be playing to itself. Someone screamed upstairs and my head automatically snapped towards the sound. I was the only person in the room who reacted. Even the orderlies didn't really react. They paused in mid-conversation for a moment, then started up again like nothing had happened. The screamer let rip with another high-pitched, tortured shriek. It was impossible to say with any degree of certainty if they were male or female.

"So how's it going, Sarah?"

Sarah stared through the glass, seeing but not seeing. Her chest rose and fell in line with the instructions being sent out from her medulla oblongata. Her hair was sleep-tangled and a stringy line of drool had escaped from the corner of her mouth. I'd brought a packet of tissues with me this time and used one to wipe the drool away.

Outside, a groundskeeper tidied up leaves. The footprints in the virgin snow showed where he'd been, and there were tyre tracks from his small tractor, neat parallel lines like rail tracks. A monkey puzzle tree stretched strong and tall into a slate-grey sky. The world on the other side of the glass was sheened with the dull matt of winter.

Sarah didn't see any of this. She probably had this same spot every day, the same view. The seasons would come and the seasons would go and she would be oblivious to it. That was depressing enough, but what made it worse was the fact that Sarah would never complain about her unchanging view.

I sat back and crossed my legs and waited.

It didn't take long.

Amanda Curtis came into the room. Light, defined footsteps on the wooden floor. She picked up a chair on her way across the room and placed it next to her daughter's. There were stress lines etched into her face, crow's feet around her sad brown eyes. The grey in her hair had been hidden with dye. She looked a lot like Sarah Flight, only older.

Like her daughter, Amanda also had an empty space on her ring finger. This was the ripple effect in action. Something I was all too familiar with. You got the victim, then you got the victims of the victim, that poison rippling outwards from the unsub like radiation from a nuclear blast, completely invisible and just as destructive.

"Morning, sweetheart."

Amanda Curtis brushed Sarah's hair back from her forehead, uncovering a patch of skin where she could plant a kiss, then sat down and stared out at the grounds. For a while she just sat and stared and said nothing. I wondered what she was seeing, what memory she'd lost herself in.

"The first day Sarah was here, they left her in a chair facing the wall." Amanda was talking to her reflection in the glass. "I know it's silly but I was so angry. Almost as angry as I had been when I first heard what happened to her."

"It's not silly," I said.

"I like to think there might be a piece of the Sarah I knew and loved still in there. I know that's not the case, but even still." Her voice trailed off and she took a moment to catch her thoughts. "Sarah would have liked this view. She always loved the outdoors. As a child she was happiest when she was outside. She used to love riding horses. Watching her fly around on the back of a horse, going over all those jumps, used to worry me half to death. She was absolutely fearless. I would never have stopped her, though, because that would have been like taking away one of the things that made her who she was."

Amanda reached out and placed a hand on her daughter's. The gesture brought her out of her memories and back into the room. She turned her sad brown eyes in my direction.

"So what can I do for you, detective?"

"I've come to ask permission to kill your daughter," I said.

# CHAPTER
# THIRTY-EIGHT

There were four scars in total. One on her stomach, one on each arm, and the fourth on her thigh. They burned into Rachel's skin, branding her. The longest and deepest was four inches long and ran down her left biceps. She'd passed out by the time Adam started cutting into her thigh and didn't remember that one. That final scar was the shortest, only an inch in length. When she'd stopped screaming, he'd stopped cutting.

While she'd been unconscious, Adam had tidied up her wounds with disposable stitches and disinfectant. The smell of TCP clung to her skin. Rachel was still in the dentist's chair but the restraints had been removed. She was naked and cold, her muscles stiff from sitting awkwardly for so long.

The lights slammed on and Rachel's heart rate rocketed. Her eyes immediately turned towards the dog flap and she waited for Adam's voice to boom from the speakers, waited for something to be pushed through the flap. Nothing happened. She got up too quickly and almost collapsed. Her head was spinning from dehydration and the after-effects of the drugs, and she felt weak. She stumbled over to the nearest corner and stared into the black eye of the camera.

"What do you want from me?" she screamed.

The speakers stayed silent.

"What do you want?" she whispered.

Rachel slid down the wall onto her knees and curled into a ball. Hot tears slid down her cheek and she swiped them away with the back of her hand. The reality of the situation suddenly hit her, and it hit hard. She was never going to see the sun again, never feel it warm her skin on a summer's day, never feel hot sand between her toes. She would never again waste time gossiping with her friends, sharing laughs over a bottle of wine, never eat in her favourite restaurant.

Then there was the future she would never have. She had taken it for granted that she would have children one day, maybe even two or three. Jamie had led her to believe he wanted the same thing, but whenever she brought up the subject, he would come up with some lame excuse why it wasn't the right time.

She wasn't going to miss Jamie, she realised, and this made her cry even harder. Tears for all those wasted years. Her father was right. She could have done so much better. At the time she thought he was being overprotective, but now she saw he had a point. She wiped away the last of her tears and lifted her head. This was her world now. A twenty-metre-by-twenty-metre cell with a cold tiled floor, a stained mattress and that bloodstained chair, her future defined by Adam's whims.

"Stop it," she hissed to herself. "Stop it, stop it. Stop it!"

Rachel realised she was talking out loud and stopped as abruptly as she'd started. Things were really bad when you started talking to yourself. Only crazy people talked to themselves. Did that mean she was going crazy? And if she was, would that be a bad thing? If things got so bad that her mind snapped, maybe that would be the next-best thing to escaping. She considered this for a minute, then decided it wouldn't be better, it would just be the next-best thing to giving up.

The dog flap clattered and Rachel looked over to see a bucket being pushed through. She waited for her instructions, gave it a long couple of minutes, but the speakers remained silent. She gave it another minute because she was worried that Adam was toying with her.

More silence from the speakers.

Rachel got up and made her way tentatively across the room. She gave the dentist's chair an even wider berth than usual, but couldn't stop herself glancing at it, her eyes hypnotically drawn to the bloodstained armrests. There were more stains than before. She reached the door and looked down into the bucket. It was filled with soapy water, a sponge floating amongst the bubbles. There was a towel and a change of clothes next to the bucket, and a tube of antiseptic cream.

"You'll feel better after you've had a wash," Eve whispered. "There's some cream to stop your cuts getting infected."

"Thank you."

216

"I'm sorry Adam hurt you. I asked him not to, but he just laughed at me. He says I'm stupid."

"You're not stupid, Eve."

"I am stupid. Stupid, stupid, stupid." Eve's voice was edged with inwardly directed anger.

"Does your brother know you're here, Eve?"

The silence went on long enough to convince Rachel that Eve wasn't going to answer.

"He's gone out. He told me to make sure you were cleaned up before he got back. You need to wash or I'll get into trouble."

Rachel heard the distress in Eve's voice. She could imagine how horrific Eve's life with Adam was. She'd been here a couple of days and had started talking to herself. What would it be like to be with Adam for years?

"It's okay, Eve. I'll get washed."

Rachel undressed and began sponging herself down. The water was hot and smelled of lavender. She scrubbed away the dried blood and grime, moving carefully around the cuts so she didn't knock any stitches out. She washed her face, paused, then ran the sponge over her bald head, the heat from the water quickly turning cold. She dropped the sponge back into the bucket, towelled herself dry, then smeared antiseptic cream on her wounds, wincing when they stung. Rachel got dressed in clean clothes that were identical to the dirty ones she'd taken off. A grey sweatshirt, grey jogging bottoms, plain white panties. No socks or shoes or slippers. She wondered how far

217

she should push things and decided she should just go for it.

"If I met you away from here I think we could be friends, Eve."

"No we wouldn't." Each word was clipped. Eve sounded angry, only this time all that anger was aimed right through the door. "We would never have been friends because you're beautiful and I'm ugly."

"You're not ugly."

"And how do you know? You've never seen me."

Before Rachel could respond, the basement lights went out. She heard Eve stomp angrily down the corridor, heard her footsteps on the wooden stairs, heard a distant door open and close.

Great.

Rachel was furious with herself. She'd pushed too hard too soon. She'd always been impatient. Always. The best she could hope for now was that she hadn't done too much damage to her relationship with Eve. Without Eve on her side she didn't see how the hell she was ever going to get out of here. Rachel was just about to head back to the mattress when she realised there was one sound missing from the series of sounds she heard when Eve left.

She hadn't heard the click of the dog flap being locked.

# CHAPTER
# THIRTY-NINE

I shook a cigarette from my pack and wedged it between my lips. A sharp wind was blowing south from the Arctic and I had to shield the Zippo to keep the flame burning. The clouds were darker and greyer, lower, too. It was like being trapped in a concrete tomb. There was a promise of snow on the breeze.

The Jag was parked in the same place as earlier, the driver hidden behind the pages of a tabloid newspaper. The words CUTTING JACK were printed in big bold letters on the front page. It wasn't a surprise that they'd picked up on the nickname so quickly. The media loved that sort of thing. The linebacker saw me and nudged his buddy. The driver snapped the newspaper shut, folded it in two, tossed it over his shoulder. I walked over to the Jag and got in the back.

"Take me to your leader," I said.

The two guys up front shared a dopey look. This scenario obviously hadn't been part of their briefing. They'd been told to follow and observe, they hadn't been told to play taxi driver. The skinny guy shrugged at the linebacker, and the linebacker shrugged back. The skinny guy was obviously the brains of the operation, the one who called the shots. He glanced back at me one last time then made his decision. He fired up the car and we pulled out of the parking lot and bumped along the drive to the main road.

I killed time by flipping through the driver's newspaper. The unsub had laid claim to pages one through four, and I recognised my own voice in some of the words. The only logical explanation was that the leak had come from one of Hatcher's team. My money was on the grizzled old detective. His glory days were long behind him and he would have got a buzz from seeing a story in print and knowing it had originated from him and that he'd got one over on everyone. It was sad and pathetic, not to mention counterproductive.

The front page was taken up with a large photograph of Rachel Morris and the only text was the capitalised headline: CUTTING JACK'S LATEST VICTIM. I hadn't seen this photograph before, which meant it probably originated from Donald Cole rather than Scotland Yard.

The picture had been touched up using a computer. Rachel's skin was as smooth as a model's. The colour had been played around with to give her a healthy glow. This was a mistake. You wanted to humanise the victims, not dehumanise them. It's the imperfections that make us human. The stories of our lives are told through the lines and wrinkles we accumulate. Aside from that, it was a typical shot. Rachel was smiling a happy carefree smile for the camera, eyes shining. Everything about the picture shouted out that this was someone with everything to live for, someone with a whole world of possibilities stretching out in front of them.

We pulled up in the lot behind Cole Properties' Stratford HQ and parked next to Cole's Maserati. The skinny guy and the linebacker accompanied me to the third floor. We walked along the corridor side by side, the skinny guy on my left, the linebacker on my right. Cole's PA took over when we reached the office. She knocked on the door and a deep, muffled voice from the other side told us to enter. The aroma of cigar smoke drifted under the door.

The driver had called ahead so Cole was expecting me. The big man dismissed his PA with a nod, and the door gently closed. He was sitting on one of the leather sofas, which told me he wanted to keep things informal. There was a pile of paper on the glass-topped table and my name was on the top sheet. He'd checked me out, and wanted me to know it. Interesting.

Cole was smoking a cigar, something big and expensive. Given his love of obvious status symbols, it was probably Cuban. I lit a cigarette and sat down on the sofa that formed the bottom part of the L. There were pictures of Cole's race-horses on the walls behind each sofa.

Donald Cole had aged a decade in the last twenty-four hours. He looked like crap. I'd seen this before. It was the cumulative effect of shock and stress, and the sorrow of being stuck in an endless cycle of what-ifs. He was hurting and the only thing that could take that hurt away was the safe return of his daughter.

"The Met are a bunch of muppets," Cole growled. "I wouldn't trust them to find their arseholes with a map." He stabbed the air in front of him with the cigar. "You, on the other hand, you get results."

"Call off your bodyguards. I don't need babysitting."

"This isn't about what you need, this is about what's got to be done to get my daughter back."

"I can look after myself. I don't need any bodyguards."

"Yes you do, and I'll tell you why. Anything happens to you and I'll never see my little girl again. So, what's being done to find Rachel?"

"Everything that can possibly be done."

Cole made a disdainful snorting noise. "And what the hell's that supposed to mean?"

"Look, I understand how frustrating this is for you. I get it. You're used to calling the shots and now you're in a situation you can't control. To make matters worse, you've got money. Not a good combination. At the moment, you think you're helping, but you're not. What you're actually doing is sabotaging this investigation."

"Are you a father? Have you got kids?"

I shook my head, flicked the dead ash from my cigarette into the crystal ashtray on the table.

"Then you don't know anything."

Cole gave me the hard stare.

"Are you done?" I asked.

"I want my little girl back."

"Well, at least that's something we agree on." I took another drag on my cigarette. "Look, I'm going to get

Rachel back, but to do that I need you to back off and let me do my job. That means no more rewards and no more babysitters. You get an idea in your head of something that you think is going to help Rachel, I want you to forget it straight away, because whatever you're thinking is not going to help her. I can guarantee that. In fact, I'll go one step further. You'll probably end up killing her."

Cole stared at me and there was nothing of the hard man in this stare. For a second he looked like the hundreds of other stunned parents I'd met over the years. I wondered when anyone last talked to him like that, wondered if anyone had ever talked to him like that. If they had, they probably weren't breathing.

"If you don't get her back safe, I'm holding you personally responsible. You realise that, don't you?"

"Are you done?" I crushed my cigarette out in the ashtray and nodded to the pile of paper on the table, acknowledging it for the first time. "You've done your homework. You know I get results."

"Not all the time."

"More often than not."

"Let's hope this is the rule rather than the exception," he said.

"Let's hope so."

I got up to leave.

"Wait a second."

Cole went over to his desk and took a business card from one of the drawers. He wrote something on the back with a gold-plated pen, then handed me the card.

"My personal number," he said. "You can get me on this twenty-four/seven. If there's anything you need, anything at all, just call me."

# CHAPTER
# FORTY

"Where the hell have you been?"

"Good to see you, too, Hatcher."

"Seriously, Winter, where have you been?"

We were in Hatcher's office, a small cubicle on the fourth floor that was within shouting distance of the incident room. The office was as cluttered as Professor Blake's, but without any of the bookish charm. The desk was covered in files and paperwork and there wasn't an inch of laminated wood showing. The furniture was cheap, practical rather than aesthetically pleasing, the styles tracing a visual timeline stretching from the eighties onwards.

Templeton was hovering near the doorway, ready to make a quick getaway. Her body language made it obvious that she didn't really want to be here, and her puzzled expression made it obvious she had no idea why I'd brought her along.

"I want you to call a press conference," I said.

"You're kidding, right? Have you seen the papers today? A press conference is the last thing we need."

"Sarah Flight's dead. This is now a murder investigation."

"What are you talking about? If Sarah Flight was dead, I'd know."

I pulled a sheet of paper from my pocket and handed it to Hatcher. Hatcher read what was written on it then frowned.

"Is this some sort of joke?" he said.

I shook my head. "No joke. What you've got there is written permission from Amanda Curtis saying that we can tell the press her daughter is dead."

"And why the hell would we do that?"

"To drive a wedge between the unsubs. They're already escalating. It's time to up the pressure."

"We can't say someone's dead when they're not."

I shrugged.

"It's unethical."

Another shrug.

"We'd be lying to the press."

"Which is bad because the press never, ever lies about anything," I said.

Templeton chuckled. She tried to hold it in, but it was out there before she had a chance to stop it.

Hatcher looked at Templeton like he'd just noticed her. "What are you doing here anyway?"

"She's doing the press conference," I said.

"No way," said Templeton. "Absolutely no way." In the space of those five words the pitch of her voice had gone up by half an octave.

"You'll do fine."

"Read my lips, Winter. No way. I'm not doing it."

"Templeton!" Hatcher said sharply.

Templeton glared at him.

"Go. Now. I need to talk to Winter. Alone."

Templeton looked from Hatcher to me, then back to Hatcher again. Her face was tight, lips pursed. The look in her eye could have been anger, or it could have been hate, or fear. It was difficult to tell. She sighed and shook her head, then left the room. Hatcher watched the door close then turned to me.

"Remember what we were talking about this morning? All that stuff about me being taken off the investigation? If I pull a stunt like this, I won't just get taken off the investigation, I'll end up fired."

I took out my cigarettes and Hatcher flashed a warning.

"Don't you dare."

He looked as serious as he sounded, so I pushed the pack back into my pocket, then moved a pile of folders from the office's only spare seat and sat down.

"You're not going to get fired, Hatcher. Worst-case scenario, you'll go through a disciplinary and get busted back down to detective constable and bang goes your chance of ever being commissioner."

"This press conference isn't going to happen."

"*You* brought me in to advise on this case. Okay, I'm advising you to hold a press conference so you can tell the media that Sarah Flight is dead, and that this is now a murder investigation."

Hatcher sighed. "Have you tried this tactic before?"

"It'll work," I assured him.

"That's not what I asked."

"These unsubs are devolving. They're vulnerable right now. If we apply pressure in the right place, then we can destabilise their relationship. Keeping the victims alive is important to the submissive partner. If she believes one of her dolls has died, she's going to be devastated. The guilt will push her over the edge."

"And what's the risk to Rachel?"

"It's negligible."

"Define negligible."

I shrugged.

"So there's a risk we could make things worse for Rachel?" said Hatcher.

"Of course there is. Every move we make has some risk attached to it. Even doing nothing comes with an element of risk. This can work, Hatcher. You've got to trust me here."

"Okay," said Hatcher. "Let's do it. Maybe being a DC again won't be so bad."

"It's a lot less responsibility," I said. "So who gets to break the good news to Templeton?"

"That'll be you."

"By the way, the old guy who was giving me grief at the briefing, you need to transfer him to whatever your equivalent of Alaska is."

"Why? Because he was giving you grief?"

"No. Because he's leaking information to the press."

"And you know this how?"

"Because someone's leaking information, and it's him."

"I'm going to need proof."

"No you don't. As far as your team is concerned you're God, which gives you licence to smite with impunity."

Hatcher laughed.

"You know your team," I said. "If anyone's going to leak information, who's it going to be? That young DC with her whole career ahead of her? Or someone whose career stalled at detective sergeant, and who would do anything to get back at the organisation that screwed him over, particularly if it's going to earn him a few quid in the process?"

Hatcher sighed then frowned, his tired face folding in on itself like a black hole. "I'll get the paperwork sorted," he said.

# CHAPTER
# FORTY-ONE

Rachel pressed a hand against the dog flap and felt it give. She pushed hard enough to open it an inch, then gently closed it again, guiding it back into place with both hands, convinced it was going to creak. She leant against the wall, her heart beating wildly. Her lungs felt too big for her chest and breathing was an effort. She closed her eyes to shut out the dark and told herself to calm down, whispered the words under her breath, over and over. *Calm down, calm down, calm down.* It worked. Her heart rate steadied and her breathing got easier.

She replayed the conversation she'd had with Eve in her head. Eve said Adam was out and would be back *soon*, but what did that mean? It was one of those vague terms that could be measured against a length of string.

Would he return in an hour or the next five minutes? Rachel had no idea. What she did know was that sitting here like this, talking herself around and around in circles, was wasting precious time. This could be her chance to escape. This might be her only chance. Whatever the consequences, she had to at least try because if she didn't she'd just end up torturing herself with what-ifs the next time Adam strapped her to the dentist's chair.

She pushed the dog flap open, all the way this time. She was aware the clock was ticking, but made herself wait so she could listen for any signs of Eve, or Adam. All she heard was the gurgle of the ancient heating system, and the occasional creak of old wood settling. Way in the distance, she thought she could hear the wind whistling around the outside of the house.

Rachel put her head through the flap, squeezed one shoulder in and then the other. She went through diagonally since there was more room that way, but it was still too tight. She tried to move forward, wriggling from side to side, but she was stuck. Images of the chair and the cane and the knife flashed through her head, one after the other. Bang, bang, bang. Adam would find her stuck here, half in and half out of the dog flap, and then he would punish her.

She didn't want to think about what he might do because whatever he dreamt up was going to be so much worse than what he'd already done. Rachel wriggled harder, desperate to get free, the plastic scratching her arms and chest, fear driving her through the pain. Then suddenly she was all the way through and lying flat on the cold floor, breathing fast and hard, panic replaced by euphoria.

The corridor was as dark as the room, a degree or two warmer. Rachel crawled across the concrete floor until she found a wall, then stood and followed it along the corridor. The brickwork was rough beneath her hands. She moved as quickly as she dared because she had no idea what obstacles might be waiting to trip her up.

Twenty metres from the door there was a sharp ninety-degree left turn. Rachel stopped and listened for any signs of Eve or Adam before continuing. The flight of stairs a couple of metres on from the turn were cold and rough like the corridor floor. The glint of light that crept beneath the door at the top of them was the first daylight she'd seen since Wednesday afternoon, however long ago that was.

Rachel forced herself to climb the stairs slowly. It wasn't easy. She just wanted out of here. She could see freedom in that thin glimmer of daylight, she could feel it in the gentle breeze blowing down the stairs. But it wouldn't matter how close she was to freedom if she fell and broke her neck, so she made herself take it slow. She reached the door and even before she tried the handle she knew it would be locked. Luck had got her this far but it was only a matter of time before that luck ran out.

She tried the handle.

The door opened.

She stepped through the doorway into a narrow hallway with a high ceiling. The house was big and old, just like she'd imagined, that sense of space she'd experienced back in the basement more pronounced. Time seemed to crawl along much slower here than it did in the rest of the universe, reminding her of a museum. Muted daylight streamed in from a window she couldn't see, and there was cold, shiny wood beneath her bare feet, the boards worn smooth over the years. The smell of furniture polish and oranges filled the air.

Rachel paused and listened for any signs of life, then walked towards the daylight. She turned a corner and found herself in a large, open hall. Off to her right was a wide staircase with a red carpet and ancestral portraits in gilt-edged frames. She did a double take at the painting that hung at the top of the first flight of stairs. The resemblance to Adam was uncanny.

Straight ahead was the front door.

Rachel paused again. Listened. Where was Eve? Upstairs? In one of the downstairs rooms? The kitchen, perhaps? Wherever she was, she wasn't making a sound.

Perhaps she was hiding somewhere, watching her?

Rachel shook this last thought away. Her paranoia was creating fantasies, making her see ghosts in the shadows. That's all that was happening here. Her imagination had gone into overdrive, fed by fear and anxiety. Rachel walked quickly towards the front door. She'd covered half the distance when something caught her eye and stopped her dead.

A telephone sat on the small antique occasional table opposite the stairs. The phone was a faded cream colour, old-fashioned but not obsolete. It had a push-button keypad and a springy coiled cable that attached the receiver to the base unit. The wire from the phone was attached to a socket in the skirting board.

Rachel ran over and ripped the receiver from the cradle. Her first thought was to call the police, her second thought was to call her father. She jammed the receiver against her ear. No dial tone, just static. Out of the static came a thin, crackly voice. Rachel recognised it straight away. Her blood froze, her legs gave way, and she slid to the floor with the telephone receiver still pressed to her ear, the words she'd just heard rattling around her head.

"Hello Number Five."

# CHAPTER
# FORTY-TWO

"You're going to do fine," I said.

Templeton just glared. If looks could kill I'd be lying on a mortuary slab right now. The brunette wig and brown contact lenses made her look like a different person and the uniform added an air of authority. The wig and lenses were for the benefit of the submissive unsub. When she looked at Templeton she'd think about her dolls. Hearing that one of them was dead would hit hard, and hearing this from someone who looked like one of her dolls would add more weight to the blow. The harder the blow, the more pressure this would place on the partnership. Apply enough pressure to exactly the right spot and you can break anything. Even diamonds break when hit right.

"You'll be fine," I said.

"Easy for you to say. You're not about to be fed to the lions." Templeton pulled at the collar of her jacket and shucked the sleeves. "This thing's like a bloody straitjacket."

Before she could say another word, I opened the door and shooed her through. "Break a leg," I whispered.

Templeton hit me with another death stare, then strode into the room like a pro, calm and confident, hiding her nerves well. She climbed the steps to the podium and the room fell silent. The place was packed with journalists, every seat taken.

I closed the door and sat down in front of a small monitor. There was only one camera in the room, and there was a twenty-second delay before the footage was filtered through to the news channels. The panic button would kill the feed dead if I didn't like what I saw or heard. A ten-second delay would have been enough but we'd opted for overkill because there was no room for mistakes here. This was strictly a one-shot affair. For this to work we needed complete control over the information going out, and that meant controlling what went out to the TV channels. Nobody listened to the news on the radio, and by the time the stories appeared in tomorrow's newspapers nobody cared. TV was all that mattered. If a photograph was worth a thousand words then a moving picture was worth ten thousand.

The press conference had been timed so it would hit the lunchtime news bulletins. As long as there were no major terrorist incidents or superstar deaths, it would be the lead story at the top of the hour, and remain the lead story right the way through to the six o'clock news, and beyond. Maximum impact, maximum exposure.

"She looks good up there," said Hatcher. He was in the chair next to mine, staring intently at the screen. "I should get her to do more of these. Particularly when we've got bad news to deliver. It's always easier to hear bad news when it's delivered by someone with a pretty face."

"Works for me," I agreed.

Templeton looked straight at the camera and introduced herself as Detective Inspector Sophie Templeton.

Hatcher groaned. "Your idea, I suppose."

"It adds more weight to the statement if it comes from a DI," I replied, eyes glued to the screen.

Templeton began reading from the statement I'd prepared. She ignored the journalists and talked to the camera like it was the only thing in the room. She appeared relaxed. No staring, eyes soft, breathing easy, just like we'd discussed.

The statement was short and to the point. Sarah Flight had died overnight as a result of the brain injuries she sustained while she was in captivity, and the police were now treating her case as murder.

Templeton then went on to talk about Rachel Morris. She gave a detailed breakdown of her last movements from the time she left work all the way through to the time she left Springers, and finished with a standard appeal for any members of the public to come forward with information.

This was the cue for the packed group of journalists to attack her with questions. They'd been told there would be no questions, but they couldn't help themselves. Templeton handled the situation like she'd been doing this her whole life. She didn't flinch, didn't show fear. She just ignored the questions, offered a quick, clipped thank you, then walked off the podium, leaving the room as confidently as she'd entered.

The second she stepped through the door, she ripped off the wig and threw it on the floor, tore off the hairnet, shook her blonde hair free, then tied it back in the most severe ponytail I'd ever seen. She unbuttoned her jacket, shook herself out of it, then dumped it on a chair.

"Give me a cigarette. Now!"

She snatched my pack from me, lit a cigarette, took a long drag. Her hand was shaking. For once Hatcher kept his mouth shut.

"You did good," I said. "Real good."

"Don't, Winter. I was awful. Worse than awful, I was useless."

"Winter's right," said Hatcher. "You did a good job."

Templeton opened her mouth to tell him to go to hell, but common sense kicked in and she closed it again. Telling your boss to go to hell did nothing to improve your career prospects. I knew all about that one. Templeton took another drag and when she exhaled all the stress she'd been holding on to drifted away on a cloud of smoke.

She glared at Hatcher. "Don't ever make me do anything like that again."

Templeton looked around for somewhere to lose her cigarette, but couldn't see anywhere. She gave me a dirty look then dropped the butt into my coffee. The cigarette went out with a sizzle and a hiss. Without another word, she turned and stomped from the room.

"She'll calm down eventually," said Hatcher.

**238**

"I hope so." I was staring down at the cigarette butt floating in my cup and wishing she hadn't done that. The coffee had been really good. Just the right amount of bean, just the right strength, and it hadn't been stewing in the pot too long.

"You realise how many holes there are in this little illusion of yours, Winter? If anyone talks to Amanda Curtis then it's game over."

"That's why Amanda Curtis is currently staying at a luxury spa hotel under a fake name. You guys are paying, by the way."

"And what about the staff at Dunscombe House? Are we going to send them all off to a luxury spa, too?"

"The illusion doesn't have to hold up for ever. It just has to hold up long enough for the submissive partner to think one of her dolls is dead."

"When the media work out we've been using them, they're going to crucify me. You realise that, don't you?"

"Not if we catch the unsubs. Then you're a hero." I grinned. "You know something, Hatcher, you worry too much."

"And you don't worry enough. So what now?"

My grin disappeared and my face turned serious. "Now we wait."

# CHAPTER
# FORTY-THREE

Nobody gave me a second look when I walked into the incident room because everyone was too busy with the telephones. One-sided conversations came at me from all sides. Lots of yes sirs and yes madams, interspersed with the occasional "can you tell me exactly what you saw?" The downside of the press conference was that there were plenty of members of the public coming forward with information, and almost all of it would turn out to be useless.

At the front of the room was a gallery of photographs pinned to a board. Five women smiled happy carefree smiles on the top row, four stared blankly from the bottom row.

Someone had replaced the photographs I'd taken with identical copies of the originals. Everything was the same. The swollen eyes, the slack faces, the bleached look that had as much to do with the subjects as it had to do with the way the police photographer had shot them. My eye was drawn to the blank space beneath Rachel Morris's picture. I could imagine what she was going through right now. The agony, the terror, the uncertainty. The uncertainty was the real killer, not knowing what was going to happen next.

People use patterns and routine and familiarity to help them get through the day and when those routines are removed the end result is chaos. Everything Rachel had held as solid and true had been taken away and replaced by a new world order she had no control over. Every aspect of her life would now be dictated by her captors. When she slept, when she ate, what she did, what she wore. The elements that made Rachel who she was would be stripped away until all that was left was a broken doll. It was the psychological equivalent of a lobotomy.

Sarah Flight, victim number one, had been held for four months.

Margaret Smith, victim two, had been held for two months.

Caroline Brant, victim three, had been held for three months.

And Patricia Maynard was held for three and a half months.

The amount of time the victims were held bothered me because it appeared random. When dealing with organised offenders, there was no such thing as random.

The first victim should have been held for the shortest length of time. There was a logical reason for this. With the first victim, the unsub would finally be acting out fantasies he'd been developing for years. He would be making things up as he went along and invariably things would get messy and mistakes would be made. It was common for an element of panic to come into play. He would hurry and dump the victim

241

sooner than he'd like. He would do a lot of things wrong, and when he'd cooled down he would promise himself that next time he would get it right.

Because the one thing you could be certain of was that there would definitely be a next time. Now that he'd crossed the line there was no turning back. As the unsub gained in confidence, as the fantasies progressed and evolved, as techniques were perfected, the amount of time the victims were held for increased. The unsub would want to take his time, he would want to disappear into his fantasy and stay there for as long as possible.

In this case the first victim was held longest. Even factoring in my belief that there were earlier practice victims didn't help. There was no pattern. But something needed to happen to make the unsub decide it was time to lobotomise his victims and dump them. There needed to be some sort of trigger. There was a reason behind everything an organised offender did, an underlying logic. The trick was understanding that logic.

Broken dolls.

I thought about this. It was possible the dominant unsub held on to his victims until he had broken their spirits. Once that had happened they would be no use to him. The dominant was a sadist and if he didn't get the reaction he craved it would be time to move on to the next victim. The theory was a good one. It didn't explain why he lobotomised the victims, but it accounted for the variations in the amount of time he held his victims. Everyone had a different pain

242

threshold. It also explained why Sarah Flight was kept the longest. The unsub wouldn't have been so sure of himself back then. He would have held back. He would have pulled his punches.

I moved along the wall to the map of London and stared at it, trying to find patterns but not seeing any. The green pins indicated the last known location of the victims and the red pins indicated where they were dumped. The single red pin in St Albans stood out because it was an anomaly. My relationship with anomalies was a love/hate one. Love them because it means the unsub has stepped outside his comfort zone. Hate them for the same reason. That anomaly was only useful if you could figure out why the unsub had stepped outside his comfort zone.

One of the green pins had been moved since the profile meeting. Hatcher's people had been visiting bars in London's more upscale areas, showing pictures and talking to staff. They'd got one hit so far. Sarah Flight was last seen in a bar in Chelsea. The pictures had jogged the memory of a barman. He remembered she'd been on her own and his impression was that she'd been stood up. Just like Rachel Morris. This was good news since it meant the abduction MO was holding up. On the downside, there was still no sign of the unsubs' practice victims, and, although there were plenty of people who'd been kicked out of med school, Hatcher's people had yet to come across anyone who matched the profile.

I was so engrossed in the map I didn't hear Templeton sneak up behind me. It was her perfume that gave her away. The uniform was gone and she was dressed casually in jeans and a blouse. Her expression was neutral. She had a great poker face. She intrigued me because I had no idea what she was thinking.

"How's it going?" she asked.

Her voice was as neutral as her expression. There were no clues in her tone, no tells to indicate her mood. "We've hit the lull," I replied.

"The lull?"

"It happens in every investigation. Everything that can be done has either been done or is being done. All the bases have been covered."

"There's always something else we can do."

I nodded to the map and the pictures, to the whiteboards covered with scribblings in a variety of handwriting. "If you can see something I've missed, I'd like to hear it."

Templeton studied the boards for a while then shook her head. "Nothing," she said. "Not a single thing."

I stared at the map a little longer, but still couldn't discern any patterns. The idea that we'd missed something nagged at me. The lull was always accompanied by doubt. Had we done everything that could be done? Had we actually covered all the bases? Inaction always made me uneasy. In a perfect universe Hatcher would have unlimited resources and everything would happen that much faster. But this wasn't a perfect universe, and the reality was that every investigation hit a lull, often more than one.

"You'll have to forgive me eventually," I said to Templeton.

"I already have."

I looked at her. "Your lips are saying one thing, but your body language is telling a different story."

"I'll admit it, I was pissed off with you, Winter, but I've got over it. The press conference was a good idea."

"It's only a good idea if we get a result. Otherwise, it's a dumb idea."

We went back to staring at the boards.

One minute.

Two minutes.

"We don't talk much about the subservient partner," Templeton said eventually.

"So talk," I said.

"It's like she's the invisible woman. Like she doesn't exist."

"She exists," I assured her. "But the fact you've brought this up means you've been thinking about it. So, let's hear what's on your mind."

"Cutting Jack is a control freak, right?" She looked at me for validation and I nodded for her to go on. "He has her emotionally locked down to the point where she's scared to breathe. He belittles her at every opportunity, calls her names, bullies her. Basically, he's waging a psychological war, and she's the enemy. She learnt long ago to keep her opinions to herself because anything she says is met with ridicule and hostility. The fact is that she barely talks at all these days because she's too terrified to speak."

"Why?"

"Because the only person she has contact with is Cutting Jack. He won't let her see anyone else."

"That's pretty much how I see it," I said. "Okay, here's something else for you to think about. Did she end up like this because of her relationship with the unsub? Or was she already like this before they met?"

Templeton smiled. "The fact you've brought this up means you've been thinking about it. So, let's hear it."

"My money's on the latter. I'm betting she suffered similar abuse as a kid, most likely from her father. That's why she was attracted to the unsub in the first place. Unresolved daddy issues. We're talking moths and flames here. When the unsub walked into her life she didn't stand a chance."

The door suddenly clattered open and we both looked over to see Sumati Chatterjee burst in carrying a laptop. Her face was flushed and she was breathing hard. Whatever had got her agitated was urgent enough for her to choose to sprint up the stairs rather than wait for an elevator. She spotted me at the front of the room and made her way over.

"I've got a name for you," she said. "Tesla."

# CHAPTER
# FORTY-FOUR

Rachel heard Adam's footsteps on the stairs, slow, measured footfalls softened by the carpet. This was someone with time on their side, someone who had total confidence in how things were going to play out. Rachel dropped the telephone receiver and it hit the wooden floor with a plastic clatter. She scrambled to her feet and sprinted to the front door, grabbed the knob and twisted hard. The door wouldn't open. She tried again and again, twisting and pulling and banging her fist against the wood. Adam was calling out "Number Five, Number Five" in a sing-song voice. He reached the landing of the first flight then slowly descended the stairs to the hall.

She looked around, desperate for a way out, saw a corridor off to her right and ran down it. Every door she passed, she tried. All of them were locked. Adam was getting closer. She could hear his footsteps behind her. Rachel reached the door at the end of the corridor. This one was locked, too. She was trapped. Nowhere left to run. Rachel thumped a fist against the door and howled her frustration. She kicked it with her bare feet. Adam was right behind her now. She smelled his aftershave, heard his breathing.

"Number Five will turn around."

Rachel didn't move. She stood there with her palms flat against the door and her forehead resting on the wood, completely defeated. The sharp pain in her side was so sudden it stole her breath away. She collapsed to the ground, her nerve endings buzzing and sparking. Somehow she managed to turn her head. She saw Adam hovering over her, saw the cattle prod in his right hand. Rachel curled into a ball and shut her eyes. She just wanted to die and for all this to be over. She'd never wanted anything so badly.

Adam used the cattle prod again, keeping it pushed into her stomach until her screams turned to sobs. Rachel bucked and thrashed, pain coursing through her body. She tried to suck in a breath, but her lungs wouldn't work. The more she tried to get air, the more her chest tightened. The world turned grey around the edges, grey slowly fading to black. Rachel felt herself slipping towards unconsciousness and did nothing to stop the slide.

The first thing she saw when she regained consciousness was Adam's smile.

"Number Five will get up and go back to the basement."

Rachel struggled to her feet. It was one of the hardest things she'd ever done, a major test of endurance, like climbing a mountain or running a marathon. She stumbled slowly back along the corridor. More than once she almost fell, but the walls helped her stay upright. She kept going, one uncertain footstep after the other. She didn't trust her legs to hold her up. The electricity had upset her brain chemistry, causing her to twitch involuntarily, violent spasms that took her breath away.

She reached the hall, saw the front door through the veil of her tears. So near, yet so far. On the other side of that door was the world she had left behind, a world she was convinced she would never see again. Adam saw where she was looking and grinned. Then he jabbed at her with the cattle prod to get her moving. Rachel braced herself for the next jolt of electricity to fire through her body, but all she felt was the sharp jab of the cattle prod. She looked at Adam. He was still grinning. He held up the cattle prod, made sure she got a good look.

"Number Five will go back to the basement. Do I need to tell you again?"

Rachel started walking, one slow, painful metre at a time. She was trembling all over and could hardly see for the tears. The edge of her vision was filled with grey static and every breath was a dry gasp, her lungs rattling like they were filled with dry paper. Adam followed a few steps behind. He marked her progress with the cattle prod, a muted *tap tap tap* on the side of his leg that made her think of the cane tapping on the basement floor. She wanted to scream at him to stop, but she bit her lip, kept quiet. Adam pushed open the door that led down to the basement and switched on the light.

She glanced back and Adam smiled at her. He pushed the tip of the cattle prod gently into the small of her back, and she went down the stairs. She moved carefully, still using the wall for support. Reached the bottom and shut her eyes. For a brief moment she could see the beach and the sunshine. She could smell the salt on the breeze and feel her father's rough hand wrapped around hers.

Then she heard Adam's footsteps on the stairs and the dream dissolved. She opened her eyes and saw Adam staring at her.

"Number Five will keep moving."

Rachel glanced back up the stairs at the thin strip of light glowing beneath the door and wondered if this would be the last time she ever saw daylight. She took a deep breath and struggled along the corridor. Adam unlocked the basement door and Rachel went inside. The room was a bright white blur through the tears.

She was trembling harder than ever. Adam was going to tell her to sit in the dentist's chair. Then he was going to strap her down, pump her full of drugs and go to work on her with the knife. She glanced over at him, waiting for the order. Dreading it. Adam was staring at her from the doorway, his expression unreadable.

"I'll be back when I've thought of a suitable punishment," he said.

The door closed, the lights went off, and Rachel was left alone.

# CHAPTER
# FORTY-FIVE

ladyjade: how will i no its u?
tesla: I'll no u
ladyjade: seriously?!?
tesla: I've got dark hair and I'll be wearing a long black woollen trench coat.
ladyjade: eyes???
tesla: brown
ladyjade: red rose in the lapel??? LOL ☺
tesla: soz allergic to roses ☺
ladyjade: send a photo pleeeeezzzzzz
tesla: sorry I h8 having my pic taken
ladyjade: cant w8 to cu
tesla: cant w8 to cu 2
ladyjade: xxx
tesla: xxx

I held out the laptop and Templeton took it so she could read through it a second time. Sumati Chatterjee was grinning and wouldn't stand still. The combination of adrenalin and the run up the stairs and her discovery of the fragment on Rachel Morris's computer had put her in a state of perpetual motion. All around me, the incident room was a chaos of noise. Voices bounced off the walls and the ceiling, hitting me from all angles, but I barely noticed. All that mattered were the words on the laptop screen.

My first real glimpse of the unsub.

"Good work," I said.

Sumati's grin got even wider. She was practically glowing. "Thanks."

"Was this on Rachel Morris's laptop or her work computer?"

"Her work computer. It was in a Word file." Sumati was talking at a hundred miles an hour. "She'd cut and pasted it from an IM conversation. Something you might find interesting. She'd removed all trace of the file from the Recent Documents list."

"How?"

"She kept loading files until it disappeared from the list. When I checked the files in Recent Documents, a whole load had last been accessed within three minutes of one another."

"Did you find anything else?"

"Not in Word. But now I've got some screen names to work with, I'll go back through her computers with a fine-tooth comb. I thought you'd want to see this straight away. I'm going to take another look at the other victims' computers, too. Maybe I'll come up with something there."

"We need to find where this conversation originated from," I said. "Start by looking at chat groups dealing with infidelity. In particular, any forums that deal with revenge cheating."

"I'll get right onto it."

252

Sumati held out a hand and Templeton returned the laptop. She hurried out the room, a woman on a mission, and the door swung shut behind her.

"Okay," I said. "We've got some new information. How does it help?"

Templeton thought for a second, then said, "Well, for starters we've got that screen name to work with. Tesla."

"You're right, that's interesting. But not for the reasons you think."

"And how the hell do you know what I'm thinking, Winter?"

"You're thinking that we could go back to the other victims' computers and look for references to Tesla. You're also thinking that we can go fishing on the internet for Tesla. You've probably got some fantasy going where we could set up a cyberghost, someone who's been cheated on and is looking for revenge, and use that to lure our unsub out."

Templeton's eyes narrowed and a faint blush settled on her cheeks. "Wouldn't that be the logical thing to do?"

"It would be logical. But it would also be a waste of time. Tesla is the name he used with Rachel Morris. He would have used a different screen name with the other victims, and he'd have used a different name with whoever he'd targeted next. It would be stupid and unnecessary for him to keep using the same screen name, and our guy is definitely not stupid, or unnecessary."

"So the name doesn't help."

"Of course it helps. Names are special. They have power. This name wasn't chosen at random. So, the unsub called himself Tesla. Why?"

"Does there have to be a reason?"

"There's always a reason. Organised offenders never do things just for the sheer hell of it. Every act, no matter how bizarre it might seem, has a reason behind it. Reason and forethought. Plenty of forethought. You hear the name Tesla, what's the first thing you think of?"

"The inventor."

"He wasn't just any old inventor, though. Nikola Tesla was a genius. For me, he's right up there alongside da Vinci and Thomas Edison. His theories were crucial in the development of wireless communication and radio. He was also highly influential in the development of alternating current as a viable power source."

"Are you saying that Cutting Jack is a genius?"

I shook my head. "No way. I think he's overcompensating for his low self-esteem. He'd like to believe he's some sort of genius, that he's superior to the rest of the world, but deep down he knows that's not the case. By calling himself Tesla, he's trying to convince himself that he's more than he actually is. His low self-esteem drives his need to torture his victims. There's a lot of anger there and he needs to channel it."

"What's the root of his low self-esteem?"

"My money would be on the parents, or whoever the main parental influence was in his life. Something this entrenched has to be rooted in the way he was brought up. Nurture as opposed to nature."

Templeton thought about this a moment. She was chewing her lip in a way that was both sexy and way too distracting. She looked vulnerable and intelligent all at the same time. A neat trick. She stopped chewing and said, "What about Rachel Morris's screen name?"

"I'm going to throw that one back at you," I said. "The fact you're asking means you have a theory. So, let's hear it."

"Lady Jade," she said. "It's aristocratic, classy. She wants to be seen as someone whose status is higher than it actually is."

"That makes sense," I said. "Donald Cope is working-class through and through, but he definitely aspires to get higher up the greasy pole."

"And he would have passed that attitude on to Rachel," Templeton finished for me. "Maybe Cutting Jack isn't the only one who's overcompensating."

"Without a doubt," I said. "And the internet is the perfect place to do that. To some degree, when we go online we all become avatars. We're constantly reinventing ourselves. So what else have we learned here?"

"He didn't want to give Rachel a photograph."

"But he has given her a photograph of sorts, only this is a photograph made from words."

"It's pretty ambiguous, though," said Templeton. "Dark hair, brown eyes, a woollen trench coat. Like you said yesterday, he's not giving anything away. At least, nothing useful."

"You're missing the point. By the time they had this exchange Rachel was desperate to know what he looked like. Remember that long, drawn-out 'please' when she asked for a photo. Why did she feel the need to keep this conversation? Why did she hide it?"

"Because it's the next-best thing to a photograph. And the reason she hid it was because she wanted to keep it all to herself."

"No. The reason she hid it is because the unsub has coached her to cover her tracks. He would have told her to delete any evidence of their conversations. He would have used her husband as the reason, telling her that she couldn't leave any evidence behind in case Jamie Morris found it. That's why it was on her work computer. Rachel figured that the chances of Jamie finding it there were zero. Okay, what else?"

Templeton was chewing her lip again, thinking. She shook her head. "I've got nothing, but I'm guessing you've got something."

"The unsub's use of language is interesting."

"And interesting is good."

"Interesting is always good," I said. "Okay, there's a lot of mirroring going on. When Rachel uses N-O for know instead of K-N-O-W, the unsub uses it in his response. She uses an eight and a two when she says she can't wait to see him, and he fires that right back at her. Then you have those clusters of kisses when they're signing off. Mirroring would make Rachel feel comfortable. She'd feel like she'd met somebody who really got her, something that's missing from her marriage. The unsub will have been doing this all the way through the grooming process. Line four was the most interesting line in the whole exchange: I've got dark hair and I'll be wearing a long black woollen trench coat."

"It isn't written in textspeak," said Templeton.

"Got it in one," I agreed. "There are no numbers being substituted for letters and everything's spelt correctly. It's grammatically correct, too. There are even capital letters and a full stop. This tells us two things. Firstly, it confirms that the unsub is educated. Secondly, it was important to him that Rachel got this piece of information."

"Because he needed her to recognise him outside Springers."

I nodded. "So, how are you at breaking and entering? I think we need to find out more about Rachel and Jamie Morris."

"Please tell me you're not being serious, Winter." She looked at me and I answered all the questions in her eyes with a single grin. "Jesus, you are being serious."

"Grab your coat," I said. "Let's go have some fun."

# CHAPTER
# FORTY-SIX

Templeton pulled up to the sidewalk and killed the BMW's engine. She was parked illegally on a set of double yellow lines, but we'd been driving around for five minutes and it was the only space she could find. Camden had a cosmopolitan, bohemian vibe that made me think of Greenwich Village before the money, or Venice Beach before the tourists took over. There was a vitality to the area, a buzz in the air. The shopfronts were brightly coloured and the bars were busy even though it was half past three on a Friday afternoon. The sky was as dark as ever, though, and the low clouds made it feel like it was already night.

I got out the car but Templeton stayed where she was, frozen to the seat, her hands on the wheel at a five-to-one position.

"I shouldn't be doing this," she said.

"Interesting choice of words. 'Shouldn't' implies that you're going to do this, so why don't we skip all that toing-and-froing where I pretend to talk you into something you've already decided you're going to do?"

Templeton unbuckled her seatbelt and got out the car. She hit a button on the key and the immobiliser activated with a quick *beep-beep*. I lit a cigarette and offered the pack to her. She took one, lit it, blew out a plume of smoke.

"I could get fired for this," she said.

"And if you get fired you could always become a model."

"I'm serious, Winter."

"So am I."

Rachel and Jamie Morris lived in a two-bedroom apartment that overlooked Camden Lock. This was telling in itself. Donald Cole had money and liked to throw it around. He liked people to *know* he had money and he would have wanted his daughter to have the best. This was not the sort of place he would have bought for her. He would have gone for something bigger, something grander, something that reflected his status. For starters, it would have been a house rather than an apartment, somewhere with plenty of bedrooms for future grandkids, and a yard for them to play in.

So either Rachel had chosen not to take handouts and go it alone, or Cole had not approved of her choice of husband and had withheld his money on a point of principle. Having met Jamie Morris, I was veering towards the latter reason.

Jamie was staying at a friend's place in Islington, which meant the apartment was empty. Allegedly. I pressed the buzzer for number eight anyway, since it was possible he'd changed his mind, or was lying. No response. I tried again and still got no answer. I didn't try a third time. When your wife has been kidnapped you tend to answer on the first ring.

The keypad was pretty standard. Type in the correct four-number code and you were good to go. The problem was that ten numbers gave ten thousand possible combinations, which meant the chance of hitting the right code at random was slim. I checked the door in case it was open, but it wasn't. Then I took a closer look at the keypad.

Six of the numbers were black, and four had been worn down to the metal. The two, four, seven and eight. Four numbers gave twenty-four possible combinations. I checked right, checked left. No one was about. We were halfway down an alley that led off the main road. To my right, a hundred yards away, a steady stream of traffic and pedestrians flowed past the entrance to the alley. Occasionally someone would glance our way, but no one seemed interested in what we were doing. I started with two, four, seven, eight and got a red light.

"So, this is your grand plan for getting in," said Templeton. "You hit numbers at random until you get the right combination."

"Nothing's ever random." Two, four, eight, seven got me another red light.

"It looks random to me."

"That's because you can't see the underlying logic." I punched in two, eight, four, seven and got a green light. The lock clicked and the door opened.

"You were lucky," Templeton said as she breezed past me. "Admit it."

"I don't believe in luck."

On the top floor there were two doors, one blue and one red. Number eight was behind the blue door.

"So what now?" said Templeton. "We kick the door down?"

"Nothing so crude."

Inside my pocket was a small leather wallet that contained my lock picks. The FBI guy who taught me had drilled me until I could crack a Yale lock like this one in twenty seconds. That guy could do it in less than five, faster than most people managed with a key.

I pushed the tension wrench into the keyhole and applied a little pressure, gently adjusting the amount until it felt right. Then I inserted the pick and went to work on the pins, listening carefully. The first pin gave way with a tiny metallic click, then the second. I worked my way through the other three pins, then applied a little more pressure to the tension wrench. The lock released and the door opened. Thirty seconds to crack the lock. Not bad, but not brilliant.

Templeton shook her head and her ponytail bounced from side to side. "I'm not even going to ask. So what exactly are we looking for?"

"I'm not sure, but we'll know when we find it."

Templeton closed the front door, shutting us into a gloomy world of grey shadows. Four doors led off the hallway, all closed. The first one opened on a small, functional bathroom that had just enough room for the toilet, bath and sink. I checked the cabinet and found nothing more interesting than painkillers, birth control pills and Jamie Morris's shaving kit. The windowsill was a bust, too. Bottles of shampoo, conditioner, bubble bath, and a whole load of other lotions and potions.

The next door led to the master bedroom. There was a king-size bed and a line of fitted wardrobes along one wall. Lilac walls and purple curtains. Like the hallway, the flooring was laminate. The bedroom was tidy. There were no clothes scattered across the floor, everything was squared away.

"Notice anything interesting?" I asked.

"The bed's made, which means Morris didn't sleep here last night."

"No he didn't. You discover your wife's missing, the last thing you're going to do is make the bed."

"The fact his wife's missing is irrelevant. I've yet to meet a man who knows how to make a bed."

I went clockwise around the room and Templeton went counterclockwise. We checked drawers and wardrobes and the space under the bed, and met at a point halfway along the wardrobes.

"Nothing," said Templeton.

"Nothing," I agreed.

The next door led to the second bedroom. This was a multi-purpose room, part office, part spare bedroom. It was three-quarters the size of the main bedroom and decorated in warm yellows and oranges. The desk pushed into one of the corners had a filing cabinet alongside it and the bookcase was crammed with books. A futon was pulled down and a duvet had been left in a heap in the middle, pillows abandoned at the top end.

262

"Well, at least we know where Jamie Morris slept last night," said Templeton. "Do you think this is a regular thing?"

I looked at the pile of dirty washing and estimated there was at least three days' worth. "It's a regular thing," I said.

We started from the door again. This time I went counter-clockwise while Templeton went clockwise. I gave the filing cabinet a good going-over, taking out the drawers to make sure there wasn't anything hidden in the cabinet itself, checking the undersides of the drawers in case anything had been taped there. Thoroughness had been drilled into me during my years with the FBI.

"Nothing," I said.

"Nothing," Templeton agreed. "We should hurry. If Morris comes back then I might as well kiss my career goodbye."

"He won't come back. He's staying at a friend's place."

Templeton gave me a look.

"No hurrying," I said. "There's something here."

We went through the living room next, checking everywhere, behind the wall-mounted TV, behind the cream leather sofa, under the sofa. I stuffed my hand down its sides, but found nothing except fluff, a few coins and some organic matter of dubious origins. There was nothing in the DVD rack, nothing in any of the DVD cases. The kitchen was accessed through the living room, and that was a complete bust, too.

"Come on, Winter. Let's go."

"There's something here."

"Why? Because you say there is. Look, I'm going. If you want to keep looking, fine. I'll wait in the car."

Templeton headed for the hall. I took one last quick look around the kitchen then followed her. Sunlight filtered into the hall from the living room and reflected off the laminate floor. Something caught my eye. Scuff marks on the flooring. The loft hatch was directly above the scuff marks. Templeton had already reached the front door.

"Wait," I called out, and jogged back to the kitchen to grab a chair.

Templeton was waiting in the hall, tapping her foot. Her body language screamed with impatience.

"We've got to go, Winter. I've got a bad feeling Morris is going to turn up any minute."

I ignored her and climbed onto the chair, pushed the hatch open and peered over the lip. The tin sat right by the opening. Small, silver, square. I lifted it out, then climbed down off the chair and prised the lid off. Inside was a cellphone and a bank statement in the name of Jamie Morris. The statement started on November first and went through to the thirtieth. It showed an initial deposit of two thousand pounds followed by four weekly payments to someone called Simon Stephens. Different amounts, but they all went out on a Friday.

The cellphone was a cheap model. No bells or whistles. No qwerty keypad or touch screen. There was only one number in the call directory. During the last week Morris had called that number eight times. Three of those calls had been placed yesterday morning.

Templeton hovered at my shoulder, her hand on my arm, her breath warm on my neck, impatience replaced with fascination. I hit the button to connect the call, hit another button to turn on the speakerphone. Three rings then a recorded message kicked in.

"You've got through to the offices of Simon Stephens, private investigator. Sorry I'm not here to take your call, but if you leave your name and number I'll get back to you as soon as I can."

# CHAPTER
# FORTY-SEVEN

Rachel thought she'd been scared before, but that was nothing to what she was experiencing now. She was absolutely terrified. The terror was bigger than she was and had turned her into a child again. She huddled into the corner and buried herself under the blankets, wishing and praying and making bargains with herself.

Adam said he would be back when he'd thought of a suitable punishment, but what did that mean? What was a suitable punishment for trying to escape? Was this the point where he cut into her head? Rachel's imagination conjured up the buzzing of the saw and that grisly animal stink of burning bone. She saw Adam slicing up her brain and the image was so real she could almost feel it happening.

Maybe Adam would drug her again, like he'd done before he cut her.

The thought was out there before she could stop it, and the more she tried to force it away, the more it struggled to stay out in the open. The drug had amplified the agony so much that when he cut her it had felt like someone was blasting away at her nerve endings with a flame-thrower. How much worse would it be if he was sawing into her skull? Could he adjust the drug dosage to intensify the pain?

The lights banged on and Rachel shrank deeper into the corner. She stared up at the nearest camera, eyes wide and terrified. She was shaking and trembling all over, teeth chattering.

Her eyes moved from camera to camera, from speaker to speaker, her head tracing anticlockwise circuits around the room. The lights had been on for almost a full minute now and the speakers were still silent. The silence unnerved her, but waiting to find out what Adam had planned was worse. He was playing mind games, and the worst part of it was that it was working. Rachel wanted to scream at him to leave her alone, but she forced herself to stay quiet because that was exactly the sort of reaction he was looking for.

Like before, the glass was crystal, the cutlery silver, and there was a neatly folded white napkin. The food was served on a china plate. Spaghetti hoops, straight from the tin.

Rachel looked at the glass and her head filled up with more of those black thoughts. She could smash the glass against the wall and use one of the shards to cut along the length of her femoral artery. That would be the quickest and most effective way to kill herself. She would bleed out in no time. The compulsion was so strong that when she looked at her leg she half expected to see blood seeping through the grey jogging bottoms. Rachel pushed the thought away and told herself to get a grip. She lowered herself to the floor and sat cross-legged with her back against the wall.

"Is that you, Eve?"

There was a long silence, then Eve spoke in her quiet whisper. "I'm sorry. He made me do it."

"Do what, Eve?"

"He made me leave the dog flap open."

Rachel shut her eyes, a sinking feeling in the pit of her stomach. She should have known better. Adam had wanted her to escape so he could get off on chasing her around the house with the cattle prod.

"He said he would hurt me if I didn't do what I was told."

"It's okay, Eve. You didn't have a choice."

"I could have stood up to him. I could have told him no."

"And then he would have hurt you."

Another long silence. Rachel wanted to fill it, but made herself hold back.

"They said he killed one of the girls," Eve said eventually. She sounded on the verge of tears.

"Which girl?"

"The first one. Sarah. She was so pretty. She used to let me do her make-up."

*Sarah.*

Rachel filed the name away. Sarah had been just like her. She'd had a life and hopes and dreams, and now she was dead. Except that didn't make sense. Adam was a lot of things, none good, but he wasn't a killer. The girls at work had made a big deal about that. He kidnapped and tortured his victims, and then he lobotomised them and set them free. She remembered

**268**

that because the general consensus was that his victims would have been better off dead.

Suicide wasn't an option, but a mercy killing was a definite possibility. Perhaps a friend or relative had finished what Adam started. Or maybe Sarah had died from her injuries and it had just taken a while.

This last thought sent a shiver of fear through Rachel. She'd seen what Adam was capable of, and she didn't want to think about how bad things might get. Surviving meant taking things as they came. Her future was too bleak to contemplate, and if she started looking for answers there she might as well give up now.

"How do you know she's dead, Eve?"

"They said so on the news."

"Do you know how she died?"

"I don't want to talk about it."

"That's okay, Eve, we can talk about something else." Rachel paused, wondering what to say next. "I'm glad you came back. I like talking to you."

"Do you? Really?"

"I meant what I said last time. I really would like us to be friends."

The silence went on long enough for Rachel to think she'd pushed too hard again.

"I think I'd like that, too." Eve hesitated. "Could I do your make-up some time?"

Rachel smiled to herself. This was what she'd been hoping for. The walls were coming down, bridges were being built.

"Of course you can, Eve. I'd like that."

"Your dinner is getting cold."

Steam rose up from the food and Rachel's stomach did a backflip at the smell. Thinking about what Adam was going to do had stripped away her appetite. A question occurred to her. She debated whether she should ask it or keep her mouth shut, then thought what the hell and asked it anyway.

"Is the food drugged, Eve?"

"I'm sorry."

"Don't be."

Rachel picked up the fork and began to eat.

# CHAPTER
# FORTY-EIGHT

Simon Stephens PI didn't have offices, plural, he had a rented office, singular. It was above a tattoo parlour in a run-down street in a run-down part of Tottenham. I pressed the bell and waited. No answer. I gave it ten seconds then pressed again, holding my finger down long enough to annoy Simon Stephens if he was in, or wake him up if he was asleep at his desk. Still no answer. On to plan B. Templeton saw me pull out the leather wrap that contained my lock picks and muttered something under her breath.

"You can wait in the car if you want," I said.

"Yeah, like that's going to happen."

The Yale on the front door took twenty-five seconds to beat, but the five-lever mortice lock on the office door was sturdier and more of a challenge. I inserted the turning bolt first, a T-shaped device made from top-grade stainless steel, then used the pick to move the levers.

This type of lock took patience, feel, practice. The first lever disengaged, then the second. I took my time, forced myself not to hurry. Act like you've got all the time in the world and you can beat a lock like this in a minute or two, hurry and it would take all day.

Templeton was at my shoulder watching intently, holding her breath without realising. The last lever gave and the lock released.

"Piece of cake," I said.

"That does it," said Templeton. "I'm getting a bank-vault door fitted to my house."

"It wouldn't do you any good. If someone is determined enough to get in, they're going to get in."

"Could you be any less reassuring? Anyway, how come you know all this stuff?"

"The FBI is a great believer in that saying about knowing your enemy. The way they see it, if you can think like the bad guys, it's going to make it easier to catch them."

"And where do you draw that line?"

"Well, I've never flayed a person alive, but I have skinned a dead pig."

"You're kidding, right?"

I answered with a smile and Templeton shook her head.

"You know something, Winter, let's pretend this conversation never happened."

Stephens's office was meticulously tidy, the space well utilised. The desk in front of the window was made from real wood rather than laminated chipboard. It was old and scuffed and had probably come from a thrift store. The computer was a tower rather than a laptop, but it was bang up to date. The chair was a cheap executive model covered with fake leather.

There was a clock on the wall opposite the desk so Stephens could keep track of all those billable hours, a

Picasso print on another wall. The blinds were halfway closed, set to let in the daylight but reduce the sun's glare to a minimum. Not that there had been any sun today. It was full dark now, so Stephens was either out and would be back soon, or he'd already clocked off for the day.

There was a hatstand in the corner and this told me more about Stephens than anything else in the office. Either he was a white male in his late fifties who'd watched too many crappy black-and-white detective shows as a kid, or he was a thirty-something fantasist who thought he was living in a crappy black-and-white detective show. Looking around the office, the latter was more likely.

I took the filing cabinet while Templeton took the computer. The cabinet was grey and made from steel, four feet high with three deep drawers. The top drawer was filled with crisp green folders, all of them neatly alphabetised, the clients' names printed in Stephens's tidy handwriting. The same black pen had been used each time, and I added anal retentive to his profile.

The first drawer covered A through G. I pulled a couple of files at random. Both were infidelity cases. The first was a cheating husband, the second a cheating wife. There were grainy pictures taken through long-distance lenses, typed transcripts of conversations. The transcripts of online conversations in the cheating husband's file got me wondering. I put the files back and went straight to the middle drawer and tried J for Jamie and M for Morris. Nothing and nothing. There was nothing under R for Rachel in the bottom drawer, either.

"How are you getting on?" I called over to Templeton. She was sat on the fake leather chair with her cellphone wedged between her shoulder and cheek so she could use both hands on the keyboard. Sumati Chatterjee was giving her a crash course on how to break into a computer without wiping the hard drive.

"Almost there," she called back. "Okay, I'm in."

She said a quick thanks and bye to Sumati then hung up. I walked over to the desk and perched on the edge.

"Find anything?" she asked.

"Nope."

Templeton fixed me with those fantastic blue eyes. "You don't seem too depressed about that," she said.

"I was kind of expecting it." I nodded to the screen. "Less talk, more work."

"You're not expecting to find anything on here either, are you?"

"Let's just take a look."

We checked all the obvious places for any references to the Morrises, and when we came up empty there, we tried the unobvious places. To make sure we hadn't missed anything, Templeton called Sumati, but the computer wizard drew a blank as well.

The downstairs door opened and slammed shut and Templeton jumped to her feet like someone had shot a couple of thousand volts through her. While she was busy banging the mouse violently in all directions, desperate to shut the computer down, I slid into the still-warm chair and listened to Stephens's heavy footsteps on the stairs. He was either big, or tired out after a long day sleuthing.

"Relax," I said.

"Relax!" Templeton's head darted from the window to the door then back to the window again. "That's Stephens. We've got to get out of here."

"I'd forget the window. We're one floor up. Jump out of there and you'll break your neck."

"How can you be so calm?"

"Because I need to talk to Stephens and this saves me the trouble of finding him."

"You really don't get it, Winter, I'm going to lose my job."

"If you do you can always go into the PI business."

"This is no time for jokes," said Templeton. "This is serious. Prison serious."

"You're not going to lose your job. And you're not going to prison."

I rocked back in the chair, put my feet on the desk, smiled at Templeton. She glared at me then glanced over at the window again like she still considered it her best chance of escape. Stephens had reached the top of the stairs. He stopped outside the door and a few seconds later a key rattled in the lock. There was a moment's hesitation. He was probably wondering why the door was unlocked, wondering if he'd forgotten to lock it when he went out.

The door opened slowly.

# CHAPTER
# FORTY-NINE

Stephens was a white male in his early thirties. He was taller than me, six-three. Bulky, too, all gym muscle. His hair was buzzed military-short and he reminded me of one of those Texan gun nuts who patrol the Mexican border. He wasn't stupid, though. There was a quick brain ticking away behind those hazel-coloured eyes. He looked at me, looked at Templeton, looked at me again.

"Who the hell are you?"

"A couple of potential clients who want to hire you," I said.

"Yeah, right."

"Okay, you've got me there. I need to see everything you've got on Rachel Morris."

"Who?"

The lie was delivered smoothly. I kept Stephens's gaze, waited until the PI broke off first.

"I should call the police," he said.

"Did I forget to mention that we are the police?" I nodded to Templeton. She pulled out her ID and held it up. "I need to see everything you've got on Rachel Morris."

"Where's your warrant?"

I shrugged. "I must have left it in my other coat."

Stephens grinned. "I want you out from behind my desk. And I want you to get the hell out of my office."

"And here was I hoping we could do this the civilised way."

Stephens's grin turned into a laugh. "Was that supposed to be a threat? You're a cop. What the hell are you going to do? Come back with a warrant and then we'll talk."

"I need to see everything you've got on Rachel Morris," I said. "I've asked three times now, and I've asked nicely. I won't ask again."

"Get a warrant."

Stephens looked me up and down, and grinned. I could see where he was coming from. The PI had six inches and a hundred pounds on me. He'd run through all the likely scenarios in his head and come out a winner each and every time. He had the upper hand both physically and legally. Stephens opened his mouth to speak and I held up a hand for him to be quiet. Whatever he had to say, it wasn't anything I wanted to hear.

"Okay, if you want to do this the hard way that's fine by me," I said. "Let's discuss this whole blackmail thing."

"What blackmail thing?" Stephens's eyes narrowed. A touch of uncertainty had crept into his voice.

"You've hidden your files on Rachel Morris so you can blackmail her husband."

"You don't know what you're talking about."

"See, that's where you're wrong," I said. "I know exactly what I'm talking about. Jamie Morris has asked you to keep quiet, and you've no doubt agreed a price. But since then you've heard that Rachel Morris has been kidnapped by a very bad man who has already kidnapped and lobotomised four women. Now let's add the fact that Rachel Morris's father is Donald Cole to the mix, and Jamie suddenly turns into your own personal ATM."

"Prove it."

"I don't have to. And I'll tell you why. I've met Donald Cole's minders. One of them has three inches and sixty pounds on you and could take you down without breaking a sweat. The other looks like he'd take great pleasure in pulling out your fingernails with pliers. How do you think Donald Cole's going to react when he finds out you've been withholding information that might help to get his daughter back? Do you think he's going to demand proof?"

Stephens's face turned white.

I shook my head, tutted, took a sharp intake of breath. "You really didn't think this through, did you?" I turned to Templeton. "He really didn't think this through."

"No, he didn't," she agreed.

Stephens swallowed hard. It was like watching a rattlesnake swallow a mouse. "If I give you what you want, you won't say anything to Cole."

"My lips are sealed."

"How can I trust you?"

Another shake of the head, another tut, another sharp intake of breath. "That's the thing, you can't. The only thing you can be certain of is that I will go to Cole if you don't give me what I want."

Stephens walked over to the Picasso and lifted it off the wall to reveal a small safe that was set flush with the plaster-work. It had a steel door and a rotary dial. Fireproof but not bombproof. Stephens spun the tumbler left then right, left then right, slowing down each time he closed in on the correct number. He pulled the door open, took out a green folder and a small black USB flash drive, and reluctantly handed them over.

The folder had Rachel Morris's name written on the tag in Stephens's neat handwriting. The only real difference between this one and the other two I'd looked at was that this one was thinner, presumably because this was a newer case. Inside were some pictures of Rachel Morris and a couple of pages of background information. All in all, nothing to get excited about.

"The good stuff's on the flash drive," Stephens said, like he'd read my mind. "Pictures, transcripts, everything."

"And there isn't anything else?" said Templeton.

Stephens shook his head. "That's everything."

We headed for the door.

"Remember we've got a deal," Stephens called after us.

"If I were you I'd consider skipping the country," I called back. "It might be an idea to change your name, too. Maybe get some plastic surgery."

We went outside and the cold went straight to my bones, freezing me right through. The streetlamps gave my skin a sickly orange tinge. My sheepskin jacket was pulled in as tight as it would go and the hood of my top was up, but it didn't help. The next time I took a case in England I'd do it in the summertime. London in June I could cope with, but London in December was killing me.

"This was why you got kicked out of the FBI, wasn't it?" said Templeton. "For pulling stunts like this. You know, I've lost count of how many crimes we've committed this afternoon."

"You've committed two," I said. "I'm up to three. If you count the fact we were illegally parked in Camden, then that's another one for you, which makes us even at three apiece. And for the record, I quit the FBI, I wasn't fired."

Templeton shook her head, but she was smiling. "You're impossible, Winter."

"And that's a good thing, right?"

"The jury's still out on that one. Jamie Morris is in big trouble," she added. "I can't believe he'd withhold information like that. What the hell was he thinking?"

"He was thinking that since his wife was cheating on him she should get what's coming to her."

"But she's going to be tortured and cut up, and if we don't get to her in time, she'll be lobotomised. Jesus, Winter, that's really messed up." Templeton pulled out her cell. "I'm going to have him brought in."

I thought about Sarah Flight wasting away in that mental institution. Then I thought about her staring out of the same window every day for the next fifty years, and I thought about Rachel Morris being butchered for kicks. I thought about Donald Cole's business card in my wallet.

"Hold off on that call," I said.

"Morris needs to be held accountable for what he did."

"Agreed. But think about it. Bring him in now and all that happens is he gets charged with perverting the course of justice. If he gets himself a halfway decent lawyer, which he will, all he'll end up with is a slapped wrist. He's never going to see the inside of a prison cell. That's not right."

Templeton's eyes narrowed. "You're serious about going to Cole, aren't you? You weren't bluffing."

"Sometimes the justice system doesn't work. We catch the bad guys, but they manage to sneak out through some legal loophole. That's as true here as it is in the States."

"You didn't answer my question."

"I'll do what I think is necessary." I nodded to Templeton's cell. "Just like you'll do what you think is necessary."

Templeton looked at the phone, then slipped it back into her pocket. "This doesn't mean I agree with what you're doing. I just need time to think about what I'm going to do."

"Understood."

My cellphone buzzed in my pocket and I fished it out. Hatcher's name was on the screen.

"Where the hell are you, Winter?"

"Probably best you don't know."

"Well, wherever you are, get out to Maidenhead pronto. We've found ourselves a disgraced medical student who fits your profile."

# CHAPTER
# FIFTY

The surveillance van was parked a couple of streets from William Trent's large riverfront house, far enough away so we wouldn't spook him when he returned, but close enough so we could be there in less than thirty seconds. I was sitting squashed into the van with Hatcher and Templeton. The detective looked years younger. The stress was still there, the tension, that greyness, but it had all been dialled down a couple of notches.

All three of us were wearing Kevlar jackets with POLICE in large letters across the chest. It was a dumb place to put a logo, like painting on a target. Kevlar stopped most bullets. *Most*, not all. The van smelled of old sweat, old coffee, old fast food and stale cigarette smoke.

Only one monitor had a picture and all eyes were fixed on it. Nothing much was happening. The picture was being beamed in from the discreet camera set up opposite the main gate, the only way in and out. We had a good view of the drive and the front of the house and the empty gravel courtyard.

The house could have been in the Mediterranean. Italy or Spain or the French Riviera. It had white walls and a terracotta-tiled roof and was surrounded by a forest of palm trees. The property was on the banks of the Thames and had its own private mooring. There was a speedboat tied up to the jetty, but Trent wouldn't be using that to escape. If he did, he wouldn't get far.

"William Trent has a thing for dead bodies," said Hatcher. "When he was in medical school he liked to sneak into the hospital morgue at night and cut up the corpses. The hospital put in a CCTV camera and caught him in the act but they kept it all hush-hush because they were worried about the fallout. Leaving your body to medical science is one thing. Leaving it so some sicko can slice it up for kicks is another matter altogether. Apparently there's a shortage of people wanting to leave their bodies to medical science. This sort of thing gets out and it's not exactly going to have people lining up to offer their corpses."

"What else can you tell me about Trent?" I asked.

"He fits your profile to a T. He's a white male, aged thirty-three and he comes from money. His father owned a chain of supermarkets that he sold to Tesco for ten million quid. That was fifteen years ago. Three years later Trent senior and his wife were killed in a car accident. Trent inherited everything."

"Any suspicious circumstances?"

Hatcher shook his head. "Nope. It was a drink-driving case. Open and shut. Trent senior was three times over the limit and was driving too fast and lost control of his Merc. He came off the road and hit a tree. No one else was involved. And before you ask:

284

although there was obviously motive on Junior's part, there were no cut brake cables or anything like that."

"Where did he go to med school?"

"Ninewells Hospital in Dundee. He lasted two whole months before he was kicked out. When he was asked why he did it he said he liked the way it felt to cut into flesh. I mean, how twisted is that?"

"Is he married?" I asked.

"Four years. The wife's name is Marilyn. And get this. He beats her. She's gone to the police a couple of times, but she always ended up dropping the charges before it even got close to going to court. You know how it is."

"When did she last go to the police?"

Hatcher picked up a sheaf of papers and flipped through them. "Last July. She had a broken nose and a black eye, a couple of broken ribs, too. She started off saying Trent did it, then she said she tripped and fell down the stairs. There's a woman in the house at the moment. We've had a visual on her and we're pretty sure it's Marilyn Trent."

"Any idea what's happening in the basement?"

"Afraid not."

"So Trent could be down there with Rachel Morris."

"No, he's not," said Templeton. "He's just got home."

On the monitor a black Porsche hung a right and accelerated up the drive. Hatcher gave the order to go. Outside, engines burst to life and tyres squealed. I was up and out of the van in a heartbeat. We sprinted towards Templeton's BMW and climbed inside.

Templeton hit the gas. The tyres spun then bit, creating a loud screech that cut across the howl of the engine.

There were three squad cars up ahead, blue lights flashing, sirens wailing. We joined the rear of the procession and turned fast and tight into Trent's drive and came skidding to a halt in the courtyard, gravel spitting up from the tyres. The three squad cars were fanned out so they blocked Trent's Porsche in.

There were six cops on the ground, all wearing Kevlar and helmets. Three were armed, their guns aimed at William Trent. He stood frozen in front of the house's large double front doors, keys in hand.

The cops were all shouting the same thing at different times, telling Trent to get down and put his hands behind his head. We'd reached the flashpoint. Either things would work out right, or everything was about to turn bad. The blood was up, and all it would take was one itchy trigger finger applying an ounce too much pressure and Trent would end up in the ICU or the morgue.

Trent stood rooted to the spot, a rabbit caught in the headlights. More shouts to get down and I was convinced he was going to do the stupid thing. Then he slid to his knees and put his hands behind his head. Two cops rushed in, cuffed him and dragged him off to the nearest squad car.

We found Marilyn Trent cowering on her knees next to the large American-style fridge in the kitchen. She had a carving knife with a six-inch blade clutched in her trembling hands, eyes wild, strung out and terrified and completely wired.

The kitchen was a cold, sterile space that was brightly lit with dozens of small halogen spots. Black marble floor tiles, black marble worktops, black cupboard doors. Lots of steel and chrome. A man's kitchen rather than a woman's.

Marilyn Trent had a faded bruise around her left eye from the last time she'd taken a tumble down the stairs or walked into a door. She was wearing a pyjama set, short shorts and a T-shirt top. There were faded knife scars covering her legs and arms, a criss-crossing mess done by someone who liked the way it felt to cut into flesh rather than the neat parallel lines of a habitual self-harmer.

I stayed by the door with Hatcher and two of his team while Templeton edged towards Marilyn. Slowly. Carefully. Templeton got the job because she was the only female cop in the room. Marilyn was scared half to death and holding a knife, and much more likely to be spooked by a man. Templeton's palms were up and open to show she wasn't armed, that she wasn't a threat. She spoke quietly, stringing together a constant stream of meaningless words designed to reassure. She spoke like she was talking to a scared child or a dangerous animal. Marilyn Trent cowered further into the corner created by the fridge and the wall and made herself as small as possible.

"Leave me alone," she whispered.

"Hey, it's going to be okay," said Templeton.

"Please, leave me alone."

"Put the knife down, Marilyn. William won't hurt you again. I promise."

Marilyn looked at the knife and there was surprise on her face, like she couldn't work out how it had got there. She let go of the knife and it clattered to the floor. Templeton kept moving forward, slow, slow, slow, taking her time. She kicked the knife out of reach and it skittered across the marble floor. Then she crouched down in front of the cowering woman and helped her to her feet. Marilyn resisted to start with, but Templeton's gentle persistence paid off.

"Sir, you've got to see this!"

Marilyn froze to the spot, startled. Her eyes darted in the direction the voice had come from. She was looking down at the floor like she could see through the black Italian marble. Another shout, the voice urgent with excitement. I sprinted from the kitchen, Hatcher on my heels. We found the basement door and hurried down the stairs.

A short corridor led to a room that was as brightly lit as the kitchen. Black was the dominant colour here, too. The walls were black, the ceiling, the PVC floor covering. There was a rack, an iron maiden. The large king-sized bed had a black leather mattress and plenty of places to attach knots. A clothes rail held a variety of outfits in leather and PVC. Maids' outfits, nurses' uniforms, a one-piece affair in red leather with a matching gimp mask. There were shelves for Trent's extensive collection of sex toys and gadgets and DVDs. The TV fixed to the wall was huge, at least sixty-inch.

The room smelled stale and musty like a locker room, a choking mix of sweat, blood and semen.

"Looks like we've got our guy," said Hatcher, and for once he almost smiled.

# CHAPTER
# FIFTY-ONE

"Wakey-wakey Number Five."

Rachel's eyes flickered open and she saw Adam smiling at her. There was so much she hated about him, but that smile was right at the top of the list. She had eaten all the spaghetti hoops and, even though the last couple of mouthfuls made her gag, she'd forced the food down because she wanted the full dose of the drug.

A few hours' escape from this hellhole had seemed like a good idea at the time, except it didn't work like that. Drug sleep wasn't like real sleep, it was more like an alcohol-induced sleep. You didn't wake up feeling refreshed, you woke up feeling like crap, like you'd lost a slice of time.

Rachel remembered crawling onto the thin, stained mattress and pulling the blankets over her, and then nothing until now. She felt cheated and wished she hadn't eaten the food. Her head was filled with cotton wool and her limbs were heavy. She felt detached from her body and was having trouble thinking straight. Messages were going out from her brain but they weren't getting through.

"You must be thirsty, Number Five."

Rachel nodded and Adam held a large two-litre bottle of water to her lips and motioned for her to drink. It crossed her mind that the water might be drugged, then she realised she didn't care. She took a greedy sip, and another. Adam pulled the bottle away.

"Number Five will drink slowly."

He held out the bottle again and Rachel took another sip, slower this time. It didn't taste as though it had been tampered with, but how would she know? She'd heard of Rohypnol, but didn't know if it had a taste or not. Her experience of drugs was limited to over-the-counter painkillers and a few prescription medicines. Adam screwed the lid back on and smiled his charming smile.

"I've decided what your punishment will be," he said.

Rachel felt the water churn in her gut. "Please don't hurt me. I'll do anything you want."

"I know you will."

"Anything," she repeated.

"Denial, anger and now bargaining," said Adam. "You've done well, Number Five. The others reached the bargaining stage much sooner. Next we'll get depression, which tends to be the longest part of the process. And then, finally, we reach acceptance. I'm looking forward to breaking you."

"Please don't hurt me."

She hated herself for begging, but couldn't help it. She wanted to be unconscious again, wanted to lose herself in the dark. Adam was here to punish her and there was nothing she could do to stop him. It was payback time.

"Number Five will get in the chair."

Rachel got unsteadily to her feet and the room swayed all around her. She reached out for the wall and used it to steady herself, shutting her eyes until the vertigo passed. Then she took a long, deep breath and walked towards the chair. Adam's eyes followed her, and she fought the urge to turn around and look at him. She didn't want to give him the satisfaction.

Rachel had almost reached the dentist's chair when she stumbled and fell. She tried to put her arms out to break her fall but her reactions were too slow. She hit the ground face-first. The sickening thud of her head hitting the tiles was accompanied by a sudden, urgent pain that left her breathless. When she turned over, Adam was crouched down beside her, studying her face. He reached out to touch her nose and she shrank away from him.

"Stay still."

She froze. Adam sounded different. His usual self-possession was gone, the confidence, the arrogance. He sounded concerned, and he hadn't called her Number Five. It was the first time since they first met that he'd spoken to her like she was a person. Adam reached out and Rachel forced herself to keep still. He ran his fingertips over her nose, checking it carefully from bridge to tip. His hands were soft, the hands of someone who'd never done a day of work in their life.

"You're lucky. It's not broken. Number Five will be more careful in future." The confidence was back, the arrogance. "The chair," he said.

292

It took Rachel three attempts to struggle to her feet. She didn't want to crawl. It was a matter of principle. Whatever shred of pride and dignity she still possessed, she wanted to keep. She made her way to the chair carefully, one foot after the other. More than once she almost fell, but somehow she kept going.

She reached the chair and collapsed into it. Adam fastened the straps. Legs, arms and head. He checked them one at a time, pulled them tight to make sure they were secure, then left the basement. He returned with the heart monitor, switched it on, fitted the cuff over her finger, then left again. The beep from the monitor jumped around the room, slow and steady, the remnants from the sedative keeping her pulse in check. If she hadn't been drugged it would be racing into dangerous territory by now. Heart attack territory.

"Would that be a bad thing?"

Rachel tried to look over her shoulder to see who'd spoken, but the straps had reduced her movement to a series of spastic jerks. It was a woman's voice, that much she was certain of. Had Eve snuck in here? She almost called out Eve's name, but then she realised that it wasn't Eve's voice she'd heard, it was her own. Rachel couldn't believe how close she'd come to calling out Eve's name. That would have been bad for Eve. Bad for her too. What would Adam do if he discovered they'd been talking? Would he beat them? Would he stop Eve bringing food?

She glanced up at the nearest camera and imagined Adam sitting in a room watching her struggle against the straps, imagined him listening in while she slowly lost it. She took a deep breath, did a slow count to ten, told herself to get a grip. Time passed. How much, she wasn't sure. She tried to count off the minutes and seconds, but her head was too foggy to keep track.

Rachel heard the distant sound of Adam's footsteps and blinked back the tears. Her throat turned to sand and she felt sick. The noise got louder, the volume creeping up one slow notch at a time. When Adam reached the basement, his footsteps became more defined, the sound echoing off the tiles. Other sounds joined in. The gentle clatter of the objects on the metal trolley, the squeak of the rubber wheels on the tiles.

He crossed the room and stopped the trolley in front of the chair, positioning it so Rachel could see everything on it. She tried not to look but couldn't stop herself. She saw the syringe, saw the rubber tubing, saw the knitting needle with the blackened tip, saw the large knife he'd used on her last time. Her blood had been cleaned off and the edge shone again, winking under the halogens.

"Number Five shouldn't have tried to escape."

"I'm sorry," Rachel whispered.

"No you're not. But you will be."

Adam tied the length of rubber tubing around Rachel's arm and tapped up a vein. He pierced the vein with the needle then pushed the plunger and untied the tubing. The beep of the heart monitor sped up past a hundred and a wave of euphoria washed through her. This time she knew what was coming and the euphoria was mixed with dread. Her breath came in sharp, short gasps and her skin felt electric.

She watched Adam pick up a knife and balance it point-down on his index finger. He moved it back and forth so the lights reflected off the blade. A smile, a shake of the head, then he placed the knife carefully back on the trolley. Next he picked up the knitting needle and ran the heat-blackened tip slowly up her cheek. Rachel shut her eyes tight and moved her head back as far as she could. The knitting needle dropped back onto the trolley and she opened her eyes.

"Maybe next time," he said.

Adam picked up a tool that was about eight inches long. It had a sharp point at one end and looked old. The other end was flat and designed to be hit with a hammer or a mallet.

"This is an orbitoclast," he said. "When the time comes I'm going to use this on you. I'm going to go in above your eyeball and through the skull at the back of the socket, and then into your brain. And you're going to be awake when I do this. Very, very awake. I'm going to turn you into the invisible woman."

Rachel stared at the object in Adam's hand, her heart racing. She knew Adam would follow through on what he said. He'd done it four times already. All she could do was try to stay alive for as long as possible and hope the police found her in time, or she somehow managed to escape. It wasn't much of a plan. It wasn't any plan at all.

Adam smiled again and put the orbitoclast back on the trolley.

"That's one for another day, though. Today I've got something really special lined up."

He reached for the garden snips and looked at Rachel's left hand. There was a blissed-out expression on his face and a faraway look in his eyes. Rachel followed his gaze and saw the bloodstains on the vinyl. She looked at the garden snips.

"No," she said.

"Yes," said Adam.

He brought the blades of the snips together twice. *Snick-snick. Snick-snick.* It was the sound of a tool that had been well cared for and sharpened regularly. Rachel could smell the oil. She curled her hand into a tight fist, fingernails digging into the flesh of her palm. Adam took hold of her little finger and bent it away from the others. He opened the snips as far as they would go.

# CHAPTER
# FIFTY-TWO

"I want my solicitor."

"And I want a supermodel girlfriend and a Caribbean villa," I said. "Life's full of little disappointments, I guess."

William Trent was on the opposite side of the table from me, Hatcher was to my left. The recording light on the camera aimed at Trent was lit red. We were in the same interview room where we'd talked to Jamie Morris. The room was just as depressing as it had been yesterday. Same scarred table, same battered chairs, same air of despair. The smell of cigarettes lingered, making me crave one. Hatcher saw me dip a hand into my pocket. He coughed and shook his head.

"So what's this?" said Trent. "Good cop, bad cop?"

"You watch too many movies," I replied.

"I know my rights. I don't have to say anything until my solicitor gets here."

"Like I said: you watch too many movies."

For a while I sat and sipped my coffee and said nothing. I looked at my watch and followed the second hand as it ticked around the dial. Six degrees for every passing second. Three hundred and sixty degrees for every minute. 21,600 degrees every hour. 518,400 degrees every day. 189,216,000 in a standard year. 189,734,400 in a leap year.

"So what?" said Trent. "We just sit here? Aren't you going to try and get me to confess or something?"

I drank some more coffee. Then I reached into my pocket and fished out the after photographs I'd stolen from the evidence board. I dealt them out in the order the women had been abducted, slapped them down like they were playing cards. Sarah Flight, Margaret Smith, Caroline Brant, Patricia Maynard. I watched Trent for a reaction, but got nothing except mild curiosity. The last photograph dropped down onto the table. Trent looked up at me and grinned. He was completely relaxed. Too relaxed. He was breathing easy and there were no twitches or any other signs of stress.

"Are those your girlfriends? They don't smile much, do they? I can see why you want a supermodel."

"You think this is funny," said Hatcher.

"Actually, I do think it's funny." Trent grinned again. "You know, when I get out of here I'm going to sue you for wrongful arrest. I should get myself a nice six-figure sum for all the pain and suffering I've been put through. I've got a great lawyer. The best." Hatcher's hands balled into fists and then relaxed again. Trent saw this and his grin widened. "What are you going to do, Mr Policeman? Are you going to beat me up? Break an arm, maybe? A leg? A couple of ribs? I reckon that would add at least another twenty grand to the settlement, maybe even thirty."

"Where's Rachel Morris?" said Hatcher.

"She's that woman who was kidnapped, isn't she? The one who's all over the news?" Trent paused and looked Hatcher straight in the eye. "The one who's going to get sliced up and have her brain cut out."

"Answer the question. Where is she?"

Trent shook his head. "No idea. I've never met her."

I drank my coffee and watched the two men go back and forth like this for a while, winding each other up. Hatcher's face had turned red and he kept clenching and unclenching his fists. The vein in his neck was pulsing. I was watching Hatcher particularly carefully, ready to jump in if he blew up and took a swing at Trent. Hatcher getting suspended on some dumbass disciplinary charge would be a disaster.

I waited until the moment was right, then asked the question I'd been waiting to ask. My voice stayed casual, like I was asking about the weather, or today's specials.

"So what does it feel like to cut into flesh?"

Trent turned and stared at me. "I wouldn't know."

"Yes you do. I know why you were kicked out of med school. I saw Marilyn's scars. So what's it like?"

"I wouldn't know."

"Skin's quite easy to cut through, isn't it? It's when you dig deeper that you meet resistance and things get a bit tougher. Cutting into muscle, now that's where the real fun begins. You can't really do that with your wife, though, can you? So what's the deal? Have you got a thing going with a funeral parlour? I mean, you have money, and money can buy you whatever you want, right? Even some quality one-on-one time with a corpse if you know the right person. And my guess is you've made it your business to know the right person."

Trent looked deep into my eyes, trying to outstare me. There was puzzlement in his gaze, like he couldn't work out where the hell I was coming from. Trent broke away, then looked back at me. For a fraction of a second his grin morphed into a knowing smile. His eyes lit up and he licked his lips, his hands slid down towards his lap. Then the mask came back down, and his hands went back onto the table.

"I've no idea what you're talking about," he said.

I was finished here. Trent had told me everything I needed to know. Hatcher followed me into the corridor. The walls were grey, the linoleum was scuffed and past its best, and the strip lights cast a dull glow over everything because the covers hadn't been cleaned since for ever.

"He's not our guy," I said.

"He's got to be," said Hatcher.

"It's not him. Did you see how excited he got when I started talking about slicing up dead bodies? I thought he was going to start jerking himself off."

"Which is as good as a confession in my book. We know that Cutting Jack gets off on using knives on his victims."

"His *live* victims," I corrected. "Trent gets off on cutting up dead bodies. Granted, he's a sicko, but he's not our sicko."

"What about the wife? She was covered in knife scars."

"The wife's a poor substitute for the real thing. He uses her to hold his urges in check while he's waiting for his connection at the local funeral parlour to come up with the goods."

"It's got to be him."

"It doesn't matter how many times you say that, Hatcher, it won't make it true. William Trent is not the unsub. Did you see how calm he was?"

"So he's a sociopath," said Hatcher.

"He's not a sociopath. He's just a pervert with a couple of million in the bank. Big difference."

"I'm not convinced."

"Okay, where's Rachel Morris?"

"He's got her hidden in a secret location. Hell, maybe he's got a dozen places and he keeps moving her around to make it harder for us to find her. He's got the money to do it."

I shook my head. "You're clutching at straws, Hatcher. This guy needs to keep his victims close by. He *wants* to keep them close. He wants to be able to go and have fun with them whenever the urge strikes him. That means his house. You've been through Trent's house. Did you find a single trace of Rachel Morris?"

Hatcher shook his head. "That doesn't mean it's not him."

"Okay, here are two more reasons. First, his house was on the south bank of the Thames. The unsub lives north of the river."

"Come on, Winter, that's pretty tenuous."

"Our guy lives north of the river," I repeated. "Second, did you notice Trent's reaction when I showed him the photographs? He barely registered them."

"So he'd make a great poker player."

"I've used that trick dozens of times, Hatcher. It's foolproof. Show a serial criminal pictures of their handiwork and you're going to get a reaction. The reactions you get range from indignant denial all the way through to out-and-out bragging. You wouldn't believe how proud some of these assholes are. This is their masterwork, the highlight of their miserable little lives, and they can't wait to tell you all about it. The one reaction I have never seen is indifference. Read my lips, Hatcher: William Trent is *not* our guy."

# CHAPTER
# FIFTY-THREE

"Hatcher's furious," Templeton said as we rode the elevator down to Scotland Yard's subterranean levels. "He's crucifying people left, right and centre. I got away just in time. I reckon I was next in the firing line."

"Cut him some slack," I said. "Hatcher's got a lot on his plate and now he's got to deal with the fallout from William Trent shouting wrongful arrest at anyone who'll listen. That's one headache he could do without."

"I really thought Trent was our man."

"So did a lot of people."

"But not you."

"He looked good on paper."

"That's an evasion, not an answer."

"When it comes to suspects, I never get too excited. I've been disappointed too many times. I like to sit down and talk to them before I make a final decision." I thought about the child-killer from Maine who'd chosen suicide by cop, then added, "That's assuming they make it into custody."

"Are you telling me you can work out who's guilty or innocent just by talking to them?"

"I haven't been wrong yet."

Templeton laughed. "With a superpower like that, maybe we should get rid of the justice system altogether. Save ourselves a fortune."

"The justice system has nothing to do with guilt or innocence," I said. "You know that as much as I do. It's all about which side can afford the best lawyers."

The elevator bumped to a gentle stop, the doors concertinaed open, and we started along the corridor side by side.

"If Trent's not our guy, then that's us back at square one again," said Templeton. "We need to go back and review everything. There must be something we're missing."

"Agreed, but we also need to be careful that we're not looking at the forest and seeing only trees," I said. "The best thing you can do is to try and let this go for now."

"Easier said than done."

I cracked a smile. "Tell me about it."

"Okay, how about we meet up at your hotel this evening and throw some ideas around?"

"Sounds like a plan. It would probably be best to meet in my room, though."

Templeton gave me a look. Her left eyebrow was arched and she had a strange little half-smile on her face.

"So we can spread our stuff out," I added quickly.

"Okay, let's say eight. That'll give me time to shoot home and shower and get changed and feed my cat."

"You've got a cat?"

"That surprises you?"

I thought about this then shook my head. "It makes sense. You're not wearing a wedding ring, so chances are you're not married. You work long hours and you're ambitious, neither of which is conducive to a successful long-term relationship. My guess is you live alone, but like company, so it makes sense you'd have a pet. Dogs are high-maintenance and fish are boring. That leaves a cat. Cats are independent and low-maintenance. They're practical pets, and you strike me as a practical person."

Templeton laughed and shook her head. "They say men are from Mars and women are from Venus, but what the hell planet are you from, Winter?"

We reached the computer room and Templeton did a quick three-beat knock on the door then pushed it open. Sumati Chatterjee had her head buried in her monitors on one side of the narrow room while Alex Irvine was manning the workstation opposite her. They both looked up together, but this time Alex was a little ahead of Sumati. I tossed the flash drive to Sumati, who caught it two-handed. She looked surprised and shocked, like I'd tossed her a live grenade.

"I need to see what's on this," I said. "I don't think it's rigged to wipe itself clean, but be careful."

"I'm always careful."

Sumati plugged the flash drive into a USB slot. She clicked and pointed with the mouse, then her fingers flew over the keyboard with precision and grace. Alex pushed away from his desk and rolled across the room to join us.

"Okay, I'm in," said Sumati. "And I'm happy to report there were no viruses or any other nasty surprises."

"What have you got?" asked Templeton.

"Four pictures and a bunch of text documents, and that's about it. What do you want first?"

"It's got to be the pictures," said Templeton.

"While we look at the pictures can you print out the text files?" I said to Alex.

"Of course I can."

Alex gave me a look like he couldn't believe he'd been asked to do something so menial, then sighed. He held out his hand and made *come on, come on* gestures to hurry Sumati along. She quickly downloaded the pictures and gave him the flash drive. Alex pushed himself away from Sumati's desk and scooted back across the room. I could hear his heavy fingers thrashing the keyboard, the heavy click of the mouse, the long sighs. The laser printer in the corner of the room made a rhythmic *whirr-click* sound as it spat out a steady stream of paper.

"Okay, what have we got?" asked Templeton.

The excitement in her voice was infectious. All three of us crowded in closer to the screens. Sumati clicked the mouse and the first photograph appeared on her left-hand screen. The picture showed Rachel Morris going into Springers. She was in profile, so we only got half her face, but we could see enough to be certain it was her. Templeton muttered a quiet "Jesus" at my shoulder, one word that spoke volumes. I pictured the street Springers was on and worked through the angles in my head.

"This wasn't taken from Mulberry's," said Templeton.

"It wasn't," I agreed. "There was a restaurant further up the street. A little Thai place called, funnily enough, The Little Thai Place. I'm betting he was there, because, one, the unsub had beat him to the best seat at Mulberry's. Except at that point in time Stephens wouldn't have known he was the unsub. Two, Stephens was multitasking and had decided to grab a bite to eat while he was watching Rachel Morris."

"And the third reason?"

"He could charge the meal to Jamie Morris. Okay, what's interesting about this photograph? And I'm talking really interesting."

Templeton shrugged.

"Let me put it another way. How did Stephens know that Rachel Morris was going to be at Springers? He's not following her. He's got himself settled in all nice and comfortable in The Little Thai Place, and he's waiting for her to show up."

Templeton's big blue eyes lit up a shade bluer. "Because he's got a spyware program fitted to her computer."

"Alex," I called out, "I'm going to need those printouts ASAP."

"Working on it," he called back, prickly and annoyed.

The next photograph showed Rachel Morris leaving Springers. She was standing in the entrance, looking left up the street for her date. Even now she was still clinging to the hope that there was a good reason he hadn't shown up. Stuck at work, stuck in traffic, struck down with amnesia following a nasty bang to the head. She was looking in the direction of The Little Thai Place and I could see her whole face. The definition wasn't good enough to read her mood from her expression, but it was good enough to read her body language. She was experiencing a real mix of emotions. Wound up, angry, pissed off, not to mention feeling stupid.

The third photograph was just plain frustrating. It showed Rachel with the unsub, but they were walking away from the camera and all we could see were their backs. Stephens had obviously seen Rachel leave alone and thought he was done for the night. He'd paid his bill and reached the street in time to see Rachel wasn't alone. The problem was that he was at the wrong end of the street to get a picture of their faces.

"This is useless," said Templeton.

"Not completely useless," I said. "Rachel is five-seven and the unsub is taller. I'd estimate five-ten. We can see that he's medium build. So there's two things we now know for definite."

"Give me a moment and I'll give you a third thing," said Sumati. She clicked and typed and the photo slowly changed. Everything sharpened and got clearer. The colours became more defined. A final point with the mouse, a final click. "There you go. He's got brown hair."

The fourth picture was almost as frustrating as the third. It showed the back of a Porsche as it headed away from the camera, and the fact that Stephens had included this picture meant the car belonged to the unsub. It looked black, but it could have been dark red or dark green, any dark colour. It was definitely a Porsche, though. Porsches have their engines in the trunk, which gives them a very recognisable shape. This was good news since it tallied with what was on the parking ticket.

"I can zoom in on the number plate," said Sumati.

"No point," said Templeton. "We already ran it and it's a false one. Are you able to do anything with the picture so we can find out what colour the car is?"

"No problem." Sumati ran the photo through an enhancement program. She pointed and clicked and zoomed and had an answer in thirty seconds. "It's black," she said.

Alex rolled over to join us. He handed me the printouts.

"Nice wheels," said Alex.

"I need you to narrow down the model and year of manufacture as best you can," I told him. "I want a list of everyone north of the Thames who owns one." I paused and thought about that red pin in St Albans. The anomaly. "Let's go a little further. Expand the list so it takes in a ten-mile band around the outside of the M25."

"No problem." Alex rolled back across the room and went to work.

The first printout was a transcript of an IM conversation Rachel Morris had had with the unsub. It was dated three weeks ago and came from her work computer. Stephens had installed a program that monitored keystrokes so we only got Rachel's side of the conversation. I could fill in the blanks, but what I filled them with were my own words and that didn't give a true picture of the unsub. I moved on to the next sheet, then the next. It took less than a minute to go through all of them.

"So what have we got?" Templeton asked.

"He's good," I said. "He had Rachel Morris sharing all sorts of stuff with him, things she probably wouldn't even tell her best friend. He knew how to push her buttons, when to dig deeper and when to hold back. He took his time and was careful, and only when the time was right did he reel her in. It's a masterclass in grooming. The first mention of Springers was two days before he abducted her. He chose the venue. No surprises there. He would have checked the bar out. If we had a face shot, we could have run that against the footage from the security cameras and found out when. It would have been recent, so chances are one of the bar staff could have remembered him. Of course, the problem with that is we don't have a face shot."

"He got lucky there, Winter. Admit it."

"Luck doesn't come into it. This unsub is careful, organised and meticulous. Everything he does is done with two goals in mind. He wants to keep on doing what he's doing, and he doesn't want to get caught."

"Anything else?"

"Yeah. This one's for Sumati." The computer wizard's ears pricked up and she turned to look at me. "The website they were using was cheatinghusband.com. Cheatinghusband is all one word. A lot of these sites keep copies of their users' conversations. See if this one does and if it does get hold of copies of Rachel Morris's chats with the unsub. I'd really like to see his side of these conversations."

Templeton shook her head. "It's just so bloody frustrating. If Stephens had got a face shot we'd have Cutting Jack and his girlfriend in custody by morning."

"Why not just contact Stephens and ask him for a description?" said Sumati.

"Do you want to field this one?" I asked Templeton.

"Chances are he never saw his face because of the angles," said Templeton. "He followed Rachel Morris from the bar. At some point Cutting Jack fell in behind her. But Stephens would have been behind him, so he wouldn't have seen his face."

"And even if he had seen his face," I added, "it probably wouldn't have done any good. Eyewitnesses are completely unreliable. Ask a dozen witnesses to describe someone and they'll tell you he's short and tall, white and black, skinny and fat with blond hair that might have been black or brown or even grey. Hell, half of them will tell you that your he was a she."

"Ask a stupid question," Sumati said.

"It wasn't a stupid question. At this stage in the game there's no such thing as a stupid question."

"On the bright side," said Templeton, "I guess we're further ahead than we were."

"Not far enough for my liking." I turned back to Sumati and Alex. "As soon as you guys have got anything, anything at all, call me. I don't care what time of the day or night it is."

"No problem," they said, almost in unison. Neither looked up. Their eyes were glued to their screens, their heads lost in cyberworld.

We left the computer room and took the elevator up to the fourth floor. My cellphone buzzed and Hatcher's name lit up on the screen.

"What have you got for me, Hatcher?"

"You were right about the first victim. We drew a blank with the coroners so I got someone to pull the files on any unsolved murders that happened over the last couple of years. One stood out. Charles Brenner was a seventeen-year-old rent boy who worked out of the King's Cross area. He was snatched eighteen months ago and killed with a hammer. Whoever did it really went to town. They smashed his head and face to a pulp."

"And the reason it stood out was because there were no obvious injuries to any other part of his body. At least none that could be tied to his murder."

"How did you know that?"

"That's what you're paying me those big bucks for," I said. "Let me guess. Because of his profession it was written off as a sex attack. After all, there was plenty of evidence of sexual abuse to back that up. The police went through the motions but they didn't try too hard. They had a body and they had a story that made sense. There was nobody who missed Brenner enough to push for the killer to be found. If there was he wouldn't have been turning tricks in King's Cross. Where was his body dumped?"

"Barking."

"Is that north of the river?"

"It's north of the river," said Hatcher. "I can't say for sure if this is our guy, but it feels right."

"This is our guy, Hatcher. The timing works, and the geography works. What else have you got?"

"Who says I've got anything else?"

"You've still got that smile in your voice."

"Screw you, Winter."

"You're still smiling."

Hatcher laughed then said, "An orbitoclast was stolen from Glenside Museum in Bristol. It happened just before Sarah Flight was kidnapped. The bad news is that the police didn't take the theft seriously. Nothing else was taken. They thought it was a student prank."

"How long would it take to get to Bristol?"

"This time of day, you're looking at a couple of hours, an hour and a half if you use the blue lights and put your foot down."

That meant losing a total of five hours, and four hours of that would be spent in a car. We'd be lucky to get back by midnight. There were better things to do with our time. "I'm going to need a helicopter," I said.

"And I need a McLaren F1."

"I'm serious, Hatcher."

"I can't get you a helicopter, Winter."

"I only need to borrow it for a couple of hours. I promise I'll give it back. Cross my heart et cetera, et cetera."

"I can't get you a helicopter."

"Of course you can. You're the boss. You're the next-best thing we've got to God, remember. You can do whatever you want."

"For the third and final time, Winter, I can't get you a helicopter."

"The signal's breaking up. I can't hear you." I ended the call and pushed my cell back into my pocket. "We're going to Bristol," I said to Templeton. "By helicopter."

"Cool."

# CHAPTER
# FIFTY-FOUR

The roar of the Eurocopter EC145's engines filled my head. Even with the headphones on they were still deafening. My body was vibrating in time with the beat of the blades, a deep, dull throb that went right through me. The clouds were dark and low, and the helicopter skirted the bottoms of them, bumping and pitching through pockets of turbulence.

The guy at the stick was a working pilot so passenger comfort was way down on his list of priorities. He'd been told to get from A to B as quickly as possible, and that's exactly what he was doing. He flew hard and fast, like he was headed into a war zone to pick up the wounded. It was like being on a rollercoaster, only way more fun. We hit another patch of turbulence and Templeton rolled her eyes. Her knuckles were shining white from gripping her safety harness.

We came in slow and low over the hospital, nose down, tail up. The pilot levelled out and we hovered suspended in the air for a couple of seconds, then landed gently on the grass. The engines whined down to nothing and the blades slowed to a stop, but it still took a moment to register that what I was now hearing was silence. Bristol was a hundred miles from London as the crow flies. From takeoff to touchdown the journey had taken forty-five minutes, half the time it would have taken in a fast car in good traffic with the blue lights flashing.

Glenside Hospital had started life as a lunatic asylum.

During the war it was used as a military hospital, and these days it was part of the University of the West of England. The old asylum buildings could still be seen interspersed amongst the newer buildings. Glimpses of the Gothic, shadows of the manic and the mad.

The museum was housed in the church. It was past closing time, but Hatcher had got someone to call ahead to say we were coming. Templeton knocked on the heavy oak door. It was dark and cold, and I wanted to be in California more than ever. I stamped my feet to get my circulation going, flapped my arms against my jacket in a vain attempt to find some warmth. Templeton didn't notice the cold, or, if she did, she wasn't letting it show.

A key rattled in the lock and the door swung open. Elizabeth Dryden introduced herself and waved us inside. Dryden was well past retirement age, seventy plus, maybe even eighty. She was thin and birdlike and moved in slow motion like she was suffering from arthritis. Her white hair was tied up in a severe bun and she wore a tweed suit. A pair of spectacles hung from the chain around her neck and she spoke with a plummy BBC accent that was straight out of the fifties.

The building still smelled like a church, old wood and incense and candle smoke imprinted into the

**316**

stones. The pews were all gone, replaced with static displays that traced the history of psychiatric care from the late 1800s onwards.

"The police weren't particularly interested in the theft before," said Dryden. "Why the change of heart?"

"We believe it may be linked to a current case," I said.

"An important case, judging by the fact you've flown all the way from London. When the theft originally happened, it took the best part of a day to get a policeman out in a car. Your accent. You're American."

"Originally from Northern California."

"And now you work for the Metropolitan Police."

"I've been brought in to consult on a case."

"This has something to do with those women who were lobotomised, doesn't it? You think our orbitoclast was used on them?"

"That's right," I said.

"Of course I'll help in any way I can."

"Can you show us the display the orbitoclast was stolen from?"

"Certainly. This way."

Dryden led us through the nave and turned right into the south transept, her keys rattling in time with her footsteps. She stopped at a static display that depicted a man strapped to a table. Thick leather straps held his arms and legs in place, and another strap was fixed across his forehead. His head was tilted back as far as it would go to give easier access to the eye sockets, and there was a man in a white coat and a white mask to give the illusion that this was a medical procedure. A small glass-topped display case contained the equipment used. An orbitoclast had pride of place in the middle of the cabinet.

Dryden saw where I was looking and said, "Obviously that's not our original."

"Can I see it, please?"

"Certainly."

Dryden unlocked the display case and lifted the lid. She used both hands to pick up the orbitoclast, handling it like it was a religious artefact, and passed it to me.

The orbitoclast was lighter than I expected, but at the same time it felt heavier. I had a sense of its history, a sense of the atrocities that had been carried out with it. The metal had blackened and roughened over the years. I studied it carefully, looking at it from all angles, then passed it to Templeton. She didn't want to take it. She gave it a perfunctory once-over then handed it back to Dryden like she couldn't get rid of it fast enough. Dryden put it back in the case and fussed with it, moving it a little left and a little right until she was satisfied it was in the exact same position as before.

"What happened?" I asked her.

"The thief walked up to the display case as bold as brass, smashed the glass, grabbed the orbitoclast then ran out. It was all over very quickly."

"Can you tell me anything about the man who did this? Anything at all?"

Dryden's face wrinkled into a puzzled frown. "I'm afraid you've got your wires crossed there. It wasn't a man who stole it, it was a woman."

**318**

Templeton glanced at me and her eyes flashed with excitement. We were both thinking the same thing: the subservient partner.

"I noticed the security cameras when we came in," said Templeton. "I don't suppose you caught her on film?"

"I did. Would you like to see it?"

"That would be great," said Templeton.

Dryden took us to a small room that had once been the vicar's office. Everything was made from heavy dark wood, lots of carvings and frills and ostentatious ornamentation. There were faded religious paintings on all the walls, and a large crucifix hung behind the desk. Chances were nothing had changed since the building was used as a church. Dryden sat down at the computer and pulled up the CCTV footage.

"Sorry, but we only have a couple of cameras," said Dryden. "Usually we keep the footage for seventy-two hours, but we archived this footage for insurance purposes." She fired a pointed look in Templeton's direction. "We also kept it in case the police ever decided to treat this as a real theft as opposed to a student prank."

"We'd like to see whatever you've got," said Templeton.

The footage was black and white, grainy. The cameras were old with a low frame rate so the picture jumped around like a badly shot silent movie. There were two short clips, neither one longer than twenty seconds.

In the first clip the unsub walked up the nave with her head angled to the left, away from the camera. She was wearing a hat and her coat collar was pulled up high. Black thick-framed spectacles. Maybe she needed the glasses, maybe it was part of her disguise.

The second clip was a long shot taken from a camera in the north transept. We couldn't really see the unsub, but we could see what she was doing. The scene played out exactly how Dryden had described it. The woman walked up to the case, smashed the lid, grabbed the orbitoclast, then made a run for it.

"She knew where the cameras were," I said.

"So either she'd already scoped the place out, or her partner had," said Templeton.

"Could you play the first clip again, please?"

"Of course," said Dryden.

I was watching closely, looking for anything that would help build a clearer picture of the unsub. Dryden played the clip a third time and I leant in closer to the screen. I told her to pause when the unsub reached one of the pillars. The pillar gave me a rough idea of height and size.

"Not good," I said.

"What?" said Templeton.

"Either we're looking at a woman who's five feet ten with a heavier than average build. Or we're looking at a man who's medium build, five-ten and has brown hair. I know which one my money's on."

# CHAPTER
# FIFTY-FIVE

Rachel pulled the blankets around her for comfort. There was so much pain, more than she could bear. She couldn't think straight. Her hand was on fire and even the smallest of movements sent new blazes raging across her nerve endings. Most of the pain was located in her missing finger, which was impossible. How could something that wasn't there hurt so much?

She shut her eyes and tried to find the sunshine, but the sunshine eluded her. She tried to imagine her father was with her, but she couldn't find him, either. She tried to remember what her mother looked like, her brothers, her friends, but all she saw were dark shadow faces that had been warped and twisted by the pain. Adam had already taken so much from her and now he'd stolen her memories.

The lights suddenly came on, bright and blinding. Rachel glanced at the cameras and the speakers. She glanced at the door, glanced at the dentist's chair, then looked back at the speakers and waited for her instructions.

The speakers stayed silent.

"What do you want from me?" A whisper rather than a shout, the words drowned by tears.

Silence.

"What do you want?"

Rachel looked at her hand. The blackened cauterised stump contrasted brutally with the chipped red nail polish on her other fingers. Her hand was ugly. Even if she did get out of here, she would never fully escape. Not really. Every time she looked at her hand she would think of Adam. He'd scarred her for life. What had happened here would stay with her until the day she died.

Another wave of pain hit, scattering Rachel's thoughts. She closed her eyes and prayed for the sunshine and this time she found it. She was walking along that golden beach, her hand wrapped in her father's, the sand warm beneath her feet. He smiled down at her and told her that everything was going to be okay, and, for a brief moment, Rachel believed him.

"I'm sorry," a voice whispered.

The sunshine dissolved and Rachel opened her eyes. The whisper had come from behind the door. Gentle, nervous, apprehensive. Eve rather than Adam. Rachel's relief eclipsed the agony. She couldn't have dealt with another visit from Adam, not so soon after the last one.

Rachel struggled to her feet and stumbled across the basement. She reached the dentist's chair and paused for breath. Her hands were on the bloodstained armrest, palms down, supporting her weight. She saw the fresh tracks of her own blood and a fresh jolt of pain shot through her hand. Rachel took a long breath and stumbled across to the door. She slid to the ground and pulled a blanket around her shoulders like a poncho.

"Does it hurt much?" Eve asked.

*Of course it bloody well hurts.* Rachel shut her eyes, took a deep breath, got her emotions back in check. She didn't want to upset Eve again. Not after last time.

"Yes, it hurts," she said.

"Would you like something for the pain?"

"I don't want to get you into trouble with your brother."

"Adam's gone out. He'll be gone for ages. Wait here, I'll be back in a minute."

There was a shuffling on the other side of the wood. Footsteps faded down the corridor. *Wait here.* Where exactly did Eve think she was going to go? It was an asinine, naive thing to say, but that fitted with the picture Rachel had built up of Eve. Eve wasn't that bright. She reminded Rachel of a female version of George from that old Steinbeck novel she'd studied at school.

More pain.

Rachel shut her eyes until the dizziness passed. The pain was still there when she opened them and she hoped Eve would hurry up.

Time passed slowly.

Footsteps in the corridor coming closer, a shuffling behind the door as Eve settled back down. The dog flap opened and a syringe dropped onto the floor. Rachel's hand shook as she picked it up. She'd expected pills, not this. She hated needles.

"You need to tap it to get rid of the air bubbles," said Eve. "Then you inject it into your hand."

Rachel held the syringe with the tip pointing up and tapped the air bubbles to the top. She pressed the plunger and a small jet of clear fluid spurted out. She looked at the needle, looked at her shaking hand, then, before she could change her mind, she stabbed the needle into her hand and pushed the plunger. Her head spun, her vision blurred and there was a strange buzzing sound in her head. Somehow she managed to stay conscious.

"Jesus," she muttered under her breath.

"You shouldn't say that," said Eve. "It's not nice."

"I'm sorry, Eve. I won't say it again."

"Put the needle back through the flap."

Rachel did as she was told. Eve took the needle from her and their fingertips touched. Eve's skin was soft and warm. It was the first human contact she'd had with someone who wasn't Adam since she got here.

"Thank you, Eve."

"That's okay."

Rachel leant back and waited for the drug to kick in. She hoped it would work soon, prayed it would. The pain was worse than ever.

"I mean it, Eve. Thank you for everything you've done."

"Can I do your make-up now?"

"Of course you can, Eve."

Eve shuffled to her feet on the other side of the door, the lock disengaged with a click and the door opened. Rachel looked up and saw Adam standing there.

"Hello Number Five."

The face belonged to Adam, but the voice was all Eve.

# CHAPTER
# FIFTY-SIX

Hatcher was sitting in the Cosmopolitan's bar, nursing a whisky at a secluded table at the side of the room and looking even more worn down than ever. I took the chair opposite, picked up the drink he'd got for me, saluted him with the glass, then took a sip.

"If ever I saw a man who needed a drink," I said.

"One drink? Try a dozen. They've taken me off the investigation, Winter."

"They can't do that."

"They can and they have." I looked over at the bar while I processed this. The barmaid was different but the same. Young, blonde, attractive.

"Templeton wouldn't like it if she caught you staring," said Hatcher. He smiled a challenge at me, daring me to deny it.

"There's nothing going on between me and Templeton."

"The rumour mill says there is."

"The rumour mill is wrong."

"So you're not meeting her later? And you didn't meet her last night, either?"

I didn't know where he'd got his information from, but wasn't surprised he'd got it. Gossip spreads around a cop station quicker than wildfire, and it doesn't take much tinder to get the blaze started.

"There's nothing going on," I said.

Hatcher narrowed his eyes. "You sure about that?"

"I'm sure. It's not going to happen, Hatcher. We're from different worlds. End of story." I sipped my whisky. "Okay, tell me what happened."

"William Trent was the final nail in the coffin. He's going to sue, and he's going to get a payout because his lawyers are better than ours, and I'm the place where the buck stops because I authorised the arrest."

"You said the final nail. What else did they use against you?"

Hatcher sighed. "The press conference. It's out that it was a sham. There are a lot of reporters calling for my blood."

"They'll get over it."

"Easy for you to say."

He had a point. "Give it a couple of months and all this will be forgotten."

Hatcher drained his glass and shook his head. "No it won't. It doesn't matter how many successes you have, how many arrests you make, it's the cases you screw up that everyone remembers. You know the score."

I did, only too well. Too many good careers had been ruined because one stupid mistake got blown all out of proportion.

"They shouldn't have taken you off the case," I said.

"Go tell that to my boss."

"I will if you think it'll do any good."

"You're serious, aren't you?"

"I'd go toe to toe with the Commissioner if I thought it would get you reinstated. You're a great cop and you've got great instincts. Hell, look at your record. There was a reason they gave you this case. Thirty years' worth of reasons."

Hatcher forced a smile. "Thanks again for the vote of confidence."

"I'm not saying this to be nice. You're the best person for the job. End of story."

"Whatever you say." Hatcher drained his glass. "Another?"

"Why not?"

Hatcher made his way over to the bar. His shoulders were slumped and his feet were heavy. He looked totally defeated. This job could do that, even to the best. I hated seeing Hatcher like this. It was a waste of resources. To catch these unsubs, we needed our best players on the field, not on the sidelines. I glanced at my watch. It had just gone eight. Because of the unscheduled trip to Bristol I'd arranged to meet Templeton at nine instead of eight. Hatcher came back with our drinks and sat down.

"Who's replacing you?" I asked.

"Detective Inspector Daniel Fielding. He's a safe choice. He's closing in on retirement and he'll play everything by the book."

"Playing by the book won't work. These unsubs have read that book and that's one of the reasons you haven't caught them." I sighed. "This is all about politics. I hate politics. What else can you tell me about Fielding?"

"He looks great on TV and the press like him." Hatcher shook his head and rubbed his tired eyes. "Who am I kidding? Fielding will smile and say all the right things, and everyone will eat up whatever crap he decides to serve them. But when it comes to actual police work he's incompetent."

"He wouldn't be your first choice, then?"

"First choice? He wouldn't be my last choice." Another shake of the head, another rub of the face. "Rachel Morris is going to end up like all the other victims."

"And I guess this is the point where you tell me it's all your fault."

"It is my fault, Winter. I could have done more. Hell, Winter, I *should* have done more."

"Okay," I said, "enough feeling sorry for yourself. Here's what you're going to do. You're going to drink up and go home, and you're not going to drink any more tonight. I want you with a clear head in the morning. Tomorrow we're going to find this guy and bring him in."

"What part of 'I've been taken off the case' don't you get?"

"That's just a detail. What's the worst that can happen?"

"Well, they could suspend me from duty. They might even fire me."

"They'll try and they'll fail," I said. "Anyway, since when have you been worried about losing your job?"

"I've got my pension to think about, Winter."

"A minor detail."

"No, a big detail. Also, didn't I mention that I've been taken off the case and given a new assignment?"

"And London will sleep just fine at night if all those parking tickets don't get chased up. Look, you're going home now and you're going to get a good night's sleep. In the morning you're going to phone in sick. I want you back here at seven sharp."

# CHAPTER
# FIFTY-SEVEN

The best room always came with the best view, and the view from my balcony stretched way into the distance. Lights shone behind windows, from cars and buses and cabs and vans, from streetlamps. Christmas lights dotted the night with a rainbow of colours. The city looked like a pattern in a kaleidoscope. There were millions of people out there. Some were bad, some were good, and most fell somewhere between those two extremes, but there were only two that interested me right now.

I took a drag on my cigarette and the tip flared orange. Quarter to nine. Fifteen minutes until Templeton was supposed to arrive, which meant it would be twenty minutes until she actually got here since she'd no doubt want to be five minutes late again.

Sounds filtered through the night, a gentle symphony of traffic and trains and people going about their business. The day was winding down, bringing with it that heavy sensation in my chest that I got when the investigation was slipping into another lull.

Everything that could be done had been done. All the bases were covered.

The press conference hadn't made the evening news at six, but it had been the lead story from midday all the way through to five. Five hours was long enough for the unsubs to see it. Organised offenders follow the news religiously because they love to hear that they're outsmarting the police. They can't get enough of it. That was a big part of the game.

How was Rachel Morris coping? Had she worked out who'd taken her yet? Probably. The story had been all over the news, which meant she'd have a good idea of how her future was going to pan out. Torture, mutilation and a lobotomy. I wondered how strong she was and decided it didn't really matter. However strong she was, the unsub would eventually break her.

Unless we got her back first.

I flicked my cigarette over the balcony and headed back into the warmth. The second movement of Mozart's clarinet concerto was playing on my laptop. This movement had always been my favourite piece. That mournful clarinet pulled at my heart in a way that was utterly breathtaking. Mozart had written twenty-seven piano concertos but only one clarinet concerto and my guess was that he'd decided to quit while he was ahead. It didn't get any better than this.

I had already showered and changed into a clean Doors T-shirt. All that was left to do was wait. Waiting pisses me off. It always has. I like motion and action. I like to keep busy. When I stop, my brain goes into overdrive, and that isn't always a good thing. According to my watch it was only five to nine. Ten minutes until Templeton got here.

To kill time I checked my emails. There were the usual requests for help in my inbox, some spam. One of the requests came with a bunch of attachments. Curiosity got the better of me and I opened them up.

This request came from the sheriff of a county in Alabama that I'd never heard of. Two thirteen-year-old girls had been abducted and murdered and the sheriff didn't want a third. I scanned the crime and autopsy reports, and the pieces started falling into place almost straight away. The answer was in the details. On the surface the two murders appeared identical. They weren't. Someone had gone to a lot of trouble to make them appear that way, and that someone was the stepfather of the first victim.

Both girls had been stabbed twenty times and the positioning of the wounds was almost identical. The first difference was in how far the knife had penetrated. The wounds were deeper with the first victim, on average a couple of inches deeper. The second difference was that the second victim had been stabbed in the heart first, which meant that none of the other nineteen wounds were necessary because she was already dead. The killer had needed her dead so she would lie still while he got the other nineteen wounds in the right place.

The first girl had been killed in a frenzy. It was a very personal murder. The second girl had been killed in cold blood. The rage from the first murder was missing in the second. The second victim was a smokescreen, another unfortunate soul who could be filed away under wrong time, wrong place.

I clicked back to my email account, hit the reply button and started typing. The first thing I told the sheriff was that the unsub was the stepfather. The second thing I told him was that he didn't have to worry about a third victim since this guy was stopping at girl number two. Then I told him that he would find the knife hidden under a stash of porn magazines in the garage at the first victim's house.

The clock on the screen said it was ten after nine, but I checked my watch anyway in case it was wrong. It wasn't. I took out my cell, but decided to give it another five minutes. I laid the phone next to my laptop and waited. Five minutes passed. Still no sign of Templeton. I found her number. Five rings then her cell went to voicemail. The message I left was brief and cheerful. *Hi there, wondering where you've got to.*

Ten minutes late became fifteen minutes late and I called her cell again. Her phone rang out and the voicemail kicked in. There was no point leaving a message because the excuses were starting to sound hollow. Templeton's cell wouldn't be buried at the bottom of her bag. No way. She was switched on and plugged in, a twenty-first-century girl all the way. She wouldn't go anywhere without her phone, and it would be somewhere she could get to within a maximum of three rings. If she was going to be late she would have called me.

I tried Scotland Yard next since it was possible she'd detoured via the office. Possible but unlikely. If she'd gone back to work she would have called. The person I spoke to told me the last time he'd seen her was that afternoon. He did a quick shout around but nobody else had seen her either.

I went out onto the balcony for another cigarette and wondered who the hell to call next. I didn't have Templeton's home number, and didn't know any of her friends. Basically, I didn't know anything about her life outside work. I assumed she had one, but she was a cop so there were no guarantees there. Being a cop was a vocation, not a career choice.

My next call was to Hatcher. The detective answered on the first ring.

"I need Templeton's home address and phone number," I said.

"Why? I thought she was supposed to be meeting you."

"She never turned up."

"I'm sure there's a good reason. She's just running late."

"She's not running late. Something's happened to her."

"You're worrying unnecessarily, Winter. Nothing's happened to her."

"She's not here, she's not at work and she's not answering her cell. You tell me, Hatcher, does that sound like nothing's happened?"

A sharp intake of breath. A sigh. A pause. It was the sound of a heavy decision being made. "Okay, sit tight. I'll come and pick you up."

# CHAPTER
# FIFTY-EIGHT

Templeton lived in a small red-brick Victorian house on the end of a terrace of identical red-brick houses. The buildings looked old, but they also looked well cared for. This was a nice neighbourhood. Prosperous, middle-class, clean. The road was narrowed by the cars parked on both sides.

The house lights were on, upstairs and downstairs. Not good. Templeton was too diligent to go out and leave her lights on. Hatcher had given me her home number, but all I got was her answerphone. Her cell was now going straight through to voicemail, which meant it was either switched off or the battery had run down. Hatcher bump-parked between an SUV and a Mini and we got out.

"I've got a bad feeling about this, Winter." Hatcher was looking up at the glowing windows, no doubt reading the situation the same way as me. The facts spoke for themselves. There was no room for misinterpretation. He shook his head and rubbed his tired eyes. "I should call this in."

"Let's see exactly what we're dealing with first."

"The lights are on, Templeton's not answering her phone, what do you think we're dealing with?"

"Worst-case scenario, Templeton's dead. Best case, she's been kidnapped. Either way, ten minutes isn't going to matter."

"Christ, Winter, that's cold."

"Ten minutes."

Hatcher nodded. "Okay, ten minutes then I'm making that call."

We checked the front of the house first. The door was locked and there were no broken panes of glass in the bay window. The curtains were closed so we couldn't see inside. Nobody had broken in through the front. Not that I'd expected anything different. We were too close to the street here. Having so many people passing by, on foot or in cars, made it much too risky.

We made our way around back. The kitchen light was on and the blinds were up and the glow from the kitchen lit up the tiny backyard. It was twenty feet by twenty feet and paved with uneven concrete slabs. There was some moss and a few stray blades of grass growing in the gaps between the slabs, but that was the only green in amongst a whole lot of grey. There were some empty plant pots and a padlocked mountain bike. High fences for privacy.

The broken window confirmed what I'd already guessed.

To minimise the noise and mess, the unsub had placed strips of tape across the small top panel before breaking it. Once the top panel was out all he had to do was reach in, unlatch the bottom part of the window and climb inside.

The back door was locked.

I remembered Templeton joking about getting a vault door fitted, and my response was that it wouldn't make a difference because if someone wanted to get in, they'd get in. For once I hated being right.

"I need to call this in," said Hatcher. He had his cellphone out and was thumbing through to the directory.

"Ten minutes," I reminded him.

"That was five minutes ago."

"The clock starts now."

"Okay, okay. But if we're going inside we need to wear these."

Hatcher pulled some latex gloves and booties from his pocket. It was like watching a magic trick. I slipped the gloves and booties on, and boosted myself up onto the windowsill. Then I put my arm carefully through the window, unlatched it and clambered inside. Clean dishes were piled up on the draining board and small diamonds of broken glass glittered in the sink. The key was in the back door. I unlocked it and let Hatcher in.

"Nine minutes," said Hatcher.

"Nine minutes," I agreed. "But I'm going to need you to shut up so I can do my thing."

It's dark when I arrive because I like to work in the dark, but it's still early in the evening because I need to get a parking space before the after-work rush begins. I'm alone because I don't know how long I'm going to be here for. It would be too suspicious to have my partner hanging out in the car waiting for me. Someone might notice and remember.

**338**

The lights are off, which means Sophie Templeton's not home. I head straight to the backyard, walking fast but not too fast. Hurrying gets you noticed. Act like you belong and nobody ever asks questions. The high fence offers privacy from the downstairs windows of the neighbouring houses, but not the upstairs windows.

No upstairs lights. The coast's clear.

I tape up the window, break it, let myself in.

For a minute I stand there and acclimatise myself to the sounds and smells. The house is rented rather than owned. It's part-furnished and there's a very definite distinction between Templeton's taste and what the landlord has left behind. I go through the house a room at a time, looking for the best place to stage an ambush. The kitchen is out because it's too narrow and there are too many things that can be used as weapons. Knives and pans and heavy things. This target is a cop, which puts her in a different league from the others. There's no point taking unnecessary risks.

The front room is one possibility, but I'd have to wait somewhere else because the door opens directly onto the street and there's nowhere to hide. The upstairs bathroom is out because it's too small and the spare room is out because it's filled with junk. I walk into the main bedroom.

No corpse on the king-size double bed. No corpse on the floor. The smell of death is absent.

The large wardrobe is filled with clothes and the chest of drawers is crammed to overflowing. Junk

**339**

and dust bunnies under the bed. There's an indent in the duvet near the top and the pillows have been fussed with.

This is where I'll sit and wait for Sophie Templeton to return.

I open the window a crack and the noise from the street rushes in. Then I go back to the bed to sit and wait. Every time a car passes my ears prick up. Whenever someone walks by on the sidewalk my ears pick up.

Footsteps on the path that leads to the front door.

A key rattles in the lock.

There are two ways this can play out. Either she'll come in and head straight upstairs to change out of her work clothes, or she'll head to the kitchen to feed the cat. I move quickly out onto the landing so I can be ready for both possibilities.

So near, yet so far. I stared at the indent in the duvet and realised that if we'd arrived two hours earlier we'd be looking at the unsub right now. A seventy-year lifespan can be measured out at 613,620 hours, so two hours is nothing. A faint trace of aftershave lingered in the air. That's how close we were. Hatcher was at my shoulder, his gaze fixed on the indentation, and from the way he was staring it was a safe bet he was thinking along the same lines as me.

I could picture the unsub sitting on the bed. Medium build, five-ten, brown hair. All that was missing was his face. Templeton's cat padded into the bedroom and

340

jumped onto the bed. It stared at us like we were a lower form of life, then meowed for food. According to the collar tag his name was Mr Bojangles. I tickled him under the chin and he let out a long, satisfied purr.

"Acquisition is the riskiest part of any abduction," I said. "There are too many things that can go wrong. Somehow the unsub incapacitated Templeton and got her from the house to his car, and he did all this without anyone noticing. How?"

"I've got to call this in, Winter."

"No, what you've got to do is answer my question. You've already told me that Fielding is incompetent. That means it's up to us to get Templeton back. Which means doing our job. So, focus. How did he do it?"

"He drugged her."

I shook my head. "Then what? He carries her out the front door to his car without anybody noticing? Not going to happen, Hatcher. Not in an area like this."

"Okay, maybe he was armed with a gun or a knife."

"A gun is a false threat. If he fired a gun around here a hundred cops would descend on this place within minutes. The unsub would know that, and so would Templeton. The problem with knives is that they are really only effective at close quarters. Templeton is trained in self-defence and she would have had a good idea who the intruder was. She would have fought him. Can you see any signs of a struggle?"

Hatcher shook his head. "So how did he do it?"

I tickled Mr Bojangles under the chin and he gave another meow. "Good question."

# CHAPTER
# FIFTY-NINE

The lights slammed on, the door opened and Rachel shrank back into the corner. There was a woman with Adam, and to start with Rachel was convinced her mind was playing tricks. She blinked but when she opened her eyes the woman was still there. This was no hallucination, this was real.

The woman was walking unsteadily, her head wobbling from side to side like she was having trouble supporting its weight. Adam led her to the dentist's chair and strapped her in. She was more or less the same height as him. Long legs and long blonde hair. Beautiful, too. Even dishevelled and drugged, there was no disguising that fact.

Rachel's hand throbbed in time with her heart and each beat brought fresh waves of pain. The last thing Adam said during his previous visit was that the syringe had contained a saline solution. She'd stabbed that needle in her hand for nothing. Another game, another way to mess with her head.

She glanced at the open door and pictured the route to the front door in her mind. Along the corridor, up the stairs, along the high-ceilinged corridor that led to the entrance hall, past the staircase, then out through the front door to freedom. She glanced at Adam, glanced at the open door again.

"How far does Number Five think she's going to get?"

Adam didn't even bother looking over. He made no move to shut the door. They both knew she wasn't going to try anything, not after last time. Rachel sagged against the wall and pulled a blanket around herself.

"Number Five thinks she can't take much more, but she's wrong. She's stronger than the others. Much stronger."

"Go to hell."

Adam reached the mattress in four long strides. He brought his leg back and Rachel cowered against the wall. She shut her eyes and braced herself. Nothing happened. Rachel opened her eyes and saw Adam hunkered down in front of her.

"That's a bad word," he said in Eve's voice, and laughed.

Adam went back over to the blonde woman in the chair and slapped her face a couple of times.

"Wakey, wakey."

"Leave me alone," the woman mumbled. The words were indistinct and mashed together.

"Wakey, wakey!" he screamed in her face. He grabbed hold of her ponytail and pulled hard, kept on pulling until her eyes were wide open and he had her full attention.

"Sarah Flight isn't dead, is she?" he said.

"I don't know what you're talking about."

Adam wrapped the ponytail around his hand and pulled harder. "Let's try that again. Sarah Flight is not dead, is she?"

"She's dead." The words came out as a gasp.

"That's what they said on the five o'clock news. It was the lead story. And then at six, there's no mention of her whatsoever. Doesn't that strike you as odd? It strikes me as odd. So, I asked myself what was going on, and, I have to say, the conclusions I reached weren't good. Third and final time: Sarah Flight is not dead, is she?"

The woman met Adam's gaze. "No."

"Do you think I'm stupid?"

"No, I don't think you're stupid."

Adam moved in closer. "I was clever enough to find you, wasn't I? I've known where you lived from the start. I know where you all live. I saw you in the park where I left Number One, and I saw you at work, and I followed you to that pathetic little hovel you call a home, and you didn't suspect a thing." He straightened up again. "You definitely look better as a brunette, though."

Adam took a deep breath, then smiled. Rachel almost shouted out a warning. When Adam smiled like that, that's when he was at his most dangerous. She looked at the space where her little finger had been and kept quiet. If Adam was hurting this woman, then he wasn't hurting her. Rachel stared at her hand, guilt-ridden and conflicted. She kept staring at it so she wouldn't have to look at the blonde-haired woman in the dentist's chair.

**344**

"I'm afraid it doesn't work like that," said Adam. "Here's how it does work. I'm going to hurt you and you're going to tell me what I want to know. Everything. Then I'm going to hurt you some more because I don't like liars. And then I'm going to hurt you some more because I can."

He took the orbitoclast from his pocket and held it up for the woman to see. "Do you know what this is for?"

"Yes," said the woman.

"When I'm done hurting you, I'm going to use this on you. And then I'm going to deliver you back to your colleagues. Maybe they'll think twice before they try playing me again."

"If you do that they'll just come after you twice as hard. Kidnapping me was a mistake."

"We'll see."

Adam left and the lights went out.

"Are you okay, Rachel?"

Rachel started to say yes. It was an automatic response. She stopped and thought about what the woman just said. "How do you know my name? Who are you?"

"My name's Sophie Templeton. I'm a police officer."

All Rachel heard was one word: police. She glanced through the dark in the direction of the nearest camera then moved carefully over to the chair.

"You've got to be quiet." Her lips were right up against Sophie's ear, her voice more breath than sound. "I think the room's bugged. Are you working undercover? Nod if you are."

Sophie shook her head.

"What do you mean no? Someone must know you're here?"

Another shake of the head.

"The police are coming, though? They must know where you are."

"They're going to find us, Rachel."

Rachel pulled the blanket more tightly around herself. "They're not coming, are they? Nobody's coming?"

"They'll find us. You've got to believe that."

# CHAPTER
# SIXTY

"The bedroom light was on," I said.

"And?" said Hatcher.

"And that means this is where he staged his ambush. Templeton came in and switched on the light and the unsub attacked her."

"I thought we'd already established that."

"No, what we'd established was that he waited for her here. I couldn't decide whether the actual abduction happened downstairs or up here. But it must have happened up here because Templeton switched the light on. It couldn't have happened any other way. There's no way the unsub switched it on. He waited for her in the dark."

"How can you be so sure about that, Winter?"

"Because if the light had been on when she got back from work she would have noticed it from the street. Just like we did."

"Assuming you're right, how did he incapacitate her?"

"Hold on a second. We're getting ahead of ourselves here." I put Mr Bojangles down on the bed, gave him a stroke and got a purr for my troubles. "The cat is the big problem here. The second Templeton stepped through the front door he would have been all over her, demanding to be fed. She would have gone through to the kitchen, and she would have seen the broken window, and she would have got the hell out and called for back-up."

Hatcher asked a question and I shut my eyes to block out the distraction. A good hunter will always choose where to stage their ambush. If you control the environment, you stand a better chance of success. The unsub had chosen to ambush Templeton here in the bedroom. I was sure of it. Earlier I'd thought the living room was a possibility, but there was no way he could have got down the stairs quickly enough. Also, because of the layout of the house, he would have been ambushing her after she'd seen the broken glass in the kitchen. By that point, she would have been on her guard, and possibly armed. It was a complete non-starter.

The bedroom made much more sense. But how did the unsub lure her up here? The cat would have started shouting for food the second she stepped through the door, and he would have kept on at her until she relented and fed him. He would have had Templeton conditioned to feed him, because that's what cats did.

Unless he wasn't downstairs.

"The cat was in the bedroom with the unsub," I said. "Templeton got in from work and the first thing she heard was Mr Bojangles calling out from upstairs. The unsub probably tugged his tail, something like that. Anyway, Templeton assumes that the cat has shut himself in one of the bedrooms so she rushes up the stairs."

I closed my eyes again and pictured the scene. Ran scenarios until I found one that worked.

"The unsub would have been standing behind the door when Templeton came in," I said. "That's the most obvious place to hide. She would have opened the door and switched on the light and seen the cat. Then she would have marched in and headed straight over to the cat and picked him up. She would have been talking to him, telling him off for getting himself locked in the room. By the time she realised she wasn't alone it would already have been too late. Which brings us to our earlier question. How does he incapacitate her?"

"We've already ruled out guns and knives," said Hatcher.

"My money's on electricity."

"A taser?"

I nodded. "That would be my guess. He zaps her with 50,000 volts before she even knows he's there."

"That still doesn't explain how he got her to his car."

"The most likely scenario is that he did drug her, but rather than knock her out completely he used a smaller dose, just enough to keep her compliant. The effects of a taser wear off pretty quickly, but so long as he moved fast he would have had enough time to inject her."

"Okay, so what happens next?"

"Once the drug takes effect, the unsub can get her out to the car. And once she's strapped into the car, he gives her the full dose of the drug and knocks her out.

Then they drive off to wherever the hell it is he takes his victims."

"Somewhere north of the Thames," said Hatcher.

"Somewhere north of the Thames," I agreed.

I put the cat on the bed and headed for the landing. Hatcher made his call as we retraced our route through the house to the backyard. He finished his call and closed the phone. I took off my latex gloves and booties, balled them up and stuffed them into a pocket. Hatcher did the same.

"We need to wait here," said Hatcher.

"No we don't. What we need to do is find Templeton. And we're not going to do that by hanging around here answering a whole bunch of useless questions. I have no intention of finding out first-hand how incompetent Fielding is. I'm happy to trust your judgement on that one, Hatcher."

Hatcher sighed. "Where are we going?"

"My hotel's not far. We can work from there."

We hurried around to the front of the house and out onto the quiet street. The snow had held off for the best part of the day but it wasn't going to hold off much longer. The clouds were lower than ever and the air was heavy and oppressive. There was a cold wetness in the air that chewed at my bones. I climbed into the car and buckled up, and fifteen minutes later we were back at the Cosmopolitan.

While Hatcher parked up, I hurried to my suite. There was no way Hatcher would approve of what I was planning. He would try to talk me out of it, and I would ignore him and do what I was going to do anyway. My way saved time and energy. I dumped my coat on the back of a chair, then fished out my wallet and found Donald Cole's business card. Cole answered on the first ring, like he had the phone in his hand and was just waiting for my call.

Our conversation lasted less than twenty seconds.

# CHAPTER
# SIXTY-ONE

I was on the phone ordering coffee from room service when Hatcher got back. This was gearing up to be an all-nighter so we'd need caffeine, and lots of it. I switched on my laptop and wired in the printer, then logged on to the internet and found a map of North London. I printed the map across four sheets and pinned these to the wall. The walls were made from sheetrock and the pins went in easily. The downside of sheetrock was that we could hear the couple next door having sex.

The abduction sites got marked in green, the dump sites in red. Templeton's house got a green cross, and the location where Charles Brenner's body was found was marked with a theatrical black cross. I pinned the after photos of Sarah Flight, Margaret Smith, Caroline Brant and Patricia Maynard next to the map.

The coffee arrived, two cafetières and two mugs. I tipped the girl who brought it and told her to bring the same again in an hour. My blood sugar level was taking a dive so I added three sugars to my coffee, then raided the minibar and came up with some peanuts and a candy bar. I tore open the peanuts and ate a handful. Ripped open the candy bar and took a bite.

352

"So, where the hell do we start?" asked Hatcher.

"We go right back to the beginning," I said. "With Templeton's abduction the unsubs deviated from their MO. That's great news. It means all bets are off. It means we get to wipe the slate clean. We challenge every assumption, every theory, and we see where that leads us."

"He snatched Templeton because of the press conference, didn't he?"

I nodded and ate another handful of nuts.

"She could be dead," said Hatcher.

"She could be," I agreed.

"And you don't feel guilty about that?"

"Guilt isn't going to help us get Templeton back. Right now that's got to be our primary focus. Until we hear otherwise, we assume she's alive."

"Did you know this was going to happen?"

"If you're asking whether I used Templeton as bait, then the answer is no. If I'd done that I would have made sure she was protected."

"But?" said Hatcher.

"But when you push an unsub, they don't always act in ways that you can predict. In hindsight I can understand why he's done what he's done. He's angry at us because we lied to him, and Templeton is the focal point for that anger."

"Jesus."

Hatcher's voice had shrunk to a whisper and there was a faraway look in his eyes. I knew where he'd disappeared to. He was watching the flash of a blade as it cut into flesh. He was seeing the blood seep and drip and gather into pools.

"Hatcher!" I called out, loud and sharp to get his attention. "The guilt and the what-ifs and the finger-pointing we deal with later. Right now the only thing that matters is getting Templeton back, okay?"

"Okay," he said.

We drifted into a short silence that was punctuated by the moans and groans from the couple next door. They sounded like they were just about there. I hoped they were. The fewer distractions, the better. I tipped the rest of the peanuts into my mouth and finished the candy bar in three bites. My blood sugar was on the way up again. I felt energised, and the low-grade headache that usually preceded a crash had gone.

I got a fresh packet of cigarettes from my suitcase and lit one. Hatcher glared but kept his mouth shut. I smoked my cigarette and drank my coffee and did my best to stop myself thinking about what Templeton was going through. All that stuff I put into a box and nailed the lid on tight. If things went bad, I would take the lid off and deal with it then. Like I'd told Hatcher, all that mattered was getting Templeton back.

Hatcher's cellphone rang and I plucked it from his fingers before he had a chance to answer it.

"What the hell, Winter!"

I turned the phone around so Hatcher could see the number. "Fielding?"

A nod.

I switched the phone off and tossed it back to Hatcher.

"I can't think of anyone I need to speak to right now," I said. "That means there's nobody you need to speak to either. We don't need any distractions."

Hatcher didn't look convinced, but he put his cell away.

"Okay," I said. "The biggest assumption we've made is that there are two unsubs. I still believe that's the case."

"Even though we only have actual evidence of one person."

"There are two very different signatures. That means two unsubs."

I found a black marker and a clean section of wall and wrote TWO SIGNATURES TWO UNSUBS in big, bold letters. Hatcher gave me a look.

"Can you see a whiteboard anywhere?" I said.

Hatcher shrugged. *Whatever.* "Maybe he's got a split personality," he said.

"Unlikely. You see that sort of thing in movies and books because it makes the writers' job easier, but in real life it's extremely rare."

"If Cutting Jack does have a partner then she's keeping very quiet."

"As all good little submissives do. Which leads us to another assumption. We're assuming the female partner is the submissive. Pairings are governed by a complex set of dynamics. Usually the male is the dominant partner, but not always. Take the Wests. It was originally believed that Fred was the dominant partner. These days it's widely acknowledged that Rose called the shots. What if the female is the dominant partner here?"

"Is there any evidence to back that up? Anything at all?"

"Templeton's abduction." I was thinking on my feet here, brainstorming. "The male unsub stepped way outside his comfort zone there. The MO was completely different. This was the first time he'd taken someone from their own home. It was done quickly, too. Usually he takes his time. He stalks his victims over the internet for months before he abducts them. Templeton's abduction was planned and executed in a matter of hours."

"Which proves what, exactly?"

"It proves he's not calling the shots," I said. "Okay, we know he abducts the victims. The way he usually does this is risky enough, but Templeton's abduction took the risk factor up to a whole new level. The female partner has no appreciation of the risks because she's not involved in the abductions. She's sat nice and safe at home waiting for him to come back with the victims. She doesn't know what it's like to be out there on the front line, your heart racing, the threat of capture constantly there."

I nodded to myself, liking the way this was slotting together. "If it had been left to the male partner, he wouldn't have gone through with the kidnapping. But it wasn't his call, it was his partner's. There's a good chance he tried to talk her out of kidnapping Templeton, but he might as well have been talking to a brick wall. She wouldn't have been listening. She wanted Templeton, and nothing was going to stop her."

356

I crushed my cigarette out in the saucer. FEMALE DOMINANT PARTNER went on the list. So did MALE PARTNER LOW SELF-ESTEEM.

"Another thing," I said. "The change in MO is further proof that these unsubs are devolving."

"Which you said is a good thing."

"Yes and no. It's good because it means we're going to catch these assholes, and we're going to catch them soon. But it's bad because it means their behaviour will become increasingly erratic."

Hatcher sighed. His whole body seemed to sag as the exhalation left his body. "Which could be very bad news for Templeton."

"Forget about that, Hatcher. It's not going to help. Focus on the here and now. What other assumptions have we made?"

"We're assuming they're lovers," said Hatcher.

"Good," I said. "The Hillside Strangler turned out to be two cousins. Kenneth Bianchi and Angelo Buono. We could be dealing with cousins here, or a brother and sister, or a mother and son."

"Or they could be lovers."

"Or they could be lovers," I agreed.

LOVERS went onto the list. So did COUSINS, BROTHER/ SISTER and MOTHER/SON.

"We're not looking at an all-male partnership then?"

I shook my head. "No. The use of knives is a male signature. Playing dolls is a female signature."

"And you're still convinced he lives north of the Thames?"

"No question about it." I nodded to the map. "The river forms a natural boundary, and all the abduction and dump sites are north of the river. That's his hunting ground. He's acting on some primal instinct here, something that's been with us since we lived in caves. He won't even be aware of what he's doing. So what do we know for certain?"

"We know he's five-ten, has brown hair and a medium build."

MALE UNSUB 5'10" MEDIUM BUILD BROWN HAIR went on the list.

"We know he's a sadist," said Hatcher. "And we also know he's careful and methodical."

"Agreed," I said, and added those points to the list. "Even with Templeton's kidnapping he was still careful. I'll bet forensics don't find anything. Okay, what do we know about the female unsub?"

"Hardly anything. She might as well be a ghost."

I considered this for a moment then added FEMALE UNSUB GHOST to the list.

"Which brings us on to the one thing that's been bugging me about this case from the start. The lobotomies. We need to disassociate from the horror of this act. How many dead bodies have you seen?"

Hatcher snorted. "More than I care to remember."

"And if we were dealing with dead bodies here it would be easier to disassociate since that's what we're used to. The fact that the victims are alive has thrown us a curveball. When I saw Patricia Maynard back at the hospital I couldn't stop wondering what it would be like to end up like that. The thing is, if she'd been laid

358

out on an autopsy table, I wouldn't have been fazed. I would have been considering useful things, like how she'd got there and what her death told us about the unsubs."

"So, imagine she's dead. What does it tell us?"

I looked at the cold bleached-out picture the forensic photographer had taken of Patricia Maynard. "I've no idea," I admitted.

# CHAPTER
# SIXTY-TWO

"Can you undo these straps, Rachel?"

"I can't. If I do that Adam will hurt me again." Rachel stared through the darkness in the direction of the dentist's chair. "I'm sorry."

"You don't have to be sorry. I shouldn't have asked. That wasn't fair."

"It's okay."

"How are you holding up?"

"How do you think I'm holding up? I've been kidnapped and tortured, and I've had one of my fingers cut off, and my head's been shaved."

"You've been very brave."

"You think I'm brave, try stupid." Rachel snorted a little half-laugh and shook her head. "I arranged to meet some guy I didn't know over the internet, and I didn't tell anyone where I was going. That's pretty stupid."

"You're not stupid, Rachel. You made a mistake. None of this is your fault."

"Nice of you to say so, but it doesn't change anything. Adam will keep torturing me and then he'll lobotomise me. Just like he did with the others."

"We're going to get out of here."

"Stop saying that. It's not going to happen."

"We're going to get out of here, Rachel. You've got to believe that."

"No I don't. You don't know what he's like."

A thought occurred to Rachel, one that froze her blood. What if the woman in the chair was another Eve? What if this was like the telephone in the hall all over again? What if this was another of Adam's mind games? She thought about what she'd said to this woman, replaying every word to see if she'd said too much. Sophie kept going on about getting out of here. Was that part of the game? Was Adam listening in, waiting for her to agree with Sophie so he had an excuse to torture her again?

"You're working with him, aren't you?" said Rachel. "You're not really with the police."

"I'm a police detective, Rachel. You've got to believe that."

"Prove it."

Silence, then a sigh. "I can't."

"See, you are working with him."

"And that's exactly what I'm talking about. Whatever I say you're going to twist around until it proves what you want it to prove."

"And that's exactly what I'd expect you to say."

"I know you're scared, but you have to trust me here. I'm on your side."

Rachel snorted out another small half-laugh and pulled her knees more tightly into her chest, hugging herself hard. "You don't know anything," she whispered. "But, if you are who you say you are, then you will."

"Hopefully we'll get out of here before I have to find out."

"There you go again. More lies. Adam's not going to hurt you."

"My name is Sophie Templeton. I'm a detective sergeant with the Metropolitan Police. Right now, there's an army of cops searching for us."

"More lies. If there really was an army of cops looking for me, why haven't they found me yet? Why didn't they find the others?"

"Because I'm a police officer and that changes everything. When something like this happens to one of our own then we're relentless."

"Great," said Rachel. "So there's one law for the police and another law for everyone else. Maybe if they'd taken my kidnapping more seriously I'd be out of here by now. Maybe I'd still have all my fingers."

"I'm not saying it's right, Rachel. I'm just telling you how it is."

"No. What you're doing is lying. You're not a detective, and you've never worked for the police, and there isn't an army of cops out looking for us." Rachel shrugged off her blankets then stood up and stared through the dark at the closest camera. "I'm not playing your games any more!" she screamed into the darkness. "Do you hear me? Stop messing with my head."

The lights banged on, the door opened and Adam strode into the room. Rachel slid down the wall and reached for the comfort of the blankets. Adam walked across to the mattress and grinned down at her. He tapped the cane against his palm, slow and rhythmic, *tap tap tap*.

"Number Five needs to learn to control her temper."

He lifted the cane and Rachel shrank into the corner. Adam laughed and traced its tip down her body. The bamboo scratched at her naked skin and tugged at the grey sweatshirt and jogging bottoms. He stopped when he reached her feet. A shake of the head, another grin, then the cane swished through the air and hit skin. Rachel howled in agony and pulled herself deeper into the corner and buried her feet under the blankets. They felt like they were on fire.

"Stop it," Sophie called out.

Adam walked over to the dentist's chair. He studied Sophie for a second, head cocked to the side, then he went to work with the cane. It was a brutal display of fury. The cane came down on her legs and arms and body. It swished and whistled through the air, each blow bringing more screams and crying, screams that became increasingly quiet, then stopped altogether. Rachel wanted to shout for Adam to stop but her voice wouldn't work. She wanted to run over and help the woman but she was paralysed with fear. She wanted to close her eyes, but she couldn't even manage that. All she could do was stare helplessly.

Adam stopped as suddenly as he started. Silence. A distant pipe rattled, a floorboard creaked. Rachel's head was filled with the whistle and crack of the cane. She could still hear Sophie's screams. She glanced over, convinced Adam had killed her. Sophie wasn't moving.

Her eyes were closed. She had to be dead. Adam leant the cane against the chair and took a syringe from his pocket. He jabbed it into Sophie's leg and she groaned back into consciousness.

"Tell me everything the police know," he said. "If you lie, I'll know, and there will be consequences."

Sophie told him everything and when she was done Adam left and the lights went out.

"Now do you believe me?" said Sophie.

"I'm sorry."

"We're going to get out of here."

Rachel said nothing because there was nothing to say. Right now, Sophie needed hope. She needed denial. Rachel understood this because she'd been there. She'd also been through the anger and the bargaining and the depression stages of the cycle. What she'd just witnessed had pushed her into acceptance.

She was never going to see the sun again and she was never going to walk barefoot across hot sand. All her memories were going to be taken away and it would be like she'd never existed. This was worse than death, so much worse. Rachel walked through the dark to the chair and placed a gentle hand on Sophie's shoulder. Sophie cowered from her touch, but Rachel stayed with her until she felt her begin to relax.

"We're going to get out of here," Sophie whispered again in a broken voice.

"Of course we are."

# CHAPTER
# SIXTY-THREE

My cellphone chirped to tell me a text had arrived: Alex Irvine had emailed through the list of Porsche owners. I accessed my email account, downloaded the list, printed it out. There were more than three hundred names and addresses. Hatcher groaned when he saw them.

"The good news is that one of these people is our unsub," I said.

"The bad news is that even with my full team it would take hours to get through this lot. Also, it's night so no one will be answering their phones."

I poured a fresh coffee, lit a cigarette, then scanned the names and addresses. The snow had started. It was light for now, but it was going to get worse. The weathermen were talking about drifts and blizzard conditions, motorists were being told to stay home, and Scotland and some parts of northern England were already snowed in. Small flakes floated down and stuck to the windows, hung there for a moment, then slowly melted and slid down the glass.

"We need to make this list more manageable," I said. "First off, we can get rid of all the female owners."

I used the black marker pen to score out names.

"And we can get rid of any males under thirty and over forty."

I scored out more names.

"And we can get rid of anyone whose name doesn't fit a white Caucasian profile."

I scored out another load of names and did a quick count. Forty-five names and addresses. Still not brilliant, but a hell of a lot better.

"Now what?" asked Hatcher.

"Now we hit the computer and check the satellite maps. We want large, detached properties where neighbours aren't going to be a problem."

I glanced at the list, memorised the first ten names and addresses, then tossed the list and the marker pen to Hatcher and got settled down with my laptop. The first address was a house in a cramped new development in Barnet.

"Cross James Macintosh off the list," I said. "He's not our unsub. Too many neighbours."

Twenty minutes later we'd whittled the list down to eight names and addresses. I transferred the addresses to the map, marked them with blue circles, then took a step back. I looked at the green crosses that marked the last known locations of the victims, the red crosses that indicated where they'd been dumped, then scored out one of the blue circles because it was in Essex, miles from all the other marks. It just didn't fit.

"We could send teams to all seven addresses," Hatcher suggested. "Getting enough people together would be a challenge, but we could make it happen for Templeton."

I shook my head. "Too risky. If the unsubs get even the slightest hint that we're on to them they'll panic, and that won't be good for Templeton, or Rachel Morris. We need to work out which one of these is the right address, then we go in hard and fast with a precision attack. These unsubs need to be neutralised before they know what's hit them."

"So, where are they?"

I looked at the map, then looked at the list scrawled on the wall and scored out COUSINS. Thought a bit more and scored out BROTHER/SISTER. Underlined FEMALE UNSUB GHOST.

"What are you thinking?" Hatcher asked.

I was back in the zone, acting on pure instinct. I put a line through LOVERS, then underlined MOTHER/SON and added a second and third line under FEMALE UNSUB GHOST.

"What are you thinking?" Hatcher asked again.

"You've seen *Psycho?*"

"You think Cutting Jack's being told what to do by his dead mother?"

"The mother/son relationship just feels right. More right than them being husband and wife or brother and sister."

I reached for my cell. Alex Irvine picked up on the second ring. Servers and cooling fans hummed in the background, which meant he was still at work.

"Is Sumati with you?" I asked.

"She left ten minutes ago."

"Call her and get her back in. I'm sending through a list of names and addresses and I need them checked out. Thoroughly. I'm particularly interested in what happened to these guys' mothers. How are your hacking skills?"

Alex answered with a derisory snort.

"Okay," I said. "I want you to hack into the computers of every medical supplier in the country. Big and small. See if any of them have sent anything to any of these addresses. Anything at all. I don't care what it is."

"How far back do you want us to go?"

"A couple of years. If you don't get anything try going back further. Call me as soon as you've got something."

I killed the call and tossed the phone onto the bed, then glanced over at the victim photographs and thought about Templeton. I pictured her how she was when we first met in the Cosmopolitan's bar, confident and swaggering and totally self-possessed. I pictured her how I got to know her later, softer and more vulnerable, a face she kept well hidden from Hatcher and the rest of her colleagues. This picture was followed by others, a whole host of mental snapshots I'd filed away in my memory.

I couldn't picture her like the other victims, and that was good. Whatever happened, she would not end up like that. I would do whatever it took to make sure that didn't happen.

Whatever it took.

# CHAPTER
# SIXTY-FOUR

"We think Adam has a partner. A wife or a girlfriend."

Rachel laughed. It was a dry, bitter sound. She was sitting on the mattress with a blanket pulled around her shoulders. She stared through the dark in the direction of the dentist's chair.

"What's so funny?" Sophie asked.

"Nothing's funny. Not really. Adam made me think his sister was helping him but it was just another one of his mind games. He put on a voice and pretended to be a woman, and I fell for it. How dumb is that?"

"It's not dumb, Rachel."

"It was dumb. And do you want to know the stupidest thing? I actually felt sorry for her. I thought she was being forced to help him." Rachel laughed again. "I thought I was playing her and all the time it was Adam playing me."

"Don't be so hard on yourself. Adam's manipulative and intelligent, and he's a sadist. He gets off on messing with people's heads."

"Well I wish he'd go and mess with someone else's." Rachel realised what she'd said and added quickly, "I'm sorry, I don't mean you."

"It's okay Rachel. None of this is your fault."

"I just want to go home," Rachel whispered. Fresh tears ran down her face and she swiped them away.

The lights came on with a bang and everything turned blurry. Too much brightness and too many tears. Rachel blinked away the brightness and wiped away the rest of her tears. She looked at her brutalised hand. It hurt, but not as bad as earlier. Most of the pain was still located in the empty space where her finger had been. She looked over at Sophie. The policewoman's face was pale and drawn, and the slightest movement made her flinch. The dog flap clattered open and two black cable ties dropped onto the floor.

"Number Five will pick up the cable ties."

Adam's distorted voice boomed from the speakers, loud and intrusive. Rachel looked over at Sophie and saw the panic on the policewoman's face. Her eyes were moving from speaker to speaker.

"You don't ever get used to it," Rachel told her. "You think you will, but you never do."

"Number Five will pick up the cable ties or face the consequences."

Rachel shrugged off the blanket and walked across the basement. She picked up the cable ties, then stared at the nearest camera and waited for her next instruction.

"Number Five will unstrap the prisoner."

Rachel unbuckled the straps and Sophie sagged deeper into the chair, rubbing at her wrists.

"Number Five will move the prisoner to the mattress."

Rachel put an arm around Sophie and helped her stand up. They staggered across the room together. The policewoman was leaning heavily against Rachel, feet shuffling. They reached the mattress and Rachel helped her sit down. Her breathing was ragged and she was biting back the pain.

She was trying to put on a brave face, but wasn't fooling anyone. The stress and effort of the journey from the dentist's chair to the mattress was written all over her face.

"Number Five will secure the prisoner's hands and feet with the cable ties. Hands behind back. And make sure they're tight."

Rachel did as she was told. The cable tie clicked tight but she gave it one more click just to be sure. Adam had said tight and there was no way she was going to disobey him after what he'd done to Sophie.

"Sorry," Rachel whispered. She got in close and kept her voice low so Adam wouldn't hear.

"It's okay," Sophie whispered back.

"None of this is okay."

Rachel wrapped the second cable tie around Sophie's ankles and ratcheted it tight. She stood up and stared at the nearest camera and waited for her next instruction.

"Number Five will go over to the chair and take off her clothes. All of them."

Rachel didn't hesitate. She walked over to the chair, pulled the grey sweatshirt over her head, tugged the jogging pants down over her hips, slid off the cotton panties. She stared at the floor, head cocked slightly to the right, arms tight to her sides. The door opened and

Adam came in carrying a bucket and a towel. A purple dress was draped over his left arm. He put the bucket and the towel on the floor, then laid the dress carefully on the back of the dentist's chair.

"Number Five will get washed."

A sponge bobbed in the soapy water and wisps of steam drifted up from the bucket, small clouds that broke apart then disappeared. The water smelled of lavender. Rachel picked up the sponge and washed herself down. She scrubbed away the grime, scrubbed hard enough for it to hurt.

The wounds left by Adam's knife were red and sore, but all the butterfly stitches were still in place. While Rachel got washed, Adam went over to the mattress and checked the cable ties. A single click echoed through the basement and Sophie groaned. Rachel froze, then quickly started scrubbing again. Another click, another groan. This time she didn't stop. She finished washing then towelled herself dry and waited for the next instruction.

Adam nodded to the purple dress on the chair. On top of the dress was a black bra and matching panties. "Number Five will get dressed."

Rachel put on the underwear. The panties were a size too small, the bra a size too big. The underwear was old-fashioned, decades old rather than years. The dress was old, too, fancy for its time, but that time was long gone. The shoulder pads and frills dated it back to the eighties. It smelled of mothballs.

Rachel pulled the dress over her head. It was a tight fit but she managed to wriggle into it. With a twirl of his finger, Adam motioned for Rachel to turn around so her back was to him. His fingertips brushed across her neck and she forced herself not to flinch as he fastened the clasps. He started at the bottom and worked his way up. His hands were soft and his fingers worked the clasps gently. The last one went in and Adam stepped back. Rachel breathed easier again. Adam looked her up and down then nodded to the door.

"After you, Number Five."

# CHAPTER
# SIXTY-FIVE

My cellphone rang and I snatched it up. Sumati Chatterjee didn't bother with any niceties, she just blurted out a name. It was the third name on my mental list of seven.

"Are you sure?" I asked.

"Absolutely positive."

She gave me the edited highlights in bullet points, brief and concise, her delivery rapid-fire. I hung up, grabbed the list, drew a big red circle around Darren Webster's name, then held it up for Hatcher to see.

"There's your bad guy," I said.

Hatcher grinned. "That's the best news I've had in a very long time."

I grabbed my coat and ran for the door. Hatcher caught up with me at the elevator. He was already on his cellphone, organising and planning, getting the troops rallied. He was still on his phone when we reached the ground floor. I detoured via the reception desk and asked the concierge if anything had been left for me. The concierge told me to wait a moment then disappeared into a small back office, returning a few seconds later with a small silver Samsonite case and a set of car keys. The key fob had a Maserati logo on it and the case was as heavy as I would have expected.

"We're taking my car," I said to Hatcher.

Hatcher put his hand over the mouthpiece of his phone.

"Since when have you got a car?"

"Since thirty seconds ago. It's a Maserati."

Hatcher stared at me. I stared back. He wound up his call and put his phone away. "What's going on, Winter?"

"I'll explain everything in the car."

Donald Cole's Maserati was parked near the exit of the Cosmopolitan's underground lot, nose out for a quick getaway. I'd asked for a fast car, and this was a very fast car. It had a 4.2-litre V8 engine, a six-speed gearbox and a top speed of 177 miles an hour. It could do nought to sixty in 5.2 seconds.

We got in and I dumped the Samsonite case onto Hatcher's lap. The engine roared to life and we took off, tyres squealing. Five seconds later we bumped out onto the street. Driving on the left threw me to start with, but I soon got the hang of it. The principle is the same as back home. You keep the passenger next to the sidewalk, and the oncoming traffic on the side of the driver. Do that and things usually work out fine.

I drove hard, feet dancing between the accelerator and the brake pedal. The engine revved and ebbed, and the gearbox switched gears. Horns blared and brake lights flared, and I just kept going, weaving and dodging and bullying my way through the night traffic, absolutely relentless. The wipers were on full, swiping away the snow. There were no signs of Cole's bodyguards in the mirrors.

"What's going on, Winter?"

"Open the case."

The catches clicked, one after the other, like a double tap, and Hatcher muttered a breathy "Jesus".

"What sort of guns?" I asked.

"Colt 45s. Two of them. I'm guessing they're unlicensed."

"Unlicensed and untraceable and never fired in anger."

Donald Cole had come up with the goods again, which made it two for two.

"The car, the guns, I suppose you got them from your fairy godmother," said Hatcher.

"Donald Cole would not appreciate being called a fairy."

"Christ, Winter! Donald Cole! What the hell are you playing at?" Hatcher took a deep breath and got himself back under control. "Okay, start talking. I want to know what's going on. And I want to know now."

"Darren Webster isn't the unsub."

"So, who is?"

I said nothing.

"You realise I could find out easily enough. All it would take is one call to Sumati or Alex."

"But you're not going to do that. If you were, you'd already be talking to them."

I swerved to overtake a cab, then cut back in again and hit the gas. The sound of the cab's horn receded into the distance.

**376**

"Plausible deniability," I said. "I've already told you who the unsub is, and you've been a good Boy Scout and passed that information along to Fielding, just like you're supposed to. The thing is, I'm only human. I make mistakes, just like everyone else. Like back at the hotel when I got the names mixed up."

Hatcher said nothing.

"If I give you the correct name you have a duty to pass that information on to Fielding. That would be a big mistake. He'll want to get the unsub surrounded before he goes in. He'll want everything in place before he makes a move. He'll want to make sure his ass is well and truly covered."

Hatcher still said nothing.

"Do you think for a minute that this unsub won't notice dozens of cops sneaking up on him?" I said. "Before you know it you've got a siege situation on your hands. Is that what you want? Then there's the fact that Templeton is one of your own. Emotions will be running high. Way too high. This is personal. There are too many things that can go wrong. All it takes is for one thing to go wrong and Templeton winds up dead, or worse."

"And it's not personal for you?"

"That's the wrong question, Hatcher. The question you should be asking is who you would trust with Templeton's life. Me or Fielding?"

# CHAPTER
# SIXTY-SIX

Rachel followed Adam up the wide staircase. She didn't want to, but she didn't see she had a choice. Disobeying him wasn't an option. Her legs were heavy and weak and she had to use the banister to keep herself upright, to keep moving, her hand dragging across the polished wood.

The fact they were headed upstairs terrified her. There were bedrooms upstairs. Beds. Adam had already tortured her, electrocuted and mutilated her. Was rape next? If it was, she wouldn't fight him. She'd lie there and let him do whatever he wanted and pray for it to be over quickly. Adam would be looking for a reaction. That's what got him off. Fear, hatred, desperation, anything just so long as it was a reaction. Denying him a reaction would be more effective than fighting or begging.

That was the plan, and it was a good plan because it would keep her alive. The problem was that she knew it wouldn't work. The second Adam laid a finger on her she would fight him with everything she'd got. She'd do anything to keep him away from her. Kick, punch, bite, scratch. Anything. She knew that the harder she went at him, the harder he was going to retaliate and that she might as well be signing her own death warrant, but so long as she had a single breath left in her body she would fight him.

The mirror at the top of the stairs had a gilt-edged frame, and the surface was polished to a high sheen. Rachel stopped dead and stared at her reflection. She barely recognised herself. The woman in the glass looked like a cancer victim. Her face was pinched and tight, and her eyes were dull and lifeless with large black circles around them. The dress made her look like a kid who'd raided her mother's wardrobe for clothes to play dressing up with, and her bald head made her want to cry.

Adam was at her shoulder, grinning at the way she was squirming in the glass. Rachel wished she had a knife or a gun, or a cattle prod. She wanted to hurt him like he'd hurt her, to make him suffer for what he'd done to her. She wanted him to understand her pain. Most of all, she wanted to wipe that smug grin off his face.

"Number Five will keep moving."

Adam turned right at the top of the stairs and Rachel followed him along a landing and into a corridor, past closed doors that hid darkened rooms. Snowflakes shattered against windows and the wind howled around the outside of the old house.

The air smelled like an orange grove. Underpinning this was another smell, this one fainter, a modern chemical smell that reminded Rachel of hospitals. The further along the corridor they went, the stronger it got. At the end of the corridor was another door, this one glowing from the light sneaking through the cracks.

Adam walked up to the door, knocked softly, then pushed it open. He stood aside and waved Rachel inside. Rachel didn't move. She stood frozen to the spot. That hospital smell was stronger than ever. It had got stuck in her nose and lungs. She could feel her stomach crawling up into her throat. She swallowed hard, driving the bile back down, all the time willing herself not to be sick.

"Number Five will go into Mother's bedroom."

Rachel stayed rooted to the spot.

"Number Five will go into Mother's bedroom or face the consequences."

Rachel walked through the door.

The room was decorated like a private hospital room. Pastel shades on the walls, light pink curtains on the windows, tough, practical vinyl on the floor. Extravagant bouquets of fresh flowers brought colour and life into the room.

The hospital bed was angled so Adam's mother could sit up. Her hands lay limp in her lap, one on top of the other, not so much as a twitch. Her face was sunken and gaunt, but Rachel could see the shadow of the beautiful woman she had once been. She had Adam's brown eyes, the same bone structure.

At first glance her hair looked real. It was only when Rachel looked closer that she could tell it was a wig. Her make-up was subtle, applied with care. She was wearing a cream cardigan over her white nightdress.

Four large-screen televisions were fixed to the wall opposite the hospital bed, each one connected to a basement camera, the screens filled with green and black night-vision images. Rachel could see Sophie on two of the screens. The policewoman was thrashing from side to side on the thin mattress, desperately trying to work her hands free.

The bookcase contained DVDs, the spines of the discs dated and marked with a number from one through to five. They were arranged in chronological order, a new disc for each day. The only DVD marked with a five was dated the day after she'd been kidnapped. If that one contained yesterday's footage then she had been here for two days.

On top of the dressing table were two mannequin heads and a hand. One head held a wig, the other was bald. The hand stood upright like it was waving and there were five wedding bands on it, one on each digit. Rachel's ring was on the little finger. The small camp bed in the corner of the room had been neatly made up but looked well used.

"Come and sit with me."

The old woman nodded to the space next to her. Rachel didn't move. She couldn't move. She stared at her feet so she wouldn't have to look at the old woman. Adam gave her a gentle shove and that broke her paralysis. She sleepwalked over to the bed and sat as close to the edge as she could. The old woman nodded to the space between them.

"Closer." Her voice was cultured and hinted at a different era. It was a voice used to giving orders, and having those orders obeyed without question.

Rachel glanced at Adam, then edged closer. The old woman studied Rachel carefully, her eyes examining every inch of her face and body.

"So beautiful," she said. "Do you think I'm beautiful?"

"Yes."

The old woman laughed. It was a charming sound, and Rachel had the feeling that it was just as false as Adam's smile, and just as dangerous.

"I was beautiful once, but not now. Age gets us all in the end. A word of advice, my dear, I strongly suggest that you don't lie to me. If you do then I'll get Adam to cut your tongue out." She glanced over at him. "Adam loves to play with his knives. But you already know that, of course."

Rachel stared at a patch of wall behind the bed and said nothing.

"He hates me, you know. I gave birth to him and he hates me. He wants to kill me but he doesn't have the guts. He's just like his father. His father was gutless, too. Isn't that right, Adam? You dream of putting a pillow over my face."

"I love you, Mother."

"No you don't. The only person you love is yourself. Just like your father." She locked eyes with Rachel. "Do you believe in heaven?"

Rachel thought about the sunshine and imagined warm sand between her toes. She thought about her father. "I believe in judgement," she answered quietly.

The old woman smiled. "Finally, an honest answer. What about hell? Do you believe in hell?"

Rachel glanced at the black and green images of Sophie on the screens. "Yes," she said. "I believe in hell."

382

"No you don't. Not yet. You think you believe, and you will in time, but you still have a way to go. Adam, go get my makeup bag."

Adam went over to the dressing table and returned with a large gold bag.

"You know what to do," the old woman said.

Adam took out a lipstick and Rachel shrank back from him. He held the back of her head so she couldn't get away and applied the lipstick. He took his time. Gentle, careful touches. Fussy touches.

"My son is a constant source of disappointment," said the old woman. "He destroyed my body twice. Once when I gave birth to him, and the second time when he crippled me. Never have children. You'll regret it as long as you live."

The heart monitor beside her registered ninety beats a minute. The old woman's blood pressure was up, too.

Adam was as gentle with the turquoise eye shadow as he had been with the lipstick. The blusher came next, smooth circular movements, the pad tickling her cheek.

"I always wanted a daughter. But instead I got Adam. We used to play dressing up when you were a child though, didn't we, Adam?"

"Please don't do this, Mother."

"He looked so pretty with his long brown curly hair and his big brown eyes. And he really suited pink." She smiled at the memory. "And then he got older and his body started to change and that ruined everything. It just wasn't the same any more. It didn't matter what I did, he looked too much like a boy. Adam, go and get the wig."

Rachel heard Adam's heavy steps move away from the bed, then move back again. She stared at the flowers, stared at the wall, anything so she wouldn't have to look at Adam or his mother. She knew how this game worked. Things were going to be bad when they got back to the basement, worse than they'd ever been. Adam was furious. Right now he was holding it in and squashing it down, but it was going to come out sooner or later, and when it did, she and Sophie would be on the receiving end.

The old woman in the bed knew what she was doing, she knew exactly which buttons to push. She was winding Adam up, and then she was going to sit here and watch the show on those four big-screen TVs. Adam placed the wig on Rachel's head and arranged it with his baby-soft fingers.

"Well, dear, what are you waiting for? Stand up and give me a twirl."

Rachel got up on wooden legs and turned a full circle, her movements stiff and awkward. She finished her pirouette and stood dead still, holding her breath. The old lady stared stony-faced then broke into a broad beaming smile. Rachel had the distinct impression that if she'd been able to move her hands she would have clapped with joy.

"It's just like looking in a mirror," she said.

# CHAPTER
# SIXTY-SEVEN

I put my foot down when we hit the M1 and the powerful V8 engine roared. The speedometer hit ninety and the scenery turned into a blur. Driving into snow was like flying through hyperspace, the snowflakes turning into white streaks like star trails. The outside lane belonged to me and anyone stupid enough to get in the way was hit with my full beams and horn until they got the hell out of my way.

I was driving way too fast for the weather conditions, but didn't have an option. Templeton didn't fit the victim profile and that worried me more than anything else. Whatever the unsubs planned to do, they'd do it quickly. There was a chance we were already too late.

The needle pushed towards a hundred and I stared through the windshield. All I could see were streaks of snow and the occasional red tail light. This was crazy, completely suicidal. I was driving blind. I gave the car more gas and the needle crept past a hundred.

"Who's Cutting Jack?" Hatcher asked.

"Plausible deniability," I reminded him.

"If anyone asks, I'll lie. As far as I'm concerned Cutting Jack is Darren Webster, and that's the way it stays until you realise you've made a mistake and tell me otherwise."

"You sure?"

"I'm sure."

"Okay, his name's Adam Grosvenor. I was pretty sure it was him, but I needed to be totally sure. Sumati got me the confirmation I needed."

"Why him?"

"Because of the geography," I said. "Adam lives at Waverley Hall, a large country house on the outskirts of Redbourn. The village is near junction nine of the M1, which gives him easy access to London. And it's only five miles from St Albans, which explains why he dumped Patricia Maynard there. Basically he got greedy. He dumped Patricia Maynard then twenty-four hours later he abducted Rachel Morris. He needed to cut corners, so he dumped Patricia Maynard close to home. Also, out of all the seven possible locations we had, Redbourn was furthest away from Charles Brenner's dump site. Even back then he wanted to mislead you."

"So what's the story? Is he working alone?"

"No. Adam's the submissive and his mother, Catherine Grosvenor, is the dominant."

"So, his mother's alive?"

"Just. There was a car crash two and a half years ago. Adam was driving. He ended up with a broken arm, but Catherine Grosvenor wasn't so fortunate. She suffered a C4 fracture and is paralysed from the neck down. She spent almost a year in hospital. Halo traction, operations, the works. After she was discharged she went home and Adam took responsibility for her care."

"That's why you wanted the medical companies checked out. Adam would need medical equipment to look after his mother. You suspected this had happened."

I nodded. "Either this or something similar. Something that left Catherine Grosvenor incapacitated, like a stroke, or motor neuron disease. It explains the lobotomies. Catherine Grosvenor is alive but she's reliant on Adam for everything. Eating, getting dressed, going to the toilet. She wants the victims to suffer like she's suffering."

"But they're not aware of their condition so it's not the same."

"It doesn't matter. This is a symbolic act."

"She got out of hospital eighteen months ago. That was around the time Charles Brenner was murdered."

"That was the trigger," I agreed. "Catherine Grosvenor is almost at the end of her life. Her looks have gone and now her body is failing, too. She's a very angry woman, and Adam bears the brunt of her anger. He'll have been abused since he was a kid. Psychologically and physically, but it's likely he suffered some sort of sexual abuse as well."

Hatcher was nodding. "Yeah, that makes sense."

"There's more. Get a photograph of Catherine Grosvenor in her prime and you'll be looking at a brown-eyed brunette who's confident and self-assured. Just like Sarah Flight and Margaret Smith and Caroline Brant and Patricia Maynard. And just like Rachel

Morris. It's not just Adam she's taking her anger out on. She looks at these women and sees all the things she has lost. Her looks, her youth, her mobility. So she gets Adam to torture them while she watches, and she plays dress-up with them because for a time she can remember what it used to be like to be young and beautiful."

"What about Catherine Grosvenor's husband? Where does he fit into all this?"

"He doesn't. He died when Adam was a kid."

"Natural causes?"

"According to the coroner it was a heart attack."

"But you're not convinced?"

I shook my head. "Catherine's husband cheated on her and I'm sure she murdered him, and she got away with it. Nobody worked it out at the time because nobody dug hard enough. They looked at her, saw a heartbroken, distraught widow with a young son, and they stopped looking. Dig deeper and you'll find I'm right. All the victims' husbands were unfaithful. That's not a coincidence. All the victims were angry wives whose husbands had wronged them. That's no coincidence either. Catherine Grosvenor is reliving her past, Hatcher. The victims represent the person she was thirty years ago."

# CHAPTER
# SIXTY-EIGHT

Adam dragged a chair over to the side of the hospital bed, slowly, eyes fixed on Rachel. The legs scratched against the vinyl floor covering and let out a high-pitched screech. A shiver ran through her and she tried to hide it. She stared at the wall through the nearest bouquet of flowers and told herself everything was going to be all right. Even though she knew it was a lie, she kept repeating that thought in her head. *It's going to be all right. It's going to be all right. It's going to be all right.* Adam wanted a reaction, but he wasn't going to get one. He turned the chair so it faced the television screens.

"Number Five will sit down."

Rachel complied and Adam grabbed her arms. He pulled them behind her, then fixed her wrists to the chair back with cable ties, securing them tight enough for the hard plastic to dig into her skin, but not tight enough to cut off her circulation. Next he fixed her ankles to the chair legs and clicked the cable ties tight. Rachel stared at the wall. She wanted to escape back to the beach, but the memory eluded her.

Adam left the bedroom. Footsteps along the corridor, then on the stairs. His footsteps faded out of earshot and the dead silence was filled with other sounds. The wind in the eaves, the snow hammering the windows, the creaks and groans of the old house, the rhythmic pulse of the heart monitor, the soft breathing of Adam's mother. The television screens were dark and reflective, four black mirrors that cast distorted reflections that looked like melted wax creations.

Rachel glanced over at the bed. The old woman caught her staring and smiled warmly. Rachel looked away quickly and stared at the TV screens. If they'd met outside of this time and place she would have viewed Adam's mother as just another harmless old woman who whiled away her twilight years having afternoon tea with her slowly diminishing circle of friends. She might even have felt sorry for her. And how wrong she would have been.

Like her father had told her so many times, you judged a person by their actions, not their words. How many times had she seen news reports where neighbours and friends of some psycho shook their heads and expressed their disbelief? He was just so normal, they'd say. He kept himself to himself. He couldn't possibly have done the things he's been accused of. Back then, Rachel had wondered how they could be so clueless. How could they not know? Now she knew.

"Camera four zoom in," the old woman said. Her diction was perfect, every word pronounced with care.

The picture on the bottom-right screen got larger, green and black resolving into a clearer image. Rachel could see Sophie thrashing back and forth on the thin mattress, struggling against her restraints, fighting to get free.

"Camera three zoom in."

The picture on the bottom-left screen got larger. Sophie on the mattress from a different angle, feet first rather than head first. The beep of the heart monitor had dropped back to seventy-eight. Rachel stared at the screens so she wouldn't have to look at Adam's mother.

She watched the old woman's warped reflection in the glass. The only part of her body she seemed able to move was her head. Everything from the neck down was completely still. Adam's mother suddenly started to blink rapidly and the heart monitor beeped quicker. Rachel glanced over. The old woman's eyes were watering and she was desperately trying to clear her vision. A tear slid across the make-up on her cheek. Except this wasn't a tear. Adam's mother was incapable of tears, incapable of love. The only emotions she experienced were the darker ones. Hate, anger, loathing.

Rachel could sense the old woman's frustration, her utter helplessness. The irony of the situation struck and, despite everything, Rachel felt a small wicked glow light up inside her. If she hadn't been bound to this chair, she could have helped the old woman. Then again, if she hadn't been bound to the chair the temptation to put a pillow over her face would have been too great. She had no idea why Adam hadn't done that years ago. Living with his mother must have been hell. If he chose to he could kill her easily. It wasn't like she was going to put up any sort of fight. And if he didn't have the bottle to do that he could walk away at any time, just head out the front door and keep on going and never look back.

But he chose to stay here. The old woman was completely vulnerable, yet she held all the power. Rachel didn't get it. She doubted she would ever fully understand what was going on there. The dynamic of their relationship was just too screwed-up for her to comprehend.

All four screens suddenly flared white, like the basement was ground zero for a nuclear blast.

"Night vision off," said the old lady.

The pictures changed to colour, the definition got sharper. Sophie stopped struggling. She lay there totally still on the mattress, arms pulled tight behind her back, and stared at the door. Her grey top was soaked through with sweat and she was breathing hard. Rachel glanced at the top-left screen. The door was closed, so was the dog flap. She looked back at the bottom screens where Sophie was still staring at the door, body tense, eyes wide and alert.

"Sound on."

Sophie's breathing filled the bedroom. Rapid, shallow breaths. Scared breaths. Rachel looked back up at the top-left screen and saw the door swing open. Adam entered, the garden snips in his right hand, the cattle prod in his left. Rachel had told the policewoman what had happened to her, so she knew what was coming next.

Her mind would be in overdrive right now. It would be filled with thoughts of pain and escape and

**392**

retribution, a whole jumble of random useless ideas and images. Adam walked past the chair and disappeared from the top screen, reappearing a couple of seconds later on the bottom screens. There were two Adams now. One screen favoured his left profile, the other his right.

Adam held up the snips and Sophie let out a small gasp that sounded like a shout through the bedroom speakers.

"Turn over," said Adam.

"Go to hell."

Adam held up the cattle prod. "Turn over or face the consequences."

Sophie glared and Adam lunged forward. He jammed the cattle prod into her stomach and held it there while she howled in agony, held it there longer than he needed to. The louder she screamed, the wider his smile got. He put down the cattle prod and grabbed hold of Sophie's shoulder, flipped her roughly onto her front and pushed his knee into the small of her back.

The first snip cut through the cable tie around her ankles and the second snip cut the tie that bound her wrists. He jumped to his feet and bounced back from the mattress, gracefully, keeping his distance in case the policewoman retaliated. Sophie rubbed her wrists and ankles and glared at him. She winced when she touched the raw spot on her stomach.

"Sit on the chair."

Sophie didn't move.

Adam jammed the cattle prod into her stomach and followed her as she squirmed across the mattress. Her agonised howl was worse than before, higher-pitched and more desperate. Adam stepped back and the noise subsided. Sophie was lying on her side curled into the fetal position, biting back her sobs, her breathing ragged and harsh.

"Sit on the chair," said Adam.

Sophie hesitated and Rachel was sure she was going to defy him again. Adam waved the cattle prod back and forth in a tick-tock motion. Sophie glared, then walked across to the dentist's chair. She sat down and Adam buckled her in tight.

He left the basement and returned with the trolley. He parked it in front of the chair, picked up the chef's blowtorch, lit it. Adam reached for the knitting needle and heated the tip in the flame until it glowed. Sophie shrank back in the chair. Her face was filled with fear, eyes frantically searching for a way out.

"Please stop him," whispered Rachel.

The old lady smiled sweetly. "Earlier you said you believed in judgement, my dear. *This* is judgement."

# CHAPTER
# SIXTY-NINE

It was blowing a blizzard by the time we reached junction nine of the M1. I'd eased the Maserati back to seventy, but that was still way too fast for the conditions. For the last couple of miles I hadn't said a word because I needed all my concentration to keep us alive.

The roads got progressively worse the further we drove from the M1 and the snow got deeper. My speed was right down now, but I still almost lost the Maserati a couple of times. The car wasn't designed for these conditions. It was designed for wide open stretches of straight road. What we needed right now was a 4×4, not a sports car.

High hedges had turned the lane that led to Waverley Hall into a narrow tunnel, and the wind had pushed the snow into a high bank on the right-hand side. A thick layer of snow covered the road. The Maserati crawled along at ten miles an hour, the tyres struggling for traction on the packed ice beneath the snow. The wipers were still fighting a losing battle. If this blizzard kept up, the road would be impassable within another half an hour.

Waverley Hall was surrounded by a high wall and hidden by tall fir trees that rose like spectres out of the snow. I cruised past the main entrance and peered through the gateway, stared hard into the snow and tried to make sense of the blurred white shapes. I could just about make out the driveway that cut between the trees for about twenty yards before turning sharply to the right. This tallied with the aerial image we'd gotten from the internet.

The best way to approach the house was from the east. The area to the front was too open. There was a gravel courtyard for parking cars and an unkempt lawn and too much open space. We'd be sitting ducks. Same for the area to the rear. The grounds stretched for four hundred yards, all the way to the trees that marked the southern boundary. Again, there was far too much open space. The west side was difficult to access, which left the east side.

I drove to the north-east corner of the boundary wall and abandoned the Maserati in the middle of the road. Then I reached into the passenger footwell, grabbed the Samsonite case, popped the catches and opened the lid. The smell of fresh gun oil hit me the moment the lid went up.

Donald Cole had done good. The Colt 45 was one of my favourite handguns because it was one hundred per cent reliable. Not ninety-nine per cent, not ninety-eight per cent, one hundred per cent. Back in 1911, the US army had tested some guns and the Colt 45 was the only one to fire 6,000 rounds without a single problem. Whenever it got too hot they dunked it in a bucket of cold water then carried on firing. Add in the fact that it was comfortable to handle and easy to conceal and you had one very impressive weapon.

I clicked out the magazine and checked the ammo: .45 hollow-points. Nine-millimetre rounds penetrated more deeply, but the .45 had much more stopping power. When it hit something solid all that kinetic energy was transferred to the thing it hit, whereas there was a good chance that a 9mm bullet was just going to pass straight through. According to legend, .45 hollow-points could be stopped by a wet army blanket. Swap that blanket for a body, and you could see why I preferred .45 rounds to 9mm.

I checked the guns over and dry-fired them a couple of times. My preference would be to fire some live rounds to make sure they worked, but that wasn't going to happen. I pushed the magazine back into the second gun, racked the slide and chambered a round.

The downside to keeping a round in the chamber was the possibility of an accidental discharge but it was a risk I was willing to take. If you needed to use a gun you didn't want to be messing around trying to chamber a round. Bottom line: if things got that bad then every single second would count. Chambering a round now could mean the difference between life and death later.

One of the Colts got stuffed down the back of my jeans and a spare magazine went into my back pocket. I held the second Colt out to Hatcher. The detective just stared at it.

"It's a gun," I said.

"I know it's a gun."

"You know how to fire a gun, don't you?"

"Of course I know how to fire a gun."

"You point it and squeeze the trigger. You keep squeezing until you run out of bullets."

"I know how to fire a bloody gun, Winter."

"I'd feel better if I knew my back was covered."

Hatcher snatched the Colt from me and we got out of the Maserati. The wind was so vicious it stole my breath away. Heads down, we ploughed into the blizzard. Hatcher was right beside me all the way, a ghostly presence floating through the snow.

It was hard going. I couldn't feel my feet or hands, and my eyes stung. We followed the eight-foot-high boundary wall along the eastern perimeter of the property. An inch of snow had already settled on the sloping cap. I counted off the yards in my head and when I reached 150 stopped walking. If my calculations were correct we were now perpendicular with the house.

Hatcher gave me a boost up and I clambered onto the top of the wall. Snow soaked into the seat of my jeans, freezing my ass. I reached down and, grabbing Hatcher's hand, helped him up.

We dropped down into a wood, which was good as it tallied with what we'd seen on the laptop. It also meant that we had a much better chance of getting to the house without being seen. Most of the trees were bare, but there were a few evergreens. The tall thick trunks blocked the worst of the wind, turning it into a manageable breeze, and the sudden silence was eerie, like someone had flicked a switch and turned the blizzard off. We battled through the thick undergrowth, branches snatching at our clothes, creepers and roots threatening to trip us up.

The woodland went on for about thirty yards and ended at a six-foot wall. I grabbed the top of the wall, my frozen fingers sinking into the snow, then pulled myself up and peered into the darkness.

There was a kitchen door twenty yards away. To reach it we had to cross an area that had once been used to grow vegetables, but had long been abandoned. This was surrounded by walls on three sides, and the house on the fourth side. There were two small windows on the first floor, both dark. I couldn't see any signs of life behind the glass, but kept looking a few seconds longer, just in case. Once we were on the other side of the wall we'd be easy targets. I dropped back down and filled Hatcher in.

"You ready?" I asked.

"Ready as I'll ever be."

Hatcher looked scared, but scared was good. Scared would keep him sharp. I was scared, too. If I looked into a mirror right now my expression would be identical to Hatcher's.

We clambered over the wall and sprinted for the house. Hatcher was right behind me. We were out in the open again, out in the blizzard. It seemed to hit me twice as hard as before. My lungs were filled with ice, and the snow lacerated my skin. Those twenty yards felt like twenty miles. I half expected a bullet to hit me at any second. It would slam into me and the first I'd know about it would be when I hit the ground, my blood seeping into the snow.

We reached the house and pressed up against the wall. Hatcher was breathing hard and actually had some colour in his face.

"I need to get to the gym more often," he said.

"You say that like you know what the inside of a gym looks like."

Hatcher gave me a short smile. "Screw you, Winter."

I tried the door. Locked. There wasn't a spare key in any of the obvious places, so I blew some heat into my frozen fingers, took out my lock picks and went to work. The lock took a couple of minutes to crack. It was old and heavy, in need of oil, and my fingers weren't working so well. I pulled the Colt from the back of my jeans and followed the gun inside, my wet boots leaving a trail of damp footprints.

The kitchen was big, with a stone floor and fixtures that looked old but weren't. The room was spotlessly clean. Tins of food were piled up on the work surfaces and, at first glance, they looked as if they'd been placed randomly. At a second glance, I saw the order. Soup in one group, baked beans in another, spaghetti hoops in another, and so on.

Each group was neatly positioned and made me think of Andy Warhol. Aside from the tin cans, everything was squared away and shipshape. No dirty dishes in the sink. No clutter of any sort. There was a smell of orange groves and bleach in the air. Looking around, three letters sprang to mind: OCD.

**400**

I stood completely still in the middle of the kitchen, melting snow running down my face and clothes, and listened hard. The sounds we heard were the sounds you'd expect to hear in a house this old. The pop and rattle caused by air bubbles in the water pipes, the occasional creak, the whirr of the refrigerator.

No sounds of life.

Only one door led from the kitchen. I walked over to it, placing each foot with care and distributing my weight as evenly as possible, my wet footprints following. Hatcher moved as silently as air and the only reason I knew he was there was because of his breathing. We reached the door and a noise from upstairs stopped us in our tracks.

"Any ideas?" Hatcher whispered.

I shook my head, placed a finger against my lips, then turned the handle and pushed the door open slow and easy. I went out into the corridor, my gun hand moving left to right, up and down, covering all the angles like I was back on Hogan's Alley at Quantico. Hatcher was a step behind. He had his gun out, too. I stopped and listened, all my attention focused on the upper floors.

Another noise from above, but there was no mistaking what it was this time. The sound of a scream gets inside you like no other sound. This was a female scream, long and drawn-out and filled with agony.

We broke into a run, reacting to the sound like it was the bang of a starter pistol. Someone was hurting and it was our job to stop that hurt. We sprinted into a large entrance hall then headed for the stairs, taking them

**401**

two at a time. At the top we turned right and ran into a corridor.

There was a light behind the door at the far end. The smell of hospitals got stronger the closer we got. The door was ajar and I hit it with my shoulder, slamming it all the way back and smashing it into the wall. I crashed into the room, my gun moving in all directions. The adrenalin was pumping and my finger felt heavy on the trigger. I scanned the room, taking everything in.

Catherine Grosvenor's shocked face, her mouth scrunched into a surprised O.

The five wedding rings on the mannequin hand.

Rachel Morris bound to the chair, alive and breathing and missing a finger.

The TV screens.

I could see Templeton on one of the screens. She was stripped to the waist and strapped to a wooden chair. Her sweatshirt had been cut off and lay in tatters on the floor.

Adam stood next to her with a large bowie knife in his hand. Templeton was in a bad way. There were welt marks from where she'd been beaten. Streaks of blood spread out from the three-inch knife wound that ran from the bottom of her sternum to her belly button. She was conscious but only just.

"Microphone on," said Catherine Grosvenor. "Adam, the police are here. You know what to do."

Adam walked up to one of the cameras and stared into it. His face was large on the screen. It was like he was staring directly at me. I stared back. He had a handsome face, a trustworthy face. His eyes twinkled with good humour. He didn't look like a killer, but then my father hadn't looked like a killer, either. Neither did Bundy, Dahmer or John Wayne Gacy. They never did.

I looked over at Catherine Grosvenor. "Tell him to put the knife down."

"Put the knife down or what?" Adam's voice came from the wall speakers. The volume was pushed to the point where the sound distorted.

"Put the knife down or I'll shoot your mother."

Adam laughed. "Like that's going to happen."

I pulled the trigger.

# CHAPTER
# SEVENTY

I reached the bed in two strides, clapped my hand over Catherine Grosvenor's mouth and pulled the plastic cuff from her finger. The heart monitor let out a long plaintive note, the universally recognised sound of death. There was a hole in the pillow an inch from the old woman's head, feathers floated gently back down to the bed. My ears rang from the gunshot. The smell of cordite filled the room and stung my nostrils.

Catherine Grosvenor glared at me and tried to move her head from side to side, the only part of her body she could move. Plenty of people had wanted me dead over the years, but nobody had wanted it as badly as Catherine Grosvenor did at that moment. The old woman was as insubstantial as air and I held her easily. I put her in a stranglehold that stopped the flow of blood through her carotid artery, felt her go slack, then laid her head back on the pillow.

All this happened in seconds. It happened so quickly that Adam hadn't had time to process what his ears were telling him. He'd heard the gunshot, and a millisecond later he heard the heart monitor flatline. It should have been a simple equation but grief would have made him stupid.

"What have you done?" Adam whispered. His voice became a shout, loud and filled with fury. "What have you done!"

I got up close to Hatcher, close enough for my lips to touch his ear, and gave him the three-second version of my plan, hoping that would be enough. Time was not on our side.

"We've just done you the biggest favour of your life, Adam," said Hatcher. "You don't have to do what she says any more."

"Why did you shoot Mother?"

This wasn't the response I expected. How the hell had Adam confused my voice with Hatcher's? Hatcher sounded nothing like me. It was another example of how grief had made him stupid.

"You don't have to do what she says any more," Hatcher repeated.

I ran over to the medical trolley and found a pair of scissors and a roll of bandage tape. I tossed the tape to Hatcher so he could gag Catherine Grosvenor. By my reckoning she'd be out for another twenty seconds and then the shouting would start. We needed Adam Grosvenor to believe she was dead. We needed him in a state of shock and denial. We needed him confused and not thinking straight. It was Templeton's only chance. The orbitoclast was on the trolley in the basement, and I'd seen what Adam could do with it.

I went over to Rachel Morris and pressed a finger against her lips. *Shut up.* I cut the cable ties, helped her to her feet and we headed for the corridor. Behind me, Hatcher was talking up a storm. The detective was doing a great job. He was keeping Adam in the present, keeping it personal by using his name wherever he could. He was promising the world without giving a single thing away. Textbook stuff.

"Tell me everything you can about where Adam was holding you," I said once we were out of range of the bedroom microphone.

Rachel started talking, and kept on talking until we reached the door that led down to the basement. I was impressed at how together she was, how focused. There were no questions, no recriminations, no self-pity, just precise answers to my questions. Donald Cole would have been proud.

I went down the stairs alone and jogged along the corridor to the basement door. The light switch and the dog flap were exactly how Rachel had described them. I lay down on the floor with my head right up next to the dog flap. The plastic acted as a soundboard, amplifying what was happening on the other side.

Hatcher's voice was distorted and he sounded like an angry robot. The way it had been manipulated explained why Adam hadn't been able to tell the difference between Hatcher and me. Adam's voice was quieter, more natural-sounding.

I made myself wait, made myself listen, forced myself to be patient because I needed to build up a picture of what was going on in there. It wasn't easy. I was over-adrenalised, buzzing with nervous energy. There was a mocking tone in Adam's voice I didn't like one bit, a pleading tone in Hatcher's voice I liked even less. Things were about to turn critical.

**406**

I pushed the door open and walked into the basement. The light was blinding. It reflected off the white tiles, glinted off the exposed steel on the dentist's chair. Adam was standing alongside the chair, using Templeton as a shield. His left arm was curled around her body, gripping her tight, the bowie knife in his right hand was pushed up against her throat, and his head was hidden by Templeton's. It didn't matter where I aimed, there was no clear shot.

Templeton was unconscious. The only reason she was upright was because Adam was holding her up. Blood seeped from the wound in her stomach, but it looked worse than it was, superficial rather than anything life-threatening. I stepped to the left and Adam matched my move, twisting around so Templeton's body was between us.

"Drop the knife, Adam."

"You drop the gun."

I held the gun steady, left hand supporting the right. Beyond the gun sight, all I could see was Templeton. Wherever I moved, there she was. I told myself I was back on the shooting range at Quantico, that this was a cardboard target rather than flesh and blood. Told myself to chill. Willed my heart rate back to a more manageable level.

"Not going to happen."

"Drop the gun or I'll kill her."

"If I drop the gun you're going to kill her anyway, and then you're going to try to kill me."

"Drop the gun."

"Why did you do it, Adam?" I needed to buy some time to think. I'd already played through all the scenarios in my head, every single last one of them. It didn't matter what move I made, Templeton always ended up dead.

"Why did I do what?"

"Why did you lobotomise those women? Killing them would have been so much easier."

"Mother told me not to kill them."

"But it was you who came up with the idea to lobotomise them, wasn't it?" My brain was working overtime. There had to be an answer, a way to unravel this mess that left Templeton alive. There was always a solution. Always.

"That was my favourite part." There was a smile in Adam's voice. "For a moment the lights were on, the next second, nothing. It was bizarre. They looked like people but they weren't, they were empty. They were like ghosts."

"That wasn't the real reason it was your favourite part, though, was it?"

"What are you talking about?"

"There was another reason, wasn't there?"

"And I suppose you're going to tell me what that was."

"You didn't have to hurt them any more," I said. "You didn't really want to hurt them, did you, Adam? You only did it because your mother told you to. Because she made you angry and you needed someone to take that anger out on."

"You don't know what you're talking about."

**408**

I could hear from his voice that I'd got that one right. I could also hear that we were done talking. For a moment the world stopped turning and time ground to a halt. Everything went still. Adam's fingers tightened on the knife handle. Any second now he was going to drag the blade across Templeton's throat, opening her carotid artery and killing her within seconds. Once that was done he'd drop her body and wait for me to shoot him. I'd seen this before and that was how most of them chose to go.

The solution came to me in a single bright flash of inspiration. I was thinking so far outside the box, the box had ceased to exist. I went through the moves in my head, over and over, making sure there were no errors. Just like shooting pool, I told myself.

My finger tightened on the trigger and I thought about Sarah Flight staring blankly out of a window for the next fifty years. I thought about everything she could have been and everything she would never be, all that lost potential. I thought about her mother going to visit her every day. I thought about her mother getting older and I thought about the day when her mother wouldn't visit any more. I thought about how close Templeton had come to the same fate.

Just like shooting pool, I told myself.

Cardboard rather than flesh and blood.

Alive is always better than dead.

My first bullet hit Templeton in the shoulder. By the time it reached her it was travelling somewhere in the region of 1,000 feet per second. I'd aimed for bone and hit bone, which meant that Templeton absorbed most of the energy from the bullet, a vicious punch that made her jerk back violently and sent her tumbling to the floor. The rest of the energy had to go somewhere. That somewhere was Adam. The punch that hit him wasn't as hard as the one that hit Templeton, but it was still enough to send him spinning and loosen his grip on the knife. Metal clattered on ceramic, the sound dulled by the boom of the Colt.

I dropped to my knees and counted off one and a half seconds. During that one and a half seconds Adam rotated through a full 180 degrees, just like I'd calculated. More importantly, he spun away from Templeton. It was like two billiard balls colliding, Newtonian physics in action.

My second bullet smashed upwards through the thin bone at the back of Adam's skull. Because of the angle of entry, the bullet hit the prefrontal bone, the thickest part of the skull. Rather than exit the skull, the bullet bounced around inside Adam's brain, tearing apart his prefrontal cortex, the same part of the brain that had been destroyed when he performed his lobotomies. Adam dropped like a rock and was dead before he hit the floor.

# CHAPTER
# SEVENTY-ONE

I shut my suitcase and carried it to the door. My plane wasn't scheduled to leave Heathrow for another four hours, then there would be the inevitable delays due to the snow. The runways were clear but there was still a backlog of flights to work through, so there was plenty of time to get to the airport and get checked in and go through all the security protocols that had been implemented after 9/11.

Two days had passed since I killed Adam. Two days of questions and speculation. The ducks were now neatly lined up, asses were suitably covered, and I had my escape to a sunnier place all planned. This storm would blow on for a while before it blew itself out. But that was Hatcher's problem, not mine. The bad guy had been taken down. Dead or in prison, it didn't make much difference to me. I'd still sleep as well as I ever did.

I headed to the balcony for a last smoke, my mind already on the next case. That was the way I'd always done things. Once the bad guys had been stopped they ceased to be interesting. The interesting ones were the ones who were still out there, and there would never be a shortage of those.

Someone knocked on the door. This wasn't the firm knock used by room service the world over, it was more tentative, someone seeking an invitation to enter rather than someone demanding entry because it was their job. I opened the door and Templeton stood there smiling that great smile, her arm strapped across her chest to keep it still. The surgery had gone well, but she'd be setting off airport metal detectors for the rest of her life. She looked over my shoulder at the suitcase.

"Going somewhere?"

I stood aside to let her in. "Shouldn't you be in hospital?"

She walked over to the sofa and sat down heavily, her discomfort obvious from the stiff way she moved.

"How bad is the pain?" I asked.

She made a so-so gesture with her good hand. "Right now the drugs are doing their thing so it's just about manageable. Another hour and a half or so and I'll be coming down the other side, and then it won't be so manageable."

"You weren't supposed to be discharged until tomorrow."

"I snuck out when the nurses' backs were turned." She paused and her face turned serious. She glanced away and when she looked back the seriousness was gone, replaced by an expression that contained a touch of uncertainty. It was an expression that didn't sit comfortably on Templeton. "I didn't want your last memory of me to be in a hospital. That wouldn't be right." She paused again and cracked a lopsided grin. "I wanted to say goodbye properly."

412

"And," I prompted.

"And I thought that maybe we should talk about what happened. You know, clear the air."

I kept quiet. Always the best policy when a woman says she wants to talk.

"In his final report, Hatcher said Adam Grosvenor committed suicide by cop."

Templeton was watching me carefully, her expression serious again. This time I kept quiet because we'd just stepped into a minefield. Hatcher had run his report by me before he submitted it. That report had become the final word on the subject. Everyone was happy. Hatcher's superiors were happy because the bad guys had been stopped and that made them look good, and the media was happy because they had a great story, and the relatives of the victims were as happy as they could be because they'd got something they could rationalise as justice.

The sole voice of dissent belonged to Catherine Grosvenor, who was telling anyone who listened that her son had been murdered, but nobody was listening too hard. In the end it was her word against Hatcher's.

And that was the problem, because things hadn't quite gone down the way Hatcher described them in his report. Most of what he wrote was an accurate and true account of events, but there were a couple of things that weren't. First off, he said we found the Colts in the house. And secondly, he said I warned Adam Grosvenor before I pulled the trigger. Blatant lies whose only purpose was to cover my ass.

Not that I was going to lose any sleep. Whatever happened, however things had gone down, it was a good shooting. Adam Grosvenor deserved to die and Templeton deserved to live. It was that simple. From the way Templeton was staring she obviously had her suspicions, but because she'd been unconscious at the time, that's all they were, suspicions. She nodded once to herself, an indication that she'd come to some sort of decision. Her eyes softened and the seriousness slid away and she was back to being someone I recognised.

"I'm glad he's dead," Templeton said, and the tension between us eased.

"And I'm glad you're alive."

"Thanks to you. Did you really have to shoot me, though?"

I grimaced. "Believe me, I wish there'd been another way."

Templeton laughed. "Lighten up for Christ's sake. I'm making fun of you. At the end of the day you did what you had to do."

"So you say."

"I do say. If it wasn't for you I wouldn't be here now. Thanks for saving my life."

"Any time," I said, and immediately wished I hadn't. It was one of those things that sounded way cooler in my head. Out loud, it made me sound like a dork. We fell into a short silence. Templeton had said what she'd come here to say and now the heavy stuff was out the way neither of us was sure where to go next.

"Can I talk you into staying a couple of extra days?" Templeton said, breaking the silence. "At least until

**414**

after Christmas. You can crash at my place. Nobody should be alone at Christmas."

"I won't be alone."

"The staff at the next hotel you end up in doesn't count."

That was worth a smile. "I'm not a big fan of Christmas. It's all about family and I'd rather forget about mine. I prefer to keep busy."

"I won't push it, Winter, but if you change your mind you know where I am."

"Thanks."

We went downstairs and I asked the concierge to order a couple of cabs. He made the call then told me to wait a second and disappeared into the back office. The aluminium Samsonite case he brought back with him was the same design as the one the Colt 45s had come in. The only difference was that it was larger and heavier. I handed the case to Templeton.

"You can have this," I said. "Think of it as a goodbye gift."

"What is it?"

"Open it and find out."

Templeton walked over to a table and put the case down. She popped the catches with her good hand and lifted the lid. Her eyes widened and she took a sharp intake of breath, swore to herself, then banged the lid down. She was tempted. Maybe just for a second, but she was definitely tempted.

"A million pounds?" I asked.

"I don't know if it's a million, but it's a ton of cash. Used banknotes if I'm not mistaken."

"It's a million. It's the reward for getting Rachel Morris back. Use it to pay off your mortgage, buy a new car. Take a holiday."

"I can't keep this. It's from Donald Cole. I need to hand it in."

"Hand it in and it'll end up disappearing into the system," I said. "You know how these things work. The best thing you can do is split it four ways and arrange for anonymous donations to be made to the families of the Grosvenors' victims. They're going to need the money. You can do that, can't you?"

"Yeah, I can do that."

The concierge called over to tell us the cabs had arrived. We headed out through the revolving doors and hugged at the kerb. For a second I thought that hug might morph into something more. I hoped it would, but was enough of a realist to know that it probably wouldn't. Cheerleaders and straight-A students. It was never going to happen.

And that was before I shot her.

The moment passed and Templeton got into her cab. She gave me one last smile through the window then the car pulled away. The brake lights flared red, the cab slowed then swung right, and she was gone.

I heaved my suitcase into the trunk of my cab, then climbed into the back and told the driver to take me to Heathrow. I had a plane to catch.

# Acknowledgements

My agent, Camilla Wray, has been truly inspirational. Her enthusiasm, professionalism and sharp eye for detail has been invaluable in bringing Jefferson Winter to life. I really do count myself fortunate to have the best agent in the business.

I'd also like to thank Katherine Armstrong at Faber for her superb editing skills. Her sense of humour and love of books is infectious, and this makes her a joy to work with.

My good friend Nick Tubby has been fantastic. In addition to critiquing early drafts of my work, he has tirelessly answered questions on all things related to guns, technology and websites.

In addition I'd like to thank Clare Wallace and Mary Darby at the Darley Anderson Agency, Detective Sergeant Gabriel Chrystal of the Metropolitan Police, Kate O'Hearn, KC O'Hearn, Rosie Goodwin, Ruth Jackson, and, of course, the irrepressible Wayne Brookes.

Last, but not least, my love and thanks go out to Karen, Niamh and Finn. You guys make this all worthwhile.